BITTER WASH ROAD

AVAILABLE FROM GARRY DISHER AND VIPER

Peace (October 2020)

BITTER WASH ROAD

GARRY DISHER

VIPER

First published in Great Britain in 2020 by
VIPER, part of Serpent's Tail,
an imprint of Profile Books Ltd
29 Cloth Fair
London
EC1A 7JQ
www.serpentstail.com

First published in Australia in 2013 by
The Text Publishing Company

1 3 5 7 9 10 8 6 4 2

Printed and bound in Great Britain by
CPI Group (UK) Ltd, Croydon, CR0 4YY

A CIP catalogue record for this book is available from the British Library.

ISBN 978 1 78816 507 5
eISBN 978 1 78283 696 4

In memory of Deborah Cass

1

On a Monday morning in September, three weeks into the job, the new cop at Tiverton took a call from his sergeant: shots fired on Bitter Wash Road.

'Know it?'

'Vaguely, Sarge,' Hirsch said.

'Vaguely. You been sitting on your arse for three weeks, or have you been poking around like I asked?'

'Poking around, Sarge.'

'You can cover a lot of ground in that time.'

'Sarge.'

'I told you, didn't I, no dropkicks?'

'Loud and clear, Sarge.'

'No dropkicks on my watch,' Sergeant Kropp said, 'and no smartarses.'

He switched gears, telling Hirsch that a woman motorist had called it in. 'No name mentioned, tourist on her way to look at the wildflowers. Heard shots when she pulled over to photograph the Tin Hut.' Kropp paused. 'You with me, the Tin Hut?'

Hirsch didn't have a clue. 'Sarge.'

'So get your arse out there, let me know what you find.'

'Sarge.'

'This is farming country,' the sergeant said, in case Hirsch hadn't worked it out yet, 'the sheep-shaggers like to take pot-shots at rabbits. But you never know.'

Wheat and wool country, in fact, three hours north of Adelaide. Hirsch's new posting was a single-officer police station in a blink-and-you'd-miss-it town on the Barrier Highway. Tiverton. There were still a few of these little cop shops around the state, the department knowing not to call them one-*man* stations, not in this day and age, or not within range of a microphone, but it didn't place female officers in them all the same, citing safety and operational concerns. So, single guys were sent to Tiverton—the wives of married officers would take one look and say no thanks—often, or especially, guys with a stink clinging to them.

Like Hirsch.

The police station was the front room of a small brick house right on the highway, where flies droned and sluggish winds stirred the yellowed community notices. Hirsch lived in the three rooms behind it: bathroom, sitting room with alcove kitchen, bedroom. He also enjoyed a parched front lawn and a narrow driveway for his own aged Nissan and the SA Police fleet vehicle, a four-wheel-drive Toyota HiLux mounted with a rear cage. There was a storeroom at the back, its barred window and reinforced door dating from the good old days before the deaths-in-custody inquiry, when it had been the lockup. For all of these luxurious appointments the department screwed him on the rent.

Hirsch finished the call with Sergeant Kropp, then he located Bitter Wash Road on the wall map, locked up, pinned his mobile number to the front door and backed out of the driveway. He passed the general store first, just along from the police station and opposite the primary school, the playground still and silent, the kids on holiday. Then a couple of old stone houses, the Institute with its weathered cannon and memorial to the dead of the world wars, more houses, two churches, an agricultural supplier, a signpost to the grain dealer's down a side street . . . and that was Tiverton. No bank, chemist, GP, lawyer, dentist, accountant or high school.

He drove south along the floor of a shallow valley, undulating and partly cultivated hills on his left, a more dramatic and distant range on his right—blue today, scarred here and there by scrubby trees and shadows among erupted rocks, a foretaste of the Flinders Ranges, three hours further north. Following the custom of the locals, Hirsch lifted one finger from the steering wheel to greet the oncoming cars. Both of them. Nothing else moved, although he was travelling through a land poised for movement. Birds, sitting as if snipped from tin, watched him from the power lines. Farmhouses crouched mutely behind cypress hedges and farm vehicles sat immobile in paddocks, waiting for him to pass.

Five kilometres south of Tiverton he turned left at the Bitter Wash turnoff, heading east into the hills, and here there was some movement in the world. Stones smacked the chassis. Skinny sheep fled, a dog snarled across a fence line, crows rose untidily from a flattened lizard. The road turned and rose and fell, taking him deeper into hard-scrabble country, just inside the rain shadow. He passed a tumbled stone wall dating from the 1880s and a wind farm turbine. Someone had been planting trees against erosion up and down one of the gullies. He remembered to check kilometres travelled since the turnoff, and wondered how far along the track this tin hut was.

He slowed for a dip in the road, water running shallowly across it from last night's storm, and accelerated uphill, over a peak and around a blind corner. And jammed on the brakes. Slewed to a shuddering halt in a hail of gravel.

A gumtree branch the length of a power pole lay across Bitter Wash Road. Hirsch switched off, his heart hammering. Close shave. Beyond, the road dipped again, bottoming out where a creek in weak, muddy flood had scored a shallow trench in the gravel, then it climbed to another blind corner. And there, in a little cleared area inside the fence and angled alongside a bend in the creek, was Sergeant Kropp's Tin Hut: corrugated iron walls and roof, mostly rust, and a crooked chimney. On a flat above it he glimpsed trees and the suggestion of a green farmhouse roof.

Hirsch got out. He was reaching to drag the branch off the road when a bullet snapped past his head.

His first reflex was to duck, his second to scuttle around to the lee side of the HiLux drawing his service pistol, an S&W .40 calibre semi-automatic. His first *thought* was that Kropp's anonymous caller had got it right. But then, crouched there beside the grubby rear wheel, Hirsch began to have a second thought: two days ago, some arsehole placed a pistol cartridge in his letterbox. It occurred to him now that it hadn't been a joke or a threat, but a promise.

He weighed his options: call for backup; tackle the shooter; get the hell out.

Options? They had him trapped where the road dipped between a canola crop and a stony hill. As soon as he showed himself—as soon as he got behind the wheel or clambered uphill to find the shooter or climbed the fence to run through the canola—he'd be shot. Meanwhile, police backup was in Redruth, forty kilometres away.

Hang on. Like fuck it was. The shooters were the very officers he hoped might back him up. They were not forty kilometres but forty metres away, up there on the hillside, positioned for crossfire, their radios conveniently switched off. Redruth was a three-man station, Kropp and two constables, and when Hirsch had called in to introduce himself three weeks ago, they'd called him a dog, a maggot. A silent *pow!* as they finger-shot their temples, grins as they finger-sliced their throats.

Placed a pistol cartridge in his letterbox when his back was turned.

Hirsch thought about it some more. Even if he managed to climb back in the HiLux, the tree was still across the road and there was nowhere to turn around. They'd shoot him through the glass. Discounting a full-on, up-hill assault, that left a zigzagging escape into the canola crop, a broad yellow swathe stretching to the smoky hills on the other side of the valley—but to reach it he'd have to climb the bank and then tangle himself in a wire fence. And how much cover would the crop provide?

Hirsch began to feel a strange, jittery discordance. He might have put it down to fear, but he knew what fear felt like. Was it some emanation from the wind farm? He was very close to one of the turbines. It sat on the stony hill where the shooter was hiding, the first of a ragged line stretching along this side of the valley, the blades cutting the air in a steady, rhythmic whooshing that reached deep in his guts. To Hirsch, it was all of a piece with ending his days where the world was unlovely, at the base of a scruffy slope of grass tussocks, rabbit holes and lichened stone reefs.

He glanced both ways along the road. He didn't know where the next farmhouses were or how much traffic to expect, or . . .

Christ, traffic. Hirsch cocked an ear, listening for vehicles he'd have to warn off, or protect, or mop the collateral blood from. Or run like hell from.

Which raised the question: why would the bastards ambush him here, within cooee of town? Why not somewhere more remote? 'Out east,' as the locals called it. According to the calendar hanging above Hirsch's desk, out east was a region of undernourished mallee scrub, red dirt, nude stone chimneys, mine shafts and September wildflowers. One jagged hill named the Razorback.

September school holidays, wildflowers blooming . . . Hirsch listened again, imagining he could hear a busload of tourists trundling along Bitter Wash Road.

He risked a quick glance over the passenger door windowsill. The radio handset jutted from a cradle on the dashboard. His phone sat in a drinks holder between the front seats. He wasn't obliged to call the Redruth station. He could call Peterborough, Clare, even Adelaide . . .

He heard another shot.

He froze, fingers on the door handle.

Then he relaxed minutely. What was it he'd actually heard? Not a high-powered crack but something flat, puny. Small calibre, dampened further by the huge sky and the whoosh of the wind turbine. Hardly a sniper's rifle. There had been a weak howl, too, as the bullet hit something—a stone?—and whanged away across the creek.

Nowhere near him.

A second ricochet came. He stiffened again, relaxed again. Not a ricochet at all. A kid's voice saying *peeowww*.

Hirsch did what he should have done from the start and checked out the fallen branch. No drag marks in the gravel, no saw or axe cuts, no foliage removed. He eyed the tree itself, found the break halfway up the trunk. He recalled camping trips from his childhood, teachers warning the kids not to pitch their tents under gumtrees. All that sinewy health on the outside and quiet decay within.

A bit like the police, really.

He holstered his handgun. Hunching his shoulders a little, he stepped into the middle of the road and dragged the branch into the ditch. Then he parked the HiLux on a narrow verge, leaving room for passing vehicles, and climbed the scabby hill to see who might have put him in his grave if his luck hadn't been running.

They didn't hear his approach, the boy and the girl: the wind, the rhythmic rush of the turbine above their heads, their absolute absorption as one kid aimed a .22 at a jam tin on a rock and the other stood by to watch.

Hirsch knew he should pounce on them before they sent another ricochet over the road, but he paused. The view from the base of the turbine was panoramic, exhilarating. Bitter Wash Road was clear in both directions, so he took a moment to get his bearings. The broad valley, the vigorous crops, the road running up and down the folds in the earth. And that khaki smudge back there was Tiverton with its pale grain silos poking into the haze.

There was a farmhouse above the Tin Hut, the green roof clearly visible now, and on the other side of the road was a red-roofed house. Both hedged in by cypresses, the shrubberies, garden beds and lawns quarantined: the usual landscaping out here in the wheat and wool country. The green-roofed property was extensive, with a number of sheds, a set of stockyards and farm vehicles parked on a dirt clearing beside a haystack. The place with the red roof was smaller, faded, only an attached carport and one small garden shed to brag about. Hirsch wondered at the relationship between the two properties. Maybe a farm manager lived in the smaller house. Or a couple, a man to do the gardening, his wife to cook and clean—the shit work. If those feudal relationships still existed.

Hirsch shaded his eyes. The sun passed in and out of the scrappy clouds as a few sheep trotted nose to tail across a nearby hillside.

Otherwise only the children moved, and Hirsch was betting they belonged to one of the houses. No school for two weeks and, with or without the blessing of their parents, they'd taken the .22 out for some target shooting. The location was perfect: nothing here but grass and stones, sloping down to the creek, nothing with blood in its veins. You could pretend you were in a shootout with the bad guys, and when the rifle got too heavy you could prop the barrel on a rock.

Except that bullets strike objects and howl off in unexpected directions. Or you might forget where you are and take a pot-shot at a crow or a rabbit just when a policeman is stepping out of his HiLux to shift a fallen tree.

Yeah, well, wasn't this just great? A couple of adults he could deal with: clear regulations, clear offences and penalties. But kids . . . He'd have to involve the parents; he'd maybe have to charge the parents. Jesus.

The children didn't hear him, not at first. Not until, side-stepping down the slope, he skidded and fell. Now they heard him, his curses and the tock and rattle of stones tumbling over one another, Hirsch cursing because he'd startled himself, torn his trousers and barked the skin on palm and elbow.

The children whirled around in shared alarm, mouths open, eyes shocked. They were caught in the act and they knew it, but it was how they managed it that was interesting. Hirsch forgot his discomfort and watched. The boy dropped his eyes like a beaten dog, already surrendering, but the girl grew tense. Her eyes darted to the empty hill, the boy alongside her, possible escape routes. She didn't run, but that didn't mean she wouldn't. The gaze she fixed on Hirsch was working it all out.

He held up his palm, not quite a warning, not quite a greeting. 'Don't,' he said mildly.

A faint relaxing. She was about twelve years old, skinny, contained, unblinkingly solemn, with scratched bare legs and arms under shorts and a T-shirt, her dark hair hanging to the shoulders and cropped at her forehead. Scruffy, but someday soon she'd have the looks to light dark places.

Disconcerted, Hirsch eyed the boy. Thin, similarly dressed, he could have been her brother, but his hair was straw-coloured, full of tufts and tangles, and his pale skin was flushed and mottled. Where the girl seemed to be looking for the angles, he was ready to be told what to do. But he was the one holding the rifle, and he was practised at it, keeping the barrel down, the stock in the crook of his arm, the bolt open. Hirsch counted five .22 shell casings glinting dully in the grass.

'My name,' he said, 'is Constable Hirschhausen. I'm stationed at Tiverton.'

The girl remained expressionless but Hirsch sensed hostility, and he scratched around in his head for the best way to go on.

'How about we start with your names?'

The girl's voice piped up above the whoosh of the turbines. 'I'm Katie and he's Jack.'

Katie Street and Jackson Latimer, and Katie lived with her mother in the smaller, red-roofed house that Hirsch had seen, and Jackson with his parents and older brother in the larger green-roofed house. In fact, Grampa Latimer lived on the property, too, in a house half a kilometre in from the road. 'You can't see it from here.'

Even Hirsch had heard of the Latimers. 'This is your land?' he asked, indicating the hill they were standing on, the turbine above them, the ragged line of turbines stretching away along the ridge.

Jack shook his head. 'Mrs Armstrong's.'

'Where does she live?'

He pointed to where Bitter Wash Road disappeared around a distant bend.

'Won't she be cross if she knows you're trespassing?'

They were puzzled, as if the concept hadn't much currency out here. 'It's the best spot,' Katie reasoned.

Right, thought Hirsch. 'Look, the thing is, one of your shots went wild. It nearly hit me.'

He gestured in the direction of the road. Putting some hardness into it he added, 'It's dangerous to shoot a gun so close to a road. You could hurt someone.'

He didn't say kill someone. He didn't know if the severity would work. He didn't know if he should be gentle, stern, pissed off, touchy-feely or full-on tyrant. He took the easy way: 'Do your parents know you're up here shooting a gun?'

No response. Hirsch said, 'I'm afraid I'll need to talk to—'

The girl cut in. 'Don't tell Mr Latimer.'

Hirsch cocked his head.

'Please,' she insisted.

'Why?'

'My dad will kill me,' the boy muttered. 'Anyway he's not home.'

'Okay, I'll speak to your mothers.'

'They're out, too.'

'My mum took Jack's mum shopping,' Katie said.

Hirsch glanced at his watch: almost noon. 'Where?'

'Redruth,' she said reluctantly.

Meaning they hadn't gone down to Adelaide for the day and would probably be home to make lunch. 'Okay, let's go.'

'Are you taking us to jail?'

Hirsch laughed, saw that the girl was serious, and grew serious himself. 'Nothing like that. I'll drive you home and we'll wait until someone comes.'

Keeping it low-key, no sudden movements, he eased the rifle—a Ruger—from Jack's hands. He'd disarmed people before, but not like this. He wondered if police work ever got chancy, out here in the middle of nowhere. He walked the children back over the ridge and down to the HiLux. The girl moved with a quick, nervy energy; the boy trudged, his spine and spindly arms and legs moving in a curious counterpoint, a kind of pulling back on the reins. Hirsch saw that his left shoe was chunkier than the right, the sole and heel built up.

The girl caught Hirsch looking. Her eyes glittered. 'You've got a hole in your pants.'

The kids strapped in, Katie in the passenger seat, Jack in the rear, Hirsch said, 'So, we wait at Jackson's house?'

'Whatever,' Katie said. She added: 'You could be looking for that black car instead of hassling us.'

The police were looking for hundreds, thousands, of cars at any given moment. But Hirsch knew exactly which one she meant: the Pullar and Hanson Chrysler, last seen heading for Longreach, over two thousand kilometres away. He said, 'I doubt it's in our neck of the woods.'

Katie shot him down with a look, swung her gaze away from him. 'That's what you think.'

Hirsch was fascinated by her. Dusty olive skin, a tiny gold hoop in each ear, a strand of hair pasted damply to her neck, and entirely self-contained. One of those kids who is determined, tireless, mostly right and often a pain in the arse. He tried to remember what he'd been like at that age. When it was clear that she didn't intend to elaborate, he slotted the key in the ignition.

'We saw it go past our school,' said Jack in the back seat.

Slowly, Hirsch removed his hand from the key. Had some guy waved his cock at the kids? Tried to snatch one of them? 'The primary school in town?'

'Yes.'

'When was this?'

'Yesterday.'

'A black Chrysler?'

'Yes.'

'But what were you doing at school on a Sunday?'

'A working bee. Cleaning up and planting trees.'

'Did this car stop?'

Katie shook her head. 'It drove past.'

'What time was this?'

'Nearly lunchtime.'

Hirsch pictured it. The little primary school was opposite the police station, with a large playing field fronting Barrier Highway. The entrance, car park and classrooms were off a side street. The speed limit was fifty kilometres per hour through the town, giving an observant child time to mark details. But what details had marked this vehicle out from the others that passed the school every day, the farm utes, family cars, grain trucks, interstate buses?

It was a black Chrysler, that's what. A car in the news, driven by a pair of killers.

Not a common car—but not rare either, and Hirsch said so. 'I think those men are still in Queensland.'

'Whatever. Can we just go?'

Hirsch glanced at the rearview mirror, seeking Jack's face. The boy shrank away.

'Suit yourselves,' Hirsch said, checking the wing mirror and pulling onto the road.

Speaking of observant children . . .

'Did you kids happen to see anyone hanging around outside the police station late last week? Maybe putting something in the letterbox?'

They stared at him blankly, and he was thinking he'd mystified them, when the girl said, 'There was a lady.'

'A lady.'

'But I didn't see her putting anything in the letterbox.'

'Was she waiting to see me, do you think?'

'She looked in your car.'

Hirsch went very still and braked the HiLux. He said lightly, 'When was this?'

14

'Morning recess.'

Hirsch went out on patrol every morning, and someone would have known that. 'What day?'

Katie conferred with Jack and said, 'Our last day.'

'Last day of term? Friday?'

'Yes.'

Hirsch nodded slowly and removed his foot from the brake pedal, steering slowly past the fallen branch. Seeing Katie Street peer at it, he had a sense of her mind working, putting the story together—him stopping the HiLux, getting out, and hearing a stray bullet fly past his head. As if to check that he wasn't sporting a bullet hole, she glanced across. He smiled. She scowled, looked away.

Then she said tensely, 'We're not lying.'

'You saw a woman near my car.'

Now she was flustered. 'No. I mean yes. I mean we saw the black car.'

'I believe you.'

She'd heard that before. 'It's true!'

'What direction?'

She got her bearings, pointed her finger. 'That way.'

North. Which made little sense if Pullar and Hanson had been in the car she saw—not that Hirsch could see that pair of psychopaths breaking cover to drive all the way down here to Sheepshit West, South Australia.

Still sensing Hirsch's doubt, Katie grew viperish: 'It was black, it was a station wagon and it had yellow and black New South Wales numberplates, just like in the news.'

Hirsch had to look away. 'Okay.'

'And it was a Chrysler,' said Jack.

Feeling lame, Hirsch said, 'Well, it's long gone now.'

Or perhaps not, if it had been the Pullar and Hanson car. The men liked to target farms on dirt roads off the beaten track. Suddenly Hirsch understood what the children were doing with the Ruger: they were shooting Pullar and Hanson.

He steered gamely down through the washaway and up around the next bend, to where Bitter Wash Road ran straight and flat for a short distance, the children mute and tense. But as he neared the red roof and the green, Katie came alive, snapping, 'That's Jack's place.'

A pair of stone pillars, the name *Vimy Ridge* on one, 1919 on the other, the oiled wooden gates ajar. Imposing. Hirsch supposed that a lot had occurred since 1919, though, for everything was weatherworn now, as if the money had dried up. A curving gravel driveway took him past rose-bordered lawns and a palm tree, all of the road dust dampened by last night's rain, ending at a lovely stone farmhouse. Local stonework in shades of honey, a steep green roof sloping down to deep verandas, in that mid-north regional style not quite duplicated elsewhere in the country, and sitting there as though it belonged. Hirsch eyed it appreciatively. He'd spent his early years in a poky terrace on the baked streets of Brompton—not that the miserable little suburb was miserable any longer, now the young urbanites had gentrified it.

He pocketed his phone, got out, stretched his bones and gazed at the house. It was less lovely closer up. Careworn, the paintwork faded and peeling, a fringe of salt damp showing on the walls, a fringe of rust along the edges of the corrugated iron roof. Weeds grew in the veranda cracks. He didn't think it was neglect, exactly. It was as if the inhabitants were distracted; no longer saw the faults, or blinked and muttered, 'I must take care of that next week.'

The children joined him, Jack a little agitated, as though unsure of the proprieties. Hirsch contemplated phoning one or other of the mothers but mobile reception was dicey. Anyway, nobody reacted well to a call from a policeman, and the women would return soon. So, how to fill in the time . . . He didn't think he should enter the house uninvited, and he didn't want to wander around the yard and sheds uninvited either. Meanwhile, he needed to keep an eye on the kids.

He stepped onto the veranda and indicated a huddle of directors' chairs. 'Let's wait over here.'

When they were seated he asked, 'Who owns the .22?'

'My dad,' whispered the boy.

'What does he use it for?'

'Rabbits and things.'

'Does he own any other guns?'

'Another .22, a .303 and a twelve-gauge.'

'Where are they kept?'

'In his study.'

Hirsch asked the questions casually, keeping his voice low and pleasant, but he was scanning the dusty yard, taking note of the sheds, a scatter of fuel drums, an unoccupied kennel, stockyards, a field bin in a side paddock. A ute and a truck, but no car. A plough and harrows tangled in grass next to a tractor shed. A working farm but no one working it today, or not around the house.

'So anyone could take the guns out and shoot them?'

'He locks them in a cupboard.'

Hirsch threw Jack a wink. 'And I bet you know where the key is, right?'

Jack shook his head violently. 'No, honest.'

'He's not lying,' Katie said. 'We used the gun that's kept in the ute. It's just a little gun, for shooting rabbits.'

Little and overlooked and forgotten, thought Hirsch. Not even a proper gun to some people.

He was guessing the kids had done it a few times now, waited until the adults were out then grabbed the Ruger and headed down the creek for some target practice. Bullets? No problem. They'd be rolling around in a glove box or coat pocket or cupboard drawer, also overlooked and forgotten.

To ease the atmosphere, Hirsch said, 'So, school holidays for the next two weeks.'

'Yes.'

A silence threatened. Hirsch said, 'May I see the gun case?'

Jack took him indoors to a study furnished with a heavy wooden desk and chair, an armchair draped with a pair of overalls, a filing cabinet, computer and printer, bookshelves. It smelled of furniture polish and gun oil. The gun cabinet was glass-faced, bolted to the wall, locked. A gleaming Brno .22, a .303 fitted with a sight, a shotgun, a couple of cartridge packets and an envelope marked 'licences'.

Hirsch thanked the boy and they returned to the veranda in time to hear a crunch of gravel. A boxy white Volvo came creeping up to the house as if wary to see a police vehicle parked there. Katie's mother at the wheel, reasoned Hirsch, and Jack's mother in the passenger seat, and he didn't know what the hell he should tell them. He removed the phone from his pocket. The shutter sound already muted, he got ready to photograph them. Habit, after everything that had happened to him.

2

Viewed later, the photographs on Hirsch's phone revealed women of his age, mid-thirties, and as unlike each other as their children. Katie's mother came into view first, slamming the driver's door and advancing on the house. She wore jeans, a T-shirt, scuffed trainers and plenty of attitude, throwing a glare at Hirsch as she neared the veranda. She was small-boned like her daughter; dark, unimpressed.

Jack's mother trailed behind, leaving the Volvo in stages, closing the door gently, pressing against it until it clicked, edging around the front of the car as if she was reluctant to disturb the air. Hirsch wondered if she'd hurt her right hand. She held it beneath her breasts, fingers curled.

Meanwhile Katie's mother had stopped short of the veranda steps. She threw a glance at her daughter. 'All right, hon?'

'No probs.'

'Excellent, excellent.'

Hirsch absorbed the full impact of a high-wattage gaze,

thought Fuck this for a joke, and stuck out his hand. 'Hi. Paul Hirschhausen, stationed at Tiverton.' With a grin he added, 'Call me Hirsch.'

The woman stared at him, at his hand, at his face again; then, quite suddenly, her fierceness ebbed. He wasn't out of the woods, but he'd get a handshake. 'Wendy Street,' she said, 'and this is Alison Latimer.'

Hirsch nodded hello; Latimer responded with a smile that was trying to come in from the cold. She was tall, fair; pretty in a recessive way, as if she had no expectations and understood disappointment. But what do I know? thought Hirsch. He'd misread plenty of people and had the scars to prove it.

'Is something wrong?' Alison blurted.

'Nothing too bad, but there is something we need to discuss.'

Before he could elaborate, Wendy Street said, 'You're new at Tiverton?'

'Yes.'

'And you come under Kropp in Redruth.'

'Yes.'

'Faan . . . tastic,' she drawled.

'Is there a problem?'

That might have been a shrug, then she grinned at his torn trousers, brown eyes briefly warm and lustrous. 'The kids beat you up?'

'Entirely my doing,' Hirsch said.

'Uh huh. So, you want to discuss something?'

Downplaying it, electing, for some reason, not to mention

21

Kropp's call, Hirsch explained that he'd heard shots in passing and found the children playing with a rifle.

Alison Latimer's face dropped. 'Oh, Jack.'

Jack stared at the ground. Katie stood with folded arms and stared out across the garden. But Wendy Street said, 'You just happened to be passing, in your four-wheel-drive, and heard shots.'

So Hirsch put a little harshness into it: 'A tree was across the road. When I got out to shift it, a bullet flew past my head.'

Okay?

It worked. The women were dismayed. They turned to the children, then back to Hirsch, issuing a tide of apologies and recriminations.

'Look,' he said, 'no harm done. But I think the rifle should be locked away from now on.' He retrieved it from the HiLux and handed it to Jack's mother. 'It is licensed?'

Alison nodded. She held the rifle a little awkwardly, as though her right hand lacked strength, and used her left to flip open the bolt. As she moved, a beautiful old-style diamond ring flashed a red spark. Then she gestured with the rifle, showing him the empty chamber. She was a lovely woman full of strain and privation; she held herself stiffly, as though her joints had locked up. In a low mutter she said, 'I can show you the paperwork if you like.'

'That's okay,' Hirsch said, knowing he should check. He wasn't among criminals here, though. 'Look, you run a farm, it doesn't hurt to have a couple of rifles on hand, but keep them locked up so the kids can't get at them. No unsupervised shooting.'

All through this, Wendy Street was casting tense looks at her neighbour. Alison, feeling the force of it, broke into tears. 'I'm so sorry, Wen, I didn't . . .'

'Allie, you know how much I hate guns.'

Then Street relented and touched the back of the other woman's hand. 'Please, please, *please* keep them locked up.'

'I will.'

And to the children: 'As for you two, no more shooting. Okay?'

'Okay,' Jack said.

Katie didn't agree, she didn't disagree.

Wendy wasn't finished. She clamped her fingers around Hirsch's forearm. 'Quiet word?'

Surprised, he said, 'Sure.'

She led him to her car and he waited, watching the house, the other mother, the children. 'What's up?'

'I don't know you, I don't know if I can trust you.'

There was nothing to say to that.

'I teach at the high school in Redruth.'

'Okay.'

'I've seen how Sergeant Kropp and his men treat people.'

Hirsch stroked his jaw. 'I don't know anything about that, I'm new here. What's it got to do with Jack and Katie?'

'All right,' Wendy took a breath, 'giving you the benefit of the doubt . . . I want you to know that Allie's husband is a bully. He won't handle this well when he hears about it. And he's going to hear about it because he's mates with Sergeant Kropp.'

Meaning, Hirsch thought, she'd appreciate it if I kept my trap shut.

'I assume you have procedures to follow,' Wendy said bitterly.

'Well, there are procedures and procedures,' Hirsch said.

She assessed him briefly, head cocked, then gave a whisper of a nod. And bit her bottom lip, as if thinking she'd gone too far.

Hirsch said, 'If Mr Latimer is violent to his family I can refer them to a support agency. Sergeant Kropp needn't know.'

The tension in Wendy Street shifted, but did not ease. 'What matters right now is the shooting business. If you have to report it, you have to report it—but I'd rather you didn't.'

Hirsch gave his own version of the abbreviated nod. 'How about we leave it as a friendly caution. It would have been different if someone had been hurt or the bullet had gone through the roof of my car.' He paused. 'Think of the paperwork.'

He got a smile from her but it was brief, her upper teeth worrying her bottom lip again. She cast a troubled look at the children, watching closely. They knew some kind of deal was being worked out.

'I don't know the *how*—I don't know where the gun was or where they found the bullets or whose idea it was—but I think I know the *why*.'

A car passed by on Bitter Wash Road, tyres crushing the short-lived paste of rainwater, dust and pebbles. Hirsch heard it clearly, and now he noticed the country odours: eucalyptus, pine, the roses, the grass and pollens, a hint of dung and lanolin. He realised his cut hand was stinging. All of his senses were firing, suddenly.

'Pullar and Hanson,' he said.

Her mouth opened. 'They told you about the car they saw yesterday?'

'Yes.'

Wendy folded her arms. 'It probably wasn't Pullar and Hanson, I know that, but the point is, they *are* scared. Ever since it's been on the news, Katie's been keeping a scrapbook. Jack has nightmares. The shooting is self-protection.'

A burst of staticky squawks and crackles issued from the HiLux. 'Excuse me.' Hirsch reached in and picked up the handset. Sergeant Kropp, demanding to know his current location.

'Poking around, Sarge,' Hirsch said, watching Wendy Street return to the veranda. 'No sign of anyone shooting a gun.'

'Well, get your arse up to Muncowie. Make contact with a Mr Stewart Nancarrow, on his way down to Adelaide from Broken Hill, driving a white Pajero with New South Wales plates, somewhere on the highway there.'

Hirsch scribbled the information in his notebook. 'The reason?'

'A body beside the road.'

3

Hirsch's first thought was: *Pullar and Hanson, the kids were right*, and he felt a kind of dismay mingled with excitement. 'Suspicious?'

'Probable hit-and-run.'

Hirsch made the mental adjustment: not Pullar and Hanson. 'Nancarrow?'

'No. He claims he stopped by the road for a leak, saw a dead woman lying in the dirt.' Kropp paused and added, 'Dr McAskill's on his way up there.'

'I'm on it, Sarge.'

Hirsch placed the handset in the cradle. The women and their children were watching him from the veranda. 'Got to go,' he called, climbing behind the wheel. He got a nod for his pains, a couple of half-hearted waves.

Pausing at the front gate, Hirsch fed 'Muncowie' into the GPS. It directed him not back to the highway, as he'd expected, but further out along Bitter Wash Road, which eventually made a gradual curve to the north, smaller roads branching from it. One of them looped west onto the Barrier Highway a short distance north of Muncowie.

It was a shorter route, Hirsch could see that from the map. Unsealed for most of the distance.

After twenty minutes, he found himself skirting around the Razorback, driving through red dirt and mallee scrub country, the road surface chopped and powdery where it wasn't ribbed with a stone underlay. Very little rain had fallen here last night; it was as if a switch had been flicked, marking the transition from arable land to semi-desert. Leasehold land, one-hundred-year leases defined by sagging wire fences, sand-silted tracks and creek beds filled with water-tumbled stones like so many misshapen cricket balls. You might find a fleck of gold in these creek beds if you were lucky, or turn your ankle if you were not. It was land you walked away from sooner or later: Hirsch saw a dozen stone chimneys and eyeless cottages back in the stunted mallee, little heartaches that had struggled on a patch of red dirt and were sinking back into it.

Ant hills, sandy washaways, foxtails hooked onto gates, a couple of rotting merino carcasses, a tray-less old Austin truck beneath a straggly gumtree. Weathered fence posts and the weary rust loops that tethered them one to the other. He saw an eagle, an emu, a couple of black snakes. It was a land of muted pinks, browns and greys ghosted by the pale blue hills on the horizon.

That was what he saw. What he didn't see, but sensed, were abandoned gold diggings, mine shafts, ochre hands stencilled to rock faces. A besetting place. It spooked Hirsch.

The sky pressed down and the scrub crouched. 'It's lovely out there,' one of the locals had assured him during the week, waiting while Hirsch witnessed a statutory declaration.

He passed in and out of creek beds and saw a tiny church perched atop a rise. What the fuck was it doing there, this shell of a church? Ministering to other stone shells, he supposed, left by the men and women who'd settled here and failed and walked away.

Hirsch fought the steering wheel, the gear lever, the clutch. His foot ached. Even the HiLux struggled, pitching and yawing inflexibly, taking him at a crawling pace through the back country. You had to hand it to technology, the GPS giving him the shortest route but blithely unaware of local conditions. It would take him forever to reach Muncowie at this rate, longer if he holed the sump or punctured a tyre.

Then he was out on the highway. *Muncowie 7* according to the signpost. He made the turn, heading south, the valley less obvious here, the highway striping a broad, flat plain. It gave Hirsch a sense of riding high above sea level, the sky vast and no longer pressing down, the hills a distant smear on either side. Meanwhile the crops, stock and fences were marginally better than the country he'd just passed through, more and greener grass, less dirt, as if he'd passed across the rain shadow again, moved from unsustainable life to a fifty-fifty chance of it.

And then in the emptiness he saw another car. Black. It drew closer.

Not a Chrysler. A Falcon, he saw as it passed.

Hirsch thought about Pullar and Hanson. In terms of

timing, geography and logic, it wouldn't make sense for them to have headed down here. Travel two thousand kilometres in a reasonably distinctive vehicle, away from the country they knew? Hirsch couldn't see it. But he could see how the men might hunt in a place such as this. They had been preying on roadhouse waitresses along the empty highways, housewives and teenage daughters on lonely country roads.

It had started as a local backblocks story, a Queensland story—albeit a vicious one—which quickly went viral when Channel Nine muscled in, giving the killers a voice. Back in August a forty-year-old Mount Isa speed freak named Clay Pullar and an eighteen-year-old Brisbane cokehead named Brent Hanson raped and murdered three roadhouse waitresses over a two-week period. Police tracked the men to a caravan park in northern New South Wales but arrived too late. They found the body of a Canadian hitchhiker roped to a bed. Further sightings placed the men in Cairns, Bourke, Alice Springs, Darwin . . . Nothing definite until they broke into a farmhouse near Wagga, where they raped a teenager in front of her trussed-up parents and fled north with her to a property across the border and along the river at Dirranbandi.

Feeling pleased with himself, Pullar phoned Channel Nine on his mobile phone. He'd just managed to prove who he was when the signal failed, so Channel Nine dispatched a reporter and a cameraman by helicopter, which set down on the back lawn long enough to leave a satellite phone, and took off again, circling overhead. Pullar appeared. Even through the long pull of the camera lens he looked tall, gaunt, hard, insane. He grinned and waved, showing stumpy teeth, grabbed the phone, returned to the farmhouse, and began to explain himself. An exclusive, a live interview, you couldn't ask for better. Fuck ethics, the public had a right to know. Fuck sense, too; Pullar made absolutely no sense but was full of frothing lunacy.

The police took thirty minutes to arrive. They surrounded the house, jammed the signal, chased the helicopter away—and waited. Night fell. They tried to talk to Pullar and Hanson. After a few hours of silence it occurred to them to rush the house . . .

They found an elderly man and woman unconscious and the Wagga teenager naked and traumatised. No sign of Pullar and Hanson, who had fled, on foot, to a neighbouring property where they stole a beefy black Chrysler 300C station wagon. By daybreak they were hundreds of kilometres north, apparently heading for Longreach. Another rape-and-murder team might have swapped the Chrysler for a less obvious car at the earliest opportunity; Pullar, back on the phone to Nine, had said, 'Man, this car has got some serious grunt.'

Hirsch squinted. the sun was beating hard and the road shimmered with mirages. Now a collection of tumbledown houses appeared, set two hundred metres off the highway. *Muncowie* the sign said, an arrow pointing to the little side road that took you there, to a place that seemed to have no function. Rusty rooftops, tired trees, sunlight breaking weakly from a windscreen.

Then Hirsch was through the town. A kilometre further on a white Pajero appeared, parked at the side of the highway. A man was resting his rump against it; dark heads showing inside the vehicle, behind tinted glass. Hirsch cruised to a stop, switched off and got out, stretched the kinks in his back. He could see the Pajero occupants more clearly now: a woman in the passenger seat, looked like two kids in the back. Roof racks piled with roped-down luggage.

The driver, coming around to meet him, offered a huge paw.

'The name's Nancarrow, I called triple zero.'

Powerful forearms, a nuggetty chest, sun-damaged skin, sunglasses propped above a high, shiny forehead. From Broken Hill, according to Kropp. A mine worker? 'Heading south for a holiday?' Hirsch asked. 'You and the family?'

'Two weeks,' Nancarrow said.

Hirsch strolled around to the front of the Pajero, eyed the bumper, the left and right panels. Dust, smeared insects, no dents or blood. 'You spotted a body?'

Watching him, Nancarrow said, 'Down there.'

The bitumen ran high here, raised a couple of metres up from the pocked soil, the erosion channels. Grass tussocks and a couple of hangdog mallee trees were nearby, clinging to the rim of a shallow depression. If you were a male who'd stopped for a piss, that's where you'd do it. Two damp patches side by side in the dirt. Father and son?

As if in answer, Nancarrow said, 'Me and my son went down there for a leak and saw her.'

Hirsch glanced uneasily at the Pajero. Nancarrow said,

'It's okay, he's little. I told him the lady had fallen over and the ambulance would come soon and take her to the hospital.'

'Did either of you touch her?'

'Christ, no. All I wanted to do was get my kid back to the car before he got too curious.'

'How did you call triple zero? Is there a mobile signal here?'

'Nup, dead. Zilch. I called from the pub.' He gestured vaguely back along the road.

Hirsch nodded and slipped in another question. 'Who is she?'

Nancarrow blinked. 'What? Who . . . ? How would I know?'

'Perhaps she was travelling with you? Your neighbour, babysitter, niece? A hitchhiker you picked up?'

'I know where you're coming from, and the answer's no. I stopped for a quiet leak by the side of the road and saw a woman lying there, end of story.'

Hirsch nodded glumly. Maybe they'd know her back at the pub. 'Thanks for reporting it. Thanks for waiting.'

Nancarrow gave him a sad if crooked smile. It said, 'Sooner you than me, pal,' and 'Sorry I wasn't more help,' and 'Thank Christ I can go at last.' Maybe even, somewhere in there, 'Poor woman, whoever she is.'

Hirsch noted Nancarrow's contact details. When he was alone, he grabbed the Canon stored in his glove box and stepped carefully to the rim of the depression, trying not to disturb the layers of dirt, pebbles and flinty stones. The dead woman lay a short distance in from the edge. He ran his gaze over the surrounding dirt. Last night's showers had left a speckled crust, meaning prints would show clearly. Hirsch saw no boot or shoe prints, no drag marks, just the fine tracings where animals and birds had circled the body. A fox or a wild dog had gnawed at her forearm, a crow had pecked out the visible left eye. Ants had found her. Flies. Clearly she was dead, but Hirsch was obliged to check.

He took a series of photos first, the scene from all angles, then perspective shots: the body in relation to the road, a nearby culvert, the township on the other side of a stretch of exhausted red soil. Finally he stepped down into the shallow bowl, crouched and felt for a pulse. Nothing. Her clothes were still damp.

He straightened, stepped away from the body.

She was struck while walking or hitching by the side of the road and fell into the hole; she fell from a moving vehicle; she was tossed from a moving vehicle; she was killed elsewhere and tossed down here from the road.

She lay as if sleeping, face down, her chest to the ground but her left hip cocked and her legs slightly splayed, one bent at the knee. Her right arm was trapped under her right hip, and her right cheek was stretched out in the dirt as if she were looking along her outflung left arm: looking blindly, Hirsch thought, thinking of the eye socket. Maybe her other eye was intact, tucked into the dirt. There was very little blood.

He took another series of photographs, focussing on the clothes. Tight black jeans, a white T-shirt, a tiny fawn cardigan, bare feet in white canvas shoes. The T-shirt had ridden up to reveal a slender spine, a narrow waist, the upper string of a black thong. Bruising and abrasions. A silver chain around her neck. No wristwatch but craft-market silver rings on her fingers, and in her visible ear a silver ring decorated with a Scrabble piece, the letter *M*.

What about ID? Hirsch couldn't see a bag or wallet anywhere. If she was struck by a vehicle, and knocked or carried some distance, then her bag or wallet would be further along the road. Time for that later.

He crouched, peering at the area of waist and spine between the low-riding jeans and the scrap of T-shirt, and saw a small manufacturer's tag on the thong. Her underwear was inside out. He crab-walked closer to the body and lifted the T-shirt: a rear-fastening black bra, fastened with only one of the two hooks.

None of that proved anything. It was suggestive, that's all. He could think of plenty of scenarios to explain it, some of them innocent. For example, she'd dressed in a hurry, she'd dressed in darkness, she was short sighted, she was careless or drunk, she'd dressed in a cramped space, like the rear seat of a car.

Or someone else had dressed her.

He peered at her back, but couldn't read anything into the surface damage. Dirt on her bare ankles and arms, dirt on her cheek. But you'd expect dirt if she fell or was tossed by tyres—or by hand—down a dirt incline. That's all he could tell. Dr McAskill would do the rest.

Now Hirsch brought himself to examine her head. The

outraged eye socket stared back at him as he stared at a small, fine-boned face. Small, slack mouth, tiny teeth and a swollen tongue. A pert nose. A bruised, misshapen cheek. Something had hit the girl pretty hard, and he noticed he was thinking *girl*, not *woman*—the designation given him by Kropp and Nancarrow. She's maybe sixteen, thought Hirsch. Somewhere between mid and late teens.

Then he wandered along the road in each direction. He found a small fabric bag twenty metres from the body, strap and flap torn, still damp. He photographed it *in situ* and then fossicked around the contents. A wallet with $3.65 in coins, a tampon, tissues, chewing gum, a packet of cigarettes—two left, disposable lighter, supermarket receipts. No phone. In the wallet a Redruth High School student card belonging to Melia Donovan, year 10. A hand-written card under a clear plastic window confirmed the name and gave a Tiverton address.

So, fifteen? Sixteen?

Hirsch waited for the doctor to arrive. He wanted to walk back to Muncowie and knock on doors, but couldn't leave the body unattended. He glanced at his watch: 1 p.m. A bus passed, heading north, Perth on the sign above the windshield. A couple of cars, a handful of semis. Hirsch thought of their tyres, their bull bars.

When a silver Mercedes appeared twenty minutes later, decelerating, he stepped into the road, one hand raised. The car pulled in opposite the HiLux and an unhurried, neatly-put-together man got out, hauling a doctors bag. He crossed the road, stopped when he got to Hirsch. 'Constable Hirschhausen.'

'That's me.'

The doctor stuck out his hand. 'Drew McAskill.'

He was about fifty, fingers of grey in his brown hair, dressed in a tan jacket, dark trousers, white shirt and blue tie. His hand was pale, scrupulously clean, no sign of sun damage, hard labour or mishaps, which put him at odds with the men, women and children Hirsch had encountered so far in the bush. People out here were generally blemished. Farm grime under fingernails, garden scratches, schoolyard scrapes, sun wrinkles, dusty trouser cuffs, tarnished watch straps and gammy legs. To top it off, McAskill wore gold-rimmed glasses. The overall effect was slightly scholarly.

The spotless hand slipped in and out of Hirsch's grasp. 'I understand I'm to pronounce on a body?'

McAskill ran a medical practice in Redruth and was on call for the local police. In cases of suspicious death, he'd request an official police pathologist from Adelaide, but otherwise he was there to save department pathologists a six-hour round trip. 'I'll show you,' Hirsch said, turning to go, thinking with a hidden grin that this precise, fussy man was about to get dirt on his nice clothes.

'Hold your horses.'

Handing him the doctors bag, McAskill returned to the Mercedes and took out a blue forensic jumpsuit and booties. A car passed as he dragged them on, the driver and passenger gawking.

'Ready when you are.'

Hirsch led the doctor along the road until they were adjacent to the body. 'There.'

McAskill nodded brusquely. 'Not hidden, but you'd have to be almost on top of her to spot her.'

'Yes.'

Treading carefully, McAskill edged around the rim of the depression and paused. 'Melia Donovan.'

'Sure? The damage to her face . . . ?'

The doctor was adamant: 'No. It's Melia, without a shadow of a doubt.'

Hirsch looked around at this broad, flat, sparsely nourished corner of the world, population about ten, and wondered how McAskill and the girl had ever intersected. He was about to ask when McAskill said, 'She came into the surgery a couple of times. You'd have met her eventually. She's a Tiverton girl. God knows what she was doing up here.'

Now the doctor stepped into the hollow. He crouched, felt for a pulse, poked and prodded for a while. He took the temperature of the body, rolled it onto its back, flexed the arms and legs. 'Well, I'm pronouncing death.'

Hirsch scribbled time, date, location, names and circumstances in his notebook. 'How long?'

McAskill shrugged. 'Rigor is mostly gone. Animal damage. She's been here a day or two.'

'Since Saturday night, early Sunday?'

McAskill stood, frowned. 'Possibly. The autopsy should establish time of death with more accuracy.'

Both men gazed at the slack limbs. Hirsch crouched for

another look at the thin, unformed, pretty face. The right eye was intact. Hirsch, leaning closer, said, 'Is that petechial haemorrhaging?'

McAskill said primly, 'The red spots? I'll know more when I perform the autopsy.'

Hirsch straightened. 'How old is she?'

'Fifteen? Sixteen?'

Hirsch said carefully, 'Family circumstances?'

'Only what I've heard via local gossip. There's no father on the scene. The mother's a drinker, succession of boyfriends.'

'Siblings?'

'An older brother.'

Hirsch jotted the names in his notebook. 'What can you tell me about Melia?'

McAskill grimaced. 'Pretty wild.'

Hirsch pictured the girl's home life. He could see the patterns, the dimensions. No stability, older boys sniffing around, the mother's boyfriends, too. Maybe drugs and booze.

'But a sweet kid,' McAskill said. 'Struggled at school, wagged it pretty often—I'd sometimes see her hitchhiking in the middle of the day. Arrested a couple of times for shoplifting.'

'Boys, men?' asked Hirsch.

'Who knows?' McAskill said.

He crouched again and rotated the head on its stem. 'Broken neck.' Then he lowered the head and palpated the flesh and bones of the torso, chest and spine. 'Christ,' he muttered, but didn't elaborate.

Finally he let her go and, still squatting on his heels,

said, 'Massive internal injuries. Broken ribs and spinal cord damage and no doubt some trauma to her major organs.'

'She hasn't been punched?'

McAskill shook his head. 'Nothing like that. If I was to hazard a guess I'd say she was run over.'

'Run over, or knocked down?'

'I take your point. Indications are she was upright when it happened, and I'd guess the force of it tumbled her in to the windscreen. I've seen it before.'

'Facing away—hit from behind?'

'You'll have to wait for the autopsy, but my feeling is she was in the act of turning around.'

'So no way of knowing if it was deliberate or not?'

McAskill grinned. 'Got your work cut out for you.'

He stood, brushing dust from his hands. 'Would you like me to notify the family? I am their doctor.'

Hirsch didn't think about it for long. 'Thanks—though I will need to speak to them myself, eventually.'

'Of course.'

Both men looked up at the road, hearing a motor. 'The hearse,' McAskill said.

He turned to Hirsch. 'As I said, she liked to hitchhike. Did it a lot, if that's any help to you. Anywhere, any time. I even gave her lifts myself. Everyone did, just ask around. A sweet kid who sometimes had a bit too much to drink, drugs if she could get hold of them. I can see her staggering along the road with her thumb out, trying for a lift home, and you know the rest.' He gave Hirsch a look, partly philosophical, partly distasteful, partly grieving.

'A lift home from *here*?' said Hirsch.

'That's for you to find out, sorry,' McAskill said.

The doctor scrambled up onto the road to greet the hearse. Hirsch stood where he was, ruminating. How did she get here? Had she been at the pub? A party at a nearby house? Someone brought her here, and later this same someone couldn't or wouldn't take her home, so she set out to hitchhike in the early hours and was hit by a vehicle that failed to stop. Or it wasn't an accident, she was killed elsewhere and dumped here.

He climbed up onto the road. The hearse driver and his offsider were dragging out a stretcher. McAskill was in his car, a mobile phone clamped to his ear.

When the hearse had left and he was alone, Hirsch turned to the HiLux, and the first thing he saw was a crack in the windscreen, a shallow crater and a couple of minor tributaries, smack in the middle. Roadside gravel flipped up by a passing car or truck. Life on the frontier.

Sighing, he called Kropp. The sergeant was a couple— or possibly a couple of dozen—steps ahead of him. 'About time, hotshot. Melia Donovan, of this parish.'

Hirsch waited a beat. 'The doctor told you?'

'Finger on the pulse.'

'You knew her, Sarge?'

A snake in his voice, Kropp said, 'I been here twelve years, of course I fucking knew her. Caught her shoplifting more than once.'

'Apparently she liked to hitchhike.'

'Everyone knew that.'

Hirsch waggled his jaw in thought. 'We'll need to know if she was drugged or raped or beaten . . . Maybe some of her injuries aren't consistent with vehicle impact . . . Stuff like that.'

'What, you're back in plain clothes?'

'Come on, Sarge.'

'She'll be in good hands. McAskill will do the right thing by her.'

Hirsch was doubtful. 'Shouldn't the body go down to the city?'

'McAskill's been slicing and dicing for years.'

'Okay. So who briefs the coroner?'

'Me, sunshine, all right? What I need *you* to do is stay put until the accident team arrives, then head on back to Tiverton and follow up on McAskill's visit to the family. Think you can manage that?'

'Sarge,' said Hirsch.

But Kropp had already hung up. Hirsch returned to the hollow. After a fruitless examination of the dirt that had been hidden by the body itself, he made a head-down search of the highway for a few hundred metres north and south, both sides. Looking around for anything that might have belonged to Melia Donovan or the vehicle that had delivered her here or the vehicle that had killed her. Anything, he told himself, but preferably something like a fragment of glass indicator lens with the ID number intact. There was nothing in the dirt verges, so he walked back over the bitumen. Still nothing, and no skid marks. From his work with crash investigators in the past he knew to look for dual tyre skid marks, or the scuff marks that indicate loss of control, or the skip marks of a shuddering trailer.

Nothing.

So he ran crime-scene tape around the area and sat down to wait.

It was late afternoon before the accident investigators arrived. Hirsch wanted to hang around and talk about what he'd been thinking but they ignored him. Two men and one woman conscious of the dwindling light, the sun smearing itself across the horizon, long shadows playing visual tricks. They took their photos, measured distances, crouched and poked and grid-searched and marked up their diagrams.

'You're blocking the light,' the female officer said. Her tone indicated she knew exactly who Hirsch was.

4

The Donovan house was classic 1960s small-town architecture: squat, low, double-fronted. Stubby eaves, a tiled roof, a carport, and floor-to-ceiling windows in buckling aluminium frames. It crouched in unmown grass, hedged by a rusty gas barbecue, a banana lounge, a listing red Mazda. A fence line of crumbling bricks on either side separated it from the neighbouring properties: a similar but spotless house, and a vacant lot.

Hirsch waded through weeds to reach the warped front door, the red paint losing against the elements. He knocked on the cheap plywood. Waited, knocked again. A wind had picked up since the morning. It bent the trees and, out where the Bitter Wash Road pushed into the dry country, clouds were shouldering the Razorback.

'No offence, mate, but I'd leave it for now.'

Hirsch turned. A blockish male shape at the shadowed end of the veranda, taking unhurried stock of him and quietly smoking a cigarette.

'Why's that?'

'McAskill gave her a sedative. The wife's sitting with her and I'm keeping the snakes away.'

'Snakes?' Hirsch said, heading along the cracked veranda.

'Well, a worm. Reporter for the local rag. I have to warn you he got a photo off Leanne and he'll probably sell it to the *Advertiser*.'

'It happens,' Hirsch said, sticking out his hand, announcing his name.

'Wondered when I'd set eyes on you,' the smoker responded. 'Bob Muir.'

Muir's hand was a hard slab thickened by years of manual labour, fingers like stubby cigars, but dry, warm and gentle. A square head with heavy lids over intelligent eyes. 'Live next door,' he said.

Hirsch nodded. They found themselves standing side by side, staring out at the miserable front yard and the HiLux at the kerb.

'The doc said someone run over Melia?'

'Yes.'

'Poor bloody kid.'

Hirsch could hear muted sobbing inside, another voice murmuring, and said, 'Maybe you could fill me in on the family?'

Muir went very still. Protective. Then he shrugged. 'Do my best.'

He jerked his head, indicating that Hirsch should follow him a few paces into the front yard. The better light revealed a man with a few years on him, forties probably. A tough hide, barrelly torso and small backside, dressed in comfortable faded jeans and a khaki shirt. Greying hair cropped short around the fringes of his big, genial skull.

Before Hirsch could ask his first question, Muir said, 'She was hitching?'

'Possibly.'

Muir slid his gaze at Hirsch. 'Possibly?'

'Questions remain.'

'Is that right.'

'It's possible she was hitching and a vehicle hit her. All I can say is she was found lying in a hollow near the side of the road and not noticed until today.'

Muir took the cigarette from his mouth. 'Poor little cow.' He turned to stare across the quiet rooftops of the town, a flat skyline interrupted by the grain silos at the railway station. 'Okay, ask your questions.'

'What do you know about her movements over the weekend?'

'Nothing.'

'All right, what can you tell me about her?'

'Known her all her life.'

Hirsch brought out his phone, pretending to check the screen. Waited for the patient man beside him to go on.

'A bit wild.'

'So I understand,' said Hirsch.

'Nothing mean or nasty. Sweet kid, in fact. Just a bit unmanageable.'

'What about her friends?'

An unhurried individual, Muir drew patiently on his cigarette. 'You mean boyfriends.'

'Any friends.' Hirsch paused. 'Older friends.'

'Older friends. There was a whisper she was seeing someone older, but they broke up. Me and the wife, there were times we wanted to step in, but you can't, can you.'

'Any names come to mind? Friends, ex-boyfriends, anyone at all?'

Muir stared at him and finally said, 'Good friends with Gemma Pitcher.' He checked his watch. 'Works in the shop, you might just catch her.'

Hirsch bought his groceries there, since there was nowhere else, and recalled a solid pudding of a girl stacking shelves or sitting at the cash register. If asked to bet on it he'd say she was a lot older than Melia Donovan. 'They're at school together?'

Muir shook his head. 'Gemma left school two or three years ago.' Acknowledging Hirsch's point he added, 'There are only six or seven teenagers in the whole town, mostly boys. It's not as if Melia and Gemma were spoiled for choice.'

Hirsch nodded. No jobs, no night life. Net migration would be out of the district, not in. 'Were they close?'

'Thick as thieves, always off somewhere.'

'How did they get around?'

'Gemma drives.'

'Parties? The pub?'

Muir gave him a long look. 'Wouldn't have a clue.'

'Any other names you can think of?'

'I stay out of it, mate.' Muir paused. 'Come to think of it she did turn up one day last month with a black eye, said she'd been in a bit of a crash, said it was nothing.'

Check accident reports, insurance claims, local panelbeaters.

'What else? There's a brother, isn't there?'

Like a massive ship turning on the ocean, Muir stepped around to face Hirsch. 'Mate, what's your angle here?'

He stood close, crowding Hirsch, more animated suddenly. Hirsch could smell shaving cream, talcum powder, cigarette smoke and the heat of a day's work. Not unpleasant: honest smells, given off by a decent man who was hot under the collar right now.

'If you're a mate of Kropp's . . .'

The vehemence was barely there but it registered. Hirsch put some edge in his voice: 'Mr Muir, what are you trying to tell me?'

But Muir had subsided, hands in his pockets, face turned away, muttering.

'Sorry, what?'

Muir said, very plainly, 'Kropp and his boys like to take the Abo kids out into the bush, give them a good hiding and let them walk home.'

'I don't understand.'

Muir studied him, then finally nodded. 'Maybe you don't. There are two kids in the family. Melia, white father, and Nathan, black father. Both long gone.'

He flicked his cigarette away. 'Filthy habit.'

Both men stared at the butt. Then Muir gestured at it, saying, 'Maybe you should fine me for littering. And when you've done that, breathalyse me every time I leave the house. Then scream in my face for jaywalking.'

'Why would I want to do that?'

'You wouldn't need a *reason*, not if you're one of Kropp's boys.'

Hirsch didn't want to get into it. 'I'd better speak to this Gemma.'

Muir gazed at him levelly. 'Like I said, she works in the shop.'

'Thanks,' Hirsch said. He stopped. 'Is Nathan inside with his mother?'

'Leave the poor bugger alone.'

'I fully intend to,' Hirsch said in his reasonable voice, 'after I ask him about his sister's movements on the weekend.'

Muir conceded that. 'He's not home yet, but he's probably not far away. He and a mate of his work at the grain shed.'

Hirsch nodded. Tiverton Grains, a collection of sheds in a side street near the pub. 'I'll catch him tomorrow.'

Muir, indicating the phone in Hirsch's fist, said, 'You glued to that?'

And then he was crossing into the next yard, where a severely groomed couch-grass lawn was bordered by garden beds splashed here and there with red and white. A clean, older style Holden ute was parked in the driveway, Tiverton Electrics painted on the side. Hirsch glanced towards the rear of the property. He saw a large shed, door open, fuel drums, ladders, metal shelves and coiled wire inside. Neat house, shabby house. And that was a pattern repeated everywhere.

5

Almost six o'clock. Hirsch parked the HiLux in the police station driveway, intending to walk the short distance to the shop. A mini bus pulled in next door, *Redruth District Council* stencilled along the side panels, half-a-dozen elderly people on board. The driver tooted, and here was Hirsch's elderly neighbour limping down the path from her house. Hirsch shot a glare at the driver and took the old woman's arm. He helped her up the bus steps. 'An outing?'

'A lecture at the old jail in Redruth,' she said, 'then dinner at the reform school.'

Ruins dating from the 1850s, now tourist attractions. Hirsch registered her fragility under his manacling hand and hoped he hadn't bruised her. 'Well, you belong in both places.'

She cackled and they all waved, and he was left in the exhaust gases.

He walked on to the general store, an afternoon shadow tethered to his feet. Tennant's Four Square was an off-white brick building, long, low, the shopfront glass deep inside a corrugated iron veranda, with a petrol bowser at one end, secured by a bulky brass padlock, and a chequerboard of private post boxes at the other. Nothing to entice shoppers except a dusty ice-cream advertisement on a sheet of tin and a board of daily specials. You couldn't see in: the windows were painted a greyish white. As Hirsch approached, an elderly man in overalls emerged with a litre of milk. Nothing else moved in the entire town.

The interior was a dim cave. The ceiling, pressed tin, was stalactited with hooks from the days when the shopkeeper would hang it with buckets, watering cans, coils of rope and paired boots. Refrigerator cases lined a side wall, shallow crates of withered fruit and vegetables the back, and in the vast middle ground were aisles of rickety shelving, stacked with anything from tinned peaches to tampons. The sole cash register was adjacent to the entrance, next to ranks of daily newspapers and weekly and monthly magazines and a little bookcase thumbtacked with a sign, *Library*. If you were a farmer in need of an axe or some sheep dip you headed for the far back corner. If you wanted to buy a stamp, you headed a couple of paces past the library.

No sign of Melia Donovan's friend, but Hirsch was pretty sure he'd been served by the woman seated at the post office counter a couple of times. She glanced up at him and hastily away, one forefinger poised above the keypad of a calculator as if she'd lost her place. A thin, pinched woman, full of burdens. 'Excuse me,' Hirsch said, his footsteps snapping on the old floorboards as he approached, 'are you the shopkeeper?'

She whispered, 'No,' and nodded towards the dim rear.

Hirsch set out between the racks of groceries and found a small back room furnished with a desk, a fat old computer, filing cabinets, a swivel chair and a middle-aged man, tensely thin and neat. When Hirsch knocked on the door frame, the man shot out of his chair. 'Help you?'

'Paul Hirschhausen, I'm new at the police station.'

The shopkeeper reached out a long, thin, defenceless hand. 'Yes, Ed Tennant. Thought I'd run into you sooner or later.'

And without much joy in the anticipation, thought Hirsch, returning the shake. Tennant looked as sour as the post office woman.

'I just met your wife.'

Tennant didn't reply to that. 'What can I do for you?'

'I'm afraid this is not exactly a courtesy call.'

'Oh?' said Tennant, a soup of apprehensions showing. Then he firmed up a little. 'I thought it was all sorted.'

Hirsch decided to play along. 'Depends.'

Tennant bared his teeth without humour, a stringy man fuelled by nerves and grievances. 'There was no need for Sergeant Kropp to send you.'

'Right.'

'I will give the Latimers some leeway, but they can't rely on shiny shoes and a smile to get them through forever. If they haven't got the money they shouldn't go shopping.'

Hirsch thought back to the green-roofed house he'd seen that morning, the signs of neglect. It didn't surprise him that the Latimers were in strife, he supposed. He stored that away for now and held up a palm. 'Actually, Mr Tennant, I badly need to speak to Gemma Pitcher. I understand she works for you?'

'She's not here. What's going on? She got a phone call and burst into tears and left, said she'd be back tomorrow.'

'If you could tell me where she lives?'

'Next to the tennis courts. Look, what's it about? Is she in trouble? You speak to me first, all right?'

Hirsch hardened his voice. 'Mr Tennant, I'm not about to arrest or hassle anyone. But I do need to speak to Gemma.'

'And I'd like to know what about,' Tennant said, a man of precise habits and concerns.

Hirsch sighed. 'Her friend Melia Donovan has been killed. Now, can I go about my business?'

'Oh.' Tennant subsided. 'That explains the phone call.'

Hirsch was curious. 'Did she say who called?'

'Nope.' As Hirsch moved off, the shopkeeper added, 'How did it happen? Melia?'

Hirsch stopped. 'She was hit by a car and found by the side of the road.'

He could see the man picturing it, partly avid, partly horrified. He left the shop and went in search of the dead girl's friend.

He had to get past her mother first. 'She's that upset,' said Eileen Pitcher at a peeling front door, the house peeling too, separated from the town's tennis courts by a line of overgrown cypresses.

Hirsch was tired. 'Won't take a moment, Mrs Pitcher.'

Gemma Pitcher's mother was tiny and aggrieved and didn't want Hirsch on her doorstep. 'Wipe your feet.'

She led Hirsch to a sitting-cum-dining room, semi-dark, a TV flickering and two boys crouched before it, thumbing X-Boxes. The dining table sat against the rear wall, and Gemma Pitcher was sprawled on a sofa, tissues in her fist, eyes damp. She was a plump eighteen, with a band of soft belly showing between the waistband of tight jeans and the scant hem of a T-shirt. Her navel looked sore to Hirsch, the flesh puckered around a thick silver ring. She wore her mousy hair long, a ragged fringe over her mascaraed eyes— the mascara currently leaking down her cheeks.

'Hello,' Hirsch said, telling her who he was.

Gemma was one of those teenagers who can barely speak to or look at an adult but respond to greetings with a kind of mincing grimace. Hirsch crouched so that his head was on a level with hers. 'You might remember serving me in the shop a couple of times.'

She shrugged.

Girls like this are shruggers, Hirsch thought, and they fill the world. 'Are you up to answering a few questions?'

'No, she's not,' the mother said.

'Gemma?'

'Don't care.'

'Gemma love, you've had a shock.'

'Mum, it's all right. You can go.'

Mrs Pitcher turned her hooked, distrusting features on Hirsch. Scowled, touched Gemma's upper arm as if conceding she was beaten, and left them to it.

'Perhaps we could sit at the table?' Hirsch suggested.

'Whatever.'

Gemma took one stiff dining chair, Hirsch another. She lit up a Holiday using a pink disposable lighter. The three rings in the cartilage of each ear glinted as she sucked smoke from her cigarette and jetted it out through side-pursed lips. That was all the energy she could muster. Otherwise she was helpless, scared, a little weepy.

'I don't know if I—'

'Won't take a moment. I'm trying to fill in Melia's movements on the weekend.'

Gemma's knee jiggled. An old, habitual deflection of shame or guilt? Hirsch sharpened his tone. 'Were you with her at any stage?'

Gemma didn't want to answer. Her eyes cut across to the hallway door, her purple nails picking at the hard seam of her jeans. 'Can't remember.'

'Gemma. Yesterday and the day before. Were you with her or not?'

'Might of been. For a while.'

'You went out Saturday night?'

Another shrug.

'You have a car?'

'Mum's car.'

'You took Melia somewhere?'

'I'm allowda.'

'Sure, nothing wrong with that,' Hirsch said, and he waited.

It came: 'We went down to Redruth.'

'What did you do there?'

'Stuff.'

'Pub? Friend's house? Café?'

'Didn't drink and drive if that's what you're asking.'

'Did Melia drink?'

'Her mum lets her,' Gemma said hotly.

Hirsch smiled. 'It's all right, I'm not the underage drinking police.' Which was a downright lie. 'Which pub?' he asked.

'The Woolman.'

'She was with you the whole time?'

'Friends and that.'

'There was a group of you?'

Shrug.

'You stayed there the whole evening? You, Melia, your friends?'

Gemma launched into a blow-by-blow. They'd been joined by Nick and Julie but Julie's ex-boyfriend Brad showed up so Nick told him to get lost and there was a bit of a fight and Lisa, that's Jeff's cousin, she calmed them down and Gemma's boyfriend was like, let's go to the drive-in. It made no sense and Hirsch lost interest.

'Drive-in?' he asked.

'There's one in Clare.'

'Melia didn't go with you?'

'I told you that.'

'So she was still in the pub when you left?'

'I told you that.'

'Was her boyfriend there? Ex-boyfriend?'

'What boyfriend?'

55

'Any boyfriend. How about the older guy she's been seeing?'

Gemma's gaze was sliding away at every question now, as if to escape her own evasions. 'Don't know about no older guy.'

'The one she was in an accident with,' Hirsch said, guessing.

'On the weekend?'

'A few weeks ago.'

'Wouldn't know.'

'If you think of anything,' Hirsch said, his voice on the far side of weary defeat, 'give me a call.'

He returned to the Donovan house. Another car was there, a dinged-about Commodore. Melia's brother, thought Hirsch. Or relatives or friends, and if Leanne Donovan was still sedated and the house was thick with grieving, there was no point in knocking on the door. He turned around and headed for the shop again, starving, thinking of dinner.

Hirsch's main kitchen appliance was his microwave, so he headed straight for the frozen meals. Almost closing time and the shop was relatively busy. He counted four women and two men in the aisles. Tennant's wife was at the cash register, Tennant hovering. He followed Hirsch to the freezer, watched as Hirsch selected a frozen lasagne.

'Gemma okay?'

'Bit upset.'

'We all are,' Tennant said, and Hirsch realised he'd sensed it as he'd walked through the store, a community atmosphere of fear and sorrow and whispers. By now they'd all know the who, where, what, when and why. 'Shop's busy all of a sudden.'

'It happens,' Tennant said. 'Won't complain.' He looked with miserable triumph at Hirsch. 'You're asking for a speeding ticket or whatever if you shop in Redruth. Business has picked up for me.'

What the hell was happening in Redruth? Hirsch gestured with the lasagne. 'Dinner.'

Tennant gave Hirsch and his frozen pasta a poor-bastard look. 'Your money's as good as anyone's.'

A white police Discovery was parked foursquare outside the police station. Hirsch didn't like that one bit. Hated it, in fact. Nothing in any way pleasant would come of it. And so he ignored it, unlocking the front door and shoving through, admitting late afternoon sunlight, which probed briefly, illuminating the wall cabinet, its glass doors finger-smudged with country-town boredoms and disappointments.

Checking automatically for envelopes that might have been slipped under the door, checking the message light on the answering machine, he entered his office, public notices stirring in his slipstream, a rose petal tumbling the length of the vase he'd placed on the counter earlier in the week. Time he picked another bunch. The town was half knitted together with rose canes.

As expected, footsteps came in hard on his heels, a bitten-off voice. 'Constable.'

Hirsch turned. 'Sarge.'

Kropp stood on the other side of the counter, a solid fifty-year-old with fierce eyebrows and short grey hair. 'Did you call Spurling?'

Spurling? Hirsch went blank for a moment. Spurling: right, the area commander. A superintendent based at Port Pirie. 'Not me, Sarge.'

Kropp grunted. 'Well he heard about the hit-and-run from somebody.'

'And?'

'And he doesn't want any fuck-ups.'

Hirsch waited, enduring Kropp's fury or whatever it was. The sergeant's nose had been broken and badly set sometime in the past; now it seemed to steer him in scoffing and sceptical directions. His mouth was a barely visible slash across the bottom of his face.

Hirsch said, 'So you headed up here to see if I was fucking up?'

'Don't be a cunt, son. Here to see you're settling in okay, your lovely new quarters.'

Hirsch motioned to the stiff chair that faced his desk, but Kropp shook his head. 'No thanks. Somewhere more comfortable, think you can manage that?'

Hirsch pictured his living quarters and doubted it. 'Come through.'

The connecting door led to a short corridor and a shut-in smell, no natural light, boxes hard against the wall. Edging past, Kropp said, 'You've been here what, three weeks already? You're not going anywhere else, sunshine, so you might as well unpack.'

'Had my hands full, sir.'

The corridor opened on to the cramped sitting room. 'Get your wife to do it,' Kropp said, and stopped to give his meaty head a theatrical smack. 'Oh, I forgot. She left you, I seem to recall.'

'Kind of you to remind me, Sarge,' Hirsch said, his voice full of light cadences. He opened the curtains without improving anything. He switched on the overhead light. Dust motes floated. This was a loveless place and Hirsch sometimes found himself talking to the furniture in the dark hours. Dumping Saturday's *Advertiser* from one of the armchairs, he sat in the other, better, armchair. Kropp eyed the remaining chair and lowered himself as if clenching his sphincter.

'Tea?' said Hirsch. 'Coffee?'

The sergeant shook his head, thank Christ. 'This hit-and-run. Anything leap out at you?'

'Probably she was hitching home and a vehicle hit her. *Possibly* she was killed elsewhere and dumped. Until I know what she was doing there I—'

'What's this "I" shit? Team effort. Oh, I forgot, you don't do team effort.' Kropp leaned his forearms on his knees and stared at Hirsch. 'Let the accident boys deal with the evidence and *we* will work out a plan of action to answer your questions about her movements, okay?'

'Sarge.'

'Meanwhile I want you down in Redruth at noon tomorrow for a briefing.'

'Sarge.'

Hirsch waited, Kropp watching as if to chase him if he ran.

Then the man grinned unpleasantly and stood. 'That crack in your windscreen? Get it fixed.' He paused. 'Know why?'

Hirsch's mind raced. Roadworthiness? He guessed, 'Anything we don't tolerate in the citizenry, we don't tolerate in ourselves, maybe?'

'Aren't you a boy scout. Try Redruth Automotive.'

Then Kropp was gone and Hirsch heated and ate his lasagne—talking, for want of another candidate, to the less comfortable of the two chairs.

6

What was wrong with him? Those kids this morning had seen a woman hovering around his car. He dumped his dirty plate in the sink and hurried out to the Nissan with a torch, a rag, a pair of latex gloves. After a moment's thought, he went back for a couple of evidence bags.

He started at the boot and moved forwards: toolbox, spare tyre well, under the boot carpet. Then the parcel shelf, under the rear seat, inside the door cavities, under the front seats, glove box. He found what he was looking for in an ancient, forgotten first-aid box, but continued his search inside the engine bay, just in case. Nothing there.

He returned to the first-aid box. An iPhone and a bundle of cash. First he photographed both items *in situ*, then removed them. Still some juice in the phone; it was an iPhone 5 in perfect nick. He scrolled through until he came to a screen showing the IMEI number, photographed it. The cash amounted to $2500 in hundred-dollar notes. He took the rubber band off the bundle and photographed each note, twenty-five serial numbers. Finally he stowed everything in one of the evidence bags.

The time was six-thirty. Hirsch returned to the shop, still toting the evidence bag. Tennant had a CCTV camera above the petrol bowser. Might get lucky.

He found the shopkeeper switching off lights. Tennant frowned at the evidence bag. 'You want a refund on your dinner?'

'Ha, ha. The camera above your bowser: does it work?'

'It works.'

'Video or hard drive?'

'Hard drive.'

'I need to see footage from Friday, mid-morning.'

Tennant was confused. 'Somebody broke in? I'm not missing anything.'

With a just-routine air, Hirsch said, 'Someone put a note under my door, no big deal, something about a tax cheat, as if that's the police's business, but if the lens range and angle allows it, I might get an idea who left the note, put a flea in their ear.'

Stop babbling, he told himself.

'Tax cheat?'

'Not you,' Hirsch assured the shopkeeper.

Irritated, Tennant took him to the back room and showed him the equipment and how to run a search. He wanted to hover, so Hirsch said, 'Police business.'

He was in luck: Tennant's camera had been angled to cover the bowser, but also showed the footpath and part of the police station. He saw a woman of slight build and above average height, shoulder-length fair hair swinging around her neck and cheeks, moving rapidly. No clear shot of her face, damn it all. Of course it helped that he rarely locked his old bomb, but she was in and out of his car inside a minute.

Hirsch found Tennant at the front door, anxious to lock up and go home. 'Finished?'

'I need to buy a memory stick.'

'Really? You found something?' Tennant said, intrigued, unlocking a drawer, fishing around in it and coming up with an eight gig stick. 'This do you?'

'Fine.'

'I can show you how to copy the footage.'

'I'll be right.'

So Tennant charged Hirsch twice what the device was worth and waited in a sulk at the door.

Where to stow the phone and cash? If Internal Investigations officers searched his car now—which was presumably the point—and found nothing, they'd tear the house, office and HiLux apart. And he knew and trusted no one here.

Hirsch walked around to the rear of the station, poked his head over the side fence, into the old woman's back yard. It was overgrown by weeds and roses, the little garden shed mute testament to her inability to keep up anymore. He clambered over the fence. Concealed everything in an empty paint tin, taking reasonable care not to disturb the dust that covered it.

*

Back in his office, Hirsch dialled an Adelaide number.

'We need to meet.'

Sergeant Rosie DeLisle said tensely, 'You bet we do. In fact, I was about to call you.'

That made Hirsch tense. 'What happened?'

'You tell me.'

Hirsch knew then that the Internals had some fresh purgatory in store for him: new evidence, a new slant on old evidence, something like that. Rosie had always been straight with him; ultimately she'd gone into bat for him, but he'd always skated on thin ice, the sessions he'd had with her.

'I'm being set up.'

'Is that a fact,' she said flatly.

'You show me yours and I'll show you mine.'

'Not over the phone.'

'That suits me. I can be in the city by ten.'

'Tonight? No thanks. Tomorrow afternoon sometime.'

'That works for me.'

'Somewhere off the beaten track, Paul.' She named a winery in the Barossa Valley. 'One o'clock.'

'You think your colleagues don't visit wineries?'

'Not this one.'

'Ah, somewhere nice,' Hirsch said. 'Boutique. You sure you're not on the take?'

'Just be there, all right?'

Tuesday morning, and Hirsch had things to do before he attended Kropp's briefing in Redruth. He was on the road by seven-forty, the sun laid out along the eastern horizon. A washed-clean day with vivid green on both sides of the road, the birds soaring. He lifted his forefinger to oncoming drivers, who didn't expect it from a cop. Halfway down the valley he turned right onto the road to Clare, the only town of any size in the area. It had an agency of his building society and it had a phone shop. He visited the building society first, withdrawing $2500 in hundred-dollar bills, leaving himself with $164.65 until payday. Then he went to the phone shop.

Hirsch had bought his present phone there three weeks ago on Kropp's advice. 'The first thing you need to know is we get shit mobile reception up here,' the sergeant had said. 'As much as I find it amusing to think of you stranded in the middle of nowhere with a flat tyre and no signal bars, the department would take a dim view, so get yourself a decent phone, all right?'

'Maybe the department could spring for a satellite phone, Sarge.'

'Don't push your luck with me, sunshine.'

What Hirsch remembered about the phone shop was the box of parts behind the counter: old GSM phones, cracked touch-screens, scarred plastic cases, dead batteries, iPhones with the guts stripped out.

He drove back to Tiverton with the cash and an iPhone 4 that wouldn't power past the boot logo. Cost him a completely outrageous $150, and now he had $14.65 to his name.

Half-expecting officers from Internal Investigations to jump him, half-fearing to learn they'd already carried out their search, he reached into the Nissan, found the first-aid box exactly where he'd left it, and stowed the broken phone and his hard-earned cash inside it.

7

Hirsch pinned his mobile number to the front door and headed back down the valley to Redruth. Forty minutes of wheat and canola crops spread between the distant blue ranges and finally signs of habitation, then he was drawing into a town of pretty stone buildings folded through a series of hillocks. Started as a copper-mining town in the 1840s, it was a pastoral centre now. The Cornish Jacks were long gone, leaving behind flooded mine shafts, some cottage rows and a legacy of names like Redruth and Truro. Hirsch had explored the old mine when he first arrived. Bottomless pools of water in an enchanted shade of blue; mine batteries, sheds and stone chimneys sitting licheny and eroded on the slopes above the town.

Soon he was making a shallow descent to the town centre where the shops, a pair of pubs and a garage were arranged around an oblong square containing a statue to the war dead and a tiny rotunda on a stone-edged lawn. The building frontages were nineteenth century but the hoardings and signage were purely modern, a mishmash of corporate livery in different colours and fonts. Then he was through the square and entering an abbreviated side street, directed to the police station by a sign and an arrow. At the kerb on both sides of the street were police vehicles: two four-wheel-drives, Kropp's Ford and two patrol cars.

The time was eleven-forty-five. He parked and went in. This station was no converted house, it was a dedicated red-brick building with a lockup, several rooms and a large rear yard, but inside its foyer-cum-waiting room Hirsch found a front counter like his own: scarred wood, wanted posters and out-of-date notices on the wall, a couple of desks and filing cabinets in the dim corners.

The counter was staffed by a middle-aged man in civilian clothing, an auxiliary support officer whose job it was to greet the walk-ins, hand out forms, take reports, do the filing. A dull, sleepy man, he emitted a quiver of interest when Hirsch gave his name. 'Ah, Constable Hirschhausen. Through that door.'

He pointed, and Hirsch found himself in a region of cramped rooms at the rear of the station: Kropp's office, a small tea room, a briefing room, an interview room, storage area, files. At the end of the corridor was a steel door leading to the lockup. Drawn by voices, movement, a spill of light, Hirsch headed for the tea room.

It fell silent the moment he appeared in the doorway. Two men stared at him stonily: the Redruth constables, Nicholson and Andrewartha. Hirsch gave a face-splitting grin, just to rile them. 'Hi, guys!'

Nicholson said, 'Maggot,' showing a mouth crowded with tiny teeth. He was fleshy and pink, his face veined.

Hirsch grinned again and turned to Andrewartha. Another from the porcine family, this one had moist, red-budded lips that seemed shaped to blow kisses. He stuck a stub of a finger to his temple, cocked his thumb and said, '*Pow*.'

'Good to see you, guys,' said Hirsch, pushing through.

'Arsehole.'

Two rickety plastic tables in the room, one strewn with paper cups, sports papers and skin mags, the other bearing an urn and a percolator. Hirsch poured coffee into a paper cup. Nicholson jostled him.

'Whoops, sorry mate, clumsy of me.'

Hirsch poured another cup. He grabbed a stale donut and ducked around Nicholson's tree-trunk form to stand beside the refrigerator, stashing coffee and donut on the top of it and fishing out his phone. He angled the screen and ran his fingers; not looking at the others but ready to fight if that's what they wanted.

Then, an alteration in the air, a tremor of awareness passing through Nicholson and Andrewartha, a quick subterranean nastiness. Glancing up, Hirsch saw a young female officer in the doorway, pink, tense, sprucely ironed.

'Morning.' Her voice was low and raspy, but a squeak of nerves ran through it.

'Did someone say something?' Andrewartha asked, cocking an ear.

'I didn't hear anything,' Nicholson said. He flared his nostrils: 'Hang on, there's a whiff in the air.'

The newcomer flushed, but was game. 'Maybe you've got a dose of hay fever . . . or a dose of something.'

'Now, what *is* that smell?' said Nicholson. 'Got it! Feminine hygiene product.'

'You would know,' Andrewartha said, jostling him.

Both men pushed past her into the corridor, their voices fading along it: 'They reckon she'll root anything on two legs.'

'*Four* legs.'

That left Hirsch alone in the room with her. She glanced at him without hope or interest. 'Okay, give it your best shot.'

Hirsch headed for the percolator. 'Coffee?'

'Coffee and spit, right?'

'Tea and spit if you'd prefer.'

He read her name tag, Jennifer Dee, and waited. A slender woman of almost his height. Fine bones and sharp features on a narrow face, an impression of tightness reinforced by her hair, raked back savagely and caught in a short ponytail. She looked obstinate yet nervy.

Dee was watching him right back, unblinking and intense. Abruptly a shift occurred. 'Weak black, no sugar.'

'Coming up. Donut?'

She came nearer, moving awkwardly, a young woman not yet quite comfortable with herself. Pretending she didn't know him when everyone knew him. 'I could do with a sugar hit.'

'Good thinking,' Hirsch said.

He served her. They stood there awhile. Swallowing a mouthful, Hirsch said, 'You weren't stationed here when I checked in last month.'

She shook her head. 'Just started.'

'They're giving you a hard time?'

'I can handle it.'

As if responding to an invisible signal, they sat at the empty table. Hirsch swiped the top with his sleeve, the surface layer of crumbs, racehorses and crotches and tits giving way to scratched initials and scorch marks. He raised his cup, said, 'Cheers,' and a moment later Kropp was snarling from the doorway.

'Both of you get your arses in the briefing room, and I mean *now*.' He was propped there glaring, one big hand on each upright of the door frame as if to work his chest muscles.

'Sarge,' said Hirsch, echoed by Dee.

They grabbed their paper cups and plates and followed Kropp to the briefing room, where Nicholson and Andrewartha lolled in steel chairs. Both men stared contemptuously, but Hirsch, who had been stared down by experts, blew a couple of kisses and selected the chair next to Nicholson. Dee was obliged to sit beside Andrewartha. He scooted his chair away from her.

Kropp stood at the end of the table, slapping a white pointer against his thigh. 'If you people are quite ready.'

'Sarge.'

'Let's get to it.'

The sergeant propped his hands on the back of his chair, full of scowling impatience. 'I've got a guy coming in from the accident squad, but until then here's what we know: sometime on the weekend a kid from Tiverton was killed by a hit-and-run driver up near Muncowie.'

He straightened, turned to the board and wall map behind him, and touched the tip of his pointer to a photograph clipped from that day's *Advertiser*. 'This is her, Melia Donovan. Some of you know her.'

Nicholson nudged Andrewartha. 'Some better than others.'

'If you idiots could stop fooling around.'

'Sorry, Sarge.'

Kropp paged through a mess of paperwork on the table. 'Got the preliminary autopsy here somewhere.'

That was quick, Hirsch thought. A blowfly droned through the room, smacking the window behind him. He could hear the town out there, voices and car doors slamming and the hiss of airbrakes and a radio tuned to a talkback show in the house next door.

Kropp looked up, frustrated. 'Mr Hirschhausen.'

'Sarge?'

'Go to the file room, see if I left an A4 envelope in there. Marked *Donovan autopsy*.'

'Sarge.'

Hirsch saw but couldn't read the look on Dee's face. He winked at Andrewartha as he went out.

Went to the wrong door at first, almost opened it before he saw the sign pinned at chin height: *You enter here with good looks and the truth. You don't get to leave with both.* Hirsch snorted: interview room. The next door was marked *Files*. He entered, spotting the envelope immediately, public service non-colour, flap open, angled across the top of a filing cabinet. He spotted the hundred-dollar note on the floor a moment later, when he was halfway across the room.

'Seriously?' he said.

Pocketing the note, he collected the envelope and handed it to Kropp in the briefing room. 'Here you go, Sarge.'

Seated again, arms folded benignly, he settled back to listen to Kropp.

Then smacked his forehead. 'Almost forgot. Found this on the floor.' He contorted in his seat, turning onto his left hip and, sticking his right leg out, gained access to his trouser pocket. He fished out the hundred, waved it, passed it to Nicholson. Everyone watched its progress down the table.

'It was on the floor?'

'Sure was. Should I take it to the front desk and log it in?'

'I'll deal with it,' Kropp muttered.

Hirsch beamed in his chair, arms folded again. He bumped shoulders with Nicholson, gave a little nod. 'Integrity test,' he whispered.

'Get the fuck out of my face.'

'Is that what you're calling it?'

Hirsch was having a high old time.

The accident investigator was a sergeant named Exley.

'If you find us the vehicle,' he said, 'we'll match it to the evidence.'

Hirsch hadn't seen any evidence. 'What evidence, Sarge?'

Spoiling Exley's flow. 'All in good time. I've spoken to the coroner. She intends to visit the scene during the week and on Friday open an inquest. In all likelihood she'll immediately announce a recess, but it would help if we could report on the victim's last movements and meanwhile investigate local crash repairers and motorists with a history of driving under the influence.'

Then he was gone.

Kropp was nettled; Hirsch could see it in his jaw, his whitened knuckles on the back of the chair. 'The powers that be have spoken, so let's get to it. Constable Hirschhausen, your job is to interview family and friends, see what the poor kid was up to.'

'Sarge.'

'And have a poke around in Muncowie.'

'Sarge.'

Kropp gazed bleakly at Nicholson and Andrewartha. 'Redruth Automotive. Given that you two simpletons work there in your spare time, I'll let you take care of that.'

'Sarge,' Nicholson said, swapping grins with Andrewartha.

Kropp looked at Dee sourly. 'You can tag along if and as required.'

'Yes, Sergeant.'

'Yes, Sergeant,' Nicholson said.

'Cut it out,' Kropp said.

Hirsch waved his hand lazily. 'Sarge, what's the story with the family?'

'Old story: single mum, two kids, separate fathers. What else is there to say?'

'Melia was done for shoplifting.'

'She was. Slap over the wrist.'

'I'd look at the brother,' Andrewartha said. 'Abo prick.'

'Knock it off,' Kropp said, weary.

'Well, he is.'

Hirsch said, 'Why would that make him run his sister over?'

'Why would he do anything? That's the point, there is no why.'

'Thanks for clearing that up.'

Kropp intervened. 'She liked to hitchhike,' he said, looking at Hirsch. 'Bear that in mind.'

'Sarge.'

8

Early afternoon now.

Hirsch shot out of town before anyone could intercept him, heading south. He half-expected Kropp to call him with some tiresome demand but his phone rang only once, a Barrier Highway motorist calling to report a spill of hay bales near Mount Bryan. 'Try the Redruth police station,' Hirsch said.

Better still, drag them off the road yourself.

Thirty minutes later he was at Tarlee, where he turned south-east into undulating country, giant silent silvery gumtrees watching, until finally he was driving past vines and old winery names. Another thirty minutes and he was on a potholed dirt road leading up to Rosie DeLisle's tiny hilltop winery. Out of habit, Hirsch checked the cars parked there, slotted into bays marked by old redgum sleepers. A mix of expensive German sedans and four-wheel-drives. He didn't know Rosie DeLisle's car.

German refinement and his dirty police HiLux. No

disguising that. But Hirsch did a quick number on himself. Tossed his tie, jacket and cap onto the back seat, stowed the gun belt in a briefcase, dragged on a denim jacket.

He found Rosie seated on a wooden bench at a wooden table—more old redgum slabs—under a shadecloth, the fabric whispering and slapping in a stiff breeze from the valley. Severe rows of vines stretched down into the valley and up the other side, but here in the al fresco dining area there were beds of vegetables and herbs, the air scented and bees buzzing and one magpie warbling from a trellis. There's money here, Hirsch thought—well obviously, given the cellar-door prices he'd noted on his way in.

Rosie stepped away from the table and pecked his cheek. Her movements were careful; her misgivings weren't about to evaporate any time soon. And she'd already eaten, leaving a fleck of oily lettuce in a salad bowl and a crust of pizza on a chunky white plate.

'Started without me?'

'Starving.'

Hirsch grumbled his way onto the bench opposite hers, stowed the briefcase at his feet and studied the menu. Salad, smoked salmon pizza, mineral water.

He ate, they talked.

When it all went bad for Hirsch, he'd been a detective stationed at Paradise Gardens, an outer Adelaide police station. Head of CIB was a senior sergeant named Marcus Quine. After the arrests of Quine and his team, after the raid and the charges and the media frenzy, Rosie DeLisle had been the Internal Investigations officer assigned to question Hirsch. 'One officer per corrupt detective,' she'd told him. 'We all swap notes at the end of the day, to build up our picture of what you shits have been up to.'

'What about innocent until proven guilty?'

She told him to shut up. It was clear she thought he was scum. And then, days, weeks later, her mood lightened. She believes me, Hirsch thought—or, at the very least, she's got doubts.

Finally she'd expressed these doubts to Hirsch. 'Will you give evidence against Quine?'

'No.'

She'd gnawed her lower lip, then confessed that she'd recommended no further action against him. 'But my colleagues don't agree with me, and it doesn't necessarily let you off the hook.'

No, not off the hook. A whiff clung to him. He was demoted and posted to the bush. And for all he knew, no one but Rosie and his parents thought he was an honest copper. Then, when Quine and the others were charged and punished—variously sacked and jailed; one senior constable suiciding—people asked why Paul Hirschhausen had got off so lightly. The answer was clear: he was a turncoat, a dog, a maggot. He stared at Rosie, misgivings shading her face as she drained her shiraz and slapped down her glass. 'Sometime soon, maybe as early as next week, you'll be invited to police headquarters to face another round of questions.'

'Invited.'

She shrugged.

'Why?'

'To answer fresh allegations.'

'Against me?'

'Yes. Quine's not exactly been twiddling his thumbs.'

Hirsch had heard it on the grapevine, Quine the master manipulator beating Rosie and her colleagues into exhaustion with a battery of freedom-of-information requests and demands for day-book entries, diary entries, files, notes, statements, records, reports, memos, e-mails, video and audio recordings, computer discs and memory sticks. And any and all correspondence, however vaguely connected to his twenty years in the employ of South Australia Police. A futile exercise if undertaken by anyone else, but Quine had got away with a lot for a long time and he might get away with this.

'He's saying the case against him is a soufflé,' Rosie said.

Hirsch snorted. 'So what are these allegations?'

Rosie began to chip at a fleck of cheese on her pizza crust. Nice hands, Hirsch thought. That was inconvenient. He dragged his eyes away. They'd had fun in bed, one night when it was all over, but that had no place here. He couldn't look at the vines and vegetable beds and other diners forever, though, so he turned back to watch Rosie struggle with herself. She was vivid and round and lit within, normally, her fine black hair flashing, her scarlet nails and lips avid for experiences. She was probably an affront to the men she investigated and treated seriously by no one.

'Anonymous tipoff,' she said.

'Saying . . . ?'

She looked fully at him, eaten up, you could see it in her face and upper body. 'No one will tell me anything, but I've gathered they think you pilfered stolen goods from the evidence safe at Paradise Gardens. Apparently they have serial numbers.'

'What kind of items?'

'No idea. Drugs? Cash?'

Her face twisted. She almost reached across the redgum and took his wrist. 'Paul, they seem dead certain. Is it true? Will they find something?'

'Sure,' Hirsch said, and he fished out his phone, pressed the photo gallery icon and handed it over. 'Scroll through.'

He watched a pretty forefinger flick the screen. 'The first-aid box in my car,' he said. 'The phone is an iPhone 5, and the cash amounts to two and a half grand in hundreds.'

She continued to scroll. 'Serial numbers.'

'Yes. Phone and cash.'

A twist of frustration. 'It's all going to match, isn't it?'

'Without a doubt.'

'Paul, tell me straight, did you pinch this stuff?'

'Fuck you, Rosie.'

She slid the phone back across the table. 'But who's going to believe you just stumbled on this? They'll think you took these photographs just in case, some weak attempt to say you were set up.'

'Possibly,' Hirsch said.

A young woman came by with a tray and a smile, a little frown when Hirsch bent his upper body over the phone. 'Get you anything else? Coffee? Sticky date pudding's on special.'

'Sticky date, please,' Rosie said.

'Coffee,' Hirsch said.

When the waitress was gone, tight black jeans winking, Rosie gestured at the phone. 'They'll use this. Quine has plenty of friends. Even the people I work with. You should have brought everything with you and logged it in with me.'

Hirsch took up his phone again. 'Got a little movie to show you.'

He found the file containing the CCTV footage of the woman lurking around his car. Pressed 'play' and sat back to watch DeLisle's face.

She breathed out. 'Quality's not great, but . . .'

'But it's clear what she's doing, and time and date are embedded in the original, and I have a statutory declaration from the shopkeeper whose camera took this.'

'Who is it?'

'No idea.'

'Kropp's wife?'

Hirsch went very still. He looked hard at Rosie. 'One might ask why you mention his name.'

DeLisle shut down. Eventually she said, 'Could this be the wife of one of the others? Nicholson? Andrewartha?'

'And one might wonder how you happen to know the names of everyone stationed at Redruth,' Hirsch said. 'Unless you've been checking up on me.'

Rosie DeLisle shrugged, a shrug that contained volumes. Well, fuck them all. 'When am I supposed to face the music?'

'You'll get an e-mail.'

'Not even a phone call.'

'A phone call to ensure you got the e-mail.'

Hirsch would have to tell Kropp he wouldn't be available next week. 'How long for?'

'Two or three days.'

'How will they run it?'

'They'll say some irregularities have cropped up, no big deal, but we need your help sorting them out. They'll start by taking you through your history at Paradise Gardens CIB, let you explain everything away, the corruption, etcetera, etcetera, then just when you're feeling secure, hit you with the phone and the cash.'

She'd told him. But the doubt was still there, he could read it in her. He threw a twenty onto the table and left.

9

Hirsch was back in Redruth by four-thirty. Rather than drive through the town, he turned off the highway, intending to reach Tiverton via the back roads that ran north and west of the town. A couple of the properties out there were on his watch list: an elderly farm widow and her schizophrenic son, and a farmhouse rented to a handful of dropout city kids who'd been accused of sabotaging the wind farm turbines.

His information was out of date: the widow had died and the farm was sold, the son taken in by a sister; the dropouts had returned to the city. Hirsch drove on, warm and slow from his lunch and the sun, and made the final turn back towards the highway. All of the roads out here were treacherous dirt nightmares like the Bitter Wash, so he wound down his window for a stay-alert breeze.

He came around a bend and a silver Lexus shot out of a driveway ahead, fishtailing as it gathered speed and spat pebbles at him. He backed off, hoping the dust would settle, and then accelerated gradually. He was twenty seconds or so behind the Lexus, the road otherwise empty, the air still, the dust dense, not budging. But the road coiled around the hillsides and dipped in and out of the erosion channels. He glimpsed the Lexus now and then before the dust intervened again. The driver was powering along, too fast for the conditions, and Hirsch found himself muttering, 'Slow down before you kill yourself, pal.'

Then about one kilometre before the Barrier Highway intersection, the Lexus sideswiped a guardrail. Hirsch saw the driver overcorrect, the car shooting back to the centre of the road, brake lights flaring, and he was pretty sure the driver had seen the HiLux behind him, a dim shape in the rearview mirror. The guy didn't stop but flicked around the next bend.

Fuck it. Hirsch accelerated, approaching the bend in careful stages, and found the Lexus in the middle of the road, doors open, the dust settling around it.

He braked, switched off, got out. So much drama, you'd expect an orchestra of panicky sounds, but the air was still and silent, only two hot engines ticking as they cooled. Then Hirsch's dust rolled over him and the stink of it was in his nose with his own diesel fumes.

When it cleared he saw a woman alight from the driver's seat, swinging one leg out of the footwell, then the other, emerging with the kind of fluttery relief you'd expect of a driver who'd had a close call. Or an actor.

'Oh, hello there. Whooh! My heart's going pitter-patter.'

She walked the ten metres towards Hirsch, a flirty blonde full of smiles. She was about thirty and, in a nod to spring, wore a darkish, short-sleeved cotton dress, knee-length over her tanned, tennis player legs.

She toed the dirt cutely with a sandalled foot. Red toe-nails. 'Talk about a lucky escape. These gravel roads are quite treacherous.'

Hirsch smiled, nodded, tutted his commiseration.

'Sorry about the guardrail. Of course I'll pay to have it mended.' She turned to eye the car. 'My husband and I have insurance.'

Now the husband was emerging, grinning like a madman, shaking his head at Hirsch, one bloke to another. 'If I've told her once, I've told her a thousand times . . .'

'Oh, Mike,' the wife said fondly. She rolled her eyes and turned on her smile for Hirsch, finger-hooking quotation marks in the air: 'Drive according to the conditions of the road.'

'Well, sweetheart, now you know first-hand what it means. Mike Venn,' the husband said, sticking out his hand. 'And this is Jess, my wife.'

'All right, knock it off both of you,' Hirsch said.

Venn glanced at his wife, at Hirsch. 'I beg your pardon?'

'You, sir, were driving, and you swapped places with your wife.'

'He did no such thing!'

'You've no doubt seen the drink-driving ads on TV,' Hirsch said. 'Every police vehicle is a booze bus. You can be breathalysed on the spot.'

The woman was astounded. 'You think we've been drinking?'

'I can smell it on you,' Hirsch said.

'A glass to celebrate a property sale, nothing more,' Venn said.

The wife could have left it at that. Her nose was exquisitely and maybe even naturally shaped, and it quivered now, a terrier after prey. 'What are you, some jumped-up little Hitler?'

'I'm sure if you run your mouth long enough I'll come up with another charge,' Hirsch said. He fetched a couple of breath-test kits from the HiLux, picturing the drama playing out behind his back. She glares at her husband, he glares at her, fury, a touch of panic, a pantomime of *Make it go away* and *Who do we know?*

He returned stony faced and gleeful. 'Blow into this, please, sir.'

'But I wasn't driving.'

'Don't worry, I'm testing both of you. I can't have one drunk driver replaced by another, now can I?'

Both Venns registered over .05. Hirsch announced this, and asked, 'Is there someone you can call?'

'Come on, we're clearly not drunk, and the road's not exactly crawling with vehicles.'

'You hit a guardrail, sir, and you were driving under the influence of alcohol. It would be irresponsible of me to allow you behind the wheel again today. What if you killed someone?'

'I was driving,' the wife said.

'Knock it the fuck off,' Hirsch snarled.

The clouds were high and fat and white, the sky vividly

blue. Promising a change, but just now glorious. Hirsch sought relief in the heavens, thinking there was no dust up there. He mentally listed the charges available to him. Giving a false statement, driving under the influence, reckless driving . . . There were a few.

He spelled it out to Venn, and asked again: 'Do you have someone who can drive you home? In your car, preferably. It's a hazard sitting here.'

'You clearly don't know how things work in the bush,' Venn said, hot in the face. 'A bit of live and let live, give and take. We make allowances. It works.'

Hirsch held up a warning finger. 'Before I forget, how many demerit points do you have on your licence, Mr Venn?'

That shut his mouth.

'Mike *needs* his licence,' his wife said. 'He's the Dalgety agent. He drives two or three *hundred* kilometres a day sometimes.'

'If he knew he'd accumulated enough points to lose his licence, why did he drink and drive?' Hirsch asked, telling himself he was a fool to get into it with them.

'The property market's quite depressed so we were thankful to steer a sale to fruition,' Venn said.

'And if you'd killed yourself? Killed your wife? Worse still, killed a kid on his bike?'

'All right! You've made your point. And my point is, my wife was driving.'

Hirsch glanced curiously at Venn.

'It's your intention to contest these charges before the magistrate?'

'Too right.'

'You'll testify that your wife was driving.'

'Sign a statutory declaration if I have to.'

Hirsch turned to Jessica Venn. 'You intend to perjure yourself before the court?'

She tilted back her nose, a woman forever intent on being hard done by. 'Not perjury. I was driving.'

'If you persist with this,' Hirsch said, 'and your husband loses, then I will charge you with perjury there and then, and I hope you know it could earn you a jail sentence.'

'You don't scare me. Jumped-up little Hitler.'

Well, that was a gorgeous experience. Entering the highway just north of Tiverton, Hirsch decided to head on to Muncowie.

He drove into a town more depressed than Tiverton, but laid out just like it. One shop, one pub and a handful of houses on either side of an abbreviated grid of stubby, broad streets. About eight in total, four running east-west, four north-south. Small houses, some built of local stone, others of rusting corrugated iron in the old three-room settler style, the rooms running from the front to the back with a chimney on a side wall and a dunny in the back yard. Weedy yards, cars on blocks. Hirsch felt deeply fatigued.

The pub was long and squat, the dusty cream outer wall sitting dark and deep behind a vine-hung veranda. A tin West End Bitter sign rattled in the wind. A couple of panes in the fanlight above the front door were cracked and cob-webby. The veranda floor had once been painted red but the colour had retreated over the decades, revealing glassy worn concrete—a good surface if you wanted to crack a head open.

He pushed into the pub, stepping from the concrete to creaky floorboards. Nail heads glinted brightly here and there, despite the curtained gloom of the front bar. The air was layered with stale beer fumes, cigarette smoke and the odours of rural work: diesel, petrol, grease, oil, sweat and animal odours, dung or lanolin or blood or all of it. Deeply ingrained and years old, guessed Hirsch, because the two old boozers and the publican at the bar didn't account for it.

They saw his uniform and the publican said, 'Reckoned you'd be in before too long. Pour you a drink?'

It was said with a crooked eyebrow so Hirsch took a stool and rested his elbows on the bar and said, 'Lemon squash.'

'Lemon squash, lemon squash,' the publican ruminated, as if the drink and its ingredients were beyond him.

'Bloody Mary, then.'

'That I can do,' the publican said, sticking a glass under a spigot and flipping a lever. Lemon squash frothed palely into the glass. 'Ice?'

'Hundred per cent lemon squash.'

The publican leaned back against the wall behind him, a small, narrow, beaming, efficient character, his arms folded above a neatly moulded belly. 'There goes my profit.'

Hirsch took him in, seeing the kind of small-time bustler who has virtually no personality beyond dishing up a patter of humour and inoffensive insults as he served drinks. He'd know your name and what you drank but you'd never learn a thing about him beyond the smile and the tight ship he ran. Possibly there was nothing to know. He'd have a history of pub management and maybe ownership behind him, here and there around the state. You wouldn't know why he'd chosen to buy your local pub, or why it was time for him to move on again, or why he'd left the last one, and there'd be no point in asking.

Hirsch toasted the publican and the two drinkers, bleary old-timers in crumpled work clothes and whiskers, cigarettes smouldering in the ashtray on the bar between them. They were halfway through tall glasses of beer that might have been sitting there for days, weeks. They weren't drinkers so much as drink-nursers. And yarners.

They had a few questions and knew a few half-truths about the death of Melia Donovan, so Hirsch filled some of the gaps, keeping his words, tone and delivery low key. He was hoping to read something in their responses, a tut-tut and a rueful head shake if they thought it just another tragic loss of a young life, or a flicker of something darker if they knew her or the circumstances of her death.

He got the former. 'Poor bloody kid,' they said. 'Like to get hold of the mongrel that hit her and just drove off.'

'Does her name ring a bell?'

'Not to me,' the publican said.

'Donovan,' nodded one of the drinkers, precipitating a to-and-fro with his mate about who Melia's mother, father, uncles, aunts and cousins might have been. Pretty much all hearsay, it seemed to Hirsch, but one thing was clear, the lineage wasn't covered in glory.

'Did you see her in here on Saturday night or any time Sunday?'

The publican gave a good impression of outrage. 'I don't serve kids.'

'She would have looked older,' Hirsch said, and described Melia Donovan, her size, colouring, hair.

'Mate, we don't get that many kids in here. Maybe Saturdays we'll get a couple of young blokes in after the footy or the cricket, but they hardly ever bring their girlfriends with them. Don't stay long either. They head up to Peterborough or across to Jamestown or down to Redruth, not the other way around.'

'Arse end of the world,' grinned one of the old-timers.

'So your first inkling,' Hirsch said, 'was when the bloke came in asking to use your phone.'

'That's the size of it,' the publican said.

Hirsch left his card on the bar. 'If you see or hear anything, give us a call,' he said, and went out to doorknock the town.

He got nowhere, heard nothing, and returned to the highway.

Another dead end in Tiverton. There was no answer at the Donovan house, no Commodore, no battered Mazda in the driveway. But Hirsch met Yvonne Muir, the neighbour who'd been comforting Leanne Donovan the previous day.

'Yoo hoo,' she called, a thin, edgy figure where her husband was solid and comfortable. She came across her yard and stopped at the side fence—but still in motion, her hands patting her hair, smoothing her dress, centring her necklace. She took a deep breath and said, 'You're the new policeman. You met my husband yesterday.' She added, in an expense of strength and feeling, 'Has something happened?'

Hirsch shook his head. 'A follow-up visit, that's all.'

With an air of tiptoeing through the proprieties, Muir said, 'She's at her mother's today. In Jamestown. Back tomorrow.'

Hirsch didn't pursue it. 'Have you known Mrs Donovan for long?'

'Ten years. More.'

'Are you friends, would you say?'

'Friends and neighbours. Are you sure nothing's wrong? It's not Nathan, is it? You leave that boy alone.'

Hirsch was tired. Needing to cut through the thickets, he said, 'Mrs Muir, I'm helping investigate Melia's accident, that's all. A few questions and I'll be out of their hair.'

'Please go easy on them.'

It was an entreaty, yet with some steel in it. 'Okay,' said Hirsch carefully, inviting an explanation.

'That family's been through a lot,' the woman said and she whisked back into her house.

Hirsch slipped his card into the door jamb and walked back to the highway.

Inside the general store the air currents moved sluggishly, the day's warmth coming to a head. Two cars parked snout-up to the shop veranda, two customers browsing with baskets hanging from their elbows. A teenage girl he didn't know was at the cash register, waiting.

Hirsch said, 'Is Gemma here?'

Her mouth opened slowly, she moved her head slowly. 'What?'

'Doesn't matter.'

Hirsch made his way to the tiny back office. Since yesterday the space had shrunk: hard against the walls were bundles of unsold magazines, the titles torn away, and sundry cartons of cigarettes. Tennant was behind the desk; Eileen Pitcher in the only other chair.

'Well, look who's here.'

Hirsch ignored the shopkeeper. 'Mrs Pitcher?'

Eileen Pitcher sat knees together, a cigarette in one rawboned hand, refusing to meet Hirsch's eye or return his greeting. He crouched where she couldn't avoid him. 'Is Gemma at home, Mrs Pitcher?'

The woman moved then, drawing powerfully on her cigarette. 'All your fault.'

'I don't understand,' Hirsch said mildly.

'She was that upset last night.'

'After my visit?'

She gave him a *what-are-ya?* look.

'Where is she, Mrs Pitcher?'

'She's run off, that's where she is,' Tennant said behind him.

Hirsch knee-creaked until he was upright again. 'Did she say where she was going?'

Cigarette bobbing in her mouth, smoke dribbling up the curve of her cheek and into her narrowed eyes, Eileen Pitcher leaned over to fish in her cardigan pocket. The note was warm and read: *Mum I love you but I have to go away for a while don't worry about me I am fine I will ring you I need space I done nothing wrong remember that I love you your daughter Gemma.*

'Have you tried calling her?'

'Goes to voicemail.'

'Mrs Pitcher, is there anything we should be worried about here?'

'What do you mean?'

'Did she call anyone last night or this morning?'

'Wouldn't know.'

'Did she pack a bag? Clothes, shoes, toiletries?'

'Course.'

'Things you'd expect her to take?'

'Yes.'

'What's going on?' said Tennant.

'I'm sure it's nothing,' Hirsch said. 'She's upset, it's only natural. But sometime soon I will need to have a chat with her about Melia's movements on the weekend.'

'Thought you already done that,' the mother said.

'It was a preliminary chat,' Hirsch said. 'I could see she was too upset to go on.'

'My daughter doesn't know nothing about nothing.'

'Of course not,' Hirsch said. 'Just a formality.'

He glanced at Tennant. 'If you could give me a moment with Mrs Pitcher . . .'

The shopkeeper didn't like it. 'I keep an eye on Eileen and Gemma. They don't need any aggravation.'

'That's not my intention.'

'Go easy, okay?'

'Mr Tennant.'

'All right, all right, I'm going.'

When he was gone, Hirsch closed the door, crouched by the woman's knees again. 'Mrs Pitcher, is this Gemma's handwriting?'

Pitcher began to tremble, full on, her free hand plucking at her top button, ash falling from her cigarette. 'Of course it is, what do you mean, are you saying she—'

'When did you find the note?'

'When I got home just now.'

'Where were you?'

'I help out down the pub.'

'Where was the note?'

'Kitchen table.'

'Had Gemma locked up before she left?'

Pitcher jetted smoke across the room. 'That girl never locks up, never turns off lights, never picks up after herself ...'

'Was anything disturbed or out of place?'

'You're making me scared.'

'Standard questions, Mrs Pitcher.'

'You think something's happened to her.'

'Heavens no,' Hirsch said. 'But there will be an inquest eventually and Gemma might be called and it would be good if we were all on the same page.'

How many times in his career had Hirsch waffled on like that? It was part of being a cop, he supposed. 'How about,' he said, 'you make me a list of her friends, anyone, family included, who she might visit or call. We'll contact them together.'

'She's gone off in me car. Can't you put out a whatchama-callit, alert?'

'Do you wish to report it stolen?'

Pitcher worried at it. 'Will that get her into trouble?'

'It might.'

'No.'

'Can you survive without a car for a few days?'

The woman slumped. 'I'll need it eventually.'

'For now,' Hirsch said, 'let's concentrate on those calls.'

They used her kitchen phone.

The house was as stuffy as the store, what air there was laced with cigarette smoke and emanations from the kitty litter heaped by the laundry door. As Eileen compiled the list of names and numbers, Hirsch made the calls. He figured it would be harder for people to knock back a policeman. Fifteen calls: aunts and uncles, adult cousins, school friends, grandparents, getting him nowhere.

Hirsch gave up. Maybe her Facebook page would reveal her whereabouts. 'Does Gemma have a computer?'

'Laptop,' Eileen said, taking him to a bedroom that was pretty much furnished by a floordrobe and an unmade single bed. Hirsch didn't bother stepping over the clothes. There was a printer but no sign of a laptop.

He returned to the police station. The first-aid box was missing from the boot of his car.

10

Hirsch got out of bed at six-shitty on Wednesday, drained a coffee and decided on some exercise: stretches, then a walk around the town.

Tiverton seemed deserted. Perhaps country people didn't walk or jog? He took their point: they knew the place, they worked hard at physical labour all day; what was the point? A couple of passing motorists eyed him, curtains twitched and mad dogs raced as he invaded fences and hedges. He gazed benignly at the school, the little grain business along a side street, the Catholic church and the Anglican, various back and side yards, chook sheds, a skeletal horse on a patch of dirt. Galahs screeched in the gumtrees and it occurred to him that he'd not been hearing the sounds of big city life these past three weeks. No traffic, no hoons with sound systems, no voices spilling from cafés. Only galahs in the trees.

Back in the office, he fired up the computer. One e-mail, headed *Quine hearing*: starting Monday, 10 a.m. sharp, Hirsch was obliged to present himself at the hearing into allegations of corruption against Senior Sergeant Marcus Quine and other detectives of the Paradise Gardens CIB.

Hirsch acknowledged, then fired an e-mail to Sergeant Kropp, explaining the circumstances. *So I'll be in Adelaide all next week, sorry Sarge.*

After breakfast, he made another run at the Donovans' house. The tired Mazda had returned. He mounted the veranda, reached out his knuckles and knocked.

Nothing. He looked across at the Muirs', sensing their eyes on him.

Just then the red door screeched and a woman appeared, rounded, not plump, untidily beautiful, drawing a brush through damp red hair. Taking in Hirsch's uniform she said, 'Yvonne said you'd dropped by.'

As if he'd been an old friend passing. Hirsch removed his cap and said, 'I'm very sorry, and I can't imagine what you're going through, everyone has such kind things to say about Melia, but I wonder if I could have a quick word with you and Nathan?'

He stopped, conscious that he was babbling. The door widened and he was hit by a front of stale warm air from inside the house, faintly laced with dope and beer. 'Only if it's convenient. I could come back tomorrow.'

Everything stopped. Leanne Donovan was very still in her doorway, her eyes clear and searching, then her hands moved, squeezing the end of a rope of the thick hair. Fresh out of the shower, her body was scented with shampoo and lotions and, despite himself, Hirsch was aware of her flesh beneath the green sundress.

'Nathan's not here.'

'That's all right, I'll catch him another time. Could I come inside, do you think?'

Her voice came raggedly, 'It's like a bad dream,' and her eyes filled.

'Yes. I'm very sorry.'

She dropped where she stood and might have slapped onto the cement front step if not for the door frame and Hirsch grabbing her around the waist. 'Let's get you inside. Would you like me to fetch Mrs Muir?'

'That's okay.'

Her legs found their strength and Hirsch eased her along a narrow corridor to a worn, dimly lit sitting room. A bulky old TV set dominated one wall, a detergent ad splashing blue and red over the reflective surfaces—the glass cabinet against one wall, the glossy veneer coffee table. A lived-in room, with a couple of empty bottles, an overflowing ashtray, a spill of lifestyle magazines. On one wall there was an image of Christ on the cross, on another Christ gazed soulfully past Hirsch's shoulder. But no grime or spills, and the only other furniture was a card table in the corner, crammed with a boxy old computer, a cheap inkjet printer beside it. Communal computer? He settled Leanne Donovan onto a floral fabric sofa, but it faced the television set, which continued to paint the room, so he found the remote and switched it off.

'Shall I make you a cup of tea?'

Leanne fiddled with a packet of cigarettes and a lighter. 'I'm okay.'

God, Hirsch was dreading this. 'Before I start, were you told there'll be an inquest?'

Leanne nodded. 'This lady rung me from the coroner's, she said Dr McAskill's finished the autopsy and I can have Mel back to bury.'

There was a pause. A word you can't sweeten, autopsy. Knives, saws, fluids, the peeling back of flesh. Hirsch said, 'Do you have a day for the funeral?'

'Saturday.'

'Would you mind if I came?'

'I don't care.'

Another pause, and Leanne said, 'Dr McAskill said she must of been hitching.'

Hirsch trod carefully. 'Her injuries and the position she was found in do suggest that.'

Leanne was very still and then she reeled and wailed. Hirsch waited. She swiped a sleeve across her nostrils and gasped, 'Sorry, I'm okay, it hits me out of nowhere sometimes.'

'Of course.'

'I don't understand it. She was alone up there? Someone just left her to hitch home? Was she, you know, drunk?'

'She'd had a couple of drinks.'

'Where was Gemma? She should of been looking after her.'

'They went their separate ways earlier in the evening. Are you sure you don't want a cup of tea?'

'Everyone wants to make me tea. What I want is my daughter back.'

'I understand. Perhaps we could start with what Melia had planned for the weekend.'

Hirsch strained to hear the reply. 'She didn't come home, the little devil.'

'She usually comes home after a night out with Gemma?'

'She's a good girl.'

'So you don't know what she was doing or who she was seeing in Muncowie?'

No reaction. Hirsch didn't know if the woman was taking it in or not. Maybe she had never taken an interest in her daughter's movements. 'Mrs Donovan? Does she know anyone up there? Did she mention a party she was going to, for example?'

No response, then, 'Nathan's all I've got now.'

'Did Melia have a boyfriend, Mrs Donovan? Could she have been with him on Saturday night?'

'Maybe.'

Hirsch felt his insides stir. 'Can you give me his name? I'll need to speak to him.'

She shook her head, her eyes weepy but alertness returning to them. 'It was a secret. She didn't want to jinx it, you know.'

'You didn't meet him.'

'No.'

Speak to her friends, Hirsch thought. Better still, speak to her enemies. If the boyfriend was an older man, married or single, or a farmhand, or from a town outside the district, he'd not be easy to find.

In a choked voice Leanne Donovan said, 'It was a hit-and-run?'

'I'm afraid so.'

'Would she of felt . . . Did she . . .'

'It was instantaneous, Mrs Donovan,' Hirsch said, reaching out to touch her wrist before he could stop himself. He saw her shrink away and knew she was watching a nasty movie in her head.

The voice rose. 'She shouldn't of had to hitch home. Someone should of given her a lift.'

'Yes,' Hirsch said, understanding why Gemma Pitcher had left town. 'We're still not sure of her movements after the pub in Redruth.'

'She likes a good time, why shouldn't she?'

'Think back: did she say anything about her movements, anything at all? Did she mention anyone's name, for example?'

'Not to me,' Leanne muttered, looking mad and incomplete.

'Did Gemma usually pick her up when they went out together?'

Leanne just looked at him, helpless.

'They were together in the early part of the evening but later separated. Mrs Donovan, I'd dearly love to know who she might have hooked up with. Have a think about it, will you, please? Ask around? Get Nathan to ask his mates?'

'They wouldn't know anything.'

'I found her bag, but no mobile phone. Did she leave it at home?'

Leanne scoffed. 'Her and mobiles! She loses them and I can't afford to buy her new ones all the time, plus she run up a huge bill last time.'

'So she doesn't have one at present, she's not on a plan?'

'Not unless she paid for it herself.'

Hirsch looked across at the computer. 'What about Facebook? E-mail?'

'What about it?'

'Did she use the computer in this room, or have one of her own?'

Leanne shook her head. 'We all use that one.' Looking oddly shamefaced, she said, 'Bob and Yvonne gave it to us when Melia started high school. It's their old one.'

The sadness and poverty dragged at Hirsch. The Donovans lived on the margins, and a kid like Melia would want what others seemed to have. 'Would it be all right if I borrowed it for a couple of days? I'll give you a receipt.'

He didn't tell her that he'd found a list of passwords in Melia's wallet, not that it would do him any good, for the befuddlement faded from Leanne Donovan's eyes. He could see the cogs turning: she saw dirty tricks, saw a greater darkness attending her daughter's death, quotation marks around the word 'accident'.

She shook her head adamantly. 'We need it.'

'Everything in confidence, Mrs Donovan.'

'Don't you need a whatchamacallit, warrant?'

I certainly do, Hirsch thought. 'How about if I had a quick

look at her Facebook page and recent e-mails? You can sit with me, watch I don't accidentally stray into anything private to you and Nathan.'

'It doesn't feel right. I can't think straight and I don't think you should come here poking your nose in.'

'Yes, all right, Mrs Donovan. Insensitive of me.'

Hirsch climbed to his feet, feeling the weight. 'Again, I'm very sorry about what happened to Melia. It's tragic,' he added, meaning it.

'You'll never catch who did it. How can you? Long gone by now.'

'We won't stop trying.'

Leanne Donovan drew sharply on the last centimetre of her cigarette, scathing and focussed. 'They might not even know they done it. Half asleep in the middle of the night, what was that bump? Must of been a rabbit, no big deal, no need to stop.'

Hirsch knew she had a point. 'Is Nathan at work?'

'His boss gave him the week off.'

'He works at the grain shed?'

'Yes.'

'Is that his car in the yard?'

'Mine.'

'How does he get around?'

'What is this? You think he run her over? Who the fuck do you think you are?'

Fortunately Yvonne Muir came darting in, she might even have been listening, and saved Hirsch from giving further offence.

*

He said he'd make a pot of tea and hurried into the kitchen, ignored by the women, who were lost in hugs and weeping.

They're neighbours who habitually come and go through each other's back doors, he thought, filling the kettle. The window above the sink was laced with cobwebs in one corner, the insect screen clogged with dust, but he could see the back yard easily enough: a tumbledown chook shed, rotary clothesline with two stiff tea towels hanging from a wire, a rusted car body ringed by weeds. A back gate to a laneway, some evidence of regular use in the path tracked through the patchy grass, the scraped dirt at the base, and Hirsch wondered if the girl had liked to slip out the back way at night.

Waiting for the kettle to boil, he peered at the refrigerator door. A dozen cards and photos held by cute magnets. A recent shot of Melia Donovan, looking vaguely scruffy in her school uniform, and a family grouping: Melia, her mother, her brother. The brother had dark hair and skin. Hirsch removed both photographs, placed them face up on the table, and took close-ups with his phone.

He heard a car pull up, doors slam, footsteps, and by the time he'd reached the hallway the boy in the family snapshot stood there, a slender form inside a black T-shirt and baggy jeans midway down his arse. He looked red-eyed and stunned, but the instant he noticed Hirsch's uniform, the distress faded to wariness, shame and anger.

Fear, too. Hirsch didn't have time to read it as another kid came in on his heels, a bulky ginger with pimples and weak stubble. He was alarmed to see Hirsch there, and Hirsch was about to say something reassuring when the kid raised a hand and said, 'Catch ya later, Nate.'

Nathan returned the wave. 'Later.'

The redhead shuffled away, out to a lowered Commodore that Hirsch recognised from earlier in the week. It complained away from the kerb in a cloud of toxins.

Hirsch turned back to Nathan Donovan, who'd reached the door of the sitting room. He checked that his mother didn't need him and disappeared into one of the bedrooms.

Hirsch shook his head. He didn't want to distress the kid further, but he did need to speak to him. And Nathan must know he wouldn't go away, or would soon be back if he did.

He followed the boy, knocked and entered. Nathan was already sprawled messily in the little room, on his back on the bed, arms flung wide, his huge dusty trainers trailing laces across the worn lino floor. This was his cave and he didn't move when Hirsch took another step into the room, and another.

'Nathan? My name's Paul Hirschhausen.'

After a while the boy shrugged and examined the ceiling.

Hirsch regarded him, taking in the fine-boned, olive-skinned lankiness—attractive, but you had to look for it, under the scowls. 'I know this is a bad time for you but I'm anxious to find the driver who knocked Melia over. Hoping you might be able to help.'

Too late, Hirsch wondered if saying 'I' was a misstep. What did he have to offer? And would his saying 'I' necessarily cancel his apparent ties to the despised Redruth police, in Nathan's estimation? There was silence and it grew, and he was conscious of a kind of misery and defeat in the air.

'Just a couple of questions,' he said gently. 'For example, do you know what Melia's plans were last weekend?'

'Nup. Going out. She's always going out.'

Hirsch said, 'I've spoken to Gemma. She drove Melia to the pub down in Redruth but after a while she went to the drive-in with another friend and isn't sure what Melia's movements were. Do you know? Did you see her on Saturday night or Sunday morning?'

Nathan shook his head.

'Where did you go?'

'Pub.'

'Where?'

'Spalding.'

'With the guy who dropped you off just now?'

'Yeah.'

Still Nathan was looking at the ceiling. 'What's his name?'

'Who?'

'Your friend.'

'Sam. Hempel.'

'Would he know anything of Melia's movements?'

'Nah.'

'Did you spend the night out, or did you come home?'

'Home.'

'You didn't notice if Melia was at home or had been home and gone out again?'

'She does what she does.'

'What about this boyfriend?'

'What boyfriend?'

'Older guy, apparently.'

Nathan shrugged, said, 'Dunno,' and showed no other interest.

Hirsch returned to the sitting room.

'Did you see Nathan?' Leanne asked.

Hirsch nodded. 'He doesn't know anything.'

Leanne exchanged glances with Yvonne Muir. 'Von thinks it would be okay if you looked at the computer.'

Hirsch shot the neighbour a smile. 'You can look over my shoulder if you like.'

Both women demurred, as if fearing what they'd see. Hirsch sat himself at the old monitor, switched on the box and, waiting for it to boot up, smoothed out the paper slip from Melia Donovan's wallet. The machine was slow, and no wireless.

There were two passwords: the first gave him access to a file named 'MelD' and it proved to contain a handful of school essays, saved e-mails, journal entries and photographs. He'd examined all of it within a few minutes. Nothing stood out, apart from several references to 'Cool'. A name? A concept? The second password gave him access to the Facebook page. He poked around in it. It revealed nothing of her secret life.

'Before I go, Mrs Donovan, could you give me a list of Melia's school and town friends?'

That took a while, Leanne embarrassed because the list was brief and opened gaps in her knowledge. Hirsch returned to the station and started dialling. School holidays. Half the kids on the list were away, the others said they knew nothing of Melia's movements and were astonished that anyone would think they did.

That afternoon he bit the bullet and called Kropp.

'What do you mean, missing?'

'She left a note, didn't say where she was going.'

'Unbelievable. Have you tried family? Friends?'

'No luck, Sarge.'

'What's she scared of? What's she hiding?'

'Maybe she just feels guilty for not looking after her best friend, Sarge.'

'Find the slag, all right? Drag her along to the inquest.'

'Sarge.'

'And what's this about a Quine hearing?'

'I have to attend, Sarge. All next week.'

Kropp said nothing but what Kropp was saying was *dog, maggot.*

Next on Hirsch's list was Dr McAskill. 'Sergeant Kropp gave me the short version, but I was wondering if there's anything to add.'

There was a sense of the doctor drawing himself up on the other end of the line. 'I don't feel comfortable having a side conversation about it.'

Hirsch sighed. 'The thing is, Sergeant Kropp has all of us working on it and it's my job to piece together the kid's last movements. So, anything?'

'I suppose you mean stomach contents?'

'It's a start.'

'She'd not eaten much prior to death—a hamburger and chips some hours earlier—but she had been drinking wine.'

'We'll need a toxicology report. She might have been drug affected.'

'Are you telling me my job, Constable Hirschhausen?'

Moving right along . . . 'Was it petechial haemorrhaging? The spots around her remaining eye?'

Another silence, then the stiff voice saying, 'If a vehicle struck her and tossed her aside, flipping her into the bushes, one might expect a range of crushing-type injuries, wouldn't you say? And so, in and of itself, petechial haemorrhaging is not cause for suspicion.'

'Fair point.'

'It's a motorist you're looking for,' McAskill said. 'As I suspected when I examined her by the side of the highway, she sustained severe internal injuries consistent with being struck and tossed aside by a largish vehicle.'

'Going at speed? I didn't see any skid marks.'

McAskill recited, 'All one can say for certain is that the victim sustained severe external and internal injuries consistent with being struck by a largish vehicle.'

'Truck?'

'I'd expect more damage. Possibly a van or a four-wheel-drive.'

'She wasn't punched? Struck with a blunt object?'

'If she were, and I doubt it, such injury or injuries were masked by the other injuries.'

Treading carefully, Hirsch said, 'Doctor, you say you treated Melia from time to time. I wonder if—'

'Hardly time to time. No more than a couple of times.'

'For?'

'Earache, when she was little, and painful periods, if you must know.'

'I was wondering if she was sexually active,' Hirsch said. 'Perhaps you prescribed birth control.'

'She wasn't a virgin, if that's what you're getting at.'

'Were there signs of intercourse in the hours before she was killed?'

'I don't rule it out, but she sustained massive injuries in the centre mass of her body, from groin to neck, consistent with the large, flat nose of a van or a four-wheel-drive. Am I getting through to you?'

'So, no semen.'

'Have you heard of condoms, Constable?'

'No one seems to know who her boyfriend was.'

'No good asking me,' the doctor said.

On Thursday Hirsch poked around out east for a couple of hours, buffeted by warm northerly winds, returning via Bitter Wash Road. Seeing the gates to Vimy Ridge reminded him of Katie Street and Jackson Latimer, their fear of Pullar, Hanson and the black Chrysler. Be the good copper, he thought, check to see they're okay.

A teenage boy answered at the Latimers'. He was about fourteen, solid, hair artlessly messy. Pimply, with one pimple raging at the cleft between nostril and cheek, and he could scarcely bring himself to look at Hirsch or get his words out. Craig, he said his name was.

'I was hoping to say hello to Jack. Is he in?'

'Nup.'

'Your mum?'

'Nup, and good riddance.'

Oh. So Hirsch said, 'How is Jack?'

'Good riddance to him, too,' Craig muttered.

Some school holiday thing, Hirsch thought. She's taken the younger one to Adelaide or somewhere and the older one's been left at home; grounded, maybe.

He drove to the house across the road, parked behind the Volvo and approached the house. Katie Street called to him from a hammock on the veranda. She was full of a bright force today, not suspicion. 'Poor you, finding Melia.'

Hirsch sat on the warped boards, his back to a post. 'Yes. Enjoying the holidays?'

'Yes.'

'What are you reading?'

She showed him the cover wordlessly. *To Kill a Mockingbird*.

'Seen the film?'

'Yes.'

She collapsed onto her back again and all he could see was a skinny leg hanging over the edge, a grimy, callused foot. He heard her say, 'Who's your favourite character?'

She wants me to say Scout, he thought, so he said, 'Boo Radley.'

'Huh.'

But his answer satisfied something in her. She popped up again and looked at him. He said, 'Is Jack okay? I thought you two would be playing.'

Katie closed the book and swung both feet out of the hammock. She shook her head violently. 'He's gone away.'

'Oh.'

Now she hopped to the veranda and sat with him. Sulking a bit at the dirt and grass blades between her toes, she said, 'Have you come to see me or Mum?'

'Either. Both. Just passing,' Hirsch said. 'You haven't seen that car again?'

'No.'

'There's no need to be afraid, you know. Those men are nowhere near here. Anyway, they'll be caught pretty soon.'

There was silence and, 'Me and Jack have been good.'

Hirsch grinned. 'Not too good, I hope.'

'Really *bad*.'

'That's what school holidays are for. Your mum at home?'

'Somewhere. Mum!'

Nothing. 'Where is that dratted woman? *Mum!*'

Hirsch laughed.

Pleased, Katie edged closer to Hirsch. 'Have you ever arrested anybody?'

'Yes.'

'Have you shot anybody?'

'Katie, the police don't generally go around shooting people.'

'Me and Jack were being careful that time you caught us.'

Her face was tilted up, her fine hair framing her face.

Olive skin, no freckles, beautifully shaped lips. He could see Wendy in her.

'I know you were,' he said, 'but bullets can fly in unpredictable directions if they strike something, a rock. It's called a ricochet.'

'I know what a ricochet is.'

'Okay.'

'*Mum!*' shouted the girl again.

Nothing, so she said, 'Come with me,' and led Hirsch along the side of the house to the windy back yard.

He stopped in his tracks, feeling a sudden lurch of desire. Wendy Street was battling a great flower-head of white sheets onto a clothes hoist set in the middle of the lawn. The sheets flung themselves about, enveloping and taunting, flattening against her slender limbs and filling with air again. He watched her wreathe and dance, feeling blindly for the pegs and the line.

'Toga party!' he called, but it didn't come out right.

She unwrapped herself and eyed him balefully. 'Very funny.'

Wearing jeans and a T-shirt and patches of dampness, she crossed the grass towards him, drying her palms on her thighs. 'Giving my daughter the third degree?'

'She won't break.' He shook his head. 'Should've brought the bad cop.'

Wendy Street stopped a couple of metres from him and waited.

'I've been out in the back blocks and thought I'd pop in.'

She nodded. It wasn't hostility, he thought, just wariness.

She turned to glance at Katie who, with a kind of tact, turned on her heel and disappeared towards the front of the house.

When she was gone, Hirsch took a breath. 'Actually, I was wondering if you could tell me a little about Melia Donovan.'

'Melia Donovan?'

Hirsch nodded. 'An accident team's investigating the actual hit-and-run, but I'm trying to find out how and why she ended up at Muncowie. It would help if I knew a bit more about her. Did you teach her?'

'Year 11 maths.'

'You teach maths?'

'Don't look so surprised.'

Hirsch grinned. 'What was she like?'

'Sweet—when she bothered to come to school, that is. I had nothing to do with her outside of school.'

'Any rumours?'

Wendy Street tucked a wing of hair behind her ear. Hirsch fought the impulse to help her with it. 'This and that, mainly to do with boys and partying and her mother.'

'Anything specific?'

'No, you'll have to speak to others about that.'

'Did you ever see older guys hanging around the school, waiting for her?'

'No.'

'Do you know how she got to and from school?'

'There's a bus. It runs between Redruth and Muncowie.'

'Muncowie. Was she friends with any of the Muncowie kids?'

'She wasn't friends with anyone. I don't mean she was

115

friendless, I mean she seemed to have outgrown the kids at school, she didn't need them.'

'So her friends were older? Older boys? Men? Can you give me any names?'

Wendy shook her head. 'You don't understand, I don't know anything. Try a girl called Gemma Pitcher. She lives in Tiverton.'

'She wasn't very forthcoming,' Hirsch said. Feeling that he was on thin ice, he said, 'Did Melia seem sexually active or experienced to you?'

'I'd hate to have your job. Look, I barely knew her, but I did wonder if she'd had too much experience too soon. She wasn't knowing, didn't flaunt it, just seemed a bit lost and alone, if you know what I mean.'

'Are the local kids into drugs? Binge drinking?'

'No more than city kids, and probably less, I wouldn't know.'

Silence settled between them. 'I popped in across the road,' Hirsch said.

'Is that why you're here? Checking the kids aren't out target shooting? Checking their mothers haven't let them run wild?'

Her manner wasn't quite severe; maybe it was even a little amused, but Hirsch said levelly, 'I'd hate to think they were feeling afraid needlessly, and I do need to know about Melia Donovan, and I do need to patrol out east from time to time.'

Wendy Street crinkled her eyes at him. 'All right. So you would have learned that Allie's left her husband?'

That explained the teenage boy's manner. 'Oh.'

'She's in town at her parents'. Jack, too. Craig sided with his father.'

'Permanent?'

'Seems that way.'

It was pleasant, standing in the sun with an attractive woman. Wendy Street seemed in no hurry to return to her laundry basket. She dragged her errant wing of hair into place again. A simple act—arm raised, shirtfront tightening, chin tilted, neck briefly exposed—that sank Hirsch for good.

But the uniform got in the way, as it always did.

Kicking himself for not acting on what he felt, Hirsch drove back to Tiverton, and the first thing he saw was his elderly neighbour wheeling her shopping cart into Tennant's. He ran to the back yard, vaulted the side fence and retrieved the iPhone and cash. Then he drove to Clare, hoping no one would call him to report a stolen stud ram or a cat up a tree. Entered the post office there and addressed the phone and cash to himself, poste restante Balhannah, the town in the hills where his parents lived.

11

Friday, and the town's first inquest.

Hirsch's first inquest, and his first time inside the Mechanics Institute, a fine stone building two hundred metres from the police station. Wooden floors, wooden half panelling around the walls, pastelly blue paintwork, vases of flowers on solid wooden stands, pressed tin ceilings and photographs of prize rams and former councillors here and there. A staircase to one side, a corridor of meeting rooms—the Country Women's Association, he was guessing; the RSL; council chambers. A cardboard sign sat on a plain wooden chair outside the doors to the main hall: *Inquest here today*.

He stepped through, pausing to take in the vastness of the hall. High windows, more wood panelling, good ballroom-dancing floorboards, and a stage at the far end complete with wings and a bushland scene painted on a canvas backdrop. Hirsch doubted that plays were still performed here, but the town did need a venue for the primary school concert, the New Year's Eve ball, the debutante ball, the strawberry fete,

Liberal Party fundraising events. Below the stage was a table with a microphone and two chairs. A smaller table, chair and microphone stood to one side of it. The coroner and her assistant at one table, guessed Hirsch, witnesses at the other. And there was an easel, supporting a shrouded rectangular shape. Blow-up photographs? Bird's-eye diagrams showing the road and the position of the body?

The grandeur was spoiled by a dozen rows of metal folding chairs. Someone had been optimistic: the only onlookers—great gaps of empty chairs separating them—were Kropp, Dr McAskill, one of the accident investigators, a reporter from the Redruth rag, the shopkeeper, Nancarrow the Broken Hill mine worker who had discovered Melia Donovan's body, and the Muirs, sitting with Nathan Donovan and his mother. No Wendy Street—but then, why would she be here?

Kropp turned his massive head and jerked it at Hirsch: *Get your arse over here.* Hirsch complied. His shoulder brushed Kropp's, it couldn't be helped.

'Morning, Sarge.'

'Correct me if I'm wrong, but you live two minutes' walk away.'

'Phone calls, e-mails.'

'Speaking of e-mails, yours didn't say how long you'll be away next week.'

'Could be a few days.'

Kropp grunted. 'At least we're not going through a crime wave.' He paused. 'So long as you're back by Saturday.'

'Sarge?'

'Football final. All hands on deck.'

Hirsch got a kick out of that. 'You mean Redruth actually comes alive? People on the street?'

Kropp turned quiet and nasty. 'We get lucky, someone might mess your face up a bit.'

'Looking forward to it, Sarge.'

They were silent. Hirsch fiddled with his phone and stared at the empty tables. He knew he was here at the coroner's discretion. Today's hearing would merely establish the who, when, where and how of Melia Donovan's death and invite witnesses to come forward. Then it would adjourn until the police investigation was complete, and that might take months. Footsteps; a cadaverous man appeared, stiff-backed, grey-faced. 'He was in the job,' whispered Kropp, and Hirsch could see ex-policeman in the scowling figure, who halted beside the main table and called: 'All rise for her majesty's coroner.'

They stood, the air above them clanging, crashing, a symphony of cheap metal chairs sliding and colliding, and a middle-aged woman appeared in a whisper of fabric and rubber-soled shoes, her face kindly, apologetic, almost grandmotherly, a foil to the grim-looking old cop. She gestured at them vaguely and they all sat and the man beside her boomed, 'All mobile phones off, if you wouldn't mind.'

'That means you,' muttered Kropp.

Hirsch switched off, pocketed the phone.

The coroner remained on her feet, her hands moving folders around on the table top, and now she glanced out at the rows of chairs. She looked untethered to Hirsch, lost and adrift in the vast hall. *Sit*, he begged her.

She cast her voice over their heads, full, rolling, educated: 'Thank you all for coming. You may be wondering at the choice of venue: quite simply, I wished to view the place where Ms Donovan died. I've now done that. I also want to say I welcome community involvement in the investigation into her death.'

Leanne Donovan cried out. The coroner put her hand to her throat, opened and closed her mouth. Leanne and her son thrust back their chairs and stumbled out of the hall, followed by Yvonne Muir.

The coroner, unsettled, said, 'I hereby formally open the inquest into the death of Melia Anne Donovan on or about Saturday the twentieth of September and I will presently adjourn these proceedings to enable the police to complete their inquiries and for any criminal prosecution arising to take its proper course.'

She sat at last, removing her glasses. 'What I must do today is confirm the identity of the deceased and the location, time and cause of death. Witnesses, including the pathologist and police members, will give evidence in regard to these matters and then my officer will give a brief summary of the circumstances, as far as these can be ascertained.'

The coroner replaced her glasses. 'As I said, I have made my visit to the scene of Ms Donovan's death, and I hope that opening the inquest here, in her home town, will encourage as many of her friends and family as possible to come forward and assist this court, and the police, to find the person or persons responsible for her death.'

Kropp half-turned his huge head to Hirsch. Hirsch read

the accusation: he'd already put a spoke in that wheel by allowing Gemma Pitcher to do a flit.

'Anyone giving testimony will be speaking under oath and may subsequently be required to make a formal statement to police. Of course, this is not to say you need see this morning's proceedings as in any way fraught with meaning and consequences. I wish merely to discover the truth.'

Hirsch heard backsides shift on the flimsy seats. He didn't think anyone had anything much to say, except to establish the groundwork and express grief.

Nancarrow was called first. He explained why he'd been driving south along the Barrier Highway and how he'd found the body. The coroner had no questions, and called Hirsch, who read from his notebook: times, the date, distances, the movement of personnel, the recovery of the body. Plenty of cop phrases like 'female deceased'.

'Then I remained at the scene until accident investigators arrived.'

'Had a formal identification been made at this stage?'

'Dr McAskill stated that he knew the deceased.'

'You relied on his identification?'

Hirsch glanced around at Kropp. Kropp held his hands wide, so Hirsch returned to the coroner. 'Sergeant Kropp is in charge of the investigation and will provide further detail in regard to this matter, but I do understand that he, like Dr McAskill, knew the deceased and later viewed the body and had no reason to doubt Dr McAskill's identification.'

The coroner was scribbling. She looked up. 'I am able to confirm that another method of identification has subsequently confirmed the visual identifications of Dr McAskill and Sergeant Kropp, namely dental records. Constable Hirschhausen, you may step down. I call Sergeant Exley.'

Exley summarised his team's findings at the accident scene: no tyre tracks or skid marks, no identifiable fragments from the vehicle that had struck Melia Donovan.

'Was more than one vehicle involved?'

'If you mean, was she knocked over by one vehicle and run over by subsequent vehicles, there was no evidence at the scene to support or disprove that scenario.'

McAskill was called. A man full of clarities and certainties, he confirmed identity, injuries and cause of death. 'I submit that she was struck with some force by one vehicle, the impact sufficient to kill her and throw her body to the area where she was found. The locus of the impact was her right hip, arm and trunk, which might indicate that she'd had her back to the vehicle and was in the act of turning to face it when hit. There was also a massive injury to the head, which in my experience indicates that she was flipped up and into the windscreen or onto the roof of the vehicle before tumbling off the road verge.'

'Were there indications of third-party violence to the deceased apart from vehicle impact injuries?'

In other words, had she been choked, stabbed, punched, burnt with cigarettes, tied up, poisoned, raped . . .

'There were not.'

'And the toxicology findings?'

'Indications of alcohol and cannabis use.'

'Sufficient to cause disorientation?'

'In my opinion, and taking account of her slight body mass, yes.'

Kropp was called. He confirmed identification and outlined the police investigation. He also disclosed that Melia Donovan was an inveterate hitchhiker.

The coroner thanked him and, as he returned to his seat, said, 'That completes the initial formal input. It remains for me to invite members of the community to step forward.'

The chairs shifted minutely.

She waited, glancing keenly at their faces. 'Very well, this inquiry is adjourned.'

'All rise,' the officer said.

'Fucking waste of a morning,' muttered Kropp. 'Find her slag of a friend, all right?'

'I'm in the city next week, Sarge,' Hirsch reminded him. 'The Quine inquiry.'

Kropp screwed his face at the floor, not looking at Hirsch.

12

On Saturday morning, Hirsch attended Melia Donovan's funeral. A service at the tiny Catholic church, followed by a procession of cars, lights on, to the cemetery on the hill, a windswept patch of red dirt, busy ants and gumtrees. Everyone wept; the kids from the high school were inconsolable, although Wendy Street was doing her best. Katie toed the dirt, standing next to Jack Latimer and his mother, and a couple aged in their sixties. Maternal grandparents?

Hirsch stood well back. He felt sad, but didn't mourn. He tried not to look as if he was watching people. Other than the schoolkids there were men and women, young and old. He could not name a tenth of the people there, but they all knew him. One or two nodded; others glared, symptomatic of the district's rancorous undertow. Bob Muir asked him to come to the get-together afterwards, tea and cakes in the hall, but Hirsch declined. Wendy Street caught his eye, gave him a little wave.

That afternoon he was called to a farm contractor's property a few kilometres outside the town. The man's work was largely seasonal: ploughing and harrowing, crop sowing, reaping, carting, hay baling. He mended fences and bores, crutched sheep, put up sheds, you name it. Leading Hirsch across a dirt yard to a collection of implement, hay and tool sheds, he said, 'Feast your eyes on that.'

The door to a small tin structure had been jimmied open, the wounds raw in the metal skin. 'I was at that poor lass's funeral and come back to this. The bastards pinched me son's trail bike, plus some of me tools. Chainsaw, brushcutter, cans of fuel, saw, plane, pipe wrench . . .' He glared at Hirsch. 'I bet I'm not the only one. The pricks were at the service. They clocked who else was there, knew we'd be out for a couple of hours, the cemetery and the rest of it, and snuck off and robbed us.'

Quite likely. Hirsch gave the man an incident report number for his insurance company, made no promises, and returned to town. Two more calls came in, people returning from the funeral to find broken windows, doors prised open, tools, computers and TV sets missing.

A truck or a ute, thought Hirsch, returning from the last call. In a land of trucks and utes.

The HiLux was throwing a long shadow as Hirsch returned to town, the fence posts and power poles striping the paddocks. He found a dusty Holden parked outside the police station, a woman piling out of the driver's seat, clutching a mobile phone. 'Thank God. I tried calling the number you pinned to the door but I had no signal.'

Hirsch recognised her from the funeral, the older woman with Alison and Jack Latimer. 'Something wrong?'

She looked comfortable, greying, grandmotherly; but she was in a state now, wringing her hands. 'It's my son-in-law, he's come round making a scene and I'm scared someone will get hurt.'

'Lead the way. Is it far?'

She was already climbing into the Holden. 'Better if you came with me, then I can explain.'

Hirsch thought about it. Would he need anything from the HiLux? Was this likely to end in a car chase?

'Hurry,' the woman said.

No, probably not. He slid into her passenger seat, belted himself in. 'May I have your name?'

The woman shot away from the kerb, no signalling or mirror checking. Then again, Barrier Highway was always quiet. 'Heather Rofe. Our daughter appeared on our doorstep during the week with her youngest, asking if they could stay for a while. Her marriage hasn't been the happiest so of course we said yes, but her husband keeps ringing her to come home, and a little while ago he turned up, yelling and swearing.'

'Your daughter is Alison Latimer?'

'Yes. How do you know that?'

'We met briefly,' Hirsch said. He paused. 'Is her husband violent, Mrs Rofe?'

A ragged sigh. 'I'm not sure. Ray can be overbearing, I know that much.'

Hirsch sat back as Heather Rofe swung the car into a

short street beyond the Catholic church. He counted four houses on either side, the end house on the border of farmland. Eight old houses choked with cottagey shrubs and peeling gums, small-town houses that never opened the front curtains or spoiled the quiet. A beefy green Range Rover was angled outside the end house. The man on the path between the little gate and the front door was tall, solid, wound tight, dressed for a reconciliation in grey trousers, black shirt and a sports coat. An older man stood at the door, barring him.

Rofe pulled into the kerb and Hirsch climbed out, adjusted his uniform cap and approached the house. He stopped at the garden gate, eyeing both men, who eyed him in return, the householder mostly unreadable but, sensed Hirsch, relieved—with an undertone of *I probably could have handled this*. Raymond Latimer was different, flexing his hands, a rampager not rampaging but coiled like a spring.

'Gentlemen,' said Hirsch.

Latimer ignored him. 'Heather, you fetched the police?'

'Sir,' Hirsch said, 'your business is with me now.'

Latimer shook his head like a reasonable man pushed to the limit by fools. 'You're not needed here. We can sort it out ourselves.'

Huge, flexing hands. Hirsch watched the hands, the torso, for a hint of the man's intentions. Alison Latimer's husband was savagely shaven at this late stage of the afternoon, wearing his best casual gear. A big, practical man. Out of costume now, but no joke, despite the tidy comb tracks raked across his skull. Regarding Hirsch with a kind of exalted fury, in fact, as if he'd never been challenged like this. Hirsch felt an intense expectation. His fingers flicked over the equipment strapped to his belt. He gauged distances.

'You hear me? We can sort this. No need for the police. A civil matter.'

'Ray,' said Heather Rofe, 'you were scaring us. I had to fetch the police.'

'That's bullshit Heather and you know it.'

Heather Rofe's husband said, from the veranda, 'Banging on the door, shouting and swearing, we felt threatened, Ray. You said some pretty terrible things.'

'Heat of the moment, Keith. I only want to speak to Allie, then I'll be on my way.'

'Not now, not today. Give her a bit of time.'

'I think she's had enough time already. It's a coward's way out, just slinking away from home without talking it over with your husband. I think it's in everyone's interest if Allie comes home with me now.'

'You're frightening her,' Heather Rofe said. 'And you're frightening Jack, poor little thing.'

With an effort, Latimer put aside the fury. He shook his head and stomped out onto the footpath in a huge, martyred capitulation. 'Unbelievable. A concerned husband and father tries to find a solution to a family difficulty and everyone gangs up on him and then the police are called.'

Heather Rofe slipped past him to join her husband. 'Allie needs time, Ray, all right?'

'A day? A week? What?'

'Time,' Rofe said and pushed her husband ahead of her

into the house. Hirsch sensed that the daughter and grandson were in there, peering through the curtains.

Latimer was about to climb into the Range Rover. 'Sir, a quick word before you go?'

The man paused, taking a cold, summarising interest in Hirsch. 'You're the new cop. Just so you know, your superior's a very good mate of mine. All right?'

'I'm not fully convinced that you won't hassle these people again, Mr Latimer.'

Hirsch expected hostility. What he got was a smile. 'I know all about you, you prick.'

Hirsch waited. Waiting had become one of the chief conditions of his life. He waited right through a stream of oblique and wrathful abuse because he'd heard it all before. At the end of it he nodded, said 'Sir,' and walked past Latimer to enter the Rofes' yard. He heard the Range Rover drive away as he lifted his knuckles to knock.

Heather opened the door. 'I can't thank you enough.'

'Do you wish to take out a court order against him, Mrs Rofe?'

She smiled. 'That won't be necessary.'

Hirsch gave her his card. 'Call me any time.'

13

'Got church this morning?'

Hirsch's parents had church every Sunday morning. The question was part of a pattern: he would call after breakfast, ask about church, catch up on what his sister was up to in the UK, ask after everyone's health, who his parents had seen lately . . . Every Sunday, and running behind the chatter were Hirsch's overpowering sense memories, aroused by their voices: the smell of eggs and bacon on weekends, his father's cigarettes, the play of light in the little hill towns above Adelaide, the stutter of the lawn sprinklers.

And their unspoken question: *Are you really on the take, Paul?*

Then they'd sign off, but this time Hirsch said, 'I should get there sometime after lunch.'

'Drive safely,' his mother said.

Two and a half hours to Adelaide, then a quick climb into the hills, the road fast until he turned off for Balhannah. Cooler air up here, scented with spring grasses. He'd struck some Sunday-lunch traffic but the road was quiet now. Greenery pushed in on him from both sides, and he was wool-gathering, not fully engaged, when the siren whooped.

A patrol car, in snarling white and martial black. A ninety k zone and Hirsch was doing eighty-five. All his electrics worked: brake light, indicator light. No broken lenses. No failure to stop back there at the crossroads, no failure to give way. So Hirsch woke up pretty quickly, the daydreams dissipating like smoke.

If they wanted to pat him down they'd find the Beretta around his ankle and no paper to go with it.

He pulled over onto the verge and sat there, motor running, watching the rearview mirror. Two figures on board, but the angled windscreen gave him no more than shapes, heads and shoulders. Time passed and Hirsch felt for the pistol and tucked it against his thigh, under a flap of his street directory. They could have been calling it in, he supposed, but didn't seriously think so. Or they had their windows down and were gauging sounds, here above the plain, in the land of little hill towns and doubling-back, up-and-down roads. You'd soon hear a vehicle coming. If you were here to kill Hirsch, you'd want to wait until the coast was clear.

A car did come, an unmarked white Holden. Hirsch watched it crawl past, pull over and reverse until he was hemmed in. He cranked a cartridge into the firing chamber. Flicked the safety off.

Nothing happened, and then something happened. There

were four men in the Holden, plainclothes, and one of the rear passengers held up a mobile phone, waggling it at Hirsch without revealing more than a white shirt cuff under a dark suit sleeve and a shaven bullet head.

Was he to expect a phone call? Make a phone call? Hirsch took his Motorola from the dash cradle, clamped it against the windscreen, his way of saying, 'Your move.'

The slumbering screen woke with sound and light. Hirsch said, 'Hello.'

'Hello?' his mother said.

So Hirsch said, 'Hello,' wondering how the pricks had managed to network the call.

When there was no response, he said, 'Mum, it's me.'

She didn't hear him and her hearing was perfect. The line was clear and her handset was new, a cordless he'd given his parents last Christmas. Something else was going on. The next time she spoke—'Hello,' and 'Is anybody there?'—she sounded frightened.

'Mum!' shouted Hirsch, knowing it was futile.

'What do you want?' his mother was saying. 'Why are you doing this to us?'

'Mum,' Hirsch said, and there was a click and the man in the back seat of the white car waved two devices at him, phone and digital recorder.

Then the white car was streaking away. The patrol car pulled out, too, pausing for a moment alongside Hirsch. A woman in the passenger seat. She shot him with her finger and then passenger and driver were gone, being four-year-olds with the siren again.

*

Twenty minutes later Hirsch said, 'Have you been getting anonymous calls?'

'We didn't want to worry you.'

The house sat at the end of a quiet side street and was indefensible. No alarms or window bars, flimsy locks, a bedridden old woman on one side, a weedy paddock on the other, a plant nursery behind them. Hirsch prowled from window to window and tugged at his parents' blinds and curtains.

'You're making us nervous, Paul.'

'When did the calls start?'

'A few days ago,' his mother said.

She worked for the ambulance service, a narrow, rangy, nail-nibbling woman used to dealing with drunks, addicts, the scared and the deranged. Her love for Hirsch was absent-minded, as if she were not quite sure how she'd come to give birth to him. Never mean or cross or negligent, just practical and distracted. Closer to his sister.

'Did you report it?' he said.

Hirsch's father cocked his head tiredly, a man as raw-boned as his wife, still in his churchgoing pants and shirt. He was a carpenter and had the dents, scars and arthritis to prove it. He said, in his mild rumble, 'As soon as we give them the name Hirschhausen, what do you think's going to happen?'

Hirsch said, 'I think it'd be a good idea if both of you went away for a few days.'

'Few days.'

'Until the end of the week. Or sooner. As soon as I've finished giving evidence I'll call you.'

His mother came and gave him a hug. It was there and gone. 'I don't think that will be necessary, do you?'

There was something about the main sitting room window. Hirsch crossed the room. 'New glass. Fresh putty.' He heard the accusing tone in his voice.

'A brick,' his father said.

'When?'

'Friday night. We found it when we came back from seeing a film in town.'

'Had it repaired yesterday morning,' his mother said.

'Why didn't you tell me?'

'We're telling you now.'

'No, you're telling me because I noticed it now. And don't say you didn't want to worry me.'

'Well, we didn't.'

'Just a rock?'

'A rock would have been too subtle for us,' Hirsch's mother said. 'There was a note wrapped around it, in case we missed the point.'

'Let me guess: "Tell your son not to testify."'

'Along those lines,' Hirsch's father said.

His mother said, '"Tell your *cunt* of a son to do the decent thing and keep his trap shut."'

Hirsch had never heard his mother say the word and saw a glint in her eye. She had a good poker face, his mother, but under it he realised she was worried, and he remembered the fear in her voice. Her manner was unchanged, but she was holding herself too tightly.

'Mum, please, talk sense into Dad. Go up north for a few days.'

His parents owned a time-share apartment on the Gold Coast. School holidays were finishing so they might have the place to themselves.

'Do you think your pals would hurt us?' his father said.

'If it would hurt me? Yes,' Hirsch said, collapsing into an armchair, his body tired of the tension. Planted his feet firmly, held his arms out wide, a way of saying, *Am I getting through to you?*

The legs of his jeans rode up and his father saw the Beretta on his ankle. The colour drained from his face.

Embarrassed, Hirsch stood until the hems draped over his shoes again. 'A precaution.'

'Pretty serious precaution.'

'I don't know what to do,' Hirsch said. 'If I stay here for the week like we planned, I put you at risk. If I stay somewhere down in the city, I leave you here exposed. And if I do stay with you I won't be around during the day. So I'm begging you, take a holiday for a few days. Call in sick. When it's all over they'll have no more reason to threaten you.'

'But they could come after you.'

'I'll manage.'

'Not if you get locked up, you won't,' Hirsch's father said.

Inviting—*begging*—Hirsch to say that wouldn't happen because he wasn't a dirty cop.

Hirsch looked at his mother, she looked at her husband. 'Karl,' she said.

'Eva.'

*

They were gone by late afternoon, a late cancellation on a houseboat based at Renmark. Meanwhile Hirsch supposed he was still a target. He didn't want to be killed in his childhood bed for his parents to find, so booked into a pay-by-the-hour motel on South Road and paid for four nights in advance.

'Cash or card?'

'Cash,' Hirsch said.

Then he had to turn around and hunt for a cash machine. He knew the transaction would trigger a record, but no one would know where the cash went after that. Unless there was a tracking device on his car. It did Hirsch's head in, all that thinking, and he almost forgot he still had to drive back into the hills first thing in the morning to collect his parcel from the Balhannah post office.

14

The parcel retrieved, Hirsch reached police headquarters by nine-forty-five on Monday. Marking time in the main foyer, he spotted Marcus Quine. Quine wore the look of a man setting off on a raid, strolling in his languid, dangerous way towards a huddle of men waiting at the entrance to one of the out-of-bounds corridors that riddled the building. You didn't mistake Quine for a teacher or a shopkeeper; he was a cop. Tall, proprietorial, unimpressed, full of unschooled intelligence. Not good looking—his features were too irregular—but the lopsided smile, when it appeared, was attractive. Hirsch sank down in his armchair, hoping he hadn't been spotted.

Quine stopped abruptly, seemed to sniff the air. He turned on his heel. And now he was cutting towards Hirsch, full of sharkish amusement. He halted. He grinned, no humour in it, his eyes like cracked marbles, his face all harsh planes and shadows. He said nothing. Hirsch gazed at him blankly, then started to pick his nose, really sticking his finger in. Quine moved off again, greeting the men in the corridor, a gifted backslapper.

They grilled Hirsch in a room suited to savagery, a corporate blonde-wood and cream-walls kind of room, with a nondescript carpet and a side table holding a water jug and glasses. The scent of cleaning fluids and aftershave. Two glum senior officers sat at the head of the room, facing down Hirsch, who sat alone at a small central table, a briefcase containing his laptop and the cash and the iPhone at his feet. He'd requested and been denied a lawyer: not necessary, just a few formalities, okay? And sitting in, ranged along the side walls, were a handful of officers from the various squads whose activities Quine had compromised in some way: drugs, armed robbery, fraud . . .

Rosie DeLisle was there, too, next to a woman who seemed to emit distaste and fury, as if she loathed Hirsch. Short-haired, solid, gruff, a scornful look on her face if he happened to catch her eye. He thought he knew all the Internals, but he didn't know this woman. He shot Rosie a querying glance, *Who's your friend?* Rosie gave a whisper of a shrug. Nothing for Hirsch to worry about.

A prosecutor, maybe? Someone from a specialist squad with some dirt on him, real or imagined?

Rosie's boss, an inspector named Gaddis, asked the first question. He was thin and ferrety and perfect for the job, his long fingers tapping next to an AV control box. 'What was your first impression of Paradise Gardens?'

Paradise Gardens was one of Adelaide's bleak new outer suburbs: cheap housing, struggling young families, a volatile mix. High welfare dependency but few welfare services. No jobs and nothing for the kids to do, including catch a bus or a train anywhere. But Gaddis hadn't meant the suburb, he meant the Paradise Gardens police station, which was also dysfunctional. Hirsch wondered which came first, the dysfunctional police station or the dysfunctional suburb.

'I was new to detective duties, sir, and had no clear expectations.'

Gaddis gave him a stop-stonewalling look. 'In an early interview you said you felt "an atmosphere" soon after joining Senior Sergeant Quine's CIB team at Paradise Gardens. What did you mean by that?'

Hirsch thought he might as well give a straight answer. 'Canteen and locker conversations would dry up whenever I showed my face,' he said, 'as if I wasn't trusted. I wondered if they saw me as a spy.'

Gaddis hid his sneer poorly. 'Did this atmosphere improve over time?'

'Eventually.'

The other interrogator, a man who looked drawn and ill, said, 'Please elaborate.'

Conscious of sounding a little pathetic, Hirsch said, 'At first the shunning was quite overt. I was rarely invited along on raids or to social events, for example, but left to man the CIB phones. That situation improved over time. After a while it was more like I was taken for granted. Like part of the furniture.'

'You were a junior officer,' Gaddis said, 'and someone had to be on call at the station.'

Nice try, Hirsch thought.

The other man said, 'These social events: dinner parties? Barbecues?'

'Dinner parties, barbecues, strip clubs, four-hour lunches and nightclubs,' Hirsch said.

Someone laughed. Gaddis snarled, 'By nightclub I take it you mean the Flamingo?'

'Yes.'

'A club owned by the brother of a Comancheros gang member,' Gaddis said. 'Wouldn't you expect CIB interest in the place?'

'The Paradise Gardens CIB was only interested in sex and money: the girls in the back room, the kickbacks and the Comancheros who bought the cocaine Quine had filched from the evidence locker.'

'*Senior Sergeant* Quine,' Gaddis said. He moved right along. 'Presumably you did more than man the phones all the time. You performed some CIB duties?'

'Yes.'

'Such as?'

'I helped to investigate minor crimes. Burglaries, noise complaints.'

'When investigating one such noise complaint, did you accept a bribe of five hundred dollars?'

'No, that is a lie,' Hirsch said. 'We were short-handed and I was sent to look into an after-hours pub noise complaint. The publican offered me the five hundred to turn a blind eye. I took the money and immediately logged it in at the station, along with a written report. I then informed Quine, *Senior Sergeant* Quine. It's in my report.'

'We have been unable to find that report, Constable Hirschhausen.'

'Is that a fact.'

Gaddis said, 'You might want to rethink your attitude. You're not doing yourself any favours.'

Hirsch ignored him. 'In addition to handing me five hundred dollars, the publican took me into a back room where people were playing poker and roulette. I was invited to join in. I declined, saying I had another call to investigate. It's all in my report.'

'Which no one can find. When you reported to Senior Sergeant Quine, what did he say?'

'He said, "Big Trev offered you a bribe? Doesn't sound like him." I then told Quine—'

'Senior Sergeant Quine.'

'I then told Quine that we should raid the pub's gambling room. I also thought there might have been rooms set aside for prostitution. Quine said we needed to be better prepared, and suggested I see Big Trev again, wearing a wire.'

'His name is Senior Sergeant Quine.'

'It implies a respect he doesn't deserve,' Hirsch snapped.

Gaddis breathed out. 'Did you go to the pub again, wearing a wire?'

'A week later. I was offered another five hundred. In fact, a weekly payment was suggested.'

'You had this on tape?'

'Yes.'

'You gave it to Senior Sergeant Quine?'

'I did.'

The other man coughed. Hirsch couldn't read his grey face. 'And?'

'He called me in two days later and said the equipment must have been faulty, all he could hear was static. I offered to write it up from my notes. He said, "Yeah, why don't you do that," and so I did.'

'More paperwork that seems not to exist,' Gaddis said. 'Then what happened?'

'Nothing. No follow-up.'

Gaddis smiled at him and pressed a button on the AV controls. Scratchy sounds filled the air. 'Static. Clearly your recording didn't work, so why should there be a follow-up?'

'It did work,' Hirsch said. He removed his laptop from his briefcase. He cranked the volume up and pressed play. The room heard his voice, and another voice saying, 'Five hundred now and a hundred and fifty a week, whaddaya reckon to that?'

'Trevor Dean,' Hirsch said. 'Big Trev.'

Gaddis swallowed. 'Has that recording been authenticated?'

'No.'

'Formally lodged?'

'No.'

'Then why—'

'Having determined that Quine was corrupt, I got into

the habit of making two copies of everything,' Hirsch said. 'I have never deviated from that.'

The grey-faced man glanced at Gaddis and back at Hirsch, so that Hirsch wondered if he had an ally here.

'Moving right along. In your year at Paradise Gardens did you not see a great number of successful CIB actions?'

'Yes.'

'Robberies investigated, witnesses questioned, raids mounted, arrests made?'

'Yes,' Hirsch said, and added, over Gaddis's attempts to ask a new question, 'But more often than not the team returned empty-handed from a so-called "sure thing" or carrying drugs and stolen goods that were never properly logged into the evidence safe.'

Gaddis, tensely red, said, 'More on that evidence safe later. What makes you so sure of these accusations, if you were manning the phones or whatever it was you were doing?'

'I got curious. One day I saw Detective Constable Reid make a call on his mobile before one of these raids that amounted to nothing. The next day he left his phone in the charger while he went to the pub, so I checked his call log. He'd called another mobile phone. After work I went to the address they'd raided and started calling the number. I heard a phone ringing and found it in a rubbish bin. The idiot who'd dumped it hadn't cleared any of his personal information: photos, texts, Google account, calls made, calls received. He'd been the target of the raid and Reid had tipped him off.'

'Do we take your word for this?'

After all, Reid was dead. Facing imprisonment, he'd shot himself. Not my concern, Hirsch thought, and he held his briefcase aloft. 'If you like I can show you screen shots of Reid's phone and the phone I found in the bin.'

'Surely you gave this material to an Internal Investigations officer? Sergeant DeLisle, were you shown any of this material?'

She was slightly behind Hirsch and he heard her cough and shift in her chair, and to save her he said loudly, 'Things have a habit of getting lost.'

This must have seemed like an escape route to Gaddis. With a smirk he said, 'Lost by Sergeant DeLisle?'

'No, not by her, by others under your command.'

The man with the unhealthy skin said, 'Getting back to these CIB raids. What happened when Senior Sergeant Quine's team *did* recover drugs and valuables?'

'Never properly logged, sir. Partial descriptions, under-reported quantities, that kind of thing.'

'Did you come to any conclusions regarding this?'

'It's my belief Quine and his mates would keep a portion of the drugs and the valuables and later sell them.'

'To the Comancheros.'

'The Comancheros preferred the drugs over the diamond earrings.'

Someone laughed. The grey-faced man said, 'Do you have proof that the squad kept aside stolen items for sale?'

Hirsch squirmed a little. 'I attended a raid in which a large amount of stolen jewellery was recovered. I was later handed a Rolex watch from that haul.'

'Did you sell it?'

'No.'

'Did you declare it to a senior officer?'

'No.'

'You kept it.'

'In my locker,' Hirsch said. 'I didn't know what to do about it.' And Quine was clever, appealing, Hirsch would admit only to himself. He ran rings around defence barristers and made headline arrests of genuinely bad people, and Hirsch—isolated, marriage failing—had felt himself drawn to the man for a while.

'You did nothing?'

'I made a note for my own files,' Hirsch said, waving his briefcase again. 'Time, date, personnel involved, serial numbers and so on.'

'You held onto the watch.'

'Yes.'

'It was found months later when your locker was searched.'

'Yes.'

'Tying you effectively to the other members of the team.'

Hirsch said nothing.

Gaddis said, 'So the others trusted you by this time?'

'Not entirely, but they'd stopped thinking about me. I mean they were less cautious around me. As I said, part of the furniture.'

'In the first inquiry,' the grey-faced man said, 'Senior Sergeant Quine's barrister argued for some of the squad's actions as "noble-cause" corruption. Would you care to comment on that?'

'Well, I know what it is.' Hirsch curled his lip. 'It's a weasel word for fabricating evidence in order to get a conviction in cases where you know someone's guilty but can't prove it.'

'Did you see Senior Sergeant Quine fabricate evidence in order to secure a conviction?'

'He boasted of it.'

The pale man said, 'We have statements from other sources that Senior Sergeant Quine also misplaced evidence or concocted false statements in order to protect his informants or the criminals he did business with. Can you speak to that?'

Hirsch wasn't sure what was going on. Gaddis wasn't happy with this line, but said nothing. And who these other sources were, Hirsch had no idea. He said so.

The grey-faced man sat back, a little deflated, but said, 'You got into the habit of keeping meticulous records while serving at Paradise Gardens?'

'Yes.'

'What things did you record and how were they stored?'

'Photographs and audio recordings,' Hirsch said. 'Lists, copious lists.'

'Of?'

'Businesses that offered freebies. The quantities of drugs or valuables seized on raids versus the quantities later listed at trial. Vehicle registrations. Phone numbers. Plus my own recollections of events: what was said and done, by whom, and where and when, together with my doubts and suspicions.'

'No one saw you do this?'

'No.'

'It must have been well hidden.' Meaning the raid on the station and on his house had not uncovered anything—except the Rolex.

'I used an internet storage site,' Hirsch said.

Then he had to explain how the system worked. Gaddis asked, 'Did you ever store material written by Senior Sergeant Quine?'

'No.'

'Tape recordings of the things he or his team said?'

'No.'

'Why?'

'The squad was preternaturally suspicious and wary. They rarely communicated by phone, paper or electronic means.'

'So your records are limited.'

'Yes, but—'

'It has been shown that Senior Sergeant Quine invested in restaurants, bars, home units, racehorses, the share market . . . Do you have similar investments?'

'I have a ten-year-old Nissan,' Hirsch said, which raised a bit of a snigger from the bleachers.

Gaddis said, 'Tell the members of this hearing about your involvement with Ms Eliza Ley.'

Arsehole. Hirsch swallowed. 'She's a lawyer.'

'A *drug* lawyer.'

'Yes. I didn't know that at the time.'

Eliza Ley was simply a pretty but harried-looking barrister he'd seen around the courthouse or visiting remand prisoners from time to time. They got talking. Hirsch found her appealing in a scatty kind of way. The tabloid press intimated that she was appealing in a big-breasted kind of way, but Hirsch thought she was smart, too. They met for drinks a few times and then later for sex. He'd not known until it was too late who she was. He tried to explain this now.

'You were slow on the uptake?' Gaddis said.

'Yes.'

'Your wife left you as a result?'

'We'd effectively left each other long before that,' Hirsch said. 'She moved out as a result.'

Gaddis was enjoying himself. 'So you shared a drug lawyer's bed and knew nothing about her?'

'Not until I was warned,' Hirsch said.

He'd been sitting in the pub, minding his own business, when two senior drug squad detectives, venomous with it, slid into the booth, book-ending him. 'Eliza Ley,' one of them said.

'What about her?'

They told him: cops in her pocket, drug-dealer boyfriend, fucking Quine on the side, photos to prove it. 'You're getting sloppy seconds, mate.'

Gaddis was saying, 'And you expect us to believe you had no idea who this woman really was and what she was doing?'

'Not until it was too late.'

'What else did the detectives tell you?' asked the grey man.

'They'd noticed a pattern. If one of her clients appeared on a possession charge, Quine would go in to bat for him, appear in court saying, "We've misplaced that evidence, your honour," or "We have no objection to bail in this matter, your honour." They'd raid known meth labs and there'd be no drugs or equipment or cooks or dealers.'

'They believed Senior Sergeant Quine was passing on information?'

Pillow talk was how one of the drug squad officers had put it, squeezing Hirsch's upper leg under the table. Fingers like steel clamps.

'When in fact it was *you* passing on information,' Gaddis said.

'No.'

'You were advised to drop Ms Ley?'

'Yes.'

'What did she do or say as a result?'

In all honesty, Hirsch felt Eliza had been hurt that he'd stopped returning her calls. But he didn't tell Gaddis that. He didn't say that he'd grown more vigilant, changing his locks, buying the little Beretta, obtaining a silent number and a new mobile. And he absolutely stopped drifting into the grey areas of police work. When his cousin asked him to run a numberplate after a traffic altercation, Hirsch refused. He also refused to protect a school friend from an irate creditor—and just as well, for the friend had turned out to be a cheat and a liar.

Gaddis said, 'We have mobile phone records showing that you made several calls to drug dealers.'

'I've explained that,' Hirsch said. 'Ms Ley made those calls.'

'When your back was turned I suppose?' sneered Gaddis. 'Lots of things happen when your back is turned, don't they, Constable Hirschhausen.'

15

That was Monday and Tuesday.

On Wednesday Gaddis returned to the Rolex.

'Why was the watch given to you, do you think?'

'To implicate me. To make me one of theirs.'

'And were you? One of theirs?'

'No. Perhaps they thought so.'

And yet Hirsch had shared some of the squad's contempt for the justice system; the weak, partisan and unjust nature of courts, judges, magistrates. He felt some sympathy with the notion of taking shortcuts, bending the rules, to obtain justice. Or at least punish someone. The feeling of us-against-them, an instinct to belong, had grown in him.

'You didn't wear the watch?'

'No.'

'It merely sat in your locker, ready to be found.'

'Yes.'

Officers from the Internal Investigations division had raided the Paradise Gardens police station right on the morning shift change, nabbing staff going off and on duty. Those on sick leave were taken at home. The building was cleared, locks changed, computers and files seized. Then the place was searched. Drugs were found in gym bags, guns in the ceiling cavities, bundles of cash in the air conditioning vents. Previously missing files, tapes and evidence bags were discovered under different case numbers.

'You could have declared it. It's now known that the officer in charge of Paradise Gardens was not involved in the corruption. You could have gone to Internal Investigations.'

'I didn't know who to trust. I believed then and I believe now that elements in Internal Investigations are supportive of Senior Sergeant Quine.'

Gaddis said and did nothing, a quality of stillness that seemed like fury to Hirsch.

'Instead you started babbling your innocence once the inquiry began.'

The initial inquiry sat for ten months. Hirsch had turned over his records, starting with his taped conversations with Big Trev, the publican, who'd already been named during the inquest. Hirsch was gratified to learn that the Internals already knew most things—that his material mostly confirmed that knowledge. He felt less like a dog and a maggot, he supposed.

One by one Quine's crew went down, committed to stand trial, until only Quine and Hirsch were left. Then things got dirty. Late-night phone calls, gravelly voices asking if his mother, sister, niece were in good health? Bullets in his letterbox, a truckload of cement dumped in his driveway. Breathalysed three times in one week.

Dirty in court, too. Quine's barrister cited the Rolex and accused him of holding a grudge, turning on the other squad members because he hadn't got his fair share. Hirsch thought that was a bit self-defeating, since it implied the barrister thought his client was guilty, but no one else remarked on it. Other accusations were thrown at him: failing to call witnesses, losing crucial evidence, accepting bribes and gifts, leaks to the media. And those calls to drug dealers made on his phone.

Meanwhile Quine remained on his feet while his squad went down. Two constables jailed, two committed to stand trial, a senior constable on the run, and the constable named Reid had shot himself.

The only good thing to come out of it was a kind of understanding in Hirsch. Police officers could drift over time, he saw. It wasn't always or entirely conscious; more like a loss of perspective. Real and imagined grievances festering; a feeling that the job deserved greater and better public recognition. Or at least perks, rewards. More money, more or better sex, a promotion, a junket to an interstate conference. Greater respect in general. Cynicism set it. The bad guys always got away with it, and the media hammered the cop who took a bribe rather than recognised the one who helped orphans. So why wouldn't you take shortcuts? Bend the rules?

'Are you paying attention, Constable Hirschhausen?'

Hirsch blinked. 'Sir.'

'You'd like us to believe that you were tainted because you were an innocent member of a corrupt squad? That you naively supported a corrupt senior officer, not knowing the full extent of his corruption?'

Hirsch was wary. It was coming now. 'Yes.'

Gaddis was wearing a dark blue suit today, with a pale blue shirt and mid-blue tie knotted fatly at the base of his scrawny throat. He wore gold-rimmed glasses and they glinted. He was a spotless man at odds with Grey Face, who was yet to speak this morning and looked washed-out, badly shaven and creased. He sat unmoving where Gaddis was full of motion, taking a box from the floor and crossing the room to where Hirsch was seated.

He spilled an iPhone and some bundled cash onto the table. 'These items were found concealed inside your private motor vehicle late last week. Perhaps you can account for them?'

Hirsch took out a pen and poked at the phone, then the cash. 'Never seen these before.'

Gaddis was delighted. 'Oh, really? You expect us to believe that?'

Hirsch shrugged. 'Believe what you like: I have never seen these items before.'

'Have a closer look.'

So Hirsch, using his handkerchief, lifted the phone from the table, held it in his palm and pressed the power button. He watched as the screen lit up. 'An iPhone 4,' he said at last. He was having fun but didn't show it. 'Apparently they had antenna issues.' He peered at it. 'Seems to be stuck on the boot logo. Maybe you could get a few dollars for it on eBay.'

'Stop arsing about,' Gaddis said. Reading from a file, he

said, 'That is an iPhone 5 that was last seen in the Paradise Gardens evidence safe, along with the cash.'

'Really? This is the latest iPhone?' Hirsch twisted around in his seat. 'Anyone got a five?'

Amused, Rosie DeLisle crossed the room, proffering her phone, looking spruce and intemperate in a swirling skirt. Hirsch compared them. 'See? The five is longer and thinner. This is a four. Easy mistake to make.'

He shot Rosie a look as he returned her phone: *Hope he doesn't take it out on you.* She smiled and went back to her seat. Hirsch turned his attention to Gaddis, seeing a change in his manner. He was shooting glances at a man standing at the back of the room. The man went out.

Hirsch smiled at Gaddis. 'I mean, your investigators did check the IMEI number, right? Checked the IMEI of this phone against the one that was supposed to be in the evidence locker?'

Strangling his words, Gaddis said, 'I would have thought the first-aid box a strange place to keep a phone and two and a half thousand dollars.'

Hirsch shrugged. 'Like I said, I have no idea what these items were doing in my car, if indeed they were there in the first place.'

Gaddis waved a folder at him. 'My officers conducted a proper search, every stage photographed and witnessed, with no breaks in the chain of custody.'

'Oh,' Hirsch said. 'Fair enough. So you'd have a record of all the serial numbers of each hundred-dollar note?'

Gaddis didn't bite. He froze, then left the room, giving off a 'someone's fucked up' air. The grey man contemplated Hirsch. Fidgeting and murmurs. Then Gaddis came back. He said, 'Are you pulling a swiftie on us, Constable? A dishonest man must expect dishonesty in others. You thought you'd embarrass the department by swapping the phone and the cash?'

'Well, you do investigate devious people, sir,' Hirsch said. He reached into the briefcase, took out his laptop. 'Like the devious person on this bit of CCTV footage. It shows a woman opening my car and leaning in. Don't know who she is. Your daughter, sir? Did you put her up to it?' He peered at the screen. 'She's got a little of your nervy manner.'

Afterwards Rosie DeLisle grabbed him.

'You are such a smartarse. Gaddis is furious.' She gave him a twist of her mouth. 'You come out ahead, don't you? I assume the cash they found is yours? You'll keep the original cash, change a hundred every time you buy something? You get the latest iPhone too, I guess.'

'We'll see,' Hirsch said.

Rosie shrugged. 'Either way, the stink isn't going away anytime soon.'

'Fuck them,' Hirsch said.

'Another day,' Rosie said. 'Someone I want you to meet.'

She grabbed him by the forearm, dragged him to where the hostile woman hovered. 'Paul, this is Inspector Croome.'

Hirsch went very still. Was this some new bullshit, coming on top of being grilled by Gaddis for three days?

'From?' he said. All things would flow from knowing which department Croome represented.

Croome's eyes were like pebbles. 'Sex crimes.'

Hirsch flinched. He'd had his share of underwhelming sexual encounters, but didn't think he'd broken any laws.

Rosie took pity. Her pretty hand rested on his forearm. 'We'd like you to stick around for another twenty-four hours.'

'Is that a request?'

'Not entirely,' Croome said. She handed Hirsch a slip of paper. 'Be at that address at noon tomorrow. Don't tell anyone where you're going, don't let yourself be followed.'

16

Feeling he'd amused himself sufficiently, Hirsch relinquished the original iPhone and $2500 to Rosie, together with his photographs of them *in situ*. He obtained a written receipt and returned to his motel.

The next day he took a succession of short taxi trips, ending up in the parking area of a strip of shops in Tea Tree Gully. Walked through a door marked *Maintenance* and up a flight of stairs. Knocked on the only door at the top.

Rosie DeLisle answered, leading him into a sitting room decorated in 1970s motel. 'Nice.'

'Safe house.'

Croome was standing by the window. 'Sit please, Constable.'

There were armchairs and a sofa but Hirsch chose a stiff chair at the little corner dining table. With a glance at each other, the women joined him. 'Inspector Croome has a request,' Rosie said.

'Why the cloak and dagger?'

'Things will move easier and quicker if you sit and listen and shut the fuck up,' Croome said.

She still thinks I'm bent, Hirsch thought, or at least a bit deviated. 'Language.' He folded his arms. 'Fire away.'

'You're stationed at Tiverton.'

Hirsch said nothing. She hadn't asked a question, merely stated the bleeding obvious. That was probably his personnel file in her lap. Croome shot a look at Rosie DeLisle as if wanting her to run interference.

'Paul,' DeLisle said, leaning her slender elbows on the table.

'Yes?'

'The inspector would like you to tell us about Sergeant Kropp and his crew.'

The anger came on quickly, as it often did these days, but Hirsch expressed it coldly, a withdrawal. 'I'm not a spy. I'm not a whistle-blower.'

'No one's saying you are.'

'Everyone's saying it. And you're about to ask me to blow the whistle.'

'Paul,' Croome said, 'we have a situation and no means of monitoring it.'

'Sex crimes? Kropp and his boys?'

'I'll explain in a minute,' Croome said. She was back-pedalling now; she'd expected this to be easier. 'First, do you think you could, ah, paint us a picture?' She glanced at Rosie. 'Internal Investigations have received several complaints about the Redruth police but what we lack is context.'

Hirsch stared at her. 'Before I say or do anything I need

to know if either of you are acquainted in any way, shape or form with Sergeant Kropp, Constables Nicholson or Andrewartha, or the new woman, Jennifer Dee. No bullshit, okay?'

'No connection,' Croome said.

'Never served with them?'

'No.'

'You're not a second cousin or ex-girlfriend or ex-academy buddy with any of them?'

'No.'

He glanced at Rosie DeLisle. 'You?'

'Never met them, Paul, never served with them, no relationship with them at all.'

Hirsch chewed on his bottom lip

Croome said, 'Please Constable, it's very important.'

Hirsch liked her better when she didn't use his name. 'I can give you local gossip, that's all.'

Croome's face said she'd noted the fancy footwork. If he was merely repeating gossip, he wasn't a spy or a whistleblower. 'All right.'

Hirsch gathered himself. 'Look, they're not popular. Arrogant, heavy-handed. And this is a sleepy country town. It could be argued that Kropp's been there too long. He's networked his way into it so thoroughly and has so much power, he tends to think of the place as his.'

'Like Quine?' Rosie said.

Hirsch nodded. 'Like Quine.' He considered his words: 'Kropp likes order,' he said. 'That's his style. But he and the others overdo it with the speed traps, the breathalysers . . .

On-the-spot fines, screaming in people's faces even if all they've done is jaywalk.'

Then he recalled the way Nicholson and Andrewartha had talked about Melia Donovan and her brother. How they treated Jenny Dee. He cocked his head at Croome. 'If you're a female you're probably a bit of a target.' He thought about it. 'Or black.'

They fell silent. Is Kropp another Quine? Hirsch wondered. He pictured the full, frothing intensity of Quine, the stamp of his unimaginable expertise, but couldn't quite match Kropp with that. Yet they were both hard men, and those could be found in police stations all around the country.

'Care to elaborate?'

Hirsch's instinct was to shut up. Impressions were dangerous if there was no substance to them. But impressions were all he had. 'I don't have hard facts. I don't know any of the local girls.'

'Yes you do,' Croome said, and Hirsch didn't like the way she said it. He waited.

'Melia Donovan and Gemma Pitcher.'

Hirsch waited. Was the older man in Melia Donovan's life a local copper?

'Paul,' Rosie said, 'it's been alleged the Redruth officers demand sexual favours from young girls in return for dropping charges they might be facing. Minor charges like shoplifting, drunkenness, possession . . .'

'So if you could get a bit closer to your colleagues,' Croome said, 'you—'

Hirsch ignored her and flared at DeLisle. 'The term "false pretences" comes to mind. I've helped you people enough. Consider this meeting over.'

'Paul,' said Rosie soothingly, 'there's someone we'd like you to meet.'

Croome got to her feet and entered a short corridor at the end of the room. She tapped on a door, cracked it open, stuck her head in. Hirsch heard murmurs and then she was standing back and making a this-way gesture with one arm.

A teenage girl emerged.

'Nothing to be frightened of,' Croome said, gently ushering the girl to the sofa and settling her into it. Rosie left the table and sat beside her, giving the girl a smile of warm brilliance, then Croome sat, and now Hirsch had the three of them staring at him from the sofa.

'Paul, I'd like you to meet Emily Hobba.'

Hobba looked barely fifteen but might have been older. She was pretty in an unformed, second-glance way, with a kid's open round face, long brown hair falling from either side of a ragged centre part. Her frame was thin, almost bony, inside a lilac T-shirt, a scrap of floral mini-skirt and half a dozen clanking bangles. She caught him looking and gave him a lop-sided smile, a hint of dark artfulness in her eyes. Startled, he struggled not to return it. It wasn't quite neutral, that smile.

And as if she'd immediately forgotten him, Hobba took out a mobile phone and began working it, texting crazily with a faint grin. Hirsch glanced at Croome, then Rosie. Raised an eyebrow. They shrugged minutely as if to say, *It's the way it is, nothing we can do about it.*

Rosie placed a hand on Emily's forearm. Long, tanned, slender fingers. Hirsch looked away from them, concentrated as she said, 'Late last year, Emily got involved in a . . .' she hesitated. 'A scene involving some other young girls and a number of men.'

Emily lifted her head and said clearly, eyes bright and clear, 'Sex scene.'

'Yes,' Rosie said.

'The men wore masks, we wore nothing.' She'd told this story before.

Hirsch thought he should chip in. 'Where was this?'

Emily shrugged. 'Here and there. People's houses. I mean, I was totally wasted, you know? Out of it.'

'She means Adelaide,' Croome said. 'Inner suburbs, outer suburbs.'

'Sometimes the country,' Hobba said, anxious to put her right. 'We'd get picked up in this big car and stay away a couple of days. Free drinks and whatever, party, party, party. I'd be that sore.'

The country. Hirsch said, 'Where in the country, Emily?'

'How would I know?'

Hirsch frowned at DeLisle and Croome. Croome said, 'Tell Paul what you saw in the newspaper.'

Hobba brightened. 'Oh yeah. Okay. Well, that girl that got run over, I reckernised her.'

'Melia Donovan.'

'Yeah, I knew her.'

Hirsch had a vivid memory then of Wendy Street, standing in her back yard while sheets flapped on the line, telling him that Melia Donovan seemed to be someone who'd had too much experience, too soon. 'She was at one of the parties in the country?'

'That's what I said.'

'Who else was there?'

Hobba was working her phone again. 'What? Oh, right, there was this one other chick.'

'Was her name Gemma?'

'I'm not sure. Maybe.'

Croome chimed in. 'Emily nearly died of an overdose after one of these weekend parties. Someone dumped her outside a hospital in the Barossa Valley. It threw a little scare into you, didn't it, Em? She told a counsellor and the counsellor contacted us.'

Hirsch looked to the girl for confirmation. She shrugged and gave him the whisper of a bat of the eyelashes.

'What was Gemma's role?'

A shrug. 'Anal? Golden showers? She did what we did.'

'I mean, was there any sense that she recruited Melia?'

'Nup.'

'How many times did you attend the same party as Melia Donovan?'

'I dunno, it's a bit of a blur, maybe only once.'

'When was this?'

'Don't you believe me? He doesn't believe me.'

'Em, it's all right, he's come into this new, he needs to fill in the gaps.'

'Well he can shut up with the questions.'

Croome said, 'Emily, I know it's a long shot, a lot's

happened, but if you saw photographs of the men who might have been involved, would you recognise body shape, body language? Even if you didn't see their faces?'

Emily gave a teenage shrug. 'I was like, totally out of it. I just have this feeling of like, black masks over their eyes and this one guy wearing a uniform.'

'Uniform.'

With a bit of a grin she said, '*Police* uniform.'

Croome and DeLisle stared at Hirsch as if to say, *Now can you see why we want your help?*

Hirsch said, 'He arrived in a uniform? You caught only a glimpse of it?'

Emily snorted. 'He wore it like, the whole time, like rubbing our faces in it. I need the toilet.'

She leapt from the sofa and disappeared into a room off the hallway. Hirsch watched her go. 'How did Emily get involved? Did someone recruit her?'

'A girl called Lily Humphreys, they were in a youth training program together,' Croome said. 'Humphreys got out first, took Emily under her wing when she was released. What that boiled down to was, "Would you like to party with these cool guys I know?" Emily said yes. They did this a few times over several months, city and rural locations. Sex, booze, cocaine, probably GHB. Then one day Emily wakes up in a hospital in the Barossa Valley, sore and torn and bruised. She mends slowly, but starts to have flashbacks. They scare her. She puts them together with the state of her body and talks to a counsellor who then gets in touch with us.'

'Flashbacks.'

'Men wearing masks, someone getting rough with her and another telling him to go easy, things like that.'

'So speak to Lily Humphreys.'

'Disappeared.'

'Disappeared as in she's probably lying dead somewhere, or disappeared as in address unknown?'

'The latter. Packed all her things and hopped on a plane to the Gold Coast, according to Emily.'

'When?'

'While Em was in hospital.'

'Spooked.'

'Yes.'

'Be worth checking to see if Gemma Pitcher was in youth training with either of them.'

Croome smiled. 'One step ahead of you. Humphreys and Pitcher were there at the same time, but before Emily's time.'

Hirsch glanced at Rosie DeLisle. 'Gemma's disappeared. I've done all I can to find her, you've got better resources than I have.'

'Sure.'

Hirsch nodded his thanks. 'What about Emily's parents? Siblings?'

'Paul, we're talking ex-foster kids straight out of detention. No one is looking out for them.'

Hirsch nodded gloomily. 'When did you learn about her?'

'Three months ago. We didn't know where to start the investigation, and then a couple of days ago she texted me to say she'd recognised Melia Donovan's picture in the paper.'

Hirsch fetched out his phone. 'I have a snap of Gemma Pitcher. I could show it to Emily.'

'Good idea,' Rosie said. Then she gave Croome a look. 'She's been in the loo a while . . .'

Croome blinked. 'Oh, fuck.'

She raced away, and when they heard thumps and drama, Hirsch and DeLisle ran after her. They found Croome on the bathroom floor, slapping the teenager's face.

'What did you take? Emily, come on Emily, wake up! What did you take?'

Hirsch left as Emily was coming round, groaning, and telling everyone to just push off and leave her alone.

17

Hirsch headed back to the bush that evening. Spent Friday making his rounds and at nightfall received a call from Kropp.

'A little bird tells me you came out of the Quine hearing smelling of roses. No flies on you. But given that you haven't been sacked or jailed, may I remind you that your presence is needed here tomorrow?'

'Crowd control, I remember. Football hooligans. With any luck they're going to punch my lights out.'

'Just get your arse down here for an eleven o'clock briefing.'

Saturday. Hirsch showered, pulled on his uniform and strapped his baby Beretta to an ankle holster. He drove to Redruth. Kropp said, 'Nice of you to join us, Constable Hirschhausen.'

Hirsch checked his watch. Eleven a.m. 'Am I late, Sarge?'

'On my watch you arrive *early*.'

'I'll remember that, Sarge,' said Hirsch, giving Nicholson a winning grin. Andrewartha was there, and Dee, but Kropp had also brought in two constables from Clare: Revell and Molnar. Big men, stony, full of dull menace.

'Gents,' said Hirsch with a wink.

'Stop arsing around and take a seat,' Kropp said.

He'd pinned seven photographs to the board, head-and-shoulders shots of five white and two Aboriginal men. Four of the seven were young, three in early middle age. Sullen faces mostly, full of hard-won experience, men whose work, education, relationship and financial histories were slight to non-existent. Kropp's view of them was simple. He slapped the flat of his pointer across the display. 'If there's any trouble today or tonight, it'll be down to these characters.'

'Or anyone with a Centrelink face, Sarge,' Nicholson said, looking around with a grin.

A couple of sniggers, irritating Kropp. Meanwhile Hirsch stared at the faces. They were not that different from guys like Nicholson and Andrewartha, really. Kropp's constables were poorly educated and short of work and life experience too. Just as clannish and suspicious of anyone different. Attracted to police work because it gave them standing. And it licensed the art and craft of hurting other human beings.

'As I was saying, Constable Hirschhausen.'

Hirsch blinked. 'Loud and clear, Sarge.'

'As I was saying, these magnificent specimens of Australian manhood are a nuisance when sober and an absolute nightmare when they get on the grog. Stir in a football premiership . . .'

You get blood and broken glass, mostly.

'We have some long hours ahead of us, but I have managed to get you overtime. Best-case scenario, the night turns out to be a fizzer. But if you remember, last year we had a glassing that resulted in the loss of an eye, a full-on brawl in the Woolman, resulting in hospitalisation, and a fatality from kids drag-racing just out past the motel.'

Here Kropp's voice cracked a little. Hirsch was curious. The guy seemed genuine. He rose on the balls of his feet as he spoke, lifted by his emotions, as if the town were his and he its civilising force.

One of the hard men with their fiefdoms. All around the state, men who'd turn evasive and arrogant if you tried to pin them down. Clever men, though, a witness-box headache to every judge, magistrate and barrister in the land. How long had Kropp been here? Twelve years?

Kropp slapped the pointer down and folded his arms. 'I do not want a repeat of last year. Superintendent Spurling doesn't want a repeat of last year. Understood?'

A ragged, 'Yes, Sarge,' went around the room, Hirsch thinking, the area commander's breathing down his neck.

'Questions? No? Well, get to it then.'

Hirsch glanced at his watch: almost noon, the game started at two. He glanced at Dee and mimed eating. She nodded.

'Aww,' said Nicholson, 'the first blush of young love.'

Dee ignored him but coloured, looked down as she gathered her things.

Andrewartha worked a concerned frown onto his face. 'I hope you're sexually responsible, Constable Hirschhausen.

For your convenience, a protective sheath dispenser has been installed in the men's room.'

'Nah,' Nicholson said, 'I reckon he likes to *feel* it.'

'Then he's in for a disappointment,' Andrewartha said. 'Word is, he'll find a lack of tactile integrity, if you get my meaning.'

'Totally do,' Nicholson said. 'She overused it at the academy.'

'Look at Hirschhausen, cracking the shits.'

'You're so funny,' Dee said.

'We think so.'

These clowns, Hirsch thought, deserve to be fucking informed on.

An hour later he was patrolling the Redruth oval listlessly, watching for hotheads, just as he'd done years ago as a raw cadet.

He hadn't come full circle, exactly. For a start, here in the world of small towns and farms, the spectators were few and did their drinking and fuming in private, cocooned in cars parked snout-up to a white perimeter fence. Once in a while a door would open and the occupant raised the tailgate to rummage for another can, but other than that they might have been at a church picnic. He recognised some of the Tiverton locals, including the Muirs, Ed Tennant, Ray Latimer, who was there with his sons and a solid-looking older man. The boys' grandfather? Horns tooted desultorily, a woman knitted a baby's jacket, a man sipped thermos tea, a dog pissed on a car tyre.

At quarter time knots of men appeared, standing outside their cars, yarning peacefully. Rather than face each other or make eye contact, as women did, they stood at oblique angles, as if to face off dangers. Or maybe, thought Hirsch, it was a kind of genital anxiety. God, he was bored.

When the wind came up, whipping a scarf from a car aerial, Hirsch retrieved it and handed it to the kid seated at the wheel.

'Thanks.'

He peered in at the boys in the back. 'Nathan?'

Melia Donovan's brother looked hunted, his dark eyes liquid in his dark face. The boy beside him was on Kropp's watch list, Tyson somebody. And in the front passenger seat was the boy who had dropped Nathan off that time. Sam Hempel.

Hirsch straightened his back, saluted. 'Enjoy the game.'

'Yeah.'

Hirsch turned to go and saw Andrewartha watching him.

'Mates with the boongs, eh?'

Hirsch winked. 'I'll put your name down for sensitivity training, shall I?'

'Fuck off.'

Time dragged. Hirsch's feet hurt. The game didn't interest him even though the score was close, each side kicking too few goals, too many points. With half-time due, he headed for a van parked inside the main gate and bought four spring rolls. The woman who served him was Vietnamese or maybe Thai; he watched her fry the rolls in a spitting pan. Then the siren sounded and people poured from their cars, forming a line at the van window, a pulsing pressure point. Hirsch watched tensely, but nothing happened, the queue was orderly. The Latimers appeared. Jack gave Hirsch a tiny wave, Raymond glared. The older boy was plump and hangdog, trying to appear unattached.

Then Kropp arrived in a police car, pulling up behind the food van. He got out, bent his solid back into the rear compartment, emerged with a plastic sack of spring rolls and packaged paper cups and plates. Hirsch watched him hand the bags to the woman in the van, plant a kiss on her cheek and wave goodbye. He took his time leaving, striding like a general down the queue of spectators, winking, geddaying, giving the evil eye. He shook hands with Ray Latimer, ruffled Jack's hair.

Dee materialised at Hirsch's elbow, small and perky in her uniform. 'What would you call that? Crowd management? Improving customer relations?'

'Constable, please, a little respect. Who's the woman?'

'That's his wife. She's from Thailand.'

'Nice little sideline,' Hirsch said.

'The spring rolls or the mail-order bride?'

At the final siren, Redruth was four points ahead and Hirsch broke up a shoving match. Dee's shins were strafed by spurting gravel as she dodged an irate station wagon. Andrewartha got into the face of a screeching woman. Nicholson and the other constables whisked a man off to the lockup.

And then it was all over. The knitter and the old tea drinker and the tired farming families were gone, leaving only wrappers tumbled like scrapping birds as the wind rose. 'Don't get your hopes up,' Kropp said, reappearing in his police car. 'Consider this the calm before the storm. By nine or ten o'clock the troublemakers will be spoiling for a fight. Meanwhile, grab yourselves a quick bite and then start making your presence felt.'

At six o'clock they split into two units and began to prowl the streets, pubs and through-roads of the town, Hirsch, Nicholson and Revell in one car, Andrewartha, Dee and Molnar in the other.

Hirsch was happy to sprawl in the back seat and let Nicholson drive. Up and down the streets, in and out of the town's three pubs and car parks. The streetlights were barely adequate; few cars were about. At this stage the pubs were quiet. He felt he was encroaching whenever he entered a main bar or a lounge bar. Heads would turn away, registering not him but his uniform.

At 8 p.m. he wandered through the Woolman Hotel while Nicholson and Revell had words with some kids hanging around the bottle shop. Ray Latimer was seated in a booth with a woman who was not his wife. She was tiredly pretty, dressed in black. Guessing that Latimer had sent his sons home with the old man, Hirsch nodded and returned to the car.

At eight-thirty his mobile chirped.

'Hello?'

'Mr Hirsch . . .'—the voice stumbled—' . . . Hirsch . . . hawsen.'

'Yes?'

'This is The Dugout, concerning your eight o'clock booking.'

'Sorry?'

'Table for twelve, eight o'clock.'

'I don't understand,' said Hirsch, who did.

'One of our busiest nights of the year. I'm afraid when you didn't show we allocated that table to another party.'

'I'm afraid you've been duped.'

'We cannot issue a refund, I'm afraid.'

'Forgive me,' Hirsch said, 'but I did not make a table booking. Someone is duping you.'

'You gave this mobile number. Party of twelve, eight o'clock, a twenty-dollar deposit.'

Hirsch shook off the caller and pocketed the phone. 'Trouble?' Nicholson wanted to know.

'Twenty bucks?' said Hirsch. 'You guys wasted twenty bucks on me?' He shook his head. Dumber than dogshit.

The hours lengthened. The radio crackled from car to car, car to base, base to car. Hirsch glimpsed the other patrol car sometimes, outside a pub, nosing down a street. Otherwise he dozed. He'd been awake since dawn and his stomach was heavy with fried food grabbed in passing. He wriggled to get comfortable. He'd had enough of this, the blanketing night air, the dew and the tricky half-light. Something was making him antsy—not here in the patrol car, exactly, but just out of range, in among the shadows. He supposed he was waiting for violence. Nicholson and Revell talked while he dozed.

'How long's the sheila been with you?'

'Dee?' said Nicholson. 'Couple of weeks.'

'Nice tits.'

'Get her pissed she might flash them for you.'

'Is it true, she did the whole academy?'

'Top to bottom.'

'Top *and* bottom.'

The tyres grumbled beneath them in the night.

Revell fished out his wallet. 'Ten bucks says I do her before you.'

'Dork.'

'I mean it,' Revell said. 'I saw the way she was looking at me.'

Nicholson shook his head. 'Let's make it interesting: ten bucks each for first anal, first facial, first golden shower.'

'You're on.'

'Except are we sure she's worth ten?'

'Point,' Revell said. He turned to Hirsch. 'You in?'

'I don't gamble.'

Revell stared at him a moment, turned away. 'Scumbag.'

They fell silent. The radio crackled, suspicious noises reported at 5 Truro Street. The car climbed out of the main street and up onto one of the town's little hills, where stone houses slumbered behind oleanders and ghost gums cracked the footpaths. The old copper mine was a dark excavation on the adjacent hill, moonlight flaring on the depthless black water and pushing gantry and chimney shadows down the hill. The wind was higher here, a helpless whine in the pine trees. Revell got out, knocked, no answer.

He returned to the car. 'No one in.'

'Okay, shove a card under the door.'

Hirsch stirred at last. 'Shouldn't we check around the back?'

'Oh, it speaks,' Nicholson said. 'The place is dead, all right? Got better things to do.'

'Let me check,' said Hirsch, climbing out.

'Fucking boy scout.'

Breathing in scented air from the garden beds, Hirsch strode through the gate to the side path and down it to the back yard. He was reminded of Grandma Hirschhausen's garden in Burnside, neatly cropped lawns, pansy beds, ivy trellis, a geranium in a cracked teapot, rotary clothesline.

The screen door was ajar, a weak spill of light over the concrete steps. There was something just inside it, Hirsch saw, lumpy on the lino floor. He pushed through the door and there was a woman, lying unconscious, her top half caught in the smashed glass that was the inner door. She looked about seventy-five, her dress was rucked up across her thighs, and blood was pooling. Tripped, he thought. Neighbour heard the glass break and called the police.

He phoned for an ambulance and a moment later a voice came through the darkness: 'Yoo-hoo.'

Hirsch headed for the side fence, where there was some light. 'Yes?'

An old man's creaky voice. 'Is Crystal all right?'

'She had a fall. I've called the ambulance.'

'That's good.' Pause. 'You're new.'

'Temporary assignment. I'm stationed at Tiverton.'

'I try to look out for Crystal,' the neighbour said, 'but it was dark and I suppose things are a bit rowdy tonight and I didn't want one of those policemen shouting at me for wasting his time.'

A wobbly challenge in the voice, daring Hirsch to blame him.

'My colleagues shout at people?'

'Great shouters. Pretty quick with a breath-test, too.'

Hirsch returned to the old woman. Her breath was fluttery, her pulse slow. He didn't think she was dying, but she would have been if it was down to Nicholson, the lazy shit. He heard a siren, went out to greet the ambos, just as a call came in: all officers, a brawl outside the Woolman. Well, he'd have to walk. Nicholson and Revell had left him there.

He was halfway down the street when he turned back. 'If it's on the way, can you guys drop me off at the Woolman Hotel?'

'Yeah, sure, too easy,' the ambulance driver said.

'You might even pick up some business,' Hirsch said.

Owing to the brawl, the ambulance officers set him down on the opposite side of the town square. As Hirsch passed the rotunda, where a couple of kids were sharing a bottle, he could hear shouts, see a jostling crowd, figures straggling away among parked cars.

Reaching the footpath, Hirsch broke through. Nicholson and Revell were back to back between two indistinguishable gangs of young men and women. Half-crouched, batons extended, they were lunging and retreating, screaming, *Break it up, break it up!*

'Evening, gents.'

'Took your sweet fucking time.'

Hirsch waved his baton at one ragged clump and then the other. Derision greeted it, the women screeching, the men full of spit and jutting chests.

Just then Nicholson charged, shouting, 'Got you.' Bodies retreated and a kid, back-pedalling with Nicholson in his face, sprawled onto his coccyx. He cried out, and Hirsch recognised him: Nathan Donovan. Nicholson laughed. He began to strike the boy, landing meaty thumps with his baton. Revell joined him, booting Nathan's spine.

Nicholson paused and said to Revell, 'I've got this. You go after his mates.'

'Gotcha,' Revell said. He lumbered away down the side of the pub, not quite at a run.

As Nicholson readied himself for another swing of the baton, Hirsch grabbed his arm. 'That's enough.'

'What?'

'You've made your point.'

Nicholson shook him off. The mob didn't like it either. Raw voices called to Nicholson, *'Get the cunt.'*

'Fucking Abo, smash his head in.'

'Fuck him up . . . black cunt.'

Hirsch selected the brawniest Redruth local, a kid of twenty, and charged him, windmilling his baton, up into the groin.

The kid doubled over. His mates were shocked. 'What did you do that for?'

'Piss off home,' Hirsch said. 'It's over for the night.'

'Nicko,' they said, 'tell your mate to leave us alone.'

Hirsch lunged; they retreated. One by one, they straggled away into the night.

He returned to Nicholson, who had a knee in Nathan's back, screaming into the boy's face, 'You gunna behave?'

Hirsch grabbed again. 'I said leave him alone.'

Nicholson jerked away. 'Get your hands off me.'

'Let him go.'

Nicholson stood. They were panting, Nathan prone on the ground. 'You better have a fucking good reason . . .'

'There was no need to lay into him like that.'

'Big fucking deal. You saw it, disturbing the peace, assaulting a police officer, inciting a riot.'

'I didn't see that. They were retreating,' Hirsch said. 'There was no actual fighting, nothing damaged.' He bent and hauled on Nathan's arm. 'Up you get.'

The boy complied, wincing.

'You okay?' Hirsch asked, seeing scrapes, a bleeding nose.

'Had worse from that bastard.'

'Can you get home okay?'

Nathan shrugged.

'A lift with your mates, perhaps? Have they been drinking?'

'No.'

'Off you go.'

Nicholson was disgusted. 'What a legend. A king among men.'

Hirsch ignored him. He could hear strained shouts in the night, disembodied and far away. He saw movements like

181

tricks of the light, far back in the shadows. All of the tension had leaked away, and then Revell came stumbling in from the dark, holding an injured right hand, blood dripping from his elbow. Sounding astonished he said, 'I went and fucking cut myself.'

'What happened?'

'I need stitches, I think.'

Hirsch fished for a handkerchief and pressed it against a gash in the man's palm. 'What happened?'

'Get off me,' Revell said, flinching. 'Cut myself on a piece of roofing iron.' He shook his head. 'That's me best jerking-off hand.'

'Another moron,' Nicholson said. He paused, computing rapidly. 'This is what happened. We broke up a brawl. Someone pulled a knife and slashed you with it. He got away. Too dark and confusing to see who it was.'

He shoved his chest at Hirsch's. 'Are we agreed on that version of events, *Cunt*stable?'

Hirsch shrugged. 'Whatever you like, but I don't see where it gets us.'

'It gets our mate ten thousand bucks compensation, that's where.'

'Hey, yeah,' Revell said.

'No skin off my nose,' Hirsch said.

'So long as we're on the same page.'

They drove to the hospital, bone tired now. The streets were deserted. The car made the hill climb quietly; even the radio was muted. Hirsch was lost to dreams, sprawled across the back seat in his regular position.

'They gunna buy it?' Revell asked at one point. Hirsch barely heard him; had his eyes closed.

'Piece of cake,' Nicholson said.

'Voice of experience.'

'Tell you a story,' Nicholson said. 'I was with this chick, my car, she's driving—and she prangs it.'

'Yeah, so?'

'Mate, no licence.'

Revell's light switched on. 'You said you were the driver.'

'No flies on you.'

It wasn't much of a hospital—minor procedures, a few beds—and tonight McAskill and another of the town's doctors and handful of nurses were stretched to the limit. The waiting room full, the three policemen leaned against a wall of the main corridor. A tiny surgery bustled at the end; neon lights buzzed; the white walls were blinding. Four men and a teenage girl were already seated in the plastic chairs outside the surgery, holding their heads in misery or pain. Some blood was evident, soaking through bandages. Nicholson loved it. He was like Kropp at the football, striding up and down, full of badgering mirth. Knew them all by name.

Eventually Revell came out, bandaged, pale and grinning. 'Good as new.'

'About fucking time.'

They drove down to the square, through pockets of waist-high night mist. Dew glistened on parked cars and here and there broken glass glinted in the gutters. Hirsch felt hollowed out. 'Can we pack it in yet? The town's dead.'

'Not yet, boss's orders.'

Sometime later the radio crackled: get over to the motel, possible drunk and disorderly.

Nicholson swung the wheel and planted his foot. The town dwindled behind them and on its shadowy outskirts a Budget sign came into view. Nicholson slowed to a crawl, casting an eye over the cars parked in the motel grounds. Standard police procedure. Hirsch himself had done it a million times. It was like breathing. The place looked dead. He closed his eyes again.

Snapped them open when his tired mind caught up. The police car was adjacent to the motel entrance-way and a pair of headlights was hurtling at them from inside the grounds. He cried out involuntarily. The other car struck where his left shoulder had been resting. He felt shocked, his head full of percussive sounds and sudden fright.

A ticking silence, broken by Revell: 'The cunt's only gone and run into us.'

They got out, Hirsch obliged to scoot across to the other door. He blinked to clear his head, rubbed his sore shoulder, then shuffled around to inspect the damage. It had been an almighty bang, but all he could see was a Honda with a broken headlight and dented bumper, and the dented rear door of the police car.

Meanwhile Revell was jerking the Honda driver out of his car. 'Bloody moron. You realise you hit a police car?'

'What?'

'Been on the grog, is that it? Judgment impaired?'

'What?'

The driver struggled, gaining focus, and Hirsch saw who it was. 'Mr Latimer?'

Ray Latimer, ignoring him, tried to attract Nicholson's attention: 'Nick? Nicko?'

'Don't fucking move,' Revell said. He turned to Nicholson. 'You know this bozo, Nick?'

'Who you calling a bozo?' Latimer said, shrugging him off.

'Sir, stay where you are.'

'I'm not at fault. Why the hell did you stop there? How was I supposed to avoid you?'

'Sir, I need you to calm down.'

'I am calm.'

Latimer craned his head around Revell's bulky shoulder. 'Nick, for fuck's sake.'

Nicholson had been standing back as if hoping it would all go away. He shook his head, disgusted, and came closer. 'It's okay, he's not going to do anything silly.'

'Tell this prick to get his hands off me,' Latimer said.

'You're dreaming,' Revell said. 'You're in a shitload of trouble.'

'Fuck you.'

'Just calm down, Ray, all right?' Nicholson said.

'I am fucking calm.'

Nicholson, still disgusted, turned to Hirsch and gestured at the cars. 'Don't just stand there, get this mess sorted.'

'All over it,' Hirsch said, reaching into the police car for the camera. He started snapping.

'The fuck are you doing?'

'For the insurance. For the report.'

'Don't be a moron, just clear the bloody driveway, all right?'

Hirsch climbed into the Honda, reversed it a few metres, metal shrieking, and got out. Suspecting radiator damage, he lifted the bonnet. The radiator had been pushed closer to the fan, but wasn't touching. No leaks. He took more shots with the camera, then photographed the damage to the police car. One of the rear panels was buckled and seemed to be touching the tyre.

Finally he backed the Honda into a slot outside an empty unit, his attention caught by a spill of light from a neighbouring doorway, then another, and another: guests, peering out at the racket. Catching his gaze, they retreated, curtains twitching.

One guest didn't. She stepped out of the light and crossed the dewy lawn in bare feet, wrapped in a bulky motel robe. Hirsch recognised her as the woman who'd been drinking with Latimer in the Woolman.

Closing in on the men at the street entrance, she called, 'Ray?'

Latimer stiffened, slumped. 'Oh, Christ. Finola, please, go back inside.'

She stopped. 'What's wrong? What happened?'

'Tell you later. Please, Fin, just go inside.'

She came closer. 'Did you have an accident?'

Hirsch pocketed the Honda keys and intercepted her, touched her forearm. She flinched. 'Let's leave them to it,' he said.

The tension went out of her and she let herself be turned

around and guided back across the lawn to her doorway. Number 6, noted Hirsch. Behind them, the three men were shouting now:

'Not fucking drunk.'

'Sir, will you consent to—'

'I was barely moving when I hit you. Get off me.'

'Ray, I need you to blow into this.'

Hirsch saw the woman into the room and hovered at the door. The interior was generic and held no interest, but the bed was a mess, an empty champagne bottle neck-first in a bucket of ice. He turned his attention to the woman, who perched dejectedly on the end of the bed. A tousled forty, with a pretty but weathered face, the face of someone deeply fatigued or a drinker with her good looks accelerating down-hill. An outdoors woman, he guessed, her tanned skin dark against the white of the dressing-gown. The gown gaped; she was naked under it. Her clothes were heaped on a chair. As if reading him, she pulled the towelling close around her breasts and knees. Girlfriend? Pick-up?

'He was going out to find a bottle shop.'

Hirsch nodded. Latimer's shouting had escalated, and she glanced past Hirsch, gnawing her lip.

He took out his notebook. 'Could I have your name?'

'Finola. Finola Armstrong.'

The name rang a bell. 'From Bitter Wash Road?'

'How did you know?'

'Have you been drinking, Finola?'

'I'm not much of a drinker.' She paused. 'What's that got to do with anything?'

'You might need to drive him home.'

She looked at the floor. 'What a god-awful mess.'

'Are you okay to drive? Can I call someone to come and get you?'

'No! God no. Look, does anyone have to know about this? Can you leave my name out of it? I haven't done anything wrong.'

'I'll see what I can do.'

'His wife left him, you know. Moved in with her parents.'

'I know.'

'You know? How?'

Hirsch shrugged.

'I forgot—you're all mates. Do you need a statement?'

'Brief one.'

Hirsch took it, then gave her the Honda keys and returned to the street. Latimer was swinging punches now, hitting nothing, Nicholson and Revell struggling with him, shouting at him.

Spotting Hirsch, Nicholson snarled, 'For Christ's sake move our car out of the way.'

'Don't know if it's driveable. Look.'

They looked at the edge of the rear panel, resting against the tyre. 'Fuck.'

Some of the bleariness went out of Latimer. He'd noticed Hirsch at last. 'Look who's here.'

Hirsch nodded hello. 'Mr Latimer.'

Latimer shot out his fist. Hirsch swayed neatly away, too late, the hard knuckles spending their energy on his cheekbone.

He rubbed it. 'Ouch. You want to explain that?'

Latimer took a boxer's stance, Revell jerking him back. 'Moron.' He glanced at Hirsch. 'Well?'

Hirsch sighed. 'Raymond Latimer,' he said, and ran through the formal arrest statement while Latimer struggled and Revell swore.

'Do you understand these charges, Mr Latimer?'

'You're arresting me?'

'Mate, it's already done,' Revell said. 'Weren't you listening? You've been arrested. You're spending the night in the lockup.'

Meanwhile Nicholson was shaking his head. He scraped both palms down his cheeks tiredly. 'How do we get him there if we can't fucking drive?'

'The others can come and collect us,' Revell said.

Hirsch might have been invisible. He looked back across the lawn, where Finola Armstrong was standing outside number 6. She had changed into her black dress.

Then Latimer began struggling, trying to shake off Nicholson and Revell, shouting, 'How about you call Bill Kropp, he'll sort this out.'

'How about we add another charge, interfering with a police officer in the execution of his duty,' Revell said.

'Fuck you.'

Out of the night came a pair of headlights and a whooping siren, the other patrol car rocketing alongside them, tyres scraping the kerb. The passenger side window whined down and Andre-wartha leaned out, full of humour. 'Evening, gents.'

'What took you so long?'

'Busy.'

'Doing what?'

Andrewartha exchanged a grin with Molnar, the driver. 'Showing Dee Dee the town.'

Hirsch went still. He peered in. The back seat was empty. 'What've you done with her?'

'Oh, she's on official police business,' said Andrewartha, helping to bundle Latimer into the rear of the car. Nicholson and Revell climbed in after him, Nicholson winding down his rear window to say, 'You stay with our car, okay? See if you can get it moving.'

'Shouldn't I—'

No one waited to hear what Hirsch thought he should or shouldn't do. He was alone, the road deserted and not much light leaking from the motel now. The street lighting was dim out here, blurred by mist. With a shrug, he returned to the police car and tugged on the lip of metal, feeling it move. He pulled harder and a gap opened. He ran his hand along the surface of the tyre. No damage.

Then he called Dee, and her voice in the barren night was far off and frightened. 'Hey.'

'Hey yourself. Where are you?'

'Middle of nowhere. Those pricks just left me here.'

'Where? I'll come and get you.'

He heard sounds on her end of the line: a squeaky gate, a knock on a door, murmurs. Then her voice was loud in his ear: 'Apparently it's easier if I give directions rather than a street address . . .'

A minute later, Hirsch was heading north-east, crossing the dark town to a road signposted for Morgan, a town on the Murray River, on the far side of saltbush plains. Hirsch wasn't going that far. A hundred metres down it, he turned off. There were no pretty stone houses out here. This was where people struggled on a couple of hectares of under-nourished dirt, fibro dwelling and starved pets. Midnight and the sky was densely black. His headlights picked out Dee beside a rusty fence. She climbed in. 'Thanks.'

Hirsch planted his foot, headed back to the empty streets of the town. 'What's the story?'

After a while she said, 'Sex.'

'Sex.'

'Sex, sexism and sexual harassment.'

'Okay,' Hirsch said, drawing the word out.

'I can deal with the innuendo and the bullshit. I had it all through training. But they wanted to have it off with a kid.'

'How old?'

'About fourteen, pissed out of her tiny brain when we picked her up. When I say "we", Andrewartha nabbed her for jaywalking. Has anyone been charged with that in living memory?'

'In this town, yeah,' Hirsch said.

'She was with a gang of kids, all of them a bit drunk, not doing anyone any harm. Andrewartha's plan was for him and Molnar to take her home while I stayed behind and kept an eye on the friends.'

She paused. 'You should have seen the look on her face. And her mates'. Fear, pure and simple.'

'They knew what would happen.'

'I'd say so.'

Hirsch circled the town square, the lights misty and no movement anywhere.

'So I said no way, I'm coming too, and when we got to her house I walked her to the door and checked someone was home.' She snorted. 'That's when they pissed off and left me.'

Hirsch was driving slowly; they were cocooned together in the warmth of the car. Out past the mine, back to the square, out past the motel. No sign of Finola Armstrong's Honda. Time dragged. The town was dead.

Presently Dee said, 'You do know that I know who you are.'

'Yep.'

'So is this the new you or the real you?'

He said nothing, just drove. And then at one o'clock in the morning, Sergeant Kropp came crackling over the radio: 'Okay, boys and girls, call it a night.'

Back at the station, Kropp took Hirsch aside and whispered fiercely, 'The fuck you arrest Ray Latimer for?'

Hirsch had had enough. 'So if your mates break the law they're allowed to get away with it?'

'That's not what I meant. He didn't have to spend the night in the lockup.'

'Do him some good, Sarge. And it was Nicholson who put him there. All I did was arrest him.'

Kropp shook his head as if seeing life in all its

192

stupidity. 'The magistrate's offered to hear it at ten tomorrow morning.'

Hirsch winced. Kropp smirked. 'That's what you get for being the arresting officer.'

'Sarge.'

As if it pained him to say it, Kropp muttered, 'We generally have a few beers after an operation.'

Called a 'mongrel session' at Hirsch's old station. No reason to think this one would be any different. 'Great,' he said.

They found Nicholson and the others in the tea room, herding Dee into a corner. 'Come on, love, no hard feelings, stay and have a couple of drinks with us.'

'In your dreams,' Dee said.

'Don't be like that. You need to wind down, right? We've even got a bottle of woite woine in the fridge, got it just for you.'

'Fuck off and goodnight,' Dee said, inclining her head to drag the band from her ponytail, shaking her head to free the hair, free it to swing around her neck and over her cheeks, and at that moment, Hirsch knew he'd seen that precise set of movements in the recent past.

He reached out a hand. 'You . . .' he said, about to say, *It was you who put that stuff in my car.*

He didn't. She gave him a curious look and a half smile of gratitude for looking after her. Then was gone out the door.

'Bitch,' Nicholson said.

*

Hirsch discovered he had a bottle in his hand. The hours passed and the Redruth policemen sprawled, bottles, pizza crusts and cigarette butts accumulating on the floor and the tea room table. Two o'clock, three, the air heavy. Nicholson and Kropp arm wrestled, tipping more crap onto the floor. When the chairs couldn't hold them they slumped on the floor. The phone rang unattended in the front office. Later Andrewartha found a stash of porn DVDs and Hirsch watched, absorbed for about thirty seconds, the others slightly longer, catcalling. They lapsed into talk and long pauses, then more talk, the sex a forgotten flicker in the background. When the beer ran out, Kropp staggered to his car and came back with three six-packs. Cans popped and foamed. It was the music of policemen winding down while a town sleeps, point and counterpoint.

The others would say, 'Drink up,' and Hirsch would say, 'Cheers,' and the others would say, 'Piker.'

Hirsch had played this game before. He knew the moves. He swigged, burped, swiped his mouth. He roared and laughed through until three, then four, and presently the others forgot who he was.

In those deep hours, people will come and go, you'll scarcely register their movements, you'll lose track, but at some point it occurred to Hirsch that Nicholson and Andrewartha were gone. Pikers.

He struggled to his feet. 'Time for some shut-eye.'

'The night is young,' snarled Revell.

'It is somewhere, I'll grant you that,' Hirsch said, grabbing his cap and his jacket and the belt load of crime-fighting gear that threatened to do his back in. 'Night, night, gentlemen.'

Kropp waved a bottle at him. 'Come on, get your laughing gear around this.'

Hirsch shook his head. 'I'm knackered, Sarge.'

Kropp was disgusted. 'I want you back here in time for court.'

A cold, still, silent, dampish pre-dawn, with dew beading the HiLux. Hirsch climbed in and worked the wipers and fired the ignition, then drove back through the square and out to the edge of the town with an agricultural rattle, the motor as stupefied as he was. He passed the Overlander Hotel, an antique store and two bed-and-breakfast joints, the high school, and he thought about Wendy Street. He thought about Constable Dee. He thought about his love life, which had slipped away, somehow, about the time it all went wrong.

Nicholson and Andrewartha bushwhacked him on a slow blind bend between Mount Bryan and Tiverton, flicking into his slipstream from a concealed farm gate, giving the siren a bit of a whoop. Hirsch pulled over, switched off, powered his window down. 'Guys.'

Andrewartha grinned, waving a breathalyser tube at Hirsch. 'We have reason to believe, etcetera.'

Pretending to scratch his ankle, Hirsch retrieved and pocketed the little Beretta. A desolate spot out here, the highway a black ribbon, the moon pushing shadows across the valley. Dawn was staining the horizon and there'd be early farmers and interstate truckies pretty soon, but Hirsch wasn't taking comfort from that. How would they play it? *We stopped him for driving under the influence and he just went crazy.*

But first they had to arrest him and take his service pistol. Andrewartha's face-splitting grin said he knew Hirsch's breathalyser reading would top .05. 'If you would blow into this, please, sir. We need a steady, continuous exhalation, think you can manage that?'

'Right across it,' Hirsch assured him, beginning to blow.

'Give it all you've got, pisspot,' Nicholson said.

Andrewartha retrieved the tube for testing, still with his killer grin. The grin faded. He shook the tube as if it were a thermometer. 'I don't fucking believe it.'

'Point oh nothing?' Hirsch asked sweetly.

'We're conducting the test again.'

Hirsch complied. He said, 'Maybe they're both faulty. Maybe we should go back to the station and take a blood sample.'

Andrewartha waited for half-a-dozen sour beats. 'Just fuck off home.'

Hirsch turned the key and drove sedately towards Tiverton. The patrol car trailed him for a few kilometres, a disconsolate white speck, until it turned off and Hirsch saw the red rear lights as it sped south again. A hint of the sun out east and Hirsch thought again of Wendy Street and Katie out there, the sun touching them before it touched him. He thought of the cop shop tea room back at Redruth. The sink, the pot plants, drowned in beer when no one was looking.

'One step ahead, you pricks,' he said.

18

His alarm sounded at eight on Sunday morning. Hirsch lay stunned, trying to work out who and where he was. He swung his legs out of bed and planted them on the scratchy mat beside it. Yawned and stared at the floor.

It was no good. He showered, brewed coffee and drank it with toast on a licheny chair in the back yard, a cumquat tree breathing down his neck, the filtered sunlight struggling to encourage him.

Then, still feeling pretty ordinary, he walked for thirty minutes, exploring the town, saying hello to the bony horse on its patch of dirt, a galah in a cage and an old codger squirting his roses.

'Lovely morning.'

'Remains to be seen,' the bloke said, and Hirsch thought that was about right.

Nine o'clock now, a civilised hour. Hirsch, using his office phone, said, 'Hope I woke you.'

'You'd have to get up early,' Rosie DeLisle said. 'What's up?'

'Overheard something last night,' Hirsch said, telling her about Nicholson and the girlfriend who'd crashed his car.

'No licence?'

'Which might mean she was too young,' Hirsch said.

'Excellent. This is exactly what we want from you.'

At once, Hirsch felt dirty. Less so when he said, 'And I know who planted that stuff in my car.'

When he got to Redruth there was no one in the lockup or the police station, so he walked around to the courthouse, a wood-panelled side room in the district council offices, wondering if Kropp had already released Raymond Latimer.

Not yet ten o'clock and court was already in session, the magistrate at a slightly raised table, the court reporter— a middle-aged woman—at a tiny corner desk, and Kropp sprawled with two of the overnight drunks on a bench in front of the public gallery, which at that hour on a Sunday was empty.

Ray Latimer was seated at a long table across the aisle from Kropp, next to a natty suit. Lawyer, Hirsch guessed, taking in the briefcase and files. And something cute was going on between Latimer, his lawyer and the magistrate, some sort of football banter concerning champion goals and high marks. Hirsch slid onto the bench beside his sergeant, barely covering a yawn.

The magistrate caught it. David Coulter, according to the name plate, a twinkling butterball who looked like a forty-five-year-old ex-small-town solicitor. Already dressed for Sunday golf. 'We boring you, mate?'

'Late night,' Hirsch said.

He was the centre of attention now, the magistrate, the lawyer and Latimer, all three smirking at him. But Kropp was seething. Hirsch edged away and made himself invisible.

Thirty minutes passed. The two drunks were fined. And now the court reporter was packing up, getting out of her chair, leaving with a little finger wave to the magistrate and the lawyer.

'Sarge?' murmured Hirsch. 'What about Mr Latimer?'

'Done and dusted,' Kropp snapped. 'Pleaded down to disorderly conduct and the minimum fine.'

Hirsch checked his watch. 'I didn't get here late, Sarge.'

Kropp folded his arms and snorted. Some deal had been cooked up, but why was Kropp so pissed off about it? His mate had got off with a slap on the wrist, after all. So his beef was with the magistrate and the lawyer?

The courthouse emptied, leaving Kropp, Latimer and Hirsch. And Kropp didn't want to be there. He shook Latimer's hand perfunctorily, said through his teeth: 'Well, you were lucky,' and turned to go.

'Mate, what can I say? I was an idiot.'

Kropp was almost at the door. He raised a hand goodbye.

Agitated, Latimer called, 'Mate, wait, I was hoping you could give us a lift home.'

'Ask Constable Hirschhausen.'

Fuck, thought Hirsch, and now he was on his own.

Latimer's vigour and gloss had been worn to nothing by

tiredness and a night in a cell. His clothing was wrinkled, chin stubbly, eyes bloodshot, hair in crazy tufts. But he lit up and looked keenly at Hirsch. 'Could you? Look, you have no idea how sorry I am about last night. I shouldn't have taken a swing at you.'

'I'm not a taxi service. What about your wife, father, girlfriend, lawyer?'

Latimer shuffled his feet. 'There isn't anyone. My father's taken the boys to the Jamestown air show, and obviously I can't call Allie. My lawyer's off to play golf with Dave Coulter and as for Finola, well, I might have done my dash there.'

Hirsch was cranky. 'I am leaving right this minute, all right?'

'Right then,' Ray Latimer said. 'Lead on.'

Out into the sun, down the steps and into the HiLux, the town Sunday-quiet and the air still. 'Seatbelt,' Hirsch snarled, but that expelled all of his energy and he let the four-wheel-drive trundle out of town, too tired to speed.

'Sorry about this,' Latimer said.

Hirsch ignored him. Too tired to speed, too tired to speak.

'And sorry again for last night. I got stuck into the booze after our win.'

Hirsch grunted, creeping through the empty town. Latimer, a stale lump beside him, ran commentary, swivel-necking as if he'd never been to Redruth before.

'Damn shame, Finucane's going out of business.'

A white goods shop, *Closing down sale* pasted across the windows. Hirsch couldn't give a stuff.

'It's a heartache,' Latimer said.

Hirsch wriggled his shoulders as if that would shut his passenger down.

'High costs, low returns,' Latimer said. 'When the man on the land struggles to survive, so do the local shopkeepers. There's nothing for the kids, no reason why they'd hang on, better money in the city and excellent money up at Roxby Downs or on one of the wind farms. You can't get shearers, shed hands or casual labour for love or money anymore.'

Hirsch wanted to point to himself and say, 'This is my caring and sharing face.'

'Take my property,' said Latimer. 'Been in the family for generations and now we're barely hanging on.'

And yet you keep buying things and not paying your bills. Feeling nasty, Hirsch said, 'Why not cut back on the spending?'

Latimer continued as if he'd not heard him. 'What with the economy and my wife . . .'

'How is she to blame?'

'Divorce? It'll ruin me. My father and me.'

'And yet you're giving her the grounds for one.'

Latimer snorted. 'Am I a monk? Anyway, she's unstable, mate. Tried to kill herself last year.'

'Uh huh.'

'Fifty per cent of what I own, plus child support? Where's the justice?'

Hirsch was tired. Latimer stank, stale alcohol leaching and cigarette smoke in the weave of his shirt. Flicking a switch, Hirsch dropped his window a few centimetres, wondering if he should monitor the man's movements for the next few hours. Keep him away from his wife. God he was exhausted.

'We're not made of money, we'd have to sell up if she goes through with it. A property that's been in the same family for generations.'

'Uh huh.'

'Can't catch a break. They put a line of wind generators on Finola's property, right? Not ours. Rent's worth thousands of dollars a year.'

He's going to marry Finola Armstrong, Hirsch thought. Barrier Highway was quiet. Latimer would quiver alertly from time to time, tracking a family station wagon, a ute, a truck, remarking on the driver. Hirsch had no interest. He didn't care if so-and-so in the white station wagon was a good bloke, or whosiwhatsit in the red ute had cancer. He wanted to sleep.

'Next right,' Latimer said.

Hirsch made the turn onto Bitter Wash Road, watched by a cow. Almost noon and he was starving. No rain for the past week and so for the next several kilometres, dust poured behind him and the steering wheel transmitted the surface corrugations to his hands. Then they were in the shadow of the wind turbines again, and shortly after that Latimer was pointing to his driveway entrance.

'Coming home to an empty house,' he said, drawing his palms down his stubbled cheeks, a picture of desolation.

'Your father and the boys at the Jamestown air show?'

'They headed over there yesterday, after the game,' Latimer said. 'I've got an aunt lives there.'

The old man's complicit in the son's philandering, thought Hirsch. The gravel complained under the tyres as Hirsch followed the track between the lawn beds, shrubs and silvery gums. He pulled in opposite the flagstones leading to the veranda steps and the front door, and saw that the door was ajar. He touched the man's forearm, registering briefly strength and warmth through the creased cotton. 'Did you leave your place open yesterday?'

'What?'

Latimer glanced wildly at the door and was out and powering towards the house before Hirsch could stop him. Up the steps and through the door. Oh, fuck, thought Hirsch, following him, but also thinking there'd be a vehicle if burglars were still on the premises. He paused on the veranda, hearing Latimer stomping around inside, and glanced across to the sheds, the yards, the paddocks.

And there was a glint, sunlight flashing on a windscreen, down along the creek. Hirsch shaded his eyes. How would you get a vehicle down there? Was there an access gate, a farm track?

He stuck his head in, called to Latimer: 'Anything? Damage, things missing?'

'Gun case is open. The twenty-two's missing.'

Hirsch recalled that there were two .22 rifles: the Ruger used by the kids and the Brno in the gun case. So the Ruger was still floating around somewhere, still stowed on the window shelf of the ute, probably. That's what Hirsch was thinking as he trotted across the yard and slid between the wires of the fence. He spotted fresh tyre impressions in the grass, and realised there was a farm track concealed under the spring growth. The track ran beside the fence and then down an incline to the creek, and now Hirsch had a clearer view: the Tin Hut, some ancient quince, apricot and mulberry trees. The small clearing where Alison Latimer had parked her Subaru.

He side-slipped down the bank to the edge of the creek. Reaching the car, he looked in: empty, a suitcase in the back, keys in the ignition. He straightened and ran his gaze in among the fruit trees, down into the reeds and pools of the creek, and finally over the rusted hut. He felt spooked, a shiver rippling over him as he approached the hut and came around the end wall.

He found Alison Latimer slumped against the rusted tin, half-toppled with a rifle butt between her thighs, her thumb caught in the trigger guard. The barrel tip had been in her mouth, he guessed, but she'd jerked as she died. It was not the Ruger but the Brno. No exit wound; blood over her chin and inside her shirt front. The ultimate stillness of death.

Hirsch had seen it before. But he advanced cautiously, keeping close to the undisturbed grass scratching the wall, and felt for a pulse. Nothing. Some residual warmth, so death had been no more than a few hours ago. He reversed his steps and took a series of photographs with his phone, keeping wide of the body. He had maybe a minute before Latimer arrived. Half an hour before Kropp and the doctor and everyone else arrived.

He started with a series of establishing shots of the hut, the grove of trees, the car and the creek. Then, closing in on the body, he photographed the dirt and the grass around it, the feet and legs, the rifle, the ring-less hands holding it, the bloodied chest, and Alison Latimer's head. Then the same sequence but side-on, first the left flank, then the right, as Latimer came pounding down from the track above.

'What the hell are you doing?'

Said a moment before the penny dropped. He skidded to a stop. 'What the hell?'

Hirsch put a hand to the farmer's chest. 'Mr Latimer, you can't—'

Latimer was full of trembling potency. 'She might still be alive.'

'I'm afraid she's not, Mr Latimer,' Hirsch said, maintaining the pressure, waiting him out.

Slowly the quivering chest relaxed. Latimer stepped back, mouth open in shock. 'What am I going to do?' He took a ragged breath and said, 'How do I tell the boys?'

Hirsch turned him away. 'First I need to call it in, and then I'll help you phone your friends and neighbours.'

'How do I tell the boys?'

'What time do you expect your father home?'

Latimer was slow, dull, staring at the ground. 'Late afternoon,' he said, rallying. 'He'll have his phone with him.'

They returned to the house, slipping and sliding on the grassy bank, Latimer babbling about his life now, the boys, emptiness and what might have been. 'She was going to come home, I know she was.'

Hirsch tuned him out. He trudged across the yard, a hand on Latimer's elbow. He felt mud paste to the sole of his shoes; there was a smear of it on one toe cap and his trouser cuffs.

And Alison Latimer's white runners had been pristine.

And the beautiful diamond ring: had she taken it off? A tidying act, or a gesture of meaning from a woman about to kill herself?

19

Kropp arrived first, asked for a rundown and elbowed Hirsch aside, then Dr McAskill appeared and pronounced death, and Andrewartha and Nicholson showed up with crime-scene tape and hangovers. Meaning Jennifer Dee was holding the fort in Redruth, Hirsch thought. All he could do was stand back and watch his crime scene—incident scene—be trampled over.

Then Kropp, still in management mode, began stalking up and down the creek bank, muttering into his mobile phone. Forty minutes later a hearse arrived, ready to cart the body away, followed by a flat-bed truck, *Redruth Automotive* scrolled across each door. Hirsch watched it back up to the Subaru, two men hopping out, drawing on heavy gloves.

'Sarge, what are you doing?'

'What do you mean, what am I doing?'

'We need to preserve everything. We need crime-scene people here.'

'What does this look like to you? Suicide. A tragedy. No

one needs to see it. I know the protocol, mister, I've called in Port Pirie CIB, they'll be here within the hour, and meanwhile that bloody car's in the way.'

'But Sarge.'

Kropp cocked his head. Hirsch heard it, too, a background rumble of vehicles.

'Get up there and make yourself useful,' Kropp said. 'Make sure no one wanders down here for a look see.'

Clambering up to the fence above the Tin Hut, Hirsch saw that a dozen cars, station wagons, utilities and four-wheel-drives had poured in off Bitter Wash Road to jostle for room around the house and sheds. Jesus Christ. He began to run. Clearly some kind of phone tree had been set in motion this past hour, neighbour phoning neighbour phoning football club member, churchgoer and Country Women's Association crony, and here they were, bringing cakes and casseroles and hugs and tears and nosiness.

And—if Alison Latimer had been killed at the house—trampling over a crime scene.

More cars arrived. Hirsch barged through the front door. But it was useless. At least thirty people were crowding the hallway, kitchen and sitting room, with more on the veranda or climbing out of their cars. 'Excuse me,' he said futilely.

He went in search of Raymond Latimer, finding him in a huddle with a dozen other people, enduring their embraces but aware of Hirsch, watching warily. Hirsch couldn't get through. He gestured; Latimer ignored him. And then the crowd moved and reformed and wouldn't budge, Latimer disappeared and Kropp was there, panting with effort, grabbing Hirsch by the arm. 'The fuck are you doing?'

'We're losing evidence, Sarge.'

Kropp dragged him through the room and out onto the lawn. 'What evidence? You're upsetting people. Get your arse back down to the creek.'

'Sarge,' Hirsch said, and backed away, watching Kropp apologise and shake hands.

When the sergeant had merged fully with the crush of people, Hirsch made as if to head for the creek. Walking until he was screened by a clump of oleanders, he doubled back and entered the house by the laundry door. Another door led to the kitchen, where half a dozen women were getting in each other's way. 'Need a quick word with Sergeant Kropp,' said Hirsch amiably, not stopping to gauge their reactions but bustling by them to the hallway.

The door to the main bedroom was slightly ajar. He slipped through the gap and paused and scanned the room. Latimer hadn't made the bed; dirty clothes lay heaped on the floor and a chair; the wardrobe doors were open, drawers spilling socks and T-shirts. Only a few traces of Alison Latimer remained. Hirsch crossed to the left-hand bedside table. Nestled in a dusty patterned dish were Alison Latimer's rings: wedding ring and the engagement ring he'd noticed the day he met her.

Hirsch returned to the hallway. He left via the kitchen. He wasn't challenged.

*

He was halfway across the yard when he saw the Subaru. It had been dumped beside a haystack beyond the sheds. Hirsch was fed up with it all. He stumped out of the yard and was almost to the creek when he changed his mind and returned. This time he lifted the Subaru's tailgate and unzipped the lid of the case. Women's clothing. Badly folded, which meant a lot or nothing at all. There was no reason to suppose Alison Latimer had been a neat person. No twelve-year-old boy's clothing. Hirsch closed everything and headed for the creek.

The hearse drivers sat in the sun, smoking. McAskill was still bent over the body, and when he finally eased her away from the wall for the hearse drivers, she moved like a sack of disobliging logs.

Feeling Andrewartha and Nicholson give him the evil eye from the edge of the tape, Hirsch wandered down along the creek. It was a pretty spot for a house and orchard, except that it gave him the creeps. And he supposed it was prone to flooding, that's why the Latimer ancestors had moved to higher ground. Why had Alison Latimer come down here to die? Was it special to her? He gazed at the lichen, the fruit trees choking themselves to death, the choked rushes and hoof-trampled muddy verges. A good place to die.

He took out his phone, found a number in the contacts list, and dialled.

A voice lashed at his back: 'Who are you calling?'

Hirsch whirled around. Kropp, slithering down the grassy slope. 'Sarge, we need to take Mrs Latimer's car to the lab.'

'Do we?'

'I think so, Sarge.'

'The poor cow shot herself. I'm sick of this,' Kropp said. 'I want you to piss off back to Tiverton in case someone reports a stolen lawnmower.'

'Sarge.'

'Dog,' murmured Andrewartha and Nicholson. 'Maggot.'

Alison's parents, thought Hirsch when he reached the top. Everyone's wringing their hands over the husband and the boys, but what about her parents, her friends?

The yard being choked with mourners' vehicles, Hirsch was forced to steer a slow weave out of the yard, dodging a bulk fuel tank, heaped pine posts, haphazardly parked cars and utes. He was halted by a blue heeler, prone in a dusty pool of sunlight. He stopped; looked at the dog; willed it to move. Then he brapped the horn, and when that didn't work, got out, grabbed the dog by its collar and walked it to another patch of dirt.

Climbed back into the HiLux and bumped along the driveway and immediately onto the lawn as a black Explorer shot in, followed by an unmarked Falcon, on a mission. He didn't recognise the suits in the Falcon but guessed they were the Port Pirie detectives, big men filling their seats and staring at him with the flat odium of policemen. But he did recognise the man at the wheel of the Explorer: the area commander, Superintendent Spurling. As he waited for the dust to settle, Hirsch thought his irrelevance was pretty much fully underscored now. He steered back onto the driveway, out through the gate and onto Bitter Wash Road.

It gave him a curious jolt to see Wendy Street standing beside her car in the driveway of the house with the faded red roof. The boot was open, stacked with bags of mulch, one bag out and in a wheelbarrow beside a narrow strip of unforgiving soil. She stopped what she was doing and gazed at him, and even at some distance he felt the force of her frankness, as if she'd caught him acting discreditably.

So he steered into her driveway, lifting his hand in greeting. 'Lot of cars,' she said when he got out, showing a little tension.

She doesn't know, Hirsch realised. No one has phoned her. He removed his cap and turned it absently in his hands. 'Afraid I've got some bad news.'

One hand went to her throat and she said, instantly, 'Allie? He's killed her, hasn't he?'

Interesting. Hirsch agreed that Alison Latimer was dead, but wrapped it up in some mealy-mouthed cop talk, finishing with, 'There's no reason to suppose it was anything other than self-inflicted.'

'Fuck off,' Street spat, her eyes filling with tears. 'Beside the Tin Hut? No. She hated it there.'

She gave a tearing sob and went slack, backing away from him and grabbing a veranda post. Using it as a prop, she lowered herself, sat on the edge, her hands rubbing her thighs back and forth, back and forth, as if to bring herself back under control. Hirsch waited.

She looked up. 'Who found her?'

'I did.'

Grim, intense, she said, 'And where was Ray during all this?'

'Mrs Street, he was in the Redruth lockup all last night and until lunchtime today. In fact, I gave him a lift home.'

'Don't call me Mrs Street. Has anyone told the boys?'

'That's all taken care of,' Hirsch said, not knowing one way or the other. Surely Raymond Latimer would have called his father?

Wendy shook her head. 'I can just imagine the delicate way Raymond or his father might break it: *Oh by the way, kids, your mum's shot herself.*'

'We have to give them the benefit of the doubt.'

'You do, I don't.' She bit her lip. 'How do I tell Katie?'

Hirsch glanced towards the house, wondering where the girl was. 'You'll know what to say.'

'You think so?' Her eyes were full of tears, her arms folded to ward him off. 'It's just terrible. I know he did it.'

'Did you happen to hear a rifle shot this morning?'

'Not to notice, but there's always someone shooting something. Anyway, I was mowing.'

A little Cox ride-on, parked beside the house, wearing a fresh chlorophyll skirt, damp cuttings in the tyre treads. Hirsch glanced back at Wendy Street and saw that she was biting her bottom lip, something on her mind.

'What?'

'Katie saw that car again, that black car.'

'Well, you can put her mind at ease: Pullar and Hanson stole a Holden the other day.'

Then it dawned on him. 'You think Katie sneaked the rifle out again and fired it?'

Wendy Street twisted in knots. 'Could she have?' And

then her consternation disappeared, logic taking over. 'No, she wouldn't do that.'

'Exactly,' Hirsch said. 'All indications are, Mrs Latimer shot herself. The gun was still in her hands when I found her.'

Wendy rubbed her face. 'This is just awful.'

She was glancing across at the Latimers' as if she should head there but knew she might not be welcome. To divert her, Hirsch said, 'Was Mrs Latimer more than usually down lately?'

'You mean suicidal? No. She'd made up her mind to leave Ray. Get a divorce. She seemed freer if anything.' She gasped. 'Her parents!'

'I'm off to see them now.'

'I should come with you,' Wendy said. She was this way and that. 'I need to be here for Katie.'

The younger Latimer boy might need you, too, Hirsch thought. Jack. He nodded goodbye, settled his cap on his head and reached for the driver's door.

He stopped in the act and turned around. 'I'm sorry for your loss,' he said, hating the expression but unable to think of a better one. 'I know you were friends.'

Her eyes filled again and she hugged herself. 'Thank you.'

'If you need anything . . .'

A damp smile. 'I'm okay. You need to see Allie's parents.'

Hirsch climbed in and drove away.

'Our daughter has killed herself, and he tells us over the *phone*?'

Heather Rofe was ragged, bleary, angry. Hirsch gently steered her back into the house, to the kitchen, where Keith sat, dazed, a solid man diminished, his decency more threadbare now. Man and wife, they'd been to church probably, best clothes on their backs. They'd made and poured tea but that was as far as they'd been able to take it.

'Is there anyone I can contact for you?'

Keith Rofe lifted his head. 'Our other daughter's coming over.'

Hirsch stood there, spinning his damn cap in his hands. He felt like a stormtrooper.

'How's he breaking the news to the boys?' Heather Rofe said. 'Text message?'

All kinds of statements were issued via text message these days. Your services are no longer required; by the way, your husband's having an affair; I want a divorce; here's a close-up of my pussy. Hirsch said gently, 'Alison spent the night with you?'

Keith Rofe didn't have the wherewithal to answer. He glanced helplessly at his wife, who said, 'She was in bed when we left this morning.'

'Church?'

'A christening,' Heather said. 'My niece's daughter, down in Gawler.'

Two hours distant. 'What time did you leave?'

'Seven.'

'So you were away half the day?'

Heather Rofe's tears welled and rolled down her cheeks. 'We just got back.'

'Did she tell you what she intended to do today?'

Rofe shrugged. 'Sleep in. Rest. She offered to re-pot my geraniums.'

'Didn't say anything about going out?'

'No.'

'She's not a churchgoer?'

Heather struggled. She said, 'Not lately.'

'Can you think why she'd go to the Tin Hut?'

'No, she didn't like it there . . . Please, you're grilling me. I'd like you to stop.'

Hirsch back-pedalled. 'Sorry, terribly sorry, that's not my intention.'

'No, I'm sorry, I know you do have a job to do.'

Hirsch moved his shoulders in uneasy agreement. 'One last question: was the house locked when you got back from church?'

'We don't bother, usually,' Heather said. 'Nothing worth taking, and we know everyone in . . .' Her voice trailed away.

'What?'

'It *was* locked. I had to fetch the spare key. Remember, Keith?'

'What?'

Hirsch tuned them out, letting his gaze roam around the kitchen and into the hallway and mentally retrace his route as he'd entered the house a few minutes earlier. He hadn't seen anything to suggest forced entry or a struggle, and how would he raise that question with them? 'May I see her room?'

Heather Rofe fixed him with a level stare, raw with grief but not about to lose herself in it. 'Why?'

Hirsch did his uncomfortable shoulder rotation again. 'I was wondering if she might have left some kind of goodbye.'

'Like a suicide note. Well, she didn't. Last night over dinner she was quite chirpy. Not a hundred per cent enamoured with the idea of Jack spending the weekend with his grandfather, but . . . a weight had been lifted from her shoulders over the past few days.'

Heather gave in to the grief again. Hirsch moved across and placed a hand on each shoulder. After the briefest hesitation, she let herself be consoled.

Hirsch waited, glancing over her shoulder at the husband, who was again staring sightlessly at the top of the table. Presently Heather stepped back and gathered herself and said, 'Her old bedroom, down the passage.'

A spare room now, all vestiges of the child and teenager removed. Hirsch surveyed it first and then began a search. The drawers yawned emptily, and all he found in the wardrobe was one wire hanger, a white bowls uniform in a drycleaner's bag whispering in the eddying air.

He popped his head into the adjacent room. An untidy bed, a child's trainers on the floor, warm cotton pyjamas poking from under a pillow, a laptop on top of the pillow, pasted with footballer stickers.

In the kitchen again, Hirsch said gently, 'It seems Alison packed all her things but left Jack's here.'

He saw the rapid assimilation in Heather Rofe's face.

Instead of giving him her conclusions she said, 'All right, how do *you* read it?'

Hirsch said, 'Did she give any indication she wanted to thrash things out with Ray?'

'No.'

'Leaving Jack here, where he wouldn't witness any nastiness?'

'Nothing like that.'

They took it no further than that but Hirsch could see a couple of scenarios, each ending in suicide: Alison Latimer had returned to the farm for a trial reconciliation, only to fall into a deep depression, or she'd wanted to rub Raymond's face in it.

The black Explorer was waiting for him outside the station.

Hirsch parked in the driveway, liking this visit even less than Kropp's visit the day Melia Donovan was found. Choosing to ignore it, he stepped onto the little porch, his key at the ready. Well, that triggered movement. A door slammed and footsteps stalked him. He turned: Superintendent Spurling in full uniform, a man of fifty with the bearing of an army officer. Clean, slender hands; a narrow, ascetic face.

'Sir,' Hirsch said.

'You know who I am?'

'Area commander, sir.'

'I need a word.'

Hirsch led the way into his office, hoping Spurling wouldn't insist on the sitting room. But did he offer Spurling the swivel chair behind the desk, or the stiff visitor's chair?

Spurling made no move to sit anywhere. 'I'll get right to it. This afternoon I received a phone call.'

Hirsch gave him a long look. 'Sir?'

'Anonymous caller, female, very brief: "The husband did it."'

Oh, hell, Wendy. 'Well, sir, the thing is, he was in the Redruth lockup at the time.'

Spurling grunted. 'There will be an inquest.'

Hirsch nodded his agreement.

'I need you to prepare a brief for the coroner.'

What? 'Sir, I'm new here.'

'All the better,' Spurling said, settling his lean rump against Hirsch's desk and folding his arms. 'And on the subject of phone calls, I've also been contacted about a different matter. Phone calls and letters.'

'Sir?'

'Most were from our old friend Anonymous, but a handful were not. In particular, a nurse, a couple of high-school teachers, a priest and the local ALP candidate. All from Redruth, all raising the same issue.'

Hirsch waited. He wanted to go behind his desk and sit, but that would disadvantage the superintendent, so he stood, almost at attention.

'In a nutshell,' Spurling said, 'the over-zealous policing methods employed by Sergeant Kropp and Constables Nicholson and Andrewartha. Physical and verbal abuse, harassment, unwarranted speed and drink-driving traps, etcetera, etcetera.'

Hirsch knew where this was going. All he wanted was to be free of worry and moral complications. 'Sir?'

'Don't be dim. Is there anything to these claims?'

'Like I said, sir, I'm new here.'

'Yeah, be like that. I've been hearing whispers for months now, and this afternoon I hear that Sergeant Kropp is best mates with a man who might have killed his wife.'

'I haven't been here long enough to see any patterns or—'

Spurling snarled, 'What, you're selective in which coppers you snitch on?'

'Is that why you called in to see me, sir? Want some spying done?'

An icy glitter in Spurling, and Hirsch wondered if he'd gone too far. He tensed, watching as Spurling propped his hands on the edge of the desk as if to launch himself.

The tension hung, poised. Then Spurling leaned back and folded his arms again. 'Look, I know who you are, I know your history. I'm not here to rake over the coals or ... set you up, anything like that, okay?'

Hirsch said nothing.

'Marcus Quine is a disgrace to the force. He deserves whatever's coming to him.'

Still Hirsch said nothing. He felt the skin under his right eye give the faintest twitch.

'But right now,' Spurling went on, 'I'm in a bind and I need your help. Otherwise we could be looking at a behavioural management audit, and that's the last thing anyone needs.'

Hirsch blanched. Audits were ten times worse than ethical standards complaints. Worst-case scenario, a complaint might lead to an individual officer being rapped over the knuckles, house and locker searched, finances scrutinised, but audits were applied to entire squads or police stations. Every staff member, every scrap of paper, every corner. An audit of Redruth would mean an audit of Hirsch, and he was through with being poked and prodded by the Internals.

He looked at Spurling. He saw a man whose job required him to be political, clandestine, subtle. He gathered himself to help. 'The usual rumours, sir.'

'Go on.'

'Like I said, I'm new here and there's still a lot I don't know.'

Spurling, exasperated, said, 'Look, man to man, off the record, no comeback, is there any truth to the allegations that the Redruth officers are in any way overstepping the mark?'

Hirsch drew back his shoulders. 'It's not as if this is the inner city,' he said. 'We're not dealing with bikie gangs or ethnic clans.'

Spurling nodded. 'Good. And?'

'I've heard the odd whisper, sir.'

Spurling smiled, unfolded from the edge of the desk, patted Hirsch on the shoulder. 'Thank you.'

He left Hirsch there, stepping out of the office and into the little foyer. Then he paused, propping his slender hands on the counter. 'Meanwhile, if you do hear or see anything specific, I want to know about it pronto.'

'Sir.'

Spurling assessed Hirsch briefly, then turned to go. He stopped at the front door. 'Your fleet vehicle: get a new screen fitted.'

'Sir.'

'And get it washed. It's filthy.'

Instead, Hirsch got it filthier, heading out along Bitter Wash Road again.

The Latimer house and yard were still choked with cars, but the Port Pirie detectives had been and gone, and in the meantime the Latimer children had returned with their grandfather. Hirsch found them in the main room, standing with Ray Latimer at the centre of a constantly moving press of people. Without being sure of his intentions, he began to edge through to them, pausing to grab a sausage roll from a table crammed with sandwiches, sponge cakes, beer and juice bottles, wine flagons.

The Latimer men spotted him and stiffened, acutely aware of his progress through the crowd. Why was that? They locked eyes with him, as if only they and Hirsch existed on earth, betraying nothing but stillness and vigilance. Two powerfully made, big-jawed, proprietorial men.

Then Kropp was back in Hirsch's face, red, beery and emotional. 'I thought I told you to piss off.'

'Just seeing if you wanted a hand, Sarge.'

'Is that a fact. I can read you, pal.' He poked Hirsch in the chest. 'You lay off, understand? That's an order.'

Hirsch, glancing past Kropp, saw Raymond Latimer and his father watching the exchange. They didn't smile to see Hirsch get his comeuppance, didn't look relieved. Nothing. He wondered what vaunting disappointments and ambitions drove them.

'Well?'

'Sarge, if you must know, a few things bother me.'

'Is that a fact, Nancy Drew.'

'Mrs Latimer had some odd bruises on her, Sarge. No mud on her shoes. What if this house is a crime scene? Or, if she was snatched from her parents' house, then *that* is a crime scene. The hut, the rifle, her car . . . We need prints, blood samples, tyre impressions.'

Kropp looked like he couldn't believe his ears. 'What the fuck are you talking about?'

Hirsch was distracted by an abrupt movement at the corner of his vision. He turned. Raymond Latimer had collapsed onto the sofa with his sons, Jack burrowing into his chest as if wanting to slip inside him, Craig shoulder to shoulder and looking stunned. All three looked reduced: damp, blotchy, all animation gone.

'Look at them,' Kropp said. '*Look* at them.'

'All I'm saying is—'

'The Port Pirie boys took all the samples and photos they need. Meanwhile you keep out of it. This is a peaceful community. You, you're a traveller here. Passing through.'

20

Monday began with Kropp on the line, in a mild froth. 'Just been talking to the super.'

Hirsch said nothing. He could hear yelling across the road, doors slamming: the school holidays were over.

'I'm warning you: the Latimers are decent people visited by tragedy, and Spurling or no Spurling, I'll have your guts for garters if you step out of line.'

'Yes, Sarge.'

'Why the hell he put you on it, I don't know. The mind boggles.'

'Sarge, I'm as surprised as you are.'

'Arselicker.'

Hirsch heard impotence in the sergeant's voice. 'I'll tread lightly, Sarge.'

Hirsch propped his feet on the desk, notebook in his lap, not writing but thinking.

In his view there were three essential truths to police

work: most crimes go unpunished; most crimes are solved not by forensics but chance, an admission or a word in your ear; and detection matters less than piecing together rumours and random scraps of information.

Still, a bit of method didn't hurt. Scrawling *Interviews* at the top of a blank page, he made a list: the Latimer clan; Alison's parents and sister; her doctor; her neighbours; her friends. Not knowing all of their names yet, that's how he listed them, by role and title.

Wendy Street should be able to help: friend and neighbour.

But he suspected he'd get mainly emotional, partial and impressionistic evidence from these people, proof of nothing, and it might very well lead him to one conclusion, that Alison Latimer took her life while the balance of her mind was disturbed, or however coroners liked to word it these days.

He flipped over the page and made another list: *Formal Evidence*, namely the autopsy findings and forensics. What would her body, clothing, car, parents' house, own house, rifle and the Tin Hut reveal about her death?

Finally, gut impressions. He stared at the ceiling, formulating them in his mind. The death didn't seem right to him, or to her parents or Wendy Street. Were his guts listening to them or to his own rumblings? On the surface, there was little evidence to suggest homicide, plenty to suggest suicide. Alison Latimer knew how to handle a rifle, he'd seen it himself, and she'd made a prior suicide attempt. No suicide note. But that didn't mean anything: plenty of people took their own lives without explaining themselves.

Meanwhile, what about her spotless shoes, the bruises, her thumb in the trigger guard? Why the Tin Hut? Why spend her final seconds in a place that freaked her out? On the other hand, those who might want her dead—her husband, her father-in-law, maybe even the older boy—had unshakeable alibis.

Who else? A secret lover? Wendy Street might know.

Hirsch jotted scenarios:

She committed suicide.

She was snatched from her parents' house, subdued by force, taken to the Tin Hut and shot dead, the body and gun arranged to suggest suicide.

Ditto, but she was accidentally killed during the struggle and so on.

She was lured to the farm, or the Tin Hut, and killed by accident or design and the body and gun arranged to suggest suicide.

Alison Latimer was a slight woman but not frail. Could a woman have killed her?

And so Finola Armstrong's name surfaced again. Hirsch found her address in the phone book, locked up and headed out to Bitter Wash Road.

Armstrong's house was stone with a wash of cement over it, painted white once upon a time but now mostly dust and mould, the veranda iron rusty. It sat among pine trees so high and cramped they robbed the sun, their needles starving the garden and choking the gutters. Hirsch had never seen such a miserable building, and wondered at the man or the woman, a couple of generations ago, who'd decided the pines and the cement were a good idea. The sheds, on the other hand, were in the open and expressed the busyness of a working farm.

He mounted gloomy steps. There was a hollow wind, mournful where it wrapped around the chimney, eaves and veranda posts. He was about to knock on the front door when Finola Armstrong appeared from behind a rainwater tank, removing canvas gloves. Hirsch stepped down from the veranda and eyed her carefully: jeans, a checked shirt, a scowl and an odour of diesel and silage.

She stopped a metre from his chest. 'I guessed you'd be dropping by.'

'Did you?' said Hirsch.

'Don't be coy.'

'Okay, well, perhaps you could tell me your movements after I saw you at the motel on Saturday night?'

Armstrong tilted her head, revealing a smear of chaff dust along her jaw that he itched to wipe away. 'You'd like me to say I went home in great turmoil, deciding that all my problems lay with Alison Latimer, and that I got up the next morning and did her in.'

'Well, that would simplify matters. Is that what happened?'

'No.'

'Do you think she was murdered?'

'Not for me to say, but I doubt it.'

'What did you do after I left you on Saturday night?'

'Didn't stay in that dreadful motel, that's for sure.'

'You went home?'

'I *was* in turmoil, but going home wasn't going to fix it. I went to my sister's.'

Hirsch patted his jacket pocket for pad and pen, fished them out, clicked the pen, found a blank page. He could feel her eyes on him.

'Ready?' she asked, a glint in her eye. She gave him address, phone numbers and names: sister, brother-in-law, nieces.

'They can all verify etcetera, etcetera?'

'They can.' She tilted her head again. 'Are you treating it as suspicious, the death?'

'Covering bases,' said Hirsch blithely. 'Preparing a brief for the coroner.'

'Uh huh. Bill Kropp thinks it's suicide.'

Letting him know who her friends were. 'Getting back to Saturday night.'

'I was upset. Cross. Couldn't think clearly. Told myself— not for the first time—that I should end it. So I went to the only person who'd listen and talk sense to me about it.'

'After midnight.'

'She's my sister,' Armstrong said.

'You stayed the night?'

'I stayed two nights. Got back this morning.'

By now Hirsch had pretty much discounted her. She was a hard, brusque woman—notwithstanding her need of sisterly comfort—and seemed essentially truthful. A straightforward woman, even if her love life wasn't.

Or maybe in her mind it was. 'What was your understanding of the Latimers' marriage?'

'Am I a slut, do you mean? Secretly sleeping with another woman's husband? He told me the marriage was over, she wanted a divorce.'

'When did he tell you that?'

'Ages ago. The beginning of the year, when we first hooked up.'

'Did Mrs Latimer know about you?'

Armstrong shrugged. 'We didn't shove it in her face, but yes, she did.'

'Did she have words with you about it? Angry words, upset words?'

'I barely knew the woman. Don't get me wrong, I think her death's a dreadful thing, it's sad on all levels. Those poor boys. Her parents.'

Hirsch nodded. 'How did you get involved with Mr Latimer?'

'We have an adjoining fence. There was a grass fire just after Christmas and part of the fence needed replacing.' She shrugged. 'We got talking.'

'Grass fire.'

'Passing motorist tossed a cigarette out the window? I don't know. Does it matter?'

'You got talking.'

Armstrong revealed some feeling for the first time. 'Look, he paid me some attention. I didn't go looking for it but it found me. It was nice.'

'Will you continue to see him?'

'Mind your own business.'

'How well do you know Sergeant Kropp?'

'Your boss, Sergeant Kropp? Is that the Sergeant Kropp you mean?'

Hirsch faced off the challenge with a smile. 'Yes.'

'He's mates with Ray.'

'Is that a fact?' said Hirsch flatly.

Finola Armstrong was bored with him. 'Got work to do,' she said, walking away from him, her rear shapely, a smudge of engine oil on the seat of her jeans and one pocket torn. God Hirsch was lonely.

Loneliness was more powerful than his scruples, sensibilities and good manners. Otherwise he wouldn't have slowed as he drew adjacent to Wendy Street's driveway. Nothing. No Volvo. Of course: the holidays were over; she'd be standing at the head of some classroom, pointing at the board.

21

That afternoon he doorknocked the little street where Alison Latimer had spent her last few days alive. Had anyone seen Mrs Latimer on Sunday morning, or at any time on Saturday? No one had. Had anyone seen an unfamiliar or a familiar but out-of-place car parked at or near the house at any time in recent days? Had anyone heard anything? Hirsch also invited speculations: all he got was some vague admiration of the Latimers and remarks on how well Alison had done for herself, shame about how depressed she'd been the past couple of years.

He left the Rofes alone for now.

The world turned over. On Tuesday morning Hirsch investigated the suspected theft of a hundred ewes. He found them in a neighbour's paddock, the neighbour apoplectic about the state of the complainant's fences. He calmed everyone down, returned to the town and called on the Rofes.

Heather answered, looking wrung out with grief. 'You knocked on some doors yesterday.'

'Yes.'

'Learn anything?'

'Afraid not.'

She shook her head, opened the gap in her front door. 'Come and have a cup of tea with us.'

Hirsch removed his cap and followed her through to the kitchen. Keith was there as if he was always there, still stunned, more rumpled. Heather gazed at him with a flicker of pity and irritation, told Hirsch to sit.

Hirsch drew back a chair. 'I've been asked to prepare a brief for the coroner.'

'Yes.'

'I'm afraid I need to ask about Alison in a more formal context.'

Heather turned from the sink, waved the wet spout of the kettle at him. 'Formal context? Or formal whitewash?'

The spring sunlight lit her from behind, gauzy through the little window above the sink. Hirsch had never seen so many curtained windows before moving to the bush. He said, 'There's no easy way to say this, but in the absence of foul play, everything will hinge on Alison's mental state in recent months—actual and perceived.'

'Well, that depends on who you listen to,' Keith said, stirring at last. His wife moved to him, her thigh against one shoulder and her hand reaching around to his other. As Hirsch watched, some of the man's meekness and bewilderment evaporated.

'Right now,' Hirsch said, 'I'm listening to you.'

'And we're biased.'

'So are her husband and father-in-law,' Hirsch said.

Keith cocked his head, then twisted around to share a silent communication with his wife. Asking if I'm worth talking to, Hirsch thought.

Heather gave a micro-nod and said, 'Alison these last few days was more buoyant than we've ever seen her.'

Suicides often seem that way because they've come to a decision, Hirsch thought. 'Uh huh.'

'A few weeks ago she inherited some money from a great aunt,' Keith said.

'She began to see it as a lifeline.'

'She wanted us to have some of it—'

'We said no, use it to start a new life.'

Hirsch watched and listened: Heather, Keith, Heather, Keith. They'd probably been doing it for forty-odd years.

'May I ask how much it was?'

'A hundred and sixty thousand.'

'Had she told her husband?'

'I don't think so,' Heather said.

'He'd have made her pay it all into the farm,' added Keith.

Hirsch thought it was likely Ray Latimer did know about the inheritance. 'Had she told him she wanted a divorce?'

'Yes.'

'Was it a difficult decision for her?'

Heather gave him a look. 'You mean she felt so awful she killed herself?'

'How did Mr Latimer take it?'

'He told her the only way she'd leave him would be in a box,' Heather said, and stared at Hirsch, daring him.

'Did the boys know about the inheritance and/or the divorce?'

Husband and wife glanced at each other. 'She told Jack while they were here,' Heather said. 'Maybe Craig knew and didn't approve and so he stayed with Ray, we don't know. Certainly Ray poisoned the poor kid's mind against Allie.'

Her eyes were wet with sorrow, misery and fury. Hirsch said, 'I will have to talk to both boys sooner or later.'

'If those men let you.'

Hirsch nodded that he pretty well understood what he was up against. 'When Alison came here with Jack, did you think that was it, she was never going back?'

'Yes.'

'Not even to thrash out the details?'

'Well, we told her to let a lawyer do that. But she hadn't been able to bring all her things with her. She would've gone back for the rest of her things at some stage.'

'She didn't indicate that she'd do that on Sunday?'

'No.'

'But what about Craig? She missed him, surely? Was she prepared to have the boys split up like that, Jack living with her, Craig with Ray?'

Husband and wife glanced at each other as if to acknowledge that nothing was neat. 'We're sure Craig would have wanted to live with her eventually.'

'Meanwhile . . .'

They shifted uneasily there on the other side of the

234

kitchen table. Hirsch pushed it: 'Wasn't it upsetting for your daughter, knowing she might have to challenge her husband for custody, knowing Craig chose him over her?'

'They were things that could have been worked out in time,' Heather said.

Hirsch saw movement and a grey cat padded into the room. Spotting him, it displayed apparent outrage, contempt and fear in one swift turnaround, its tail flicking as it fled the room.

'You have doubts,' Keith said.

Hirsch didn't, not really. But he wanted to present a tight brief to the coronial hearing, one that would not be challenged by Kropp, McAskill or the lawyers that Leonard and Raymond Latimer would certainly bring to court with them.

'You say you found the door locked when you returned on Sunday?'

'We never lock it.'

'But was Alison in the habit of locking it as she came and went?'

'No.'

'Remember that she hadn't lived here for some time and was in the habit of locking her house at the farm,' Hirsch pointed out, not sure if that were true or not.

Keith shook his head. 'No.'

'She arrived here with a suitcase?'

'Two cases, a big one for Jack, all his clothes and toys and school things, and a weekender for herself.'

So why, thought Hirsch, had she repacked? And why the larger case?

'I'd like to go back to her previous suicide attempt.'

Hirsch saw reluctance. They knew the earlier attempt gave credence to the view that their daughter had got it right this time.

'She'd been unhappy,' Heather said finally.

'No light at the end of the tunnel.'

'Ray and that damn father of his, they made her life a misery.'

Rather than swivel his gaze—Heather, Keith, Heather, Keith—Hirsch sipped his tea. It was tepid. 'In what way?'

'Ordered her around.'

'Monitored everything she did, every trip, every dollar spent.'

'And she got a creepy feeling if she was ever alone with Leonard.'

Hirsch nodded. 'I understand that she tried to shoot herself and Ray stopped her in time.'

'Ray? No, his mother. Meredith.'

'His mother?'

'She died late last year.'

'Do you know the circumstances?'

'You think they go around bumping off all the women in the family?' Heather gave a grim laugh. 'Cancer.'

'The circumstances of the suicide attempt.'

Heather was patting her husband's shoulder absently. 'Allie was in her car.'

'At the old hut?'

'No, she hated it there. Out in the paddock.'

'Meredith was looking out her window and wondered what the car was doing there.'

'The men were away at a clearing sale.'

'She had a bad feeling and ran down the hill and found Allie just sitting there and talked her out of it.'

'Sitting there with a rifle between her knees?' asked Hirsch.

Silence, and then Heather said, 'This changes things. You think she finally did it.'

Hirsch was non-committal. 'Tell me more about Meredith Latimer.'

'Lovely woman. Life was no bed of roses, but she stood up to Leonard.'

'Were she and your daughter close?'

'They were at the end.'

'Allie nursed her in her final months.'

'Did she feel it keenly when Meredith died? The only support she had within the family?'

'I know what you're trying to imply,' Heather Rofe said, 'and you're wrong.'

Next, the Latimers. Hirsch spent the remainder of Tuesday and all of Wednesday attempting to make contact with Ray or his father. In between patrolling his district, delivering a summons, taking reports, signing statutory declarations and investigating the theft of a drum of diesel fuel, it was a time of frustration. The Latimers failed to answer phone messages or knocks on the door of either house, and had strangers running interference, telling him to come back next week or leave the poor beggars alone.

Then on Thursday morning Hirsch knocked at the son's

door and Leonard Latimer answered. He looked very master-race in his pastoralist's uniform of cream moleskins, R. M. Williams boots and khaki shirt; a bull of a man, with wide, sloping shoulders and a thick neck.

Hirsch removed his cap. 'Mr Latimer, my name is—'

'I know who you are.'

Hirsch gave him a grave little nod. 'First, may I say how sorry I am. I know you were fond of your daughter-in-law.'

He knew no such thing, he just wanted to stir. And Leonard was stirred, his short grey hair bristled. 'What do you want?'

'I was wondering if I might have a word with Raymond. Is he in?'

'Nope.'

It might have been true. The family car was missing; silence, a sense of absence, seemed to come leaking out around the patriarch's large frame. Hirsch pictured the older man's life now, no daughter-in-law to bully or do his cooking and shopping.

'Then perhaps I could have a word with you?'

'I'm busy.'

Leonard was dressed for town, not work. Did he work, get his hands dirty, track dust and mud over his daughter-in-law's carpets? Hirsch glanced at the man's hands. Short, blunt fingers, the nails remnant stubs.

'It won't take a moment,' he said.

Leonard continued to scowl. His face had no other expression; it was the face his family saw day in and day out, seamed by long years of anger, irritation and sunburn. Pugnacious chin; barrelly chest; arms bowed as if bristling for a punch-up. Keeping his own features open and pleasant, Hirsch moved one hand closer to the equipment hanging from his belt. 'It's just that I'm preparing a brief for the coroner,' he said.

'You? It should be Kropp.'

'It's me,' Hirsch said, shrugging as if to say: *Can't do anything about it.*

'We'll see about that. It needs someone senior. It needs someone who knows us.'

Hirsch put some steel into his voice. 'No, it doesn't.'

Latimer seemed ready to throw a punch. But maybe that was his default position. Without altering expression he said, 'What do you want to know?'

'Perhaps you can tell me something of Alison's state of mind?'

A car passed by on Bitter Wash Road. Leonard cocked his head as if to identify the beat of the engine, then switched to Hirsch again. 'She was a mess.'

Hirsch got out his notebook and said, and wrote, 'A mess.' He looked up. 'In what way, precisely?'

Latimer eyed the notebook. 'In a way that caused her to shoot herself, what do you think?'

'She was depressed?'

'Depressed, agitated, anxious, suicidal.'

'She expressed these feelings to you?'

'I could tell. So could Ray. So could the kids, for that matter.'

'What if I were to inform you that others have said she'd been quite upbeat before her death?'

'That bitch across the road, you mean?'

'I've been told by more than one source that Mrs Latimer was intending to divorce your son. Leaving home was the first step to doing that.'

Nothing altered in Leonard Latimer's chemistry. 'News to me.'

'Your son didn't tell you? I'm astonished.'

'I didn't know anything about any divorce talk.'

'If Alison had divorced your son, how would that have affected the business?'

'What do you mean?'

'Legal fees,' Hirsch said, 'settlement costs, alimony. You're already struggling, money-wise, can't pay your bills. You'd be forced to sell part of the farm.'

'All academic now,' Latimer said.

No satisfaction, slyness or triumph, just the bald truth. Hirsch opened his mouth for another question and heard voices within the house. Looking past Leonard's shoulder, he said, 'Are Ray and the boys inside?'

'Leave us alone. We're grieving. And for your information the property's not struggling.'

'Perhaps I'll pop in later.'

'Perhaps you won't. The undertaker's bringing Allie home tomorrow and on Saturday we're cremating her.'

They'd released the body? Hirsch pocketed his notebook. Away to the east a helicopter clattered into view, running along the line of wind turbines on the ridge. Maybe it's partly down to the turbines, Hirsch thought. None had been erected on Latimer soil, meaning no rental income. But in the nick of time had come news of Alison's inheritance—except that rug had been pulled from under their feet when she announced she was getting a divorce and taking her money with her.

Leaving Finola Armstrong with her adjoining property and wind farm income.

Hirsch beamed at Leonard. 'I expect your son will soon find arms to comfort him.'

Hirsch went back and logged on to his e-mails. He read the one from Rosie DeLisle first. *Letting you know that Jennifer Dee's father was best mates with Reid. The suicide hit him hard, so looks like the daughter decided to do something about it.* 'But what are you going to do about *her*,' muttered Hirsch.

The next e-mail caused him to reach for the phone, dial the number for the Forensic Science Building in the city. When he got hold of a technician, he gave the reference number and heard the soft rattle of a keyboard.

'Got it,' the tech said. 'Point two two calibre Brno bolt action. What about it?'

Peering at his computer, Hirsch said, 'Says here you found the victim's palm and fingerprints on the stock and the butt.'

'Correct.'

'Not on the barrel?'

'Correct.'

'Wouldn't you expect her to grasp the barrel so she could place the end of it in her mouth? Wouldn't you expect to find prints there?'

'That's your concern, bud. I've known people to do all kinds of things when they shoot themselves. Me, I run tests. *Science*. Motives, impulsive behaviour, they don't concern me.'

Hirsch heard a young voice and pictured the guy: about thirty, breezy, loved his job, loved the science and the technology. Quite possibly crap at relationships. 'Okay, but scientists speculate, right?'

'What's on your mind?'

'You've seen the photos?'

'I have.'

'The victim's thumb is still inside the trigger guard, hooked around the trigger.'

'Yeah, so?'

'How often would you expect to see that?'

'As against what?'

'As against the body going into spasm, jerking, arms flinging out.'

'I see what you mean. But, a first time for everything. No two shootings are alike.'

Hirsch moved on, rocking back in his chair and glancing out across the front desk to the community notices. 'You found tiny amounts of gunshot residue on her hand and sleeve.'

'Correct.'

'*Tiny* amounts.'

'What about it?'

'And none in her lap or on her thighs?'

'No.'

'Wouldn't you expect to, if she sat on the ground with the gun between her legs?'

'Mate, I've seen everything.'

'And that's your scientific conclusion,' Hirsch said.

'I wouldn't want to get vague on you,' the tech said.

Next, Hirsch phoned the forensic pathologist. She was slicing and dicing, the morgue assistant said; she'd call back. Hirsch waited. He should step outside and wash the HiLux before the area commander saw it again, but he waited.

She called an hour later. Thanking her, Hirsch said, 'I understand you've released the body for burial.'

'Correct.'

The voice of a busy, short-shrift woman. Hirsch wasted no time: 'Under cause of death you put gunshot wound to the head.'

'Yes.'

'You go on to say that foul play, accident, and suicide are, quote, "unascertainable".'

'Correct.'

'May I ask what you mean by that?'

'It means exactly what it says. I do not know if another party was present, I do not know the state of the victim's mind at the time of death, I do not know the choreography, for want of a better word, of her last few moments of life. She might have been enjoying the sunshine, idly playing with the rifle until a bunny rabbit came hopping into range and, in manoeuvring the rifle, she accidentally shot herself. Or she committed suicide. Or someone staged it. Did she leave a note?'

'No.'

'Like I said, "unascertainable".'

'But suggestive?'

'You know I won't speculate.'

Please speculate, Hirsch thought.

Instead, the pathologist said, 'I can't rule anything absolutely in or absolutely out. "Unascertainable" does not mean the death wasn't suspicious or wasn't accidental. A gunshot to the head was the cause of death but an autopsy cannot ascertain the circumstances surrounding it.'

'You've informed the Port Pirie CIB?'

'I have.'

'And?'

'I have no idea what they'll do with it. I merely passed on my report.'

'Okay, what about the marks on the body?'

'I found a subcutaneous bruise just above the collar bone when I peeled back the skin on the right side of her neck, and—'

'Suggestive of someone trying to throttling her?'

'You're jumping the gun. I can't ascertain what happened. And if you will let me continue, I also found a couple of tiny abrasions on her abdomen, a small bruise on one breast, a cut on the back of her left wrist, all trivial.'

'Suggestive of . . . ?'

'A word you seem to like, Constable Hirschhausen. Suggestive of ordinary wear and tear from housework or gardening, for all I know, and so, again, "unascertainable".'

I hope someone, somewhere, is ascertaining something,

Hirsch thought. Before he could speak, the pathologist added, 'On the other hand, when people die violently—when they shoot themselves, for example—or are in a heightened mental state, they mark or injure themselves. I've seen it in cases of anxiety and panic attacks, a need to wrench at upper body clothing, for example.'

'But you've also seen women who have been forcibly manhandled.'

'Yes.'

'You can't ascertain that that happened in this case?'

'No.'

'Anything under her nails?'

'No.'

'Recent sexual activity?'

'No.'

'What about *old* injuries?'

'She'd fractured her wrist at some point in the past.'

'How? Could someone have bent it back, twisted it?'

'That I can't ascertain,' the pathologist said.

'Toxicology?'

'Negative.'

'Underlying medical conditions?'

'None.'

'You've been a great help,' lied Hirsch.

Next he called Port Pirie, the lead detective reciting him the highlights of his report: "' . . . death consistent with a self-administered gunshot wound with further investigations pending"—meaning that's as far as we'll take it. Meaning you're preparing the brief, so it's your job to tell the coroner she was nuts. Sorry, balance of whatever . . .'

'But,' said Hirsch, outlining his buts, concluding with the pathologist's claim of unascertainable.

'Exactly. It means foul play can be ruled out.'

'No,' said Hirsch, 'it means that foul play *can't* be ruled out. In other words, foul play might be ruled in, if other evidence is found.'

'Semantics,' the voice from Port Pirie said. 'And there is no other evidence.'

Three hours later, Superintendent Spurling entered the police station, propping his hands on the front counter.

'You rocking the boat, Constable?'

You came all the way down here to ask me that? 'Sir?'

Spurling calmed himself visibly. He released the counter. 'Look, Paul, I've had a word with my detectives, and they can't see that any further action is needed on Latimer.'

'So they told me, sir. I'm just trying to be thorough.'

'Yes. Any evidence of foul play?'

'No, sir. Not yet.'

'If you find anything I want to hear about it.'

'Sir.'

Spurling stepped back as if to go, then cocked his head at Hirsch. 'Do you know a Wendy Street?'

'I have met her,' Hirsch said carefully.

'And?'

'Schoolteacher, nice woman, widow, I think.'

'Not the troublemaking sort?'

'I wouldn't say so. I don't really know. Why?'

'She's called for a public protest meeting, police bullying in Redruth.'

'Oh.'

'Yes. You know the drill: keep your eyes and ears open.'

'Sir.'

'I need to know,' Spurling levelled his gaze at Hirsch, 'everything.'

'Yes, sir.'

'And get that bloody windscreen fixed.'

22

Friday morning, Hirsch parked outside Redruth Automotive.

It was a sprawling place a couple of blocks from the motel, and 'Automotive' was a catch-all term: you could buy a used car from the dozen tired vehicles in the side yard, fill your tank from one of three bowsers, get your oil changed or engine repaired in the workshop, and, in a vast, silvery shed out the back, have your scratches, dents and crumples smoothed over.

That's where Hirsch found the boss. 'Sergeant Kropp said you're the man to see about a cracked windscreen,' he said, blinking as he stepped from drenching sunlight into shadows, air laced with chemicals and the stutter and clang of machinery.

Bernie Judd grunted, muscling past Hirsch to stare at the damage. Then he shook his head as if confirming worst fears. 'She's stuffed, mate. Can't be repaired. I can replace it for you.'

He was shorter than Hirsch, older, full of twitches and

fury like a man who's giving up cigarettes. He glanced again at the windscreen, critically along each flank of the vehicle, then at his watch, Hirsch's uniform and finally somewhere past Hirsch's right ear. Stubby ginger hair on a bumpy scalp, fine gingery hair on his forearms and wrists, gingery freckles, grimy nails.

'Take long to get one in?' Hirsch asked.

Judd jerked his head. 'Got a good one out the back. Off a wreck, but there's nothing wrong with it.'

'Done,' Hirsch said. 'When?'

'Got things to do in town? Be ready in a couple of hours.'

Hirsch handed over the keys. 'We've been investigating that hit-and-run up at Muncowie. I guess the others have already asked if any vehicle has come in with—'

'Told Nicholson, nothing's come in.'

Hirsch nodded philosophically. 'Has he been working here for long?'

'Wouldn't call it working here. Him and his mate give me a hand now and then.' He glared at Hirsch. 'There a law against it?'

Hirsch shook his head. Plenty of police regulations, though. He peered into the dimness again, the hoists, paint bays, drums, workbenches. Two young and three slightly older men in overalls. The only vehicles in there were a farm ute patched with pink primer, a station wagon with a crumpled tailgate and a Honda he recognised as belonging to Finola Armstrong. 'You do small jobs? My own car's got a couple of dents.'

'We do everything. Give you a good price,' Judd said, staring at the silver watch nestled in the ginger furze of his wrist. 'Would this be an insurance job?'

'Not exactly.'

'Not exactly,' Judd said. 'Well, bring her in and I'll see what I can do.'

As Hirsch turned to go he said, 'That hit-and-run: they reckon Melia Donovan was in an accident two or three weeks prior, older boyfriend. Know anything about that?'

'Nup. See you in a couple of hours.'

'Wasn't Nicholson, was it? We were having a laugh the other day how his girlfriend crashed his car . . .'

A kind of stillness settled in Judd. As if Hirsch hadn't changed the subject he said, 'Give me your mobile number. As soon as we've fitted the glass, I'll give you a bell.'

Hirsch walked.

First to a café, where the coffee was weak, the vanilla slice gluey and the conversation limited to the weather. Hirsch thought it was going to be a long, hot summer; not that anyone asked for his opinion. Customers and staff looked away from him, the uniform. As he sipped and chewed, he tried to imagine how Wendy Street's protest meeting might play out. He saw a big room, perhaps the town hall, with Superintendent Spurling, a public relations inspector, a deputy commissioner and maybe Kropp himself seated at a large table at the head of the room, trying for smiles and patience and genial common sense. But the crowd would not have logic or patience on its side. One by one they would stand, awkward men and women who'd felt the flare of anger moments before but now, in the spotlight, tripped over their words and lost the thread of their argument. A disordered atmosphere, the crowd blurting accusations that trailed into nothing or were overheated or roamed off the point, while Spurling and the others tried to smile and reassure and give everyone a fair go and water it all down with platitudes fed them by the public relations unit.

Hirsch pushed his plate away. He left the café, strolled around the little square, bought the *Advertiser*, read it in the rotunda. Barely forty minutes had elapsed. He strolled into an op shop and immediately out again. Why did all op shops have a poorly tuned radio playing in the background? His fingers had itched to adjust the dial.

The little hillsides above the square beckoned and he found himself climbing narrow streets between stone walls dating from the 1850s. Jasmine scented the air, dense on back fences, and fake diamonds glinted where the sun struck the adzed stone.

Then down to Redruth Creek. According to a pamphlet in a plastic stand beside a plaque, huts had appeared along the creek in 1843, when Colonel Frome was surveying the northern reaches of the colony, but there was no town until 1850, when a shepherd, Alfred Tiver, spotted traces of copper oxide in the local stone. South Australia might have foundered if not for the mine. Twenty years later, the shafts were depthless blue pools of water that defeated the pumps. The Cornish Jacks had migrated to other towns and mines, but not before the hillsides and flatlands had been denuded of trees, the timber consumed by the boilers or staked deep underground against the pressing earth.

He crossed an iron bridge, guided by a map on the back fold of the pamphlet, and climbed to a museum halfway up-hill from the town. It was a converted boiler shed, shadowed by a great excavation in the hillside, remnant stone walls and chimneys, and deeply rusted iron frames and gantries. Hirsch stopped to get his breath. Below him the town threaded through the valley folds, a scattering of peaceful red roofs. There was no wind. A hawk floated.

He stepped into the museum. An elderly man turning the pages of a newspaper greeted him curtly. The main display was a diorama of the copper mine. Miners' picks hung on the walls. Shovels, brass telescopes, spears, boomerangs and woomeras. Christening gowns, napkin rings and porcelain shepherds crammed into glass cabinets. Old shop mannequins dressed in 1850s trousers, dresses, bonnets, shawls. Tables laden with crockery and knotty green and blue glass bottles. Bentwood chairs. Lamps. And several pieces from more recent times: a pedal radio, an inky school desk, dozens of photographs: Army volunteers in 1917 and 1942, shearing sheds, prize Merino rams, the cricketer Garfield Sobers visiting the primary school in the early sixties.

People would move house, or their old back-roads grandfather would die, and the museum would get anything that wasn't wanted, didn't work or couldn't be sold to a second-hand dealer. It wasn't quite junk, and was even halfway interesting, but Hirsch's interest didn't stretch past fifteen minutes. He left, aware of the grouchy gaze of the curator.

The town's hatred of Kropp and his boys was rubbing off on him, too.

Hirsch was sauntering back along the main street, draining a bottle of water, when his phone pinged: *Yr cars ready*.

He found the HiLux parked on the forecourt of Redruth Automotive, looking dusty and hand-printed with grease but with a spotless new windscreen. He entered the dimness of the panel-beating shed, benign, unprepared for the meaty forefinger that stabbed him in the chest.

'Butt out of my business, all right?'

Hirsch jumped in fright, dropped into a panicked half crouch.

Nicholson laughed. 'What, you're going to try karate on me? You a martial arts expert now?'

Hirsch straightened. They were all watching from the shadows, the overalled men and Judd and a young woman he didn't recognise. Ignoring Nicholson, he said to Judd, 'Keys in the ignition?'

Clearly Judd had called Nicholson and was expecting something else to happen. 'Er, yep, good to go.'

'Don't fucking turn your back on me,' Nicholson said.

Hirsch tried walking towards the sunlight, but Nicholson confronted him, his big paw around the woman's forearm. 'Meet Bree, arsehole. Bree, meet the cunt who dobs in his mates.'

Hirsch said, 'How old are you, Bree?'

'You prick, you absolute fucking prick.'

The punch was fast and stone hard, winding Hirsch. He

staggered, bent over, and, after a second, spewed the spring water over the floor and his shoes. He was a good target like that and Nicholson booted his backside.

'Nick,' wailed the girl, 'stop it.'

Nicholson ignored her, dancing around Hirsch, aiming kicks. 'Dog. Maggot. Slime ball. She's old enough, arsehole.'

Hirsch found a spot of oily floor and sat, his back to the leg of a metal bench. Getting his wind back he said, 'Bree, do you have a driver's licence?'

'What the fuck is this?' screamed Nicholson. 'Eh? Get out of my fucking face.'

The man's spittle flecked Hirsch's lapels and face. Hirsch swiped his forearm across his cheeks and mouth, the girl saying, 'Nicko, don't, let's just go.'

She looks about nineteen, Hirsch thought, taking in the hacked-about hair, skinny arms, a tattoo on one shoulder, rings piercing her poor pink flesh here and there. There was nothing unusual about her, she was just a young woman cowed by a bully. And he'd seen her before, he realised, serving food at the Woolman on the night of the football final.

Nicholson loomed over him. 'Stay the fuck away from me and my girlfriend and my business, all right?'

When Hirsch climbed to his feet he hurt in half a dozen places. He looked a complete fool, and he knew his uniform was a wreck. Judd and his employees had melted away, leaving the hint of silent laughter. The air in the shed was superheated and dense and silent and the noon sun, a fat block of it angling a short distance in at the doorway, was lighting up dust motes. Hirsch walked stiffly into that light, out into the fresh air.

One of the panelbeaters stood beside the HiLux, dangling the keys. Hirsch expected taunts but what he got was, 'Few things you should know.'

'Yeah? What?'

'Bree's good people, doesn't deserve the hassle.'

'I'm not going to hassle her.'

The man nodded. He was narrow faced, saturnine, slow and deliberate. 'Nicholson's another matter.'

Hirsch waited. He placed a hand on the hot metal for support. Removed his hand again.

'Him and Andrewartha,' the man said.

'I understand they work here in their spare time.'

'The odd job, yes.'

He was glancing around now, feeling eyes on his back, so Hirsch reached for the keys as if they were not having this discussion. He murmured, 'Kropp's part of it, too?'

The man shrugged. 'Probably. Behind the scenes.' His eyes shifted. 'I will deny this.'

'Uh huh. How much do I owe you?'

'Taken care of. We handle all the police repairs and servicing.'

Hirsch put away his wallet. 'Okay.'

He knew enough now. Judd, getting all of the department's business in the area, probably overcharged and shared the skim with Kropp and his boys. The after-hours work would be cash in hand. And there were always crash scenes, vehicles needing a tow, the police well placed to advise distressed motorists where they could get their car fixed.

Hirsch nodded his thanks and climbed behind the wheel. The interior was baking hot. 'Melia Donovan.'

'What about her?'

'I've heard talk of a car crash, an older boyfriend.'

'Can't help you.'

By mid-afternoon Hirsch was back in Tiverton, running a hose over the HiLux in the narrow driveway beside the station house. He squirted and swiped at the panels, trying to get rid of road dust and panelbeaters' grime. Presently he heard voices, high and sweet, cars, and car doors slamming: school was letting out across the road.

He straightened his back to watch.

Today, in the midst of spring sunshine and honest physical labour, and surrounded as he'd recently been by sudden death, he wanted reminders of blamelessness. Some kids were kicking a football around, watched by a teacher who kept glancing at her watch. Then a figure separated from the others. Katie Street. She was coming to see him, he realised. She stopped, looked left and right along the empty highway, and ran across, halting abruptly on the footpath.

'Hello there,' he said, glancing around for her mother.

'Hello.'

'Waiting for your mum?'

Katie looked briefly stricken and confused. Until recently, Hirsch realised, the person who'd dropped her off and picked her up from school most days had been Alison Latimer. Not only that, she'd been a regular visitor at the house across the road. They would have been close. 'Come and wait with me in the yard,' he said.

She entered reluctantly, Hirsch making no big deal of it but turning off the hose and dropping the chamois in the murky bucket beside a back tyre. 'Would you like a drink? A snack?'

She did what kids do, shrugged elaborately, wanting the treats but not prepared to say so outright.

'I've got Coke and Tim Tams.' Left behind by the previous tenant. He hadn't checked the use-by dates.

'Okay.'

'Stay there.'

He came back with two cans and the packet, both safe to consume. They sat companionably on the front step, where the sun warmed them as the world went by, what there was of it now that most of the parents had come and gone across the road. Hirsch eyed Katie surreptitiously. She chewed, brushed at crumbs, jumped when he crackled his empty can. Not to be outdone, she crackled hers.

Jack Latimer is off school for a few days, he thought; meanwhile, I'm a kind of security until her mother arrives to collect her. Or there's something she wants to tell me.

It came finally, the voice almost a whisper: 'I didn't shoot Alison.'

'Good grief, of course not, no one thinks you did.'

He didn't have the language or the know-how to explain a suicide to a child. Then again, why shouldn't she be told?

And maybe she had been told. That led him to secondary thoughts: What if Alison Latimer had been shot in her car, then carried to the hut? Or shot in her house, ditto. Or shot at her parents' house, ditto.

Then Katie was up and running, out onto the footpath. 'Mum! Mum!'

Wendy Street had been about to turn into the school when she caught sight of her daughter. She braked, swung the Volvo around and parked at the kerb. Gazing hard at Hirsch, she got out, passed around the front of her car and clamped Katie against her thigh. 'Hello, darling girl,' she said, eyes busy. She took in the school, the dripping HiLux, the Coke cans and Hirsch, establishing a narrative from the evidence. 'Sorry I'm late,' she said. 'Unexpected staff meeting.'

She was inviting an explanation, and Katie sensed that. 'I just came over to say hello.'

'Did you.'

'We had a treat. Coca-Cola and Tim Tams.'

Wendy shuddered. 'Nectar of the gods. Well, I'd better get you home.' She didn't move but watched Hirsch intently, Katie glued to her side. 'I understand you'll be briefing the coroner.'

Hirsch acknowledged that he was, adding, 'It would help if I could have a word with you sometime.'

'Come for dinner,' Katie said.

Her mother paused for a beat, recovered, and said, 'There you have it. Dinner. Six-thirty—country hours.'

23

Country food: lamb chops and vegetables.

Then at eight-thirty, Katie in bed, they talked, Hirsch in an armchair, Wendy on the sofa, separated by a heavy rug on polished floorboards. Bookshelves to waist height lined three walls, with photographs, prints and a single watercolour arranged in the spaces above. No television—that was in a sunroom at the back of the house. Hirsch checked the book titles: biographies, photography, art, travel, and a mix of good fiction and crap. No cookbooks, and none that he'd seen in the kitchen, thank the lord above. Vases, a couple of small brass gods from some trip to South-East Asia.

Street was watching. An ironic flicker in her face and voice she said, 'Pass muster?'

Hirsch gave her a faint grin. 'Nice room.'

'For an interrogation.'

'A chat.'

'A chat,' Wendy said, and stretched her limbs and arranged herself along the length of the sofa. Hirsch was pretty sure she was having fun with him. Her gaze was sleepy with a hint of humour.

'Fire away.'

Hirsch took a breath. 'The popular consensus is that Mrs Latimer committed suicide.'

Wendy Street dropped her mild smartarse act. She swung upright, tears filling her eyes, a faint glistening in the dim light of the floor lamp beside her. 'Can't we call her Alison?'

'Sure.'

'And as far as I'm concerned, she *didn't* kill herself.'

Hirsch shifted in his chair. 'You were close?'

'Katie and I moved here four years ago and I met her pretty much straight away. We became friends. Walking distance from each other. And she was lonely.'

'What can you tell me about her? Her health. Moods.'

'I know what you're getting at. Look, now and then she complained of stiffness in her hand, maybe arthritis. She said the wind turbines got to her, especially at night. If there was an easterly wind blowing she'd wake up in shock with her heart pounding. She said the sleep deprivation was getting to her.'

Hirsch thought of his own reaction to the turbines. 'I had a strange feeling when I stood by one of the turbines the other day. Like I was seasick.'

'Yet other people aren't affected. Katie and I sleep like babes.' A shrug. 'There's plenty of anecdotal evidence of a syndrome. It's the noise, apparently, and low-frequency soundwaves.'

'Her husband and sons weren't affected?'

'No. But her mother-in-law was. These wind farms have split families, you know. Ray and his father were dead set on getting turbines on the property; they were ropeable when the company decided on Finola Armstrong's place instead.'

'This syndrome: could it have affected Mrs Lat . . . Alison so much that she'd take her own life?'

'No. Absolutely not.'

'I can't overlook the fact that she made a previous suicide attempt.'

'Look, when I first met her, Allie was very timid. She opened up gradually and admitted things weren't great in her marriage and that she felt depressed. She'd have panic attacks and heart arrhythmia, she got very down sometimes. I told her to talk to her doctor about anti-depressants, but she shied away from that. I think she was scared her husband would find out. Then about a year ago she was found with a gun as if she intended to shoot herself.'

'Did she ever talk of suicide to you?'

'She told me once she wished she could end it all. At the time I thought she meant she wanted to get out of the marriage. I still think that. I don't think she was saying she wanted to kill herself.'

'Why didn't she just leave? Ask for a divorce?'

'The boys, I suppose. And she was afraid. No skills to speak of, no money, and there are no jobs for an unskilled woman her age around here.'

'But she did walk out a couple of times, went to stay with her parents?'

Wendy struggled with her throat, trying to swallow. 'Once late last year, and again last week.'

'What did her husband do or say? Her father-in-law, for that matter?'

'I don't know. But Ray did say to her, all the time, "The only way you'll leave here is in a box."'

'She told you that?'

'Yes.'

The statement sat there between them. 'Did he hit her? Did you see evidence of it or did she ever mention it?'

'No, but I wondered. She'd hold herself stiffly sometimes. Did the autopsy find any unexplained bruises on her?'

Hirsch knew he didn't have to answer that. 'No.'

'I'm surprised. But let's say he *had* hit her in the past. What was she going to do about it? She can't report him to the police: he's *mates* with them. Footy club mates, what's more.'

Hirsch said carefully, 'And you don't have a high opinion of the Redruth police. Even if Mr Latimer didn't have ties to them.'

She shrugged. 'They're bullies.' Then her face altered, sharpened. 'It can't hurt to tell you: I intend to call a public meeting about them—a protest meeting.'

Hirsch said slowly, 'Okay.'

'I've been in touch with your superintendent.'

Hirsch said, 'Good.'

She squinted at him, not satisfied, as if she suspected he already knew. To deflect her he said, 'How was Alison this past week? She left home again, like before, but did she seem downhearted about it?'

'The opposite, I can't describe it. Upbeat, even elated, as if her eyes had been opened. She was going to ask for a divorce.'

She hadn't been upbeat the day Hirsch met her. More like a doll: stiff, cold, powerless. He'd been in uniform, however, so she probably distrusted him, saw him as siding with her husband and Kropp.

'Did she tell you she'd come into an inheritance?'

'Of course. She knew it wasn't enough to buy a house in the city, but was enough to buy *time* somewhere, get settled, look for a job. Breathing-space money. Running-away money.'

'Did her husband know about it?'

'Motive, right?'

'You tell me.'

'He knew.'

A child's troubled cough floated down the hallway. Wendy stiffened, head cocked, ready to take to her feet. There was no follow-up cough. She relaxed again, gave Hirsch a crooked smile, and said, 'The Latimers are rich, right?'

Hirsch nodded cautiously. 'They appear to be.'

'Exactly,' Wendy said. '*Appear* to be. But it's all tied up in land and equipment. The Latimers are big spenders. The biggest and best tractor, the biggest and best shearing shed, the biggest and best stud ram.'

'Alison told you this?'

'It's common knowledge.'

'What did Alison say about it?'

'She told me there was never enough household spending

money. Always plenty for a new truck or another parcel of land, but she was never allowed to spend anything on the house. The fridge was on its last legs, the carpet needed replacing, the curtains had been there since the year dot. It did her no good to complain or beg. She said her father-in-law was a real control freak. He'd go through her supermarket receipts and ask why hadn't she bought no-brand tissues, why such expensive shampoo . . .'

'Ray put up with it?'

'Everyone did. Of course, Ray's been learning at his father's knee. He's like his dad, bad tempered, a heavy drinker, a tyrant at home. Rarely has . . . *had*, a kind word for Allie. He used to snap his fingers to get her attention.'

'I know the type.'

Wendy shuffled forward on the sofa. 'Look, everyone sees Ray as the life and soul of the party, community spirited, an all-round good bloke. But in private it's a different story. Allie said he was cold—indifferent—to her side of the family, and he'd barely talk to her or the kids except to lay down the law.'

Hirsch pictured Raymond Latimer standing over his sons and his small-boned wife, weaving threats, his voice low and insinuating when it wasn't raised, his big fingers twisting and flicking. The image came strongly and felt real. 'The other day Jack seemed terrified that I'd tell his father he'd been shooting the rifle.'

'I'm not surprised.'

'Do you think Ray hits his sons?'

'According to Allie, no, it's all verbal. Yelling, belittling . . .

Especially Craig. You should hear him at football matches. The parent from hell.'

'Everything comes back to football.'

Hirsch said it lightly, but Wendy wasn't amused. 'Football, cricket, tennis in a pinch, in that order. And because Tiverton's too small to field its own teams, the locals play for Redruth.' She shot Hirsch a mirthless grin. 'And that's how Ray Latimer became best mates with your sergeant.'

Hirsch returned the grin.

'The thing is,' she said, 'Ray was a district champion when he was young. He was going to play for a league team. Then he hurt his knee and the big dream came to nothing. Now he's trying to relive it through Craig. He keeps pushing the poor kid, but Craig's hopeless at sport, quite uncoordinated, and his heart's not in it. I bet he wishes he was still at boarding school where Ray can't bully him.'

Hirsch noted that. 'Why isn't he?'

Another grin devoid of humour. 'The official line is, homesickness. Actually they pulled him out to save on school fees.'

'We keep returning to money.'

'Don't we. I think there *was* money, a generation or two ago, but Leonard and Ray have spent it all, there have been droughts, costs have risen, incomes have fallen . . .'

Pretty much what Ray Latimer had told Hirsch. 'Apparently they owe money here and there,' he said, thinking of Tennant, the Tiverton shopkeeper.

'I'm not surprised.'

Hirsch tried to see all the angles, feel the atmosphere in

the Latimer household. 'So Craig was taken out of boarding school and now he's at Redruth High.'

'Yes.'

'How does he feel about that?'

'I see him in the yard and the corridors, looking lost and miserable. I've tried to talk to him, but he avoids me. Ray told him to stay clear, probably. I'm a bad influence, I think—some leftie feminist rabblerouser who might put ideas in his head like I did Alison.'

Yeah, she'd be full of that. Hirsch gave her a crooked smile. 'How does Craig get to school?'

'Hah! Exactly. Here I am, just across the road, willing and able, but he takes the bus.'

'And life for Jack?'

'You noticed his bad foot? That saves him from the worst of it. He was never going to be a football champion. But I imagine he's just as browbeaten as Craig.'

They fell silent. Hirsch said, 'Tell me more about Ray.'

'Well, he's a Latimer.'

'Meaning?'

'The Latimer men have a certain reputation. The moment I moved in here Leonard dropped by to introduce himself, welcome me to the district. That's nice, I thought, until he backed me up against the fridge and felt me up, wondering if I got lonely with no man in my life.'

'What did you do?'

'Shoved him away, told him I'd report him to the police, to which he replied, "Good luck with that." I haven't had much to do with him since.'

Hirsch bit his lip. 'If you don't mind my asking, is Katie's father . . . ?'

'Died. Car crash.'

'I'm sorry.'

She shrugged but she also blinked. 'Anyway, the fruit doesn't fall far from the tree. Before long, Ray made his move. Ray favours a more subtle approach. The double entendre, the insinuation, the accidental brushing against you. I'm expecting Craig to have a go next.' She waved one arm agitatedly. 'Sorry, scrub that.'

Hirsch said, 'Did, or does, Ray put the moves on other women?'

'Is that a trick question? Everyone knows about Saturday night.'

Hirsch held his palm up. 'Country grapevine. Put it this way: has he been at it for a while? Did Alison know about Finola Armstrong or his other women, if any?'

'Ray would *taunt* her. He'd stay out all night, come home without showering, make phone calls and not bother to hide what it was about.'

'What a prince,' Hirsch said. He tried to find his way into his next question. 'What's your take on Finola Armstrong?'

'Well, it's easy to condemn someone, isn't it? I don't like her much, but that has nothing to do with her sleeping with Ray Latimer. I just don't warm to her. Too hard edged and pragmatic. If it doesn't involve the seasons or the harvest or stock prices, she's got nothing to say for herself. But she is a widow, after all. She was left with a farm to run and has made a success of it.'

'A practical woman.'

Wendy laughed harshly. 'If you mean she'd stage a suicide to solve a problem, I just can't see it. I mean, what problem?'

'Removing her rival in love.'

'So she could land Raymond Latimer? It's the other way round: Allie's death will solve *his* problem.'

'Okay.'

'Please, Hirsch, look closer to home. Ray and his father are these good old boys, pillars of the community, local gentry. Underneath it, they're awful men.'

She'd called him 'Hirsch'. He liked it. 'But so far everyone with a motive also has an alibi.'

'They paid someone.'

Hirsch looked at her. Anyone else, he would have scoffed. The meal sat pleasantly in him and the light was warm and dim. Music played softly, an iPod on a shuffle—The Waifs right now, and Hirsch, lulled by the song, didn't want to go home. He stared at Wendy with her legs folded beneath her, one shapely foot resting along her thigh, and she stared at him. And there was a moment, but Hirsch let it run out like sand, with the result that Wendy, harking a little crossly to the song, said, '*Are* the wicked going to wail and weep?'

24

October gathered its skirts and raced past.

Alison Latimer's funeral attracted half the district and seemed to Hirsch an expression of confusion and heartache, an occasion that sundered, not cemented, the community. A gritty wind blew and the ants raced in the red dirt and he didn't see any hired killers lurking. The days were longer now and the sun had heat in it, and old farmers in the churchyard informed Hirsch that it was 'going to be a long, hot summer,' sniffing the air cannily. He dared not laugh. What did he know about disturbances of the bones, the air?

He settled into his small-town role of stern father, kindly father, father-confessor, bloke next door and go-to guy. All of the locals had his mobile number and some found a reason to call it. Or they knocked on his door if the HiLux was parked in the driveway. They wanted him to find their missing stock, sheepdogs, fence posts, fuel drums, motorbikes and mothers suffering from dementia. And he drove all the time, sometimes three hundred kilometres a day, investigating thefts, introducing himself at remote farms, checking on the alcoholic shearer who had a history of violence, the intellectually disabled forty-year-old whose mother and sole caregiver had just died, the alternative-healing woman who'd threatened wind farm workers, the schizophrenic who'd stopped taking his pills. He made a dash to Redruth with a gasping teenager whose asthma inhaler had run out while her parents were away in the city. He administered breath tests, doorknocked people who'd failed to renew their car registrations, had a quiet word with kids seen doing burnouts—once in front of the police station. He intercepted a ute with a stolen stud ram on board. Even helped an elderly couple get their shopping home.

It wasn't all police work. One day he confessed to a mild fondness for tennis and found himself on the tennis club committee, where he was quizzed on any letter-writing or bookkeeping skills or experience he might have. He could have been everyone's mate, but the secret to being a cop in a small rural community—the secret and the pity—was to get close to the locals but not too close. And it was never close enough.

Thus his settled life. What wasn't settled were the deaths of Melia Donovan and Alison Latimer, and they ate at him. While the accident investigators widened their search for a suspect vehicle, contacting crash repairers and hospitals, viewing CCTV tapes along Barrier Highway from Broken Hill to Adelaide, Hirsch kept the pressure on Gemma Pitcher's mother, extended family, friends and enemies. Had Gemma made contact? Phone calls? Letters? E-mails? Anything on Facebook? Was there a favourite town or holiday spot she'd liked in the past? Old boyfriend? He phoned the far-flung contacts and visited those closer to.

He also called in on Leanne Donovan. He had nothing to tell her. She asked him not to come again.

The rest of his time was spent keeping others off his back.

DeLisle, Croome, Kropp, Spurling, all wanting updates or action. He wished Wendy Street would call, wanting an update.

'I need to speak to Ray Latimer, Sarge,' he told Kropp.

'Lay off a while longer. Let the family grieve.'

'He's your mate. Ask him to phone me.'

'Lay off, I said.'

Then one day Wendy Street did call. She was friendly, but brisk, as if snatching a moment in her busy day, and related a bit of remembered conversation with Alison Latimer before signing off with a bright, 'See ya!'

Feeling unmoored, Hirsch replaced the handset. He stared at the dusty calendar, replaying the call. Had he heard a tentative quality threaded through the breezy voice, Wendy drawing on a measure of courage to phone him? More courage than I've got, he thought gloomily. Then immediately berated himself for projecting his pathetic hopes and fears onto her. It was entirely possible that she *didn't* feel the same flicker of attraction and therefore had no trouble making the call, and if there'd been anything in her voice it was a kind of resignation: she had information to impart, but clearly not to Kropp, and that left Hirsch.

When it came to tying yourself in knots, Hirsch could tie for Australia. He grabbed a pen and his notebook and pressed down hard on the page:

October 29, 3.30 p.m., telephone call from Wendy Street, recalling two statements made by Alison Latimer early this year: 'Ray thinks Jack got his bad foot from my side of the family' and 'Ray keeps saying a good stud manager culls animals that weaken the strain'.

Nasty, but it didn't prove a crime had been committed.

And Spurling dropped in again, insisting on coffee and a biscuit this time.

'Like what you've done to the place,' he said, gazing around Hirsch's sitting room.

Painted the walls, got a carpet cleaner in, replaced the curtains and light shades, hung a couple of Tiverton Primary School Community Art Fair watercolours. Wildflowers somewhere out east. The Razorback under boiling black clouds, shot by a bolt of sunlight.

'Putting down roots, sir,' said Hirsch from the kitchen.

'Good on you.'

Hirsch came in with a tray. Spurling settled himself on one of the armchairs, tatty under a patchwork quilt cover from the same art fair. He patted the fabric. 'Very pretty, Constable.'

'Made by one of the mothers at the school across the road,' Hirsch said, pouring the coffee.

Spurling nodded. 'My wife's into this kind of thing: needlework, tapestry, patchwork . . .' His slender fingers stroked a tiny square of blue with white polka dots, then he glanced up at Hirsch. 'Sit down, Paul, for god's sake. I'm not going to bite you.'

Hirsch dropped into the other armchair. 'Sir.'

Spurling blew on the surface of his coffee. 'But you will recall that I asked to be kept updated on your Redruth colleagues.'

'Sir.'

A little steel in the voice now: 'Nothing to report, it seems. Why is that, Constable?'

Hirsch shifted in his chair. 'Things have been a bit hectic, and I haven't had anything to do with them lately.'

'Uh huh,' Spurling said, his disbelief evident. He crossed his legs, spread his arms on the quilt cover. 'The Street woman's going ahead with her public meeting. No date set, but goodness, what a lovely experience that's going to be.' He waited.

Had Hirsch jolted at hearing the name? He held his tongue. He didn't want to fuck things up when the superintendent was emerging as his only potential ally in the whole mess.

Spurling broke the impasse with a curt laugh. 'Mr Inscrutable. Where are we with the suicide? The coroner can't proceed until the police hand him a brief.'

'The thing is, sir, I don't think it was a suicide.'

'Ah. All right, spit it out.'

Hirsch expressed his doubts and frustrations: the car, the rifle, the trampled-upon scene. The diamond ring. Alison Latimer's hand. Her clean shoes. The ballistics report, the pathologist's findings.

'You're light-on for evidence,' Spurling observed. 'Where's the car?'

'Sitting in the impound lot.'

'Might not be too late to have it printed and tested for fibres and fluids.'

Hirsch shook his head. 'I tried that. No joy. The windows were open, condensation had formed, too much time had elapsed.'

'You took photos?'

'Printed them out,' Hirsch said, handing Spurling a folder.

The superintendent flipped through them, stopping occasionally, glum and unimpressed. 'It had been raining, from memory?'

'A couple of days earlier.'

'Stray tyre impressions? Shoe prints?'

'Tyres, no. As for foot traffic, half of Christendom traipsed over the area.'

A pause, Spurling assessing Hirsch. 'You think it's suspicious that her shoes are clean.'

'Yes, sir.'

'And what we'll hear in court, Constable, is that people don't abandon their instincts. Here's a neat, tidy woman who, even though intending to shoot herself, didn't want to get dirty. She skirted around the mud, kept to the grass.'

Hirsch made a noise of grudging agreement. 'Maybe.'

'The same applies to the diamond ring. She didn't want it to get damaged or lost or lifted by light fingers. You say she knew about firearms?'

Hirsch shrugged. 'Farmer's wife. Country woman.'

'Still,' mused Spurling, 'not the most common way for a woman to kill herself.'

'Exactly, sir,' Hirsch tapped his forefinger on one of the photographs. 'And see the way her thumb's still hooked inside the trigger guard?'

'That's hardly compelling.'

'But she had a problem with that hand, a weakness, couldn't straighten her fingers or thumb very well. Meanwhile her prints are on the stock and butt—but not the barrel.'

Spurling shook his head. 'She did have some movement in that hand, yes? And it's not beyond the realms of possibility that she held the rifle around the trigger area with her right hand and manoeuvred the barrel tip into her mouth with the left hand holding the stock rather than the barrel.'

Hirsch grinned, rueful. 'You'd be a good defence barrister, sir.'

Spurling leaned in with a tiny smile that mirrored Hirsch's. 'Constable, I'm anticipating the questions that might get asked at the inquest—or at trial, if it gets that far, and it seems to me you don't have anyone in the frame for a crime.'

'Sir.' Hirsch hated to admit it. At the back of his mind was the thought that he'd paid too much attention to Wendy Street's viewpoint. Sympathetic because he was attracted to her.

'And remember that brain injuries cause peculiar behaviour. So does the intent to commit suicide.' Spurling paused. 'Was she checked for GSR?'

'A few flecks.'

'There you go.'

'It doesn't feel right, sir.'

Spurling sat back, mildly exasperated. 'Okay, was there anything else about the scene, the body?'

'She had some bruises and abrasions, sir.'

'Suggestive of . . . ?'

Hirsch gave a little grimace, thinking of the terse pathologist. 'Of being manhandled.'

'Or of falling over, falling against the hut,' Spurling said. 'Get a second opinion.'

'She's been cremated.'

'Ah. Well, I suppose you can always get someone else to look at the pathologist's findings.' He gave an apologetic shrug and got to his feet. On the way out he said, 'For god's sake, Paul, get that flaming vehicle washed.'

The days passed, Hirsch patrolled. On a couple of occasions he was in town at lunch or going-home time, and found himself watching out for Katie Street and Jackson Latimer in the schoolyard across the highway. Forty kids, ranging from five to twelve, full of din and discord as they flowed out of the buildings and across the playing field or into waiting cars. Sometimes they were the town's only source of sound. He'd pick out Katie Street by her animation, a quick flash of movement and intelligence. He'd pick out Jack Latimer, stunned and lost.

He watched for Wendy Street, too, determined to say hello, but somehow, when his back was turned, the children were whisked away and he didn't see her.

Get that flaming vehicle washed . . . Not wanting to get caught out again, Hirsch ran a hose over the HiLux at the end of every shift and washed it once a week, and one Friday in late October, as he sloshed and sluiced with sudsy water, the dust a stubborn film that reappeared in streaks and deltas whenever his back was turned, he heard Katie say, 'Put your back into it.'

Hirsch turned. 'Care to show me how?'

'I will if you pay me top dollar.'

She was full of life there in his driveway. Jack was with her, slow, dazed, hesitant, and it occurred to Hirsch that she'd dragged him with her in an effort to jolt some life into him.

As if I could help with that, he thought. 'You only want me for my Tim Tams,' he said, thinking Christ, why did I say that?

Katie toed a weed. 'Can we wait here till Mrs Armstrong comes?'

'Sure.'

Finola Armstrong? Was this a regular thing now? It explained why Hirsch hadn't seen Wendy Street's old Volvo outside the school. Armstrong lived near the children and there would be occasions—those staff meetings, for example—when Wendy Street might be delayed. But why couldn't Ray or his father do the school run occasionally? Too busy? Women's work?

'You guys like a treat while you wait?'

Katie Street was game. She crossed the yard with a toss of her head.

'Make yourself comfortable,' Hirsch said, indicating the front step. He went in, came out with a tray of drinks and biscuits.

But Jack Latimer was hovering at the gate, staring down the road, seeming lost, as though unsure of the steps to take now.

'Jack?'

The boy stepped from his good foot to his bad, good foot, bad. 'What if she comes and can't find us?'

'Mrs Armstrong gets a bit cross,' Katie explained.

Hirsch could picture it: the impatience, stiffness and social awkwardness of Finola Armstrong. Seeing the boy wither a little, he joined him at the gate, risked dropping a hand on his shoulder. 'How about it, Jack? Coke and a Tim Tam?'

But the high school bus was pulling up outside Tennant's. Two girls and three boys alighted, their shirts half out, socks at ankle height, shoes scuffed, hair this way and that, one girl tugging her hemline down from crotch to mid-thigh before her parents saw her. The five moved off, one girl down a side street, the other into the shop with two of the boys, the fifth to the end of the veranda, beside the mailboxes. Craig Latimer. He looked slumped, unhappy, wound tight, and Jack seemed to shrink further at the sight of him. Hirsch thought about the great gulfs in that family: the grandfather on the hill, the father at the bottom of the hill or out wild-catting with his women, the older boy giving off waves of anger, the younger boy waves of desolation.

Then Finola Armstrong's Honda came hurtling into town. It stopped for Craig and was speeding the short distance to the side-street entrance of the primary school when Jack hobbled out of Hirsch's gate, waving his arms.

Armstrong braked, U-turned, Jack stepping back to avoid it, onto Hirsch's toes. 'Sorry!'

He looked aghast at what he'd done. Hirsch clasped his shoulders gently, a brief, bolstering contact, and nodded to Armstrong through the side window of the car. Jack joined Craig in the back.

Then Katie was skipping past, crying 'See ya!' and getting into the front with Armstrong. Where the others were glum, she was a light in darkness, a ribbon of brightness.

Hirsch decided to say hello. Armstrong watched him, scowling, as he walked around to the driver's window. She wound her window down reluctantly. Not hostile, not wary; without affect. There was a placid quality to her sun-damaged face.

'Helping out?' he said cheerily.

Her whole being altered, a look passing over her that expressed disdain for some lack of knowledge. 'You could say that.'

Then Hirsch saw Alison Latimer's diamond ring flash on one careworn, farm-chapped hand. He gave her roof a little slap and stepped away from the car. Katie waved, the boys didn't. He returned to his yard and sluiced more mud onto the driveway, trying not to think too hard about what had just happened.

His next visitor was Jennifer Dee.

She banged through the main door of the police station at the end of the first week of November, startling Hirsch in the act of taking down fly-specked public notices. There were tiny spiders domiciled under a couple of them.

'You bastard. I've lost my job because of you.'

Hirsch stepped down from his stool before she kicked it out from under him. He eyed the door to his office, the door to his apartment, the front door. She was a slight, teary woman but fired up, and he didn't want to tussle with her in an enclosed space.

But Christ, whose fault was it anyway? 'You were fired because you planted evidence on me.'

'They showed me the tape, you can't even tell it was me.'

Her eyes were red, she was trembling, sweat circles under her arms, dampness at her neck. Hirsch said, 'Would you like a beer? It's beer weather.'

She blinked. 'What?'

'Beer. Juice, tea, coffee . . .'

She actually stamped her slender foot. 'Bob Reid died because of you.'

'Bob Reid died because he shot himself in the head.'

Perhaps no one had spoken to her frankly yet. She put her hands across her stomach as if he'd hit her. 'Because his life was ruined.'

'He ruined his own life. He let Quine corrupt him, and when he got found out, he couldn't cope with the strain.'

'He only got found out because of you.'

'Listen to yourself, Jenny. Are you saying it would have been okay for him to go on stealing and lying? Corrupting others? Internal Investigations knew all about him before they spoke to me.'

'You're lying.' She ran out.

He didn't follow her. In her departing words was what his life would always be. What people would always believe.

25

Coulter, the circuit magistrate, rotated through the district every couple of weeks and at noon on a Friday in mid-November, a day dry and dusty, building in heat, Hirsch headed down Barrier Highway for the Venn drink-driving case. On the outskirts of Redruth he noticed the first of several posters on power poles and crumbling walls: *Police Methods in Redruth, Voice Your Concerns* and a date in December. He was surprised: they must be going up faster than Nicholson and Andrewartha could rip them down.

Venn and his wife were waiting on the steps, together with a man Hirsch recognised as Ray Latimer's lawyer. He should have walked right on by, he knew it. But he got his phone out, thumbed the camera icon and made straight for the little group, snapping as he went.

Stopping on the step below them—at a disadvantage, psychologically—he said, 'I repeat my warning, Mrs Venn: if you persist in claiming you were the driver, I'll arrest you for perjury.'

The Venns were bright-eyed and bushy-tailed, well dressed, people for whom nothing went wrong. Jessica Venn took a pace towards Hirsch on thin, stabbing heels, the tendons flexing in her toned legs. 'You jumped up little—'

The lawyer touched her sleeve. 'Jess . . .'

'Well he is.'

Now the lawyer fixed on Hirsch, his eyes flat. 'Was that a threat I heard, Constable Hirschhausen? Directed at my client? As though I, an officer of the court, were invisible?'

'Perjury is perjury,' Hirsch said. He stuck out his hand, not sure if the man would shake with him. 'And you are?'

The lawyer was obliged to hunch over, reach down. 'Ian Logan.'

The grip was firm, almost a test, and Hirsch took stock. They were of an age, the men who ran Redruth, he decided. Early- to mid-forties, confident, smooth, full of secret knowledge. This one wore a costly grey suit, stiff white cotton shirt and paisley tie. Paisley was coming back? No one had told Hirsch. A very clean man, dark-haired, buffed to a shine. Hirsch glanced down at the slender hand: a centimetre of white cuff, a hint of neat, black, expensive wrist hairs curling there.

'Logan,' he said. 'I've seen your ads in the *Weekly*.' Wills, Trusts, Deeds, Conveyancing, Family Law, and a cheesy head-and-shoulders of the man himself.

He retrieved his hand. 'Look, I don't know what your clients have told you but—'

'We'll thrash that out before the magistrate, shall we?'

Logan said. He nodded at Hirsch's phone. 'What have you got there, pictures of the crime?'

He chortled. He was fully alert, never still, taking in the passing vehicles and pedestrians, knowing the secret business of the town. Then he went still, staring across the street. His lips moved, a silent, 'Oh, fuck.' He ushered the Venns ahead of him into the building.

Curious, Hirsch turned around. A young woman with a rope of blonde hair was parting the curtain beads at the entrance to the café fifty metres down the road. She stepped through, the beads briefly disturbed in her wake.

Then the court stenographer and general dogsbody stuck her head out to call Hirsch and he went in.

'We meet again, Constable Hirschhausen,' the magistrate said.

What can you say to that? Hirsch nodded, said 'Mr Coulter,' and glanced around the courtroom. No other cases were listed, but Kropp was there. No one else.

In the end, Hirsch had filed two charges, driving under the influence and giving a false statement to police. The damaged guardrail was a matter for the roads department; he'd sent them the details. Now, as Coulter announced the charges, Hirsch glanced at Kropp uneasily. Kropp had seemed pissed off with Coulter and Logan the last time they had been in this courtroom, and seemed so now.

Coulter was speaking. 'Mr Logan, your client has elected to contest these charges in court rather than pay the relevant fines and lose demerit points?'

'That's so, your honour.'

'Very well. Constable Hirschhausen?'

Hirsch, with another glance at Kropp, gave his account of the arrest. He turned to Logan, expecting questions, but Coulter called Venn to the stand.

Venn, duly sworn, winked at his wife and grinned at his lawyer and explained that Hirsch was mistaken, it had been his wife at the wheel.

'I'd had a couple of drinks, your honour, and thought it best not to drive and risk endangering other lives.'

'Drinks?' said Coulter. 'This was the middle of the day.'

His tone sounded wrong to Hirsch. It wasn't judicial indignation. It sounded staged, as if he'd practised his lines.

Venn said, 'We had successfully negotiated a sale, your honour. Mrs Elizabeth Jennings. You might recall she was widowed tragically two years ago and in the depressed real estate climate had been unable to sell her property. Until now.'

'Of course. Fine woman,' Coulter said. 'Mr Logan?'

'If I may, your honour, I should like to present a sworn statement made by Mrs Jessica Venn, wife of the accused, in which she states that she, not her husband, was driving the car in question on the day and at the time and on the road in question.'

The magistrate flicked his comfortable fingers. Handed the statement, he read rapidly, then stared at Hirsch, hunched and pugnacious. 'Constable? Is this statement a true account of events?'

'I have yet to read it, your honour.'

Coulter glanced at Logan, who fished another copy from his briefcase and handed it to Hirsch.

First: date, time, location and background circumstances. Then:

Mindful of his responsibilities, my husband elected not to drive and gave me the key. It was shortly after leaving Mrs Jennings' property that I got into difficulties. Unused to the potholes, gravel surface, sharp bends and narrowness of the road, I inadvertently side-swiped a guardrail. Alarmed and upset, I pulled over as soon as it was safe to do so and attempted to gather my wits, whereupon Constable Hirschhausen appeared in his four-wheeldrive. I got out at once to apologise and explain and, I must confess, seek reassurance and comfort and understanding. Instead, Constable Hirschhausen berated my husband and myself, falsely accusing my husband of driving and me of swapping places with him in order that he might keep his licence and avoid a fine.

Witnessed by a notary public in Clare.

'Your response, Constable Hirschhausen?'

Hirsch stood. 'Your honour, at the conclusion of this session it is my intention to arrest Mrs Venn for perjury, and may I state that further charges against Mrs Venn, and her husband, may be lodged at a later date.'

He sat.

'Your honour, really,' Logan said, getting wearily to his feet. 'If it pleases the court, Constable Hirschhausen made threats to this effect on the steps of the courthouse a few minutes prior to the commencement of today's session. The threats were directed at my clients in my presence and there was no mistaking Constable Hirschhausen's intent. In fact, my clients and I felt most intimidated by the constable's words and manner.'

Coulter swung his head, doing pretty convincing outrage. 'Is this true, Constable Hirschhausen? Did you threaten Mr Logan and his clients?'

'Your honour, Mr and Mrs Venn are making a mockery of this court. They—'

'You attempted to influence a witness so that she might alter her evidence before the court?'

'I attempted to help her avoid facing a serious—'

'I've heard enough,' the magistrate said with a little smack of his gavel. 'I find that Mr Venn does not have a case to answer and is free to go. As for your conduct, Constable Hirschhausen, I'm inclined to notify Superintendent Spurling.'

There was a bit of gleeful backslapping on the steps outside the courthouse. Hirsch looked on gloomily, the sun warm but unrestorative. Then the steps cleared; cars whisked the Venns and Logan away. His day shot, Hirsch headed down the steps. He was brought to a halt by Kropp growling in his ear: 'Tell me they're wrong, Constable. You did not threaten to arrest the Venn woman for perjury.'

Hirsch paused where he was, but decided he'd feel safer on the footpath than mount the steps again. 'Not wrong, Sarge.'

Kropp joined him and side by side they surveyed the town, which was doing nothing just then. The silence stretched; the bollocking didn't come. All was peace and silence and the sun beat down. Presently Kropp said, 'Jenny Dee.'

'Sarge?'

'She tried to do the dirty on you?'

'Apparently.'

'I had nothing to do with that.'

'Thought never crossed my mind,' Hirsch said. He didn't mention the hundred-dollar note on the floor of the file room. But this was the warmest Kropp had ever been with him, and he wondered how far to trust it.

They stood there. Kropp said, 'Don't worry about Spurling. I'll have a word.'

Hirsch did worry. He hadn't passed on any information about Kropp and the others. Didn't really want to, despite the fact that Spurling was the closest thing he had to a source of support. And now here was Kropp offering to put in a good word. What a confusing bloody mess. 'It's okay, Sarge. I'll wear it.'

'Suit yourself.'

A farm truck trundled through the town, hauling hay. Presently, Hirsch sneezed, and then the woman with the swinging ponytail emerged from the café, crossed the street and approached the two men. She lifted a hand to Kropp. 'Sergeant.'

'Linda.'

They regarded each other. Kropp said, 'You wouldn't be stalking your husband by any chance.'

She gave him the ghastly, fixated grin of a stalker. 'Heaven forbid.'

'That's what I thought.'

This was interesting. Hirsch looked on.

'Linda, meet Constable Hirschhausen. Constable, meet the ex-Mrs Ian Logan.'

A quick flash, a brief hint of fire. 'I do have an independent identity, Sergeant Kropp.'

'Of course. Forgive me.'

'I'll forgive you when you take Ian's guns away.'

'The court lifted the order, Linda, we had no choice.'

She snorted. 'You mean *Coulter* lifted the order.'

Kropp said nothing; Hirsch took it as assent.

'You were Coultered,' she said with a sunny smile. 'Like everyone else.'

'Thanks, Linda.'

'You're welcome. Well, I'll be off. Nice seeing you, Sergeant.'

'A hundred metres, Linda.'

The ex-Mrs Logan waved vaguely at the café. 'I was no closer than a hundred and twenty.'

'Excellent.'

When she was gone, Hirsch put his head on one side. 'What was that all about?'

'Old history. Logan got a restraining order put on her.'

'Why?'

Kropp in his brutal solid way turned slowly to face Hirsch, a fascinating contradiction playing across his face. Hirsch—the dog, the maggot—was also a fellow member who'd just been stitched up by Coulter and Logan.

Hirsch waited. Kropp, gathering himself, there on the footpath, under the early afternoon sun, said, 'Ian Logan liked to thump his wife. Just now and again, you know. Liked to forge her signature, too—banking matters, real estate contracts. Linda reported it, and when we heard he had this violent streak, we confiscated his guns. Shotgun, couple of hunting rifles. Anyway, she got screwed on the divorce and no action was taken on the issue of questionable documents and so he thought it was okay to ask for his guns back. Filled out the forms, asked to be deemed, quote, "a non-prohibited person in relation to a firearms application". Coulter approved it. Linda went ballistic and started hassling everybody.'

'They're friends, Coulter and Logan?'

'I'll tell you what else about Coulter,' Kropp said, as if Hirsch hadn't spoken. 'Last year we went into bat for a wife and kids who were being bashed pretty regularly by the husband. She turns up to court on time, we turn up on time, Coulter doesn't. Apparently he turned up in Rothwell. Redruth, Rothwell, yeah, easy to confuse the two—if you were drunk or didn't give a damn. So Coulter races back here all pissed off, blaming everyone but himself, and refuses to grant an intervention order or let the woman read her victim impact statement. A week later, her husband hospitalises her.'

Kropp turned his bristly eyebrows to Hirsch. 'And so on.'

'The Bar Council?' Hirsch said.

'It's like the police force,' Kropp said, plenty of nastiness in it. 'The first rule is, look after your mates.'

Hirsch looked away. Far off down the street, Logan's ex-wife was climbing into an ancient Toyota. The motor caught, toxins belched.

'Nice looking woman,' he said.

'Married young,' Kropp said. 'Logan likes them young, quote unquote.'

'Young as in . . .'

'Young,' Kropp said.

Encouraged by Kropp's manner, Hirsch said, 'I still need a word with Ray Latimer, Sarge.'

'How many times do I have to say it? Lay off.'

Hirsch e-mailed snaps of Venn, Logan and Coulter to Rosie DeLisle, using his phone on top of one of the town's seven hills, then bought a ham and salad roll from the café and drove slowly north. Tiverton came into view, the grain silo a stub on the horizon. The sky was huge and empty but faintly smudged out near the Razorback and then his phone came into range again.

Rosie DeLisle, saying, 'You think these characters are involved?'

'Call it a hunch. Call it webs of influence. Also the fact that Ian Logan is said to enjoy young girls.'

'I'll see what I can find.'

The next caller was Finola Armstrong, telling him that Craig Latimer was setting fires in the long grass next to her house.

26

Hirsch found a fallow paddock inside the Latimer property line, consisting mostly of dying grass, red dirt and star thistles, except for a vivid smudge of sooty earth the size of a schoolyard hard against the fence. Dirty red hieroglyphics scored the blackness, the spoor of fire-fighters and their trucks. Only one truck and four men remained now, Tiverton volunteers mopping up, together with one hopeful neighbour with a drum of water, a Honda pump, a hose and a teenage son on the back. The Mount Bryan truck had been and gone. Steam rose and hissed. Smoke wisped in the breeze.

'Could have been worse,' one of the volunteers said.

Hirsch eyed the fence. Four charred posts, drooping wires, and a metre of blackness creeping onto Finola Armstrong's property. Another hundred metres and it would have reached her sheds, her house. He could see her car in the yard. Couldn't see the Latimers' house: it lay on the other side of a rise.

All those hectares and Craig Latimer comes to the

boundary fence to light his fire? No sign of the boy or his father or grand-father. Carrying out some damage control somewhere? Presumably Jack was at school. What was Craig doing home from school?

Hirsch got behind the wheel again and headed back along Bitter Wash Road to the Vimy Ridge gates. Parked, and followed voices to the back yard, one voice bellowing, 'I'll give you something to cry about, snivelling little wretch.'

Latimer, panting, veins popping, swinging one huge paw in a back swing, the other clamped to his son's neck and, before Hirsch could act, landing an almighty whack on the back of the boy's legs.

'Mr Latimer!'

Latimer's arm froze at the top of its arc. He let it flop, straightened his back. 'Stay out of this.'

'If you strike your son again, I'll arrest you.'

'You're joking.'

'No joke.'

'Know what the little shit's done?'

'That's what I'm here to find out.'

'He was caught lighting matches and throwing them in the grass.'

'Let him go.'

Latimer shoved the boy from him, face wrenched in disgust. 'You great sooky calf, get cleaned up and go to your room. I'm not finished with you.'

'You are if you intend to hit him,' Hirsch said.

Craig was mucousy, helpless. 'Please, Dad, I didn't mean it. I was just—'

Latimer aimed a kick at him. Hirsch grabbed his arm. 'I mean it, Mr Latimer. Touch him again and I'll do you for assault.'

'It's private.'

'No it's not. It involves me, now. It involves Mrs Armstrong. It involves the firemen. Is Jack at school?'

Latimer blinked. 'What?'

'Is Jack at school?'

'Of course.'

'Why didn't Craig go?'

'I thought he had. I thought Finola had taken him to the bus.'

'Where's your father?'

'He's . . . what? He's gone to the bank, if you must know.'

Hirsch supposed it was possible the boy had heard talk of hard times and falling income, and decided a fire would bring in insurance money. The more likely explanation was a lot simpler: family circumstances, recent and historic, had messed with his head.

Latimer was still panting. His hair flopped from heat and exertion, one wing of his shirt had escaped his belt and ash streaked his trousers and boots. He looked half mad, in fact, and Hirsch stiffened in readiness—but then saw acceptance and good sense along with a dose of self-pity come creeping back through the big frame and craggy head.

'Are you arresting Craig?'

'Should I?'

'He's just a kid.'

'Let's go inside, make a pot of tea, have a talk,' Hirsch said. He saw that he had ash on his toecaps. He polished them on his trousers and thought, why did I do that?

Dust balls in the kitchen corners, a cornflakes packet on its side, a tide mark in the sink, newspapers piled on a couple of the chairs, unopened bills tucked between a pair of rotting apples in a cane basket. All of the love had gone from the room, the house, with the death of Alison Latimer.

Watching Raymond slump at the table, Hirsch filled the kettle. He could see defeat in the heavy shoulders. Then, as if sensing the scrutiny, Latimer lifted his head. 'You don't know what it's like.'

Hirsch sighed. Did he want to hear this? He pulled out a chair and sat opposite Latimer. Behind him the tap dripped and the electric kettle woke softly. 'Tell me.'

Latimer ran his hands down his cheeks as if searching for a starting point. Or choosing from many starting points. 'My son hasn't been coping very well.'

'With your wife's death.'

'Before that. He didn't want to go to Redruth High but we had no choice, the St Peter's fees were crippling us.'

'He found it hard to settle in?'

Latimer nodded glumly. 'And then Allie moved out and he felt let down. Abandoned. And then she shot herself. Maybe he felt he was to blame, I don't know.'

Latimer moved uncomfortably in his chair. 'It didn't help matters when Fin started staying over a few nights a week. I probably should have waited a bit. But it wasn't as if Allie and I had been getting on, not for years, really. I thought it would be good for the boys, a woman in the house.'

Hirsch didn't believe a word of it. 'It was Mrs Armstrong who caught Craig throwing lit matches into the grass.'

Latimer shook his head as if still amazed. 'The little bugger said he wasn't well, wanted to spend the day in bed, but when she went across to her house to do some chores, she spotted him in the paddock.'

The kettle began tearing at the silence. It shut off. Hirsch got up and hunted for mugs and teabags. 'Black? White? Sugar?'

'White and two,' Latimer mumbled.

Hirsch smacked everything onto the table. The surface was streaked and smeared, as if swiped at rather than cleaned. Latimer made no move to drink his tea. Hirsch sipped and realised the mug was greasy.

He said, 'Ray, please don't hit Craig again. What he needs is counselling.'

Latimer winced. 'How much is that going to cost me?'

Hirsch stared. 'You want him to go on lighting fires? What if someone dies?' Then he thought of the killer: 'What if someone sues you for a million dollars? One of your neighbours, for example, or the wind farm company?'

The mention of money got Latimer's attention. He brought his face back under control. 'I'll get him some help. No joke. I mean it.'

'Try the school. They'll have access to suitable counsellors. So will your family doctor.'

'McAskill,' muttered Latimer.

'There you go.'

A leaking tap got to Hirsch, drips falling with audible plinks. He pushed his chair back, stood, stepped across to the sink. The hot tap was dripping into a cereal bowl, which was piled atop three or four days' worth of cereal bowls. He twisted the tap handle, realising at once it was fully off. The washer needed replacing, and he recalled Wendy Street's words, that the Latimers spent their money on high-end farm equipment and breeding stock, not the upkeep of the house. He returned to the table.

The farmer lifted his massive head and muttered, 'Got to get that fixed.'

'Yes.'

'Is Fin going to press charges?'

'I've yet to speak to her.'

'Is she going to sue for damages?'

'Like I said . . .'

'Tell her I'll pay.'

'Tell her yourself.'

'Yeah, well, she walked out on me.'

There was a thump from the distant reaches of the house. Latimer ignored it, but when Hirsch shoved back his chair and ran, Latimer caught on quickly. Both men clattered down the hallway, an unlovely passage through the house, the wind of their passing agitating another crop of dust balls.

The sign was a relic from primary school art class, 'Craig's Room' in coloured wooden letters stuck to a board. Hirsch gave a token knock and went straight in.

Craig Latimer was handballing a slack football against the

curtain, the ball punching the fabric and falling to the floor. Over and over again. He didn't register the alteration to the air, so Hirsch grabbed his arm. 'Craig.'

The tension went out of the boy. He slid to the floor, his back against the bed, his forehead on his knees. His shoulders heaved, strangled words leaked out of him.

'Stop mumbling,' Latimer snarled.

Hirsch shot him a look and joined Craig on the floor. 'She *left* us, she just cleared out,' that's what the boy was saying, and Hirsch guessed that the father had said it first and the boy had learned to recite it.

I'm out of my depth here, he thought. And then the bed slid away on the slippery floor, responding to the pressure of their spines—as if everything was not quite right.

Hirsch swung around onto his knees. 'Your dad and I thought it might make you feel better to talk to someone. Not me, not him, not your grandparents. A nice person who will listen and not judge.'

His eyes crazy, the boy shrieked, 'I'm not crazy.'

'You'd better leave,' Raymond said.

27

Hirsch left the Latimer place and went next door, where Finola Armstrong told him a little of her recent history.

'When Eric died, men came crawling out of the woodwork. I suppose they thought I'd be an easy touch.'

'Did that include Ray Latimer?'

She shook her head. 'His *father*, randy old goat.'

They contemplated that. Armstrong said, 'I think Ray was sniffing around a nurse at the time.'

They were seated on a pair of frayed veranda chairs, behind an untamed vine. Hirsch caught glimpses of her yard and sheds and heat-stunned sheepdog and the dusty HiLux through the glossy leaves. Owing to the angle of the house, the burnt patch of grass and star thistles lay a few degrees out of sight.

He said, 'But you got talking and things developed because there'd been a grass fire.'

'Yes.'

'And now we have another fire.'

'Uh huh. But that *first* fire,' Armstrong said, 'we blamed on a cigarette tossed out a car window.'

Hirsch, his gaze alighting on the farm dog, saw it take a bite of the air and subside. A fly buzzed at its eyes. It snapped its jaws again. 'You think it was Craig?'

She smiled, unclouded by doubt. 'I'm sure of it.'

'But this time you caught him at it.'

She nodded. 'I'd just come back from dropping Jack off at school.' She paused, shook her head in disgust. 'More fool me. Why should I do the school run? Not my kids.'

'You took Jack, not Craig?' checked Hirsch.

'He didn't show for breakfast and I didn't think it was my job to get him ready for school. I mean, he's fourteen and he's not my kid. Anyway, when I get back, Ray's sitting at the kitchen table, going, "Did you think to buy milk? Did you pick up the *Advertiser*?" He wanted me to drive all the way back and get his precious milk and newspaper. Needless to say we had an almighty row and I walked out.' She shook her head. 'Call it a temporary insanity. Can't believe I contemplated moving in.'

Armstrong wore boots, jeans and a checked shirt. A practical woman, who for a time had had her head turned by a man whose sons were losing the plot and who might have arranged the murder of his wife.

Hirsch said, 'And meanwhile Craig's not in bed but out in the paddock throwing lighted matches on the ground?'

'I spotted him as I was driving in.'

'Any theories?'

'Yes. He's fucked in the head, pardon my French. Last

summer he learns he's not so special: his old man's broke and he has to attend the local high school. And this morning? Take your pick: his mother's suicide, me being around, the way his father and grandfather treat him, life at school . . . All of the above.'

'Have there been other fires?'

'Not that I know of.' She stared at him. 'That boy needs help, before it escalates. You can see how dry it is, and a hot summer coming up.'

'Mr Latimer said he'll find a counsellor for Craig.'

'They all need it,' Armstrong said, with honeyed bitterness.

'In what way?'

'Craig's a pyromaniac in the making, Jack's just sad, the old man is a bully and a sadist, and so is Ray. And lazy. He would sit around watching TV and drinking beer and expect me to cook and clean for him. I've got a farm to run. So has he, except he's stuffed that up.'

Hirsch said, 'His treatment of the boys.'

'What about it?'

'Do I need to inform children's services?'

'Ah.' Armstrong paused, and shook her head. 'Ray's hard on them,' she said, 'but he's not negligent. Not really.'

'Mrs Armstrong, where's the ring he gave you?'

'You don't miss much.'

Hirsch waited, and after a while Finola Armstrong said, 'Like I said, the youngest boy is sad, and it turns out one of the things he's sad about is the fact that I was wearing his mother's ring.'

She gave Hirsch a look, a crumpling of defences. 'I had

no idea it was hers. I thought he'd bought it specially for me.' She coughed and swallowed. 'I challenged Ray. He said the ring was special, special to *him*, it had been his mother's ring. I gave it back. Couldn't wear it.'

They each stared at nothing. Finola Armstrong broke the silence. 'That was probably the beginning of the end. The other big thing was money.'

'Money?'

'Something about his wife being due an inheritance but it hadn't been released yet and could I tide him over with a loan? Or better still, we could get married and amalgamate our properties into one big one.'

'While you cooked and cleaned.'

'Exactly.'

Armstrong rubbed her palms on her thighs, embarrassed. 'I know I went a bit crazy this year. You know, love is blind and all that, but at the same time I do have a head on my shoulders.'

She indicated the house, sheds and farmland with a little sweep of her hand, and Hirsch knew she had survived, even prospered, using her own wits. She was a good farmer, a good manager. She was canny. A partnership with the Latimers would not have been canny.

'I've just been next door,' Hirsch said, 'and Mr Latimer said he'd be happy to pay for the damaged fence.'

'I should hope so. But I imagine he wants to know if I'll take further action. Tell him no. I'm well rid of that mob.'

Hirsch got up to go. She cleared her throat, and he waited. 'I was at my sister's when Alison Latimer died.'

Hirsch agreed that she was.

'And Ray was in the lockup and his father was away with Craig and Jack.'

'Yes . . .'

'It's just that Ray and Leonard kept reminding me of that, drilling it into me, as if it might be important.' She shrugged. 'That's all. Thought I'd mention it.'

After a beat, Hirsch nodded. 'Glad you did.'

28

He returned to Vimy Ridge.

Kropp was there, waiting on the veranda, his police Explorer gleaming in the driveway. Hirsch said, 'I suppose your mate called you?'

'Don't get on your high horse, son. The man's a mess. His wife, and now this.'

Sounds from within, the wailing boy and the murmuring father. 'Sarge, I'm dealing with it.'

Kropp ignored him, stared out across the landscape to the Razorback. 'You went to see the Armstrong woman?'

'Yes.'

'And?'

'Not interested in pressing charges. Expects Mr Latimer to pay for fence repairs.'

Kropp nodded. 'Okay, this is how it pans out. A passing motorist flicked a cigarette out the window, setting off a grass fire. Local units attended, and with the help of neighbours the blaze was quickly extinguished. That's the public face. Privately, the kid gets counselling, the blokes manning the trucks get a six-pack of beer each, and everyone's happy. All right?'

'How do you know I haven't already managed to negotiate most of that? You think because I'm a dog and a maggot I'm not also a good policeman? Fuck you, Sarge.'

Kropp blinked. 'I beg your pardon?'

'You heard.'

Kropp looked amused. 'Fair enough. Now, let me sit with my friend for a while. You head on back to town.'

'I've still not spoken to Mr Latimer about his wife. He won't return calls, he won't open the door to me, and I've had enough. No more bullshit from him, and no more from you, Sarge. For Christ's sake, five minutes after his wife dies, he moves his girlfriend in? How broken up can the guy be?'

The men stared at each other. 'The super asked me to prepare a brief for the coroner and that's what I'm trying to do,' Hirsch said. 'If interested parties refuse to speak to me, how does that look? It looks like guilt, it looks like having something to hide. I don't care that Ray Latimer is your mate, stalwart of the football club and all-round good bloke, or that he suffered a tragic loss: I am not leaving until I've sat down with him and asked my questions.'

After a gap in time, Kropp said, 'I worked with Marcus Quine, you know. In the early days, Port Adelaide.'

Hirsch said nothing.

'He got the job done.'

Hirsch said nothing.

'But he did cut corners.'

Was that an admission that Hirsch had got it right about Quine? He continued to watch the sergeant.

'But in the end,' Kropp said, 'I don't care if a fellow police member swindles the Children's Hospital and violates a busload of nuns. You do not betray him.' Kropp didn't wait for a reply but banged his way into the house, calling, 'Ray? You there?'

Surprised, Hirsch followed his sergeant, catching up just as Kropp rapped his knuckles on the bedroom door, calling, 'Ray? It's Bill. We need a quiet word about Allie.'

Hirsch grabbed his arm. 'Sarge?'

'What?'

'Butt out.'

Kropp shook him off. 'What, you don't think I can do the job properly if a friend's involved? Wake up to yourself, mate.'

'Sarge, if you sit in on my interview with Mr Latimer, my report will say so. If you say one word to, or for, Mr Latimer during that interview, my report will say so. And what Superintendent Spurling or the coroner make of that I can only guess, but it won't look good.'

'You're a grade-A cunt, son,' Kropp said.

'Sarge.'

Kropp stomped out, a heavy man, brutally unhappy. The front door slammed. Hirsch heard the Explorer roar and kick up a little gravel.

Latimer insisted on using his study, a dim, unloved cave, the lone armchair a long way from the desk. 'Mr Latimer,' Hirsch began.

Latimer started talking. 'No one will tell me when or even whether I'll get the inheritance. Do you know? If the inquest shows she shot herself while of unsound mind, that won't affect the inheritance, right? It's unrelated? Only I know some insurance policies won't pay out on a suicide, but this isn't an insurance policy, it's an inheritance. The state can't touch it, can they?'

Hirsch blinked. He was always meeting men and women who had the emotional intelligence of a slab of concrete, but it never failed to surprise him. 'Mr Latimer, you agreed to talk to me about your wife. I can't advise you on the legalities or otherwise of an inheritance.'

But if you killed her I'll see you don't get a penny of it.

'I've got nothing to hide,' Latimer said.

'Very well. What was Alison's state of mind in the last few weeks and months of her life?'

'Depressed. Irrational,' Latimer said. His dark, hard man's good looks contracted. 'Made our lives a living hell.'

'In what way?'

'Didn't look after herself. The place was a mess. Forgot to cook or shop. Screaming her head off at us one minute, crying how sorry she was the next. Then in the last few days this sort of calmness came over her. I can't describe it.'

'She was happy?'

'I wouldn't say happy. More ... like she'd come to a decision.'

'A decision to leave the marriage now that she had an inheritance to fall back on.'

Latimer shook his head. 'That wasn't it. More like she'd decided to end it all.'

'Not upbeat, happy, looking forward to the near future?'

'Who have you been talking to? That bitch across the road? She wasn't here, Allie's parents weren't here, you certainly weren't here. I was. Craig was. Ask him.'

'And Jack?'

'You leave Jack out of this. He's just a little kid. He's not . . . strong.'

Unlike Craig, thought Hirsch. 'Did your wife threaten suicide at any time in the last weeks and months?'

'No. But she had tried once before.'

Had she? Hirsch was having doubts. There was no direct evidence, only hearsay. 'Was she depressed by nature?'

'Up and down.'

'What was her relationship with your father like?'

Latimer bristled. 'What relationship? What are you implying?'

Hit a nerve there, thought Hirsch. He spelled it out: 'From all accounts, she had a close and happy relationship with your mother. She had a close and happy relationship with Mrs Street across the road. That's what I mean by relationship. Was she close to your father or did they quarrel? I understand he's a . . . forceful man.'

'My father loved her like she was his own. If she was nervy around him that says a lot about her, not him.'

'Did he urge her to pay the inheritance into the business rather than leave the marriage?'

'My father's not the type to interfere like that. His view

was I was well rid of her. She was splitting up the family, taking Jack away with her. Craig chose to stay with me.'

'Well, did *you* urge her to reconsider? The farm's struggling, you told me that yourself. The inheritance would have helped carry you over until prices improve or we get some rain.'

Latimer curled his lip. 'And you know something about farming, do you? Look, we're not that far gone. It's all cyclical anyway. You wouldn't know that, being on a regular salary.' He grinned crookedly. 'Plus your other perks.'

Hirsch bit. 'Mine? Or do you mean all police officers get perks?'

'You. I know all about you. Happy to skim the cream until it goes bad, then you dob the others in to save your own skin.'

Hirsch smiled. 'So your wife's inheritance *wouldn't* have been a godsend? Surely it would have eased the pressure? Craig could have returned to his boarding school. Apparently he was happy there.'

'A hundred and sixty thousand dollars doesn't go far, not if you're on the land. All I wanted to do was save my marriage, not grab Allie's inheritance.'

'But you just said she made your lives a misery.'

'Only at the end, it would've blown over.'

'If she did make your lives a misery, perhaps it was because you had other women.'

'I still loved her.'

'Really? You told Mrs Armstrong *last year* that the marriage was over.'

'I never said that. She misunderstood.'

'You were quick to move her in.'

'Not that quick.'

Hirsch let the silence build for a while.

'She's being magnanimous about the fire.'

Latimer shrugged.

'She could have pressed charges against your son.'

Latimer grew heated. 'Didn't take her long to shoot through on me, though, did it? Didn't stay around long once the shit hit the fan. And have you seen the state the fence was in? Half-falling down, and now I suppose she wants me to spend top dollar fixing it.'

Hirsch was fascinated. 'I think the engagement ring was the final straw.'

'What do you mean?'

'She thought you'd bought it specially.'

'It was my mother's ring. Do what the hell I want with it.'

'You gave it to your wife.'

'Of course. Then when she left me I got it back.'

'She left it here when she went to stay at her parents'?'

'Yes.'

'But she had a close and loving relationship with your mother and it would have meant a great deal to her to wear the ring.'

'Who knows what went on in her mind. Can we stop now?'

'Returning to the inheritance.'

'Do we have to?'

'At the start of the interview you seemed quite concerned that you might not get it. But now it's no big deal?'

'Of course it'll help, I'm not an idiot. I've got two mouths to feed and no one to help me.'

'What were your thoughts when you heard about the inheritance?'

Latimer looked dumb. 'Nothing much.'

'Well, did you think it would save the farm from ruin? Did you fear it would give your wife a measure of independence, give her the nerve to leave you? That wouldn't look too good, would it? Make you look a bit of a fool?'

'I don't have to listen to this. Why don't you just shove off and leave us alone.'

'What time did you and Mrs Armstrong go to Redruth the weekend your wife died?'

'In time for the footy. And I was with her until I got arrested. And I was in the lockup when Allie died, okay?'

Then Latimer's face altered, a look almost of glee. 'Where are you going with this? You looking at Finola?'

'She's in the clear. But why are you pointing me at her? As far as you're concerned, your wife committed suicide.'

'That's what I think, yeah. If you'd had to live here with her, it's what *you'd* think, too. But for some reason you've got it in for my father and me, probably talking to that bitch across the road.' He shrugged. 'I'm indulging you, it amuses me.'

'Did you break your wife's hand one day, Mr Latimer? Bend her fingers back? Slam it in the car door?'

'Fucking get out.'

Hirsch thought about it. He could have gone home to talk to the furniture again. Instead, he said, 'Mr Latimer, where's the second twenty-two rifle?'

He pointed to the gun cabinet on the wall.

'What?'

'You have two rifles like that: the one that killed your wife and one other.'

'What, you checking on my licences?'

'A Ruger and a Brno. Where's the other one? In the ute? The shed?'

'Fucked if I know. Why?'

'Because your son is unravelling and might decide to shoot himself. Or you.'

That got Latimer going.

They didn't find the rifle in the ute, the sheds, the car, cupboards, wardrobes, under beds. That left one room still unsearched.

Craig Latimer was curled up on his bed, a damp, blotchy, unlovely lump of a boy, his meaty spine turned to them. Latimer sat, placed a big hand on an unresponsive shoulder. 'Son? Where's the twenty-two we keep in the ute?'

Craig rolled onto his back. 'I dunno.'

'You haven't been taking pot-shots at tin cans?'

'Not me! Jack.'

Latimer gaped. 'Jack?'

'Him and Katie Street.'

Hirsch stepped in. 'Craig, where is your brother?'

'Staying with Allie's parents,' Ray Latimer answered.

'Would he have taken the rifle with him?'

Craig scoffed. 'Nanna wouldn't let it in the house.'

'Perhaps your mum hid it.'

'Why would the bitch hide it?' Craig said.

After a moment, Hirsch said, 'Did your father teach you to talk about her like that? Perhaps she hid it because it wasn't being kept in a secure place.'

He left, stewing. The thing was, none of the Latimers could have killed Alison. They hated her enough, though. Given an opportunity to sweeten the memory, they hadn't taken it.

29

On a Sunday afternoon in late November when Hirsch was washing the HiLux again, maintaining standards, feeling stiff from yesterday's tennis, a new white Camry with Victorian plates entered town from the south. It slowed outside Tennant's store, braking next to the petrol bowser. A young man got out, rattled the nozzle. Hirsch knew Tennant locked it overnight and on Sundays and public holidays. Then the driver peered through the shop window, into the shadowy, closed, unlit interior. A young woman joined him. They pantomimed dejection, but that didn't last: now they were looking around for a way out of their dilemma. And there was Hirsch a short distance away, a hose in his hand, the police sign above his door. They climbed back into the Camry.

A moment later they were parked at the kerb and stepping onto his lawn. Hirsch released the spray-gun trigger, dropped the hose, wiped his palms on his jeans and thought *backpackers*. The clue was in the backpacks propped up like a pair of passengers on the back seat. Northern European? Tall, blonde, lithe, sun-browned, clear-eyed, quizzical, fearless—on just about every count they were not locals.

'We are not having benzene,' the boy said, his teeth white and straight. Board shorts, faded T-shirt, craft-market sandals.

'Petrol,' Hirsch said.

The girl said, 'This is so. Pet-rol.'

She was as tall as her boyfriend, vital, athletic, with cropped hair, tight shorts and a singlet top. Hirsch fell in love on the spot. Looks plus vitality plus accent.

'The shop's closed, I'm afraid.'

'We must be in Port Augusta for the famous Ghan and Pichi Richi trains,' the girl said, mangling the words charmingly.

Hirsch had a mental stab at their movements. A few weeks or months travelling around and across the continent, hitchhiking, taking buses and trains, maybe some fruit picking, bartending and waitressing along the way. Hiring a car occasionally, like this Hertz Camry. The Ghan ran from Adelaide, with a stop at Port Augusta, three thousand kilometres to the Timor Sea. But first, it seemed, they wanted to ride the old Pichi Richi train, a rickety little rattler that travelled a short distance near Port Augusta. He supposed there was a Hertz agency there where they could return the car.

'Please can you help us? The next town is too far for us and the last town is too far also. We are not having the petrol for these journeys.'

Hirsch thought this was something they didn't prepare

you for when they posted you to a one-man police station in the bush. He made a mental note to stock some emergency fuel. A jerrycan of unleaded, one of diesel. Man of the people. Who . . . ? he thought.

Bob Muir.

'I can take you to someone who might have some petrol.'

'*Dank.*'

Dutch? He squeezed in with the backpacks and directed them to the street where the Muirs and the Donovans lived.

Yvonne Muir answered. Eyeing the Camry and its occupants, quivering to know, she said, 'Bob's next door, setting up Leanne's new TV.'

Hirsch paused at the Camry to explain, and walked across the grass to the Donovans'. Leanne opened the door, looking red-eyed, uncombed, a little askew in battered Crocs, tracksuit pants and T-shirt. She blinked at Hirsch, said, 'Sorry, haven't had a shower yet,' and led Hirsch through to her sitting room, where she collapsed into an armchair. A mug of tea steamed on stool beside it, a cigarette burned in a saucer.

'Bob,' Hirsch said, nodding at Muir, who was kneeling on the floor beside a wall opposite Leanne's armchair, a screwdriver sticking out of the rear pocket of his overalls.

Muir nodded, said 'G'day,' and returned to his task. He'd run coaxial cable along the skirting board to a large flatscreen television, which had replaced the boxy set Hirsch recalled from his first visit. The old TV sat with its face to the wall with a coil of old ribbon cable, disgraced and ready for recycling. Ready for the rubbish tip, anyway.

The air was dense: both Muir and Leanne had cigarettes going. Hirsch wanted to cough, wave the smoke away, open a window. 'Need to ask a favour.'

Muir, still on his knees, produced a Swiss Army knife, took up the cable end. He peeled back a couple of centimetres of black outer casing, revealing the inner sheath, core and copper wire. 'Shoot,' he said.

Hirsch told him about the backpackers.

Muir grunted. 'Wouldn't be the first time. The last bloke always had a couple of drums on hand, one unleaded, one diesel.'

'I'll remember that,' Hirsch said.

'Go down the side of my place to the shed and you'll find a ten-litre jerrycan. There's a drum of unleaded against the back wall. How about I let them have twenty litres? Fifty bucks oughta cover it.'

'Thanks, Bob.'

Hirsch stepped over to the TV. 'You won't know yourself with this, Leanne.'

She smiled, tired, sad, thankful for small mercies. 'Present from Sam.'

'Nathan's mate?' said Hirsch, running his hand over the smooth plastic. 'Generous of him.'

'He won it at the pub. Doesn't need it.'

'Wish someone would give me a new TV,' Hirsch said, peering into the gap between the rear panel and the wall. 'All I've got is a little portable, lucky to get one channel, depending on the weather.'

There was nothing to say to that. Muir was fastening a

connector to the cable end, ready for the antenna socket. Leanne continued to watch him. Hirsch left them to it.

When the backpackers were gone and Bob had his fifty dollars—'Do I get a commission?' 'How about a second channel on your TV?' 'Done.'—Hirsch opened up the office and hunted through the burglary reports, going back one year. Then he walked across to the Tiverton Hotel: like the Muncowie pub on the outside but more appealing within. Dining room, main bar, side lounge, dartboard, snooker table, widescreen TV and no old-timers nursing beer.

And no raffle, not recently. Last Christmas, maybe? Always a ham at Christmas.

So Hirsch phoned a few other pubs in the area. Muncowie, Redruth. No raffles offering a TV set.

It occurred to Hirsch that he didn't know where Nathan's mate Sam lived, and asking around would only alert the guy. But he did know where they both worked.

At eight on Monday morning he walked across town to Tiverton Grains, a collection of storage and processing sheds around a huge untidy yard, run out of a cottage on a side street. Racked with sneezes, he entered the main shed, a vast echo chamber, almost empty but for a few pallets, jute bags and nameless items of equipment. Thick air, thick with grain dust. Seeing no one, hearing a truck motor and voices in the back yard, he continued through to a metal door in the back wall, stepping from dimness and scratchy air to drenching sunlight. The yard was a depressed expanse of fuel drums, rusted machinery and dead weeds next to a broad patch of oily dirt that served as employee parking. Four cars this morning, including Sam Hempel's lowered Commodore.

Hirsch headed across to an open tin structure against the back fence, a service bay. Inside it, nose out, was a grain truck, two overalls peering into the engine compartment. One of them saying, 'Give her another go.'

The motor ground over, didn't fire. With the bonnet up, Hirsch couldn't see who was behind the steering wheel but he said, 'Morning, gents,' as he approached.

Sam Hempel and an older man straightened, turned. 'Help you?' the older man said.

Hirsch drew incautiously nearer. When he said, 'I'd like a quick word with Sam,' Hempel spun round, punched him in the stomach and legged it, waving his hand in the air and yelping, 'Ow, fuck,' as he ran.

'Jesus, mate, sorry, don't know what got into him,' the older man said, touching Hirsch as if he might bite, not sure what to do.

Hirsch, sucker-punched twice in as many months, was bent double and gasping. He straightened and took off at a tormented shuffle, stomach muscles pulling. He followed the kid past the abandoned machinery and drums to the four employee cars. Hempel had vanished. Hirsch prowled between the vehicles, looking behind, under and into them, itching to look into the boot of the lowered Holden.

A whisper of cardboard or plywood against fabric, a soft booming sound, a sense of items shifting, compressing.

The rubbish skip.

Hirsch banged his fist against the metal flank. 'Sam? Come on out of there.'

After a while, 'Leave me alone.'

'Not going to happen and you know it.'

Hirsch waited. The morning was warm and still, the sun edging above the gums that marked the boundary between the town and the first wheat paddock. A vapour trail disintegrated as he watched it. Adelaide to Perth? Adelaide to Alice Springs or Darwin? He thought of the Dutch backpackers aboard the Ghan. Meanwhile Tiverton was silent, only a murmur in the background and Hempel trying not to disturb the rubbish.

'Sam? I won't give you up to Sergeant Kropp and his boys, okay? But if I have to call them in, it'll be taken out of my hands and I can't protect you. Understand?'

He could hear the boy thinking.

'I know you're frightened. If you had your time over again, you wouldn't punch me. Hell to pay for assaulting a police officer. But, you know, maybe we can work something out.'

'You promise you'll keep them Redruth jacks off me?'

'Yes.'

'Nicholson?'

'Yes.'

Still Sam weighed his options. Hirsch said, 'Nice gesture of yours, giving Leanne Donovan a TV set. She hasn't had a good trot, and it counts for a lot in my book that you did something kind for her.'

320

Silence.

'Even if the set was stolen, it was still a kindness to a woman who needed it.'

'She's good to me. And I felt bad for her because of Melia and that.'

So bad that you went on a housebreaking spree on the day she put her daughter in the ground, Hirsch thought.

'I understand,' he said. 'But we do have to talk.'

The load shifted, the metal skin boomed faintly and Hempel's red head appeared. He hoisted himself onto the rim of the dumpster, wild-eyed, oil on his jeans, hands and forearms. He was sweating as he gave the yard a jittery once-over.

'It's okay. Only me here,' Hirsch said.

Hempel jumped to the ground. His jeans slithered to his thighs. He tugged them up. 'Where we going?'

'To the station for the time being.'

'Not down Redruth?'

'No.'

'I didn't mean to hit ya.'

'I understand.'

They were moving towards Hempel's car now. Hirsch shepherding, ready to grab, bolster, protect or brain the kid. 'Keys?'

He lifted the boot lid. Two Blu-Ray players, a Game Boy, a laptop, a media dock, a Samsung Galaxy phone still in its box. All on the list. Hirsch slammed the lid, said, 'Get in,' and drove out of the yard.

Down they went to the main road, passing the general

store, into Hirsch's place of business, Sam looked around the station foyer and said, 'If I tell yous who run Melia over, can I go?'

30

Hirsch shook his head. 'First things first, Sam. Tell me about the burglaries.'

They were in the sitting room, the front door locked to deter callers. He switched on the digital recorder, stating names, date and location.

Hempel, a forlorn shape in one of the armchairs, looked on in dismay. 'Don't I need a lawyer?'

Hirsch got comfortable. 'You've every right to one, Sam. Of course once a lawyer's involved I'll formally charge you. And at that point I will throw the book at you: assaulting a police officer, resisting arrest, several counts of burglary. I'm sure I can think of a few more. Then I'd get Sergeant Kropp to put you in the Redruth lockup while I inform the homicide squad that you're a witness and maybe a suspect in the death of Melia Donovan. They don't mess around, those guys. They'll whisk you away and grill you for days. You won't see daylight for twenty years.'

He paused. 'That's if we go the formal route. You will still face charges, but I'd like to protect you from the worst of it, at this stage.'

Hempel gnawed at his lower lip.

'So,' Hirsch said, 'the break-ins.'

'It was me. I done them.'

'But you were at the service in the church, with Nathan and his mother. I saw you.'

Sam shifted in agreement and embarrassment. 'I was like, you know . . .'

'Checking out who else was there.'

'Yeah.'

'You knew these people would be absent from their homes for a couple of hours.'

'Yeah.'

'Didn't Nathan or his mother wonder where you'd gone?'

'Said I had stuff to do.'

'Where do you live at present?'

'At Nate's.'

'And before that?'

'With me mum sometimes, with me mates, mattress on the floor and that.'

Hirsch checked the recorder. Satisfied, he said, 'I've been looking at burglary and theft reports for the past twelve months. There have been several similar break-ins: farm properties over Easter, school holidays, Saturdays when people are playing sport. Was that you?'

Sam looked hunted. 'Thought you wanted to know about Melia?'

'Was that you acting alone, or did you have help?'

'I didn't kill her!'

'The burglaries, Sam: was that you acting alone or did you have help?'

'Me.'

'Was Nathan ever involved?'

'Nate? No way. The cops are always hassling him.'

'Yes. That would make it difficult for you.'

'What?'

'Nothing. You stole quite a lot of gear in the past few months. The stuff in your car, that's the tip of the iceberg. Where's the rest?'

'Sold it.'

'Bloke in a pub.'

'Yeah.'

'I'll need a name.'

'Dunno if I could find him again.'

Hirsch couldn't count how many times he'd had this conversation. 'What did he look like, this bloke in a pub? Which pub?'

'Can't remember. Somewhere down Adelaide.'

'You drive all the way to Adelaide to do your drinking? Don't answer that. Tell me why you gave Mrs Donovan one of the stolen TVs.'

'Like I told you, I felt sorry for her and that.'

'Sorry how?'

'Sorry Melia got killed. A tragedy.'

Hirsch gave him a look. 'A tragedy. You're close to the family?'

'Well, yeah. Me own family's fucked.'

'How do you know the Donovans?'

'Went to primary school with Nate. His mum useta let me doss down at their place when my mum was drinking or had a bloke over.'

'That's been a pattern for a while?'

'Years.'

'So you'd known Melia since she was a baby?'

'She was kinda like my sister.'

Sam had curled into the armchair. Fear, nerves and shame had shrunk him, it seemed to Hirsch. The kid's clumsy height and bulk counted for nothing. Here out of the light he was pale, very gingery, the hairs downy, no spring or verve at all.

'She was special to you?'

Sam shrugged.

'I've seen photos of her. A lovely girl. Beautiful, in fact.'

Bewilderment, loss and pain in Sam's face. He opened his mouth as if to speak, but said nothing.

'But a bit wild, right?' Hirsch said.

Sam wriggled his shoulders. 'I tried to look out for her.'

'Like a brother.'

'She's just a kid. She was just a kid.'

'Old enough, Sam. So you looked out for her. What about Nathan and his mother? Shouldn't they have been looking out for her?'

'What can they do, stuck here? I got more . . . I got more contacts and that. Driving around the place, I hear things.'

'Was it hard keeping your relationship with Melia a secret from her brother and her mother?'

Hempel's jaw dropped. 'What? What relationship?'

'She infuriated you sometimes? Wouldn't do what you wanted? There was a bruise on her face dating from before she was killed.'

'Fuck you. I never hit her, never touched her. I can tell ya who did.'

'Maybe she hit her head when she was in your car? Was that it?'

Sam got out of the chair, no longer an unprepossessing ten-year-old in disguise. 'I never done nothing to Melia.'

Hirsch used a whiplash voice. 'Sit down.'

Sam collapsed.

'Sam, were you the older boyfriend I've been hearing about?'

'What? No way.'

'All right, try this. You kept an eye out. You know who she spent time with. Boyfriends, girlfriends.'

'That's right.'

'You saw her with an older man.'

'Yep.'

'Well, who, Sam?'

'That magistrate bloke, Coulter.'

'Really? You know who he is?'

An ironic laugh. 'Sure.'

'How did Melia get involved with him?'

'She got done for shoplifting.'

'He was the sitting magistrate?'

'Yeah.'

'She caught his eye?'

'S'pose.'

'They went out together?'

'Could say that.'

'What would you say?'

'He took her to parties and that.'

'Anywhere else? A film, a restaurant, the pub . . .'

'She was fifteen. How's he gunna do that?'

Hirsch nodded. He said musingly, 'I had this girlfriend once, told me I wasn't good enough for her, wasn't making enough money, and who'd want to go out with a cop anyway?'

Hempel shifted, saying nothing.

Hirsch leaned forward. 'Did Melia say something like that to you, Sam? She tell you about her rich boyfriend, a guy with more wallet potential than you, rubbing your face in it?'

'No.'

'Gets under your skin, that kind of thing. No wonder you followed her around.'

'I was lookin' out for her,' Hempel said, with a whine of entreaty and complaint. 'Nothin' . . . filthy like you're suggesting.'

'You saw her with Coulter a few times, or only once?'

'Few times.'

'He must be what, thirty years older?'

Sam shrugged.

'But loaded, right? Big house, flash car.'

'I'm gunna get an apprenticeship,' Sam said, as if announcing a plan to float an internet start-up.

'So you were hurt that she chose a rich man over you?'

'No, I'm just sayin', he's no better than me. Least I never killed no one.'

Hirsch would come back to that. 'Did she ever reveal to you, or anyone else, that she was involved with David Coulter?'

'Dunno. Prob'ly Gemma.'

'Did she ever tease you about the affair?'

Hempel twisted about in his chair. '*Tease* me? Nah. Why? I told her she was makin' a big mistake, she told me to mind me own business. That's all.'

'What kind of big mistake?'

'I go, the guy's a creep, Mel, he's using you, he'll hurt you you're not careful.' A shake of the head.

'Did Nathan ever go with you when you followed Melia?'

'Like I said. The Redruth cops are on him like shit on a blanket.'

Hirsch checked the recorder again. 'Was Melia by herself when she saw Coulter, or did Gemma Pitcher accompany her sometimes?'

'A coupla times. Why?'

'How did it work? Gemma recruited Melia? Melia recruited Gemma? Or maybe Coulter recruited Gemma, who recruited Melia, or vice versa?'

'What are you on about?'

'The sex parties.'

Hempel floundered, opened and closed his mouth. 'Sex parties?'

'I have reason to believe that Gemma and Melia took part in sex parties with several men.'

'I don't know nothin' about that.' Hempel chewed his thumbnail and looked up. 'Explains some things though.'

'Like what?'

'Melia come running out of this house with nothing on, all upset, and—'

Hirsch held up a hand. 'I need details for the tape. Date, location, times . . .'

'Well,' Hempel swallowed and started again. 'It was the night she was killed.'

'Where.'

'This house outside Redruth.'

'Coulter's?'

'Don't think so. He lives over in Clare.'

'You followed her and—'

'Coulter took Mel and Gemma to this house. I was watching, and then Melia come runnin' out, no clothes on. A real mess.'

'In what way a mess?'

'Cryin' and that.'

'Where were you?'

'Behind this hedge.'

'Not in your car?'

Hempel shook his head. 'Mel knew it so I parked in the next street.'

'You didn't peer through the windows?'

'I'm not stupid.'

'So you were watching from behind a hedge and Melia came running out in distress. What did you do?'

'Happened so quick, I was gunna go and help her but Coulter come out. He was ropeable. He sees her runnin' down the street and he gets in his car and runs her down.'

The silence ticked. Hirsch said, 'Was it deliberate, do you think?'

Sam hoisted one shoulder fractionally. 'He was pretty pissed off.'

'What happened then? Did anyone come out to see? Did you show yourself?'

'No way. Coulter puts Melia in the boot and drives off.'

'It was definitely Coulter?'

'I reckernised him. I reckernised his car.'

'Which was?'

'Silver Land Cruiser, the flash one.'

Hirsch looked at Hempel intently. 'Were there other cars parked at or near the house?'

'A few.'

'Whose, do you know?'

'I guess.'

'Perhaps you could tell me, Sam,' Hirsch said, exquisitely patient.

'There was like, Dr McAskill's Mercedes. That real estate guy's Lexus. Ian Logan's Audi. Len Latimer's Range Rover. Plus two BMWs I didn't know who they were, and, um, this Chrysler.'

'Go back a bit: Len Latimer?'

'Him and Ray,' Sam said. He smirked. 'And was Ray in big trouble.'

'What do you mean?'

'Well, his wife was there, wasn't she?'

'At the party?'

Sam gave Hirsch a doofus look. 'No, *watchin' the place*, like me. She must of followed in her car.'

'Was she behind a hedge?'

Hempel shook his head. 'Parked up the road a bit.'

Motive, Hirsch thought. 'Tell me about the Chrysler.'

'Dunno who drove it. New South plates, but.'

'It was a New South Wales car?'

'Yeah. Big black thing.'

'Let's go back to Melia Donovan. Coulter drove off with her in the boot of his car.'

'Yeah.'

'What did you do?'

'I wasn't gunna stick around.'

'What time was this?'

'I dunno, late. Midnight, maybe.'

'Sam, when we found Melia, she was fully dressed.'

He shrugged. 'Come runnin' out starkers but had all her gear with her.'

Hirsch pictured it, the empty road in the moonlight, clumsy hands dressing a limp body before throwing it into a ditch. 'Can you think of a reason why David Coulter would drive all the way up to Muncowie to dump the body?'

'Easy, 's where I live. Me mum does, I mean.'

Hirsch closed his eyes. For want of a few key questions, he thought. And when he'd asked Leanne Donovan if she knew of anyone in her daughter's life from Muncowie, why hadn't she mentioned Sam Hempel?

Because Sam wasn't her daughter's friend, he was Nathan's.

'But what's the connection? What's it got to do with Coulter that you live there, or you did?'

'Frame me, what else?'

Not impossible, Hirsch thought. If you were sick and devious. Melia told Coulter about Sam. Probably shared a laugh with him over the sad boy who had a crush on her.

'Saddle up: we're going for a drive.'

They took Sam's car. The wrong people might recognise Hirsch's Nissan, and they'd certainly know the HiLux. Hirsch drove. The Commodore was difficult to start and it stalled a few times, then took a long while to reach ninety, at which speed it shook so hard Hirsch had to back off to eighty-five. His seat sagged. Dope, cigarette and beer odours, deep in the fabrics, came alive with his body heat. A sun-bleached dog nodded its head on the dashboard, the steering wheel belonged on a racing car and the fuel gauge didn't work. Take your hands off the wheel and the car drifted to the right. Correction: *leapt* to the right.

'Nice wheels.'

'Piece a shit,' Sam said.

Down the long, shallow valley between hills and crops to Redruth. The road shimmered. Hirsch had never seen so many mirages before this bush posting. A farmer stood in a corner of his wheat, rubbing a grain head between his palms, and then they were trundling past, waiting for the next little bit of rural business.

'Soon be harvest time,' Hirsch said, as if he had any idea.

Sam's bottom jaw peeled away from the top. It was

entirely possible that he'd lived here all his life and had no sense of its patterns. A Pioneer bus passed, another farmer, this one kicking at a clod of dirt, crows along a wire, some dust out there in the blue-smudge hills.

Then they were passing through Redruth. Hempel directed Hirsch out past the motel and up a side street that became a dirt road leading up into one of the town's many hills. Over a rise, Hempel saying, 'That one.'

A little collection of newer houses far apart, semi-farmland, small garden sheds, clumps of ornamental and native trees and a couple of reedy ponds, mostly mud now. Outside the house Sam indicated was a leaning sign staked in unmown grass. *For Sale Venn Realty*.

That made sense.

The house itself was sizeable, a pale brick structure about twenty years old, a little outmoded but solid, roomy, semi-secluded.

Hedges and shrubs.

Hirsch stopped the car. 'Where were you hiding?'

Sam pointed. The hedge was a bulky stripe of dark green along the eastern flank of the house.

'Mrs Latimer?'

A gateway fifty metres west.

'You recognised her car, or did you actually see her?'

'Both.'

'Did she see you?'

'Dunno. Don't think so.'

'She didn't go inside, remonstrate with her husband?'

'What?'

'Sam, did she get out of the car and go into the house?'

'Not while I was there.'

Spied on her husband, and a day or two later she'd gone to live with her parents. And a few days after that she had died. Been killed. Had she confronted Ray? *I saw you. I know what you're up to.*

'Where was the Chrysler?'

Sam pointed to the driveway, a grand sweep of gravel. 'They were all parked along there.'

'A big black Chrysler with New South Wales plates.'

'Yeah,' Sam said. And he rattled off the number.

31

It was afternoon now. Hirsch delivered Sam to Croome and DeLisle in Adelaide and headed back to Tiverton. A five-hour round trip. Lengthening shadows striped the crops, the highway, the hillsides. More birds on more wires. An air of waiting, of things drying, turning to dust.

It was late afternoon before he could begin tracking the black Chrysler. The New South Wales vehicle registry told him the car belonged to one Daryl Metcalfe, a Broken Hill address. One fine for speeding, but not in the Chrysler.

Next Hirsch contacted the main Broken Hill police station, jumping through various hoops until finally a sergeant agreed to talk to him.

'That car was reported stolen.'

The logical question was, 'By Pullar and Hanson?'

'What? No. Same kind of car, I guess. No, Pullar and Hanson haven't set foot in Broken Hill to the best of my knowledge. Plus their Chrysler was found burnt out near Townsville, wasn't it?'

'Okay, so . . .'

'So the car you're asking about was reported stolen here last week.'

Last week? Hirsch tried to digest that. 'Who reported it?'

Hirsch heard the clicking of keys. 'Woman called Sandra Chatterton.'

'According to the DMV it's owned by a Daryl Metcalfe.'

'Goodness, you have done your homework,' sneered the Broken Hill sergeant. He paused and Hirsch pictured him reading a screen. 'According to this, Chatterton is Metcalfe's daughter. She's looking after his place while he's overseas for six months.'

That ruled Metcalfe out. But what other men did Chatterton have in her life?

Or maybe no one borrowed the car—maybe Sandra Chatterton was another Gemma Pitcher or Melia Donovan.

'If it's the same car,' Hirsch said, 'someone was driving it in my neck of the woods back in September.'

'And that's significant how?'

'A suspicious death.' Hirsch thought about it and said, '*Two* suspicious deaths.'

'Want us to look into it?'

'Have to clear it with my boss, who will talk to your boss,' Hirsch said.

At six the next morning, Hirsch, wearing his police uniform, was driving his Nissan north along the Barrier Highway. He guessed he'd be breaching regulations in a few hours' time, conducting South Australian police business across the border in New South Wales, but he was pretty close to not giving a shit about the niceties these days. It might be days, weeks, before requests moved through official channels, and wearing a uniform would help when he questioned Chatterton. And her father, if he'd returned from overseas.

Still, he shifted a little uncomfortably, picturing Superintendent Spurling's response if he found out.

Three and a half hours, 350 kilometres, glued to the speed limit across an ochre landscape, under a vast sky. Eagles, stone chimneys silhouetted, an inclination to stone and grit, not dirt. Stone reefs, smudges of bluebush, saltbush, mallee scrub and lone demented ewes. A hawk diving, a crow watching. Road trains, trucks, cars, the emptiness ahead and behind and shimmering lakes that dematerialised as the highway slipped beneath him. Hirsch didn't like any of it, not exactly, but it felt less alien than it had when he first set foot out here. Not home, but a place vaguely familiar to him.

He'd never been to Broken Hill. It was both modern and old, bright and dull, smaller and richer and shabbier than he'd imagined. Plenty of dusty four-wheel-drives and older sedans and station wagons on streets named for the mineral wealth it was built on: Gypsum, Garnet, Argent, Silica, Calcite . . . Not a lot of green in the garden beds. Local colours: dusty reds and greys and olives. A baking noon sun.

Daryl Metcalfe's house was a low burnt-brick building with a blinding, unpainted corrugated iron roof, mostly dead garden and empty carport. And he'd not long returned from his travels, keen to tell Hirsch all about his long-service leave working for a United Nations outfit in sub-Saharan Africa. 'My field's water: conservation, drainage, irrigation, well-sinking . . .'

They were in the man's sitting room, Metcalfe about fifty, blockish but fit looking. A widower looking for some meaning in his life, Hirsch thought.

He glanced at the young woman beside Metcalfe on a huge green leather sofa, sinking into it, you'd struggle to get out. 'And Sandra's been looking after the place while you were away?'

'She lives here,' Metcalfe said, glancing at his daughter with a level of sadness.

Chatterton was a pixie, a wisp, slender, her black hair cropped to a cap around her skull. Jeans, a scrap of T-shirt that showed her pale stomach. She looked no more than seventeen, but Hirsch knew she was twenty-five.

He smiled at her. 'Someone pinched your dad's car just before he got back last week?'

She nodded, and Hirsch wondered if she didn't trust her voice.

Metcalfe patted her knee while watching Hirsch with suspicion. 'Why are the South Australia police interested?'

Hirsch kept it vague. 'A car matching the description was seen in the vicinity of an incident in the Redruth area.'

'Wasn't me,' Chatterton whispered.

Hirsch wondered about the surname. Mother's name? Maybe she was married. 'I'm not suggesting it was you, I just need to eliminate the car.'

'Consider it eliminated,' Metcalfe said. 'Sandy wouldn't

have taken it out.' He had a sweet, benighted face, a powerful frame and sun-scorched skin. Like Bob Muir, a quiet, slow, tolerant man who'd probably never committed a crime in his life. The daughter was a different matter. She'd begun exhibiting meth twitches as she sat there, her skin crawling. She looked unfinished, a wraith beside her big father, and could barely meet Hirsch's eye.

'Sandy,' he said gently, 'what day did you discover the car was missing?'

'Tuesday, when I got home from work.'

'She does odd jobs for the council,' Metcalfe said.

'And you flew in from overseas the next day?' Hirsch asked him.

'That's right.'

'You reported it to the police, Sandy?'

She jiggled, blinked and managed a nod. Metcalfe patted her knee fondly, but there was a tightness in him. 'She's a good girl,' he said. 'But she's had a rough trot these past few years. Husband used to knock her around. Health issues.'

Like addiction. She was barely holding it together now, and Hirsch thought she might fracture if he pushed. He smiled a smile that said he understood and hadn't come to judge. What he wanted to say was: 'You sold your dad's car to buy drugs, right?'

Instead he said, 'Did the neighbours see anything?'

Sandra Chatterton shook her head violently.

'Not her fault,' Metcalfe said.

The stress was there in his voice. As if he thought the sky might fall in if he didn't hold it up and he'd been holding it up for years and years and one day it would fall in despite his best efforts. He rested his solid hand on his daughter's knee, great pain in his deeply recessed eyes.

Sam Hempel had seen a black Chrysler bearing Daryl Metcalfe's plates parked at a house in the mid-north of South Australia as far back as September: over two months ago. Katie Street and Jack Latimer had seen it too, passing through Tiverton. And Katie had seen it again, a few days later, as if it hadn't left the district, or had returned.

'Do you know anyone down in South Australia, Sandra?'

She shook her head so hard the cropped hair seemed to ripple.

He said off-handedly, 'You've never been to parties down there?'

Another violent shake.

'What is this?' Metcalfe demanded, uneasy, his high forehead damp.

Then an alteration in him. He looked fully at his daughter, full of regard and suffering and forgiveness. 'Sandy?' he said, his voice a loving, low rasp, pebbles slipping off a shovel.

It was enough to flip her. Her head dropped, her hands went to her ears. 'I didn't mean it, I'm sorry.'

'You sold the car to buy drugs?' her father asked gently.

'No, I swear.'

'You owed people for drugs?'

'No!'

Hirsch was content to watch and listen. An old drama was playing out, the devoted father, the beloved daughter and her demons.

'I went on a trip,' she muttered.

Metcalfe glanced at Hirsch as if seeking permission to continue. Hirsch gave him a nod.

'Where, sweetheart?'

'I wanted to see the sea.'

Hirsch could understand that. He said, 'The nearest water is Port Augusta.'

'I went there and then I went a bit further.'

'When was this?'

Sandra Chatterton's knee jiggled. Hirsch could see the poor thin bone inside the fabric of her jeans. 'My birthday.'

The father looked pained. 'Beginning of September.'

'What happened, Sandy?'

'I ended up in Port Pirie.'

You could usually get a deal in a port town, Hirsch knew. A deal with a big shiny car as collateral. 'And?'

'I hooked up with these guys,' she told her father, full of apology.

He patted her knee.

'I wasn't using, Dad, honestly. I've been getting my act together. But it was my birthday, and you know, you weren't around . . .'

'It's all right, sweetie.'

'We got busted,' Chatterton said.

Hirsch said carefully, 'By the police in Port Pirie?'

'We were in this motel room, not making any noise or anything, not really partying or anything, and they came storming in.'

'You were charged? Fined? Jailed?'

'One of the guys I was with got six weeks. I think the other one was undercover, he just disappeared.'

'You?'

She squirmed. 'Because me and Dad've got different last names and my ID shows my old address I couldn't prove I was driving Dad's car. They rang the police here, who talked to the neighbours, who said Dad was overseas and the house was empty.' Voice and face said she'd spent her life feeling pretty much invisible.

'They accused you of driving a stolen car?'

'Yeah.'

'They confiscated it?'

'Yeah.'

Hirsch was starting to feel uneasy. 'Who did, Sandy?'

'This high-up guy who said maybe he could keep me out of jail if I'd, you know, do stuff.'

High-up guy. Hirsch felt a roaring in his ears, all light blotted out. 'A senior policeman?'

'I told him I was HIV-positive so he wouldn't touch me,' Chatterton said. She looked beseechingly at her father. 'I'm not, Dad, promise.'

'Smart thinking, sweetheart,' Metcalfe said, patting his daughter's hand and giving Hirsch a complicated look: guardedness, pity and an undertow of steel.

Battling to keep his voice steady, Hirsch said, 'Can you tell me what this man looked like?'

'Tall, dark hair. Maybe fifty?' She went on until Hirsch noticed the taste that was building in his mouth.

He cleared his throat. 'Okay, Sandy, I'm going to give you

some names: umm . . . Ringling, Wearne, Spurling, Herman, Ingleton—'

'Spurling.'

Hirsch sat there. He looked at Metcalfe. 'I'm sorry, Mr Metcalfe, but there are certain things I have to ask Sandy—'

Metcalfe folded his arms. 'I'm staying. That all right, sweetheart?'

His daughter rested her shoulder against his. She seemed calmer now, sweet and safe, and Hirsch thought he could see what Spurling would have seen in her, a gamine appeal.

'When this man said maybe he could keep you out of jail, what, exactly, was he proposing?'

She told him: parties with some fun guys, clothes, all kinds of drugs, holidays . . . 'In return for some modelling and film work,' she said. 'Sex, of course.'

'And he let you go?'

Sandy Chatterton was frightened again, tinged a little with outrage. 'He said he knew where I lived. I had no money. I had to hitch back.'

You were lucky though, Hirsch thought. Other women haven't been so lucky.

32

During the three-and-a-half-hour drive back to Tiverton, Hirsch mentally outlined the case he'd present to DeLisle and Croome.

Melia Donovan first.

Melia is adventurous, suggestible, anxious to please, her head easily turned by a man with money and charm. Coulter spends some time, money and charm on her, flatters her, lets her drive his car, gives her a fun time: alcohol, cocaine, marijuana, sex. Gradually introduces her to a group of men who like to party with underage girls. Perhaps she's reluctant, so he holds the shoplifting charge over her head, threats of youth detention.

Or he used Gemma Pitcher to bring Melia on board. Were the girls friends before this? There was the age difference; but there weren't many teenage girls of any age in Tiverton. Maybe it was inevitable they'd gravitate to each other.

Or Gemma recruited Melia Donovan off her own bat. To curry favour with the men? To share the sense of . . .

whatever it was she'd been feeling? Shame? Reflected glory? Melia being the pretty one, the sexy one? Hirsch would ask Gemma those questions—if he could find her, if she wasn't dead. The country out east was polka-dotted with mine shafts.

Something had gone wrong at the party—some abuse, something a bit too weird—with the result that Melia had grabbed her clothes and run. What was Gemma's reaction? *We've all been there, Melia. Just suck it up*? Or was she sympathetic, but too scared to intervene? Either way, she wouldn't have been complicit in what happened next.

Hirsch remembered three things about the day Melia Donovan's body was found.

One, as soon as Dr McAskill finished his examination he'd walked a few metres out of earshot and made a phone call.

Two, McAskill then drove to Tiverton, where he not only broke the news to Melia's mother but also made contact with Gemma Pitcher—who later disappeared.

Three, Kropp showed up.

None of it was coincidental. It all stemmed directly from events at the party. McAskill witnesses the incident between David Coulter and Melia Donovan. He sees Coulter chase after her. When she's found dead at the side of the road a few hours later, it's natural for him to believe Coulter killed her. Coulter assumes it'll be treated as an accident and leaves it at that, but McAskill knows it's a problem for everyone. It needs to be contained. So he calls Kropp. And Kropp duly contains Hirsch, by ordering him to stay put at the scene, giving McAskill time to contain Gemma Pitcher, probably by threatening her.

Meanwhile, Kropp ensures that McAskill will perform the autopsy. Good result all round.

Hirsch headed south, the kilometres rolling beneath him and the sun beating down, the light permanently watery out ahead on the Barrier Highway, mica-bright at the edges, broken-glass bright.

The story unrolled like the highway. What the men hadn't foreseen was a suspicious wife. Alison Latimer followed her husband, worked out what was going on and confronted him. I want a divorce. Half the farm, or I'll see you in jail.

Latimer panics, calls the others. They'll all go down if Alison Latimer contacts the police, because it won't be her husband's mate Kropp she contacts. It'll be police in Adelaide.

He doesn't *want* to kill her, but what's the alternative? And there's a bonus: his money problems solved. Nice little inheritance; no divorce payout; one less mouth to feed.

Plus, she's got a history of instability.

But who would have pulled the trigger? The Latimer men had been careful to construct unbreakable alibis. The old man taking his grandsons away for the weekend. Ray making a big public appearance with his girlfriend at the football final, then getting so obnoxiously drunk he's thrown in the lockup overnight. Easy enough for Kropp and his crew to arrange. The icing on the cake is Constable Hirschhausen, who has no stake in the matter and no relationship with Raymond Latimer, and who will be Latimer's alibi for the later part of the morning.

So who abducted and then shot her? Not Kropp: he was in Redruth. Not Nicholson or Andrewartha. No one in their right mind would rely on those clowns to organise a hit. McAskill? Coulter? Logan? Venn?

Maybe. Hirsch couldn't see it. He kept coming back with bitter certainty to Spurling. Knowledge of evidence and police procedures. Enough seniority in the region to give him some control over the investigation and the information that flowed from it. Smart, cautious enough to make sure he's in a position to contain and monitor—to disarm—anyone who might show signs of independent thinking. That's why he'd got Hirsch to prepare the brief for the coroner. An outsider, easily cut out from the pack.

Spurling could have asked Kropp to prepare the brief, though. Why hadn't he? The chance that the press or someone in HQ would question Kropp's impartiality? The rumbles about Kropp's policing methods had been getting louder, complaints becoming more public. Maybe he just wasn't a safe bet.

Managing Hirsch was a much better idea.

It was a pity for Spurling that McAskill couldn't have performed the Latimer autopsy as well, but there was no way a small-town doctor would get a gunshot death.

Hirsch's phone rang in the car cradle. He pulled over, buffeted by the wind of a passing truck. One bar of reception.

'Where are you?' Rosie DeLisle demanded.

'Halfway between Redruth and Broken Hill.'

'Can hardly hear you.'

Hirsch tilted the phone, then himself. In the end he got out and walked along the miserable verge. 'Is that better?'

Another buffeting truck, grit stinging him and a hawk slipping across the sky.

'Not much. Listen, don't talk, just wanted to fill you in. We had quite a chat with your boy—though his story's a bit all over the place.'

'Sam's not the sharpest knife in the drawer.'

'What? I can hardly hear you. Anyway, it's all on record now, so we sent him home.'

'What about the burglary charges?'

'What? Listen,' Rosie shouted, 'just letting you know we've found connections between some of these heroes. Venn, Coulter, Logan and Latimer all boarded at St Peter's. Logan met McAskill when they shared a house together at university. There've been complaints lodged against all of them at one time or another. Several against Coulter, according to the chief magistrate. Refusal to grant a police application for an AVO against a violent ex-con who was stalking his wife . . . Overturned a protection order against some school bullies . . .'

Hirsch thought that sounded like the Coulter he'd met. A crummy small-town solicitor who'd developed a gorgeous sense of his rightness in the world when he became a magistrate. No wonder Kropp didn't like him. But what about Kropp?

'What about Kropp?'

'Who? Kropp? Don't know,' Rosie said. 'Nothing on file except policing complaints. How are you doing on the Chrysler?'

'Tracked it down to Broken Hill. Owned by a guy there whose—'

'What?' Rosie sounded peeved. 'Sorry, Paul, didn't catch a word of that. Look, call me when you get a better signal.'

Hirsch climbed behind the wheel again. Nose down, the sun pouring through the glass, fatigue settling in him.

He tried to get inside Spurling's skin. A man of precision and no little charm. A crisp bureaucrat harbouring a creep, a satyr, within. Huge ego. A man who selects and rejects, controls and judges. He's been at it for a long time, Hirsch thought, and nothing's ever gone wrong. He's become complacent.

He's been the area commander for a long time. Maybe as long as Kropp's been the Redruth sergeant? Roughly the same age, so they might have known each other since the academy. Or served together early on, stayed in touch. Knew each other; knew each other's . . . tastes.

Hirsch saw the web of interests. Spurling and Kropp and his boys. Kropp and the locals—businessmen, the football club, the landed gentry. Hirsch wondered idly what the courthouse tension between Kropp and Coulter and Logan had been about. He'd know once the arrests were made.

Finally, the Chrysler.

An out-of-state car, none of the locals knew it and it hadn't been reported stolen. The owner was overseas. A perfect set of wheels for Spurling. He could come and go without anyone thinking anything but interstate driver, passing through. There were always New South Wales cars on the Barrier Highway.

Except that two children had seen the car, and it had frightened them half to death.

33

Late afternoon now, Hirsch sprawled on his sofa in a T-shirt and baggy jeans, bare heels propped on the coffee table, laptop on his thighs. He was writing up an outline of his theory for DeLisle and Croome. E-mail it, give them time to absorb it, then follow with a phone call.

After that—out of his hands.

The town was quiet, the highway, the school on the other side. Hirsch typed steadily, but before he reached the good bit, Spurling and the Chrysler, the desk phone rang.

Leonard Latimer, heat in his voice: 'I'm scared Ray's going to do something stupid.'

'Mr Latimer.' Hirsch blinked, recovered. 'Stupid how? Where are the boys?'

'Not here, thank God. Just come, will you?'

And he cut the connection. Hirsch gaped at the handset: catching flies, his mother called it.

He was shuddering his way over the Bitter Wash corrugations before he remembered the Beretta.

Idiot. But after travelling all day he'd been glad to shove his uniform in the laundry basket, dump the Beretta and his belt and service pistol and cuffs and baton and all that shit into his top drawer. He wasn't going to drag it all on again, not for the Latimers, so he'd just grabbed his service pistol. Even in his T-shirt, jeans and battered Asics he was a cop.

Would he need to draw his gun? Maybe Raymond would do everyone a favour and shoot his old man and then himself.

Leonard didn't say if guns were involved, though, did he? Arrogant old shit. Arrogant old shit who doesn't know that I know he's about to be at the centre of a major bust.

Glancing at Wendy Street's house before he breached the Latimers' stately gateposts, Hirsch spotted the old Volvo. No one in the garden or driveway or on the veranda. The old feeling crept through him: unfinished business.

He drove deeper onto the property. House and grounds had looked timeworn enough when he was last here, looking into Craig Latimer's pyromania; now the neglect was more apparent. The lawn, overgrown then, was dying. Wind debris—palm fronds, twigs, branches, plastic bags, seedling containers, a director's chair—hadn't been cleared. He steered around a bicycle dumped in the gravel. When he walked the crazy path to the veranda, he stepped over weeds, a cricket bat, dead snails. Meanwhile the gutters above him grew grass clumps and paint flakes peeled from the veranda posts. A stalactite of bird shit had set hard against one wall, dropped from a swallow's nest high on a light fitting. God knew the miseries the place contained.

Hirsch rapped his knuckles on the door.

When Leonard Latimer answered he didn't look particularly panicked. He glanced over Hirsch's shoulder at the HiLux and said warmly, 'Come in.'

Hirsch hesitated only briefly before stepping into the hallway—which was the signal for Raymond Latimer to appear on his flank, emerging from the front room with a shotgun. The man looked completely unhinged. Hirsch turned to duck outside, an instinctive urge to find cover with his service pistol.

'No you don't.' Spurling, blocking his way with an arid smile and a .303 rifle.

He came hard at Hirsch, spinning him around, pinning him to the wall. Disarmed him neatly and patted him down. Ankles included. The Beretta wouldn't have done him much good after all.

'Supe?' Hirsch said, trying not to sound bewildered, frightened.

'Shut up.'

Hirsch glanced at Leonard, the only one not armed. 'What, you're the brains of the outfit?'

The patriarch gave him the look he kept for tradesmen. 'Be quiet.'

They stood there crowding him. All Hirsch had on his side now was time. 'Where's the Chrysler, Supe?'

'Ah, the Chrysler,' Spurling said. 'Received an interesting

call about that from a CIB sergeant at Broken Hill earlier today.' His narrow face grew tighter. 'Who else knows?'

'Apart from the various people who spotted it when Melia Donovan died and again when Alison Latimer died?' Hirsch shrugged. 'Internal Investigations.'

Spurling chewed on that. 'No, I don't believe you. Changes nothing, anyway.'

'Hang on, Matthew,' Leonard said tetchily. 'What's this about your car?'

'It's not a problem, Len,' Spurling said. 'I'll disappear the car. And the witnesses . . .' He smiled. 'Well, everyone knows how reliable witness statements are. Come on.'

'Brilliant.' Latimer wasn't finished. 'What possessed you to drive something so distinctive?'

'You think I was going to roll up in a police cruiser?'

'I'm with you, Len,' Hirsch said stoutly. 'Not real smart, is it? I'd—'

Hirsch came round on the parched lawn at the side of the house.

He didn't think he'd been out long, the sun hadn't moved. But Christ, his head. Must have been Ray, with the butt of the shotgun, then they'd dragged him outside.

'Get up.'

Hirsch made a show of it, gauging the three men from where he lay: Spurling with the .303, Ray Latimer with the shotgun . . . and Leonard with a folded tarpaulin that Hirsch didn't like one bit. Spurling booted him. 'Get a move on.'

On his feet now, rocky, Hirsch said, 'Where are we going?'

He was guessing somewhere his blood and guts could be safely spilled on the tarp. Somewhere away from the house and sheds.

'Shut up,' Spurling said, driving the rifle butt into his spine.

Hirsch fell to his knees. As soon as he was upright, Spurling prodded him across the yard and out past the sheds. Hirsch scanned left and right; spotted the black Chrysler tucked behind a haystack.

When they reached the track leading down to the Tin Hut, Hirsch shook his head. 'Now there's a novel idea, stage another suicide at the site of the first one.'

'Keep moving,' Spurling said, punching again with the butt of the .303. The pain seemed to stab through Hirsch, shoot up his body and lodge behind his left eye. He stumbled.

'Quit stalling.' Spurling began to stride on ahead, calling back. 'Keep him moving.'

Downslope to the creek, which had retreated to a stretch of foetid mud between muddy pools, the edges dense with dying reeds. Sheep had tried to reach the water, churning the mud. A dead one floated in the largest pool; a live one struggled feebly in the reeds. The Latimers paid no attention.

'You clowns aren't farmers,' Hirsch said.

'What?' said Raymond Latimer. He swung the shotgun butt into Hirsch's stomach. 'What would you know?'

Hirsch doubled over, gasping, hands on his knees. 'You've run the place into the ground. Big shots in the district? You can't even pay your grocery bills, you're a laughing stock.'

'Fuck you,' Ray Latimer said.

'Will you pricks get a move on?' yelled Spurling, who had reached the flat area beside the hut's crooked chimney.

Leonard nudged his son. 'You heard what the man said, keep him moving.'

Ray edged away from his father, sulky. He prodded Hirsch. 'Move it.'

Hirsch stumbled again, falling to his knees. Hold things up, goad these losers, drive a wedge between them. It was all he had.

'You're pathetic, Ray,' he said, climbing to his feet, 'the way you've always let your old man call the shots. Just a sad little paedophile, that's how they'll remember you.'

That was stretching it, but it got a reaction. 'What? Fuck you,' Ray screamed, felling Hirsch again.

Spurling, at the far end of the hut now, said, 'Do we have to do this? Just bring him over here.'

'Yeah,' said Hirsch, looking up at Latimer, 'get on with it, Raymond. Pay attention to your orders, it's what you're good at.'

'I don't take orders from anyone.'

Spurling was wound tight as a spring. 'Can't you see what the cunt's doing? Get a move on.'

Hirsch, rolled on to his knees, peered up at Leonard, the queer blankness in the man. 'You must be proud of your boy, Len.'

Off guard, Leonard emitted the smallest of chuckles. It held, unmistakably, a flicker of complete contempt for his son.

Ray stopped. Looked at the shotgun as if it were a gadget beyond his figuring, looked at his father.

357

'You morons,' shouted Spurling, 'get him over here before someone sees us from the road.'

'Yeah, come on Ray,' goaded Hirsch, sitting back on his heels. 'Do what you're told.'

'Shut up.' Raymond sounded as if he needed time to think.

'It's easy,' Hirsch murmured. 'It's only another staged suicide, and we know what a great job old Spurls did with Alison. One fuck-up after another and you're *still* listening to him.'

'What would you know?'

'Maybe you'll do better this time. Maybe people will actually believe I came out here and shot myself with another man's gun.'

But Spurling had charged back to elbow Raymond out of the way and grab Hirsch. 'Actually, hotshot, you're going down a mine shaft.'

Hirsch shook him off. 'Same as you did with Gemma, right?'

'What? Oh, the fat girl.' Spurling slapped him casually and hauled him upright.

Hirsch thought desperately. 'Don't you idiots realise they have all your names? You, Venn, Logan, Coulter, McAskill . . .'

Ray wet his lips. 'Who has?'

'Sex crimes.'

'He's lying,' Spurling said, and began running with Hirsch, half-dragging and half-propelling him to the far end of the shed. They were hidden from the road here, visible only to the closest bend in the creek and the rocks on the other side.

358

Hirsch struggled feebly. Spurling slammed him against the wall, locked him there with one arm to his chest, waiting for the Latimers to catch up.

When Ray appeared, looking tentative and panicky, Spurling stepped back. 'All yours, Raymond.'

Hirsch's mouth was dry. He closed his eyes, opened them again, ready for the blast.

But the situation had shifted. The shotgun was a hot potato, Ray Latimer shoving it at his father. 'I can't. Dad, you do it.'

'It was your bloody wife got us into this,' Leonard said, pushing back with the tarp.

Hirsch moistened his mouth; croaked, 'You got him into it, Len. No mystery where he gets his sick ideas about sex.'

'Will one of you just kill him?' screamed Spurling. 'I did your dirty work, now you fucking do some.'

But Ray continued to shove the shotgun at his father. Leonard stepped back, outraged. 'The hell are you doing? Grow up, you snivelling great calf.'

'You must be so proud, Supe,' Hirsch said, 'the calibre of your fellow paedos.'

Spurling swatted that away and glanced at his watch, fed up with the Latimer psychodrama. '*We haven't got all day*. One of you had better come and shoot this cunt.'

Hirsch could feel the nausea churning. He swallowed, swallowed again and kept his voice even: 'I suppose you've got Kropp running damage control. What's he going to do, send in a report about my mental state? Plant some evidence, get rid of my car?'

'Kropp?' Spurling snorted. 'Kropp's got nothing to do with it. The man's a bloody disgrace.'

Hirsch let out a laugh of sheer disbelief.

One exasperated eye on the Latimers, Spurling said, 'Sometime in the next few weeks your vehicle will be found out in the dry country with an empty fuel tank. Your phone will be on the seat, flat battery. You wandered off, lost all sense of direction, no water, blazing sun, delirious, you probably fell down a mine shaft.' He paused, smiled at Hirsch. 'Meanwhile I'll have leisurely access to your office files.'

Hirsch saw how it would unfold. I'll have been corrupt all along, or off on some paranoid course of my own, wilfully misreading evidence, trying to atone for my crooked past. He felt ill and drained, his guts hurt and he couldn't breathe. He thought of Alison Latimer, her panic attacks and arrhythmia.

Spurling shouted, 'What in Christ's name are you two arseholes doing?'

Leonard and Raymond Latimer were enacting a strange, sad, wordless dance, the son pressing the shotgun onto his father almost as if proffering a gift, the father retreating in disgust.

Leonard broke first. He dropped the tarp, snatched the gun and swung it neatly to his shoulder, the bore coming around on Hirsch.

'*Stop it!*' A little voice, crying from the rocks across the creek.

Leonard did stop, but only briefly; the shotgun dipped, came up again.

So it was a good thing, from Hirsch's point of view, that Katie Street went on to clarify her demand by shooting the bastard.

The bullet punched into Leonard's belly and he *oof*ed in surprise and pain. He doubled over. He took one step back, and another, tossed the shotgun weakly away and lowered himself to the ground, taking the weight with his right hand. The collapse was slow, economical, almost graceful.

Ray Latimer reacted first, starting towards his father with a wary urgency, wanting to give comfort but expecting hostility. Too late, Spurling swung around on Hirsch with the rifle. But Hirsch had uncoiled from the starting block, leading with his shoulder, striking the superintendent full on. Spurling's trigger finger jerked, the .303 discharging a millimetre from Hirsch's ear. Deafened, hoping Katie was keeping her head down, he began a dance for possession of the .303 as crazy as the Latimers'.

He spun around and around with Spurling, manoeuvring him towards the wall of the hut. He was young and he was fit; Spurling was a fifty-something desk jockey. He slammed the superintendent against the rusty metal. Spurling bounced off, limp.

Hirsch snatched the rifle. He backed away until the three men were inside his arc of fire. Then he called, 'Katie? You can come out now.'

She emerged edgily, ready to run, taking stock before picking her way across the creek bed. Now she was sprinting towards Hirsch, stepping wide of Leonard Latimer as if he might still harm her. She reached Hirsch. She got as close to him as she could.

He hugged her thin shoulders briefly. 'Where's the gun?'

She pointed across the creek at the rocks. 'Over there.'

'It's Mr Latimer's?'

She toed the dirt. 'Yes.'

'Just as well you pinched it.'

She was indignant. 'No one would listen to me about that car. Lots of times I saw it. Today I saw it go in Mr Latimer's place.' She pointed towards the Vimy Ridge gates.

'You've been hiding the gun all this while?'

'In my tree house.'

'Listen, girlie,' Spurling said, 'this is a very bad man. Go and tell your mother to call the police.'

Katie looked up at Spurling, a scrappy kid with a tough little core of selfhood. 'He *is* the police,' she said, full of scorn.

34

Two days later, Hirsch debriefed with Wendy Street over a glass of wine. Wendy held her glass to the light a little crookedly. Her consonants had become slightly smudged. 'I have to say my daughter seems quite phlegmatic about shooting a man. "Mr Latimer was going to kill Paul so I shot him."'

'Just as well she did,' Hirsch said. 'Just as well she's not agonising over it.'

They were in Wendy's kitchen, late afternoon, Bob Dylan drifting from the speakers. The sun, seeking a way in past the blind above the sink, lit Wendy's hair, the finer, flyaway strands so burning in the light that Hirsch wanted to reach out and tame them.

'A counsellor's been offered, as they say . . . I don't know that she needs one. What do you think?'

Hirsch glanced at Katie, who was belly down, chin up before the TV set in the adjoining sunroom. 'She's clearly suffering.'

A twist of a smile. 'Joking aside, though. What if the enormity of it hits her one day?'

Hirsch took a chance and reached his hand out. Her hand, a warm claw under his, turned upwards in welcome. 'All you can do,' he said, when his pulse had settled, 'is listen and watch. Not make a big deal about it if she raises the issue.'

'Not make a big deal about it as in, it's okay to shoot people or as in, don't make her anxious and guilty?'

Hirsch was pretty sure she was smiling. 'Oh, the former.'

Now she grew serious. 'Thank God she didn't kill him. But what happens officially now?'

'She'll have to answer questions: where the gun came from, why she had it, why she shot it, that kind of thing. You'll be allowed to sit with her. Bring in a lawyer if you think things might stray into dangerous territory. But given her age and the fact the gun hadn't been secured by the owner and the fact she saved my life, then I don't think any action will be taken.' He paused. 'Ray, on the other hand, may face some kind of firearms charge. On top of everything else.'

Katie wandered in. She stood close to Hirsch's chair, bumping her shoulder against his in absent-minded affection. Wendy discreetly removed her hand from Hirsch's and smiled at her. 'Okay, sweetie?'

'Yeah, I'm good.' She wandered back to the TV.

Hirsch, feeling the absence of Wendy's hand, took it back, enveloped it. 'You going ahead with the public meeting?'

Wendy looked at their hands resting there on the table. She blinked awake. 'Sure. Superintendent Spurling won't be there for obvious reasons.'

'They'll send someone in his place.'

'The point is I want them to send someone in Sergeant Kropp's place—*and* Constable Nicholson's *and* Constable Andrewartha's. You've got your man but the situation in Redruth hasn't altered.'

Hirsch nodded. Kropp had been strangely quiet. A few weeks ago—a few days ago—the sergeant would have been ranting on the phone for Hirsch to tell his girlfriend to back off. 'Can I ask you something?'

Wendy Street tensed and slipped her hand away as if to say, 'Uh oh.' Hirsch, feeling wrongfooted, realised she was readying herself to hear something she didn't want to hear. 'I met you on a Monday,' he said awkwardly, 'the second week of the September school holidays.'

She still looked tense. 'That sounds about right.'

'Alison was with you.'

'Yes. Where are you going with this?'

'On the *Saturday*—in other words, two days before that— she'd followed her husband to a house just on the other side of Redruth where several men, including her husband and father-in-law, were having sex with Melia Donovan and Gemma Pitcher and possibly others we don't know about.'

'Yes . . . ?'

'Our theory is, she confronted Ray. He probably told his father, who told the others, and it was agreed she had to go.'

'Didn't have anything to do with the inheritance after all,' Wendy said.

'Icing on the cake, though,' Hirsch said. 'The thing is, I have a witness who saw Melia Donovan running from the house in distress, naked, carrying her clothes and shoes.'

The tension hadn't ebbed. 'And . . . ?'

'This witness said that David Coulter chased Melia in his car and knocked her down.'

Wendy tightened against the air between them. 'You think Allie should have said something?'

Hirsch said, 'It's just that I'm surprised she didn't. Was she that browbeaten, or that single-minded about leaving her husband, that she'd fail to mention something like that?'

'How do you know she saw it? It was night time, she might not have had a clear view . . . maybe she'd already left.'

'True.'

'All I know is, she was upbeat about leaving Ray and getting a divorce.'

'She didn't mention that she'd followed Ray, had her suspicions confirmed, nothing like that?'

'No.'

'She looked tense the day I met her. Scared.'

'Wouldn't you be? She assumed you were a mate of Kropp's. We all did.'

Hirsch grimaced.

'What's Coulter saying? Did he admit to running over Melia?'

'Dunno, it's out of my hands.'

'Gemma will know.'

'If I can find her,' Hirsch said. He thought about those mine shafts out east behind the Razorback. Then he decided not to think about that. He leaned towards Wendy, Wendy watching him, and kissed her. For the briefest moment she was unresponsive; and after that she wasn't.

35

When Gemma Pitcher did turn up again in Tiverton it was without fanfare. Bob Muir, on his way to fix an air conditioner one Sunday afternoon, spotted her on a swing in the playground beside the tennis courts, and called Hirsch. 'Just sitting there, mate.'

Sunday, Hirsch's day off. Still wearing his board shorts and a T-shirt, still bleary after spending the night with Wendy, he drove to the tennis courts, saw no one, and continued around to the crumbling house where the Pitchers lived.

Eileen answered his knock, her sullen face indicating that life in its entirety was a disappointment, up to and including her daughter's return.

Or maybe it's me, Hirsch thought. 'Is Gemma in?'

'Are you taking her out?'

'I beg your pardon?'

The woman looked him up and down. 'She's too upset to go out.'

Hirsch realised he should have worn his uniform. Eileen was used to men, including policemen, knocking on this door from time to time, asking for Gemma. Why should I be any different? 'It's a work matter, Mrs Pitcher.'

'I need her to help with dinner,' grumbled the woman.

But she took Hirsch through to the sitting room, where Gemma was watching one of the Twilight movies, DVD discs and covers strewn around the TV set and across the carpet. There was no sign of the boys.

'Hello, Gemma,' he said. 'Movie marathon?'

Gemma was staring dazedly at the screen, as if she'd been doing it half her life. Possibly she has, Hirsch thought. Her mouth hung open, and she lolled rather than sat, dressed in a short top and tights, the fabric stretched to within a millimetre of tolerance and revealing her soft white belly.

'What?'

'Nothing,' Hirsch said, watching the mother, who flashed him a look of bitterness and defiance before backing out of the room. Presently she could be heard in the kitchen, smacking dishes about. Hirsch said, 'Gemma, I need to ask you some questions.'

'What for?'

Hirsch stared at her. 'I have a better question: how come you're surprised I want to ask you some questions?'

Gemma looked at him blankly, as if astonished. 'But it's all over, it was on the news.'

Hirsch wondered how her mind worked. He sat beside her, sinking into the sofa cushions. Found himself pressed against over-soft, over-round teenage flesh and edged away hastily. 'Gemma, obviously we have questions to ask you. You might have to give evidence in court. You might face charges yourself.'

Beside him the girl was suddenly no longer soft but a dense, tight shape. She swallowed convulsively.

'Gemma?'

Full of tidal anxieties, her face sulky and damp, she said, 'I done nothing.'

'Gemma, I need to know who introduced Melia to this thing you had going with those men. Coulter and Venn and Logan and the others. Was it you?'

'I didn't want her there. Who do *you* reckon they all wanted?'

The fifteen-year-old beauty, not the plain, bovine eighteen-year-old. 'Did you try to dissuade her?'

'Huh?'

Hirsch sought inspiration from the stale air. 'Did you try to convince her it was the wrong thing to do?'

'Her? Yeah, right.'

'Stubborn?'

Gemma snorted.

'So who did get her involved?'

Her voice came, without conviction: 'Mr Coulter.'

'How?'

'Me and her got done for shoplifting and he let us off and asked Mel out.'

'Was she his girlfriend? Did they go out?'

'Yeah, but, you know, they had to keep it secret.'

'For how long?'

Gemma heaved her shoulders. 'I dunno, a while. Few weeks.'

'Just to be clear, they were having sex?'

Gemma's eyebrows were scathing. 'Like I said, they were *goin' out*.'

'How long after he started going out with her did he ask her to one of your parties?'

More shoulder-heaving. 'It wasn't like she went to lots of them.'

'That first time, did you tell her what kind of party it would be?'

'No.'

'You didn't try to warn her?'

'I would of got into trouble.'

'With who? Melia?'

'No—Mr Coulter. He said I had to hold her hand. He said he could still drop me in the shit because of the shoplifting and that.'

'Was she shocked, upset, when she realised what was happening?'

Gemma snorted. 'Not her.'

'Did you give her a lift or did Mr Coulter collect her? Or collect both of you?'

'Me.'

'Getting back to that first party: she wasn't scared, nervous?'

'Mr Coulter was there.'

'But so were a lot of other men and they were wearing masks, weren't they?'

'What? No.'

'They weren't masked?'

She gave a little giggle. 'Nah.'

'Never?'

'No.'

Emily Hobba had talked about masks. Maybe a one-off thing, a fetish, Hirsch thought. Or Emily had lied so she wouldn't be asked to identify anyone.

'These parties: I know you had sex with the men, but was there also music, dancing?'

'Sure.'

'Alcohol? Drugs?'

Gemma slid her eyes to a corner of the miserable room. Hirsch said, 'I'm not the drug squad. I just need to know more about the atmosphere.'

'Like you said, dancing and drinking and that.'

'And there was you, Melia . . .'

'Sometimes these other girls.'

'Apart from Emily Hobba, who were they?'

'Dunno. They came with that cop.'

'The party I'm mostly interested in is the last one. What happened?'

'Well, you know.'

'No, Gemma, I don't know.'

'I had sex and the others had sex.' A bored singsong voice.

'Melia too?'

'Sure.'

'With more than one man?'

Gemma wriggled around where she sat. 'I'll tell ya, all

right? She was with Mr Coulter and then the others wanted to gang her, all of them at once, and she got upset, all right?'

'She ran out?'

'Said she was going to tell.'

'Did David Coulter follow her outside?'

'Well, yeah.'

'Did you?'

A shrug. 'Couldn't find her.'

'She wasn't outside on the road or on the lawn?'

'Nup.'

'Did you see Mrs Latimer there?'

'What?'

'Never mind. What about Sam Hempel?'

'That loser?'

'Was he there, Gemma?'

'Didn't see him.'

'You don't sound surprised that I've mentioned him.'

'He was always like, sniffing around and that.'

'He told me he was looking out for her.'

'Yeah, right.'

'The day I first asked you questions, why didn't you mention any of this?'

'Why would I?'

'Because your best friend had just died a terrible death?'

'Dr McAskill said don't say nothin' or I'd get in trouble. Look what they done to Melia to shut her up.'

'So you ran.'

'Wouldn't you?'

'I thought you were dead.'

'Well I'm not.'

'Where have you been all this time?'

'Foster mother.'

'You were in foster care?'

'When I was like, nine.'

Hirsch's checks had uncovered a juvenile record but not the foster placement. 'She was nice to you?'

'Better than Mum,' Gemma said, drawing on reserves of hostility.

'But you came back here.'

'It's safe now though, right? Plus Mum needs her car back.'

No point in pursuing the logic. 'All right. Tell me about Emily Hobba.'

'Emily.' The big shoulders lifted to the fleshy ears. 'Met her in juvie.'

'She had an older friend who got you involved in this party scene?'

'Yeah. Look, are you nearly done?'

'Before Melia was involved, you would sometimes travel all the way down to the city for these parties?'

'So?'

'Were you paid?'

She shrugged. 'Got, you know, presents and that.'

'Were you ever paid cash, Gemma?'

The girl looked offended. 'I'm not a *prostitute* or nothin'.'

'Why did the operation move to Redruth?'

'What?'

'The parties. Why did they stop happening in the city and start happening in the country?'

'Dunno, do I? Wasn't up to me.' She paused. 'Emily said things were a bit tense.'

'People were suspicious?'

'Suppose.'

Hirsch named all of the locals and said, 'Were they there from the beginning, or new on the scene?'

'Couple of them were new. Never saw Sergeant Kropp, but it wasn't like every weekend or anything. I only went to like, six or seven parties, tops.'

Hirsch thought about it. Even posted in the bush, a senior officer like Spurling would have heard rumbles coming from sex crimes and other specialist squads, and so he'd warned the others and they'd moved the operation to Redruth. 'We'll be in touch. In the meantime, if any of the men try to contact you, call me straight away.'

Gemma stared at him. 'What?'

'Phone calls, approaches, just let me know.'

The girl looked frightened. 'I thought it was over.'

'They're out on bail,' said Hirsch gently.

He stood, said goodbye, and crossed the room. But at the door he felt the urge to glance back at Gemma Pitcher. The girl looked young, helpless. Hirsch stood there a moment, then returned to the sofa and perched beside her.

'I want you to pack a bag. Count on being away for a while.'

'Huh? How come? Where am I going?'

'I'm taking you to your foster mother.'

36

On a Thursday evening in December, Hirsch drove Wendy Street to the Redruth town hall.

She was a sour presence in the passenger seat of his listing Nissan. 'I did all the work, and now they're saying I'm compromised, can't even chair my own meeting.'

Hirsch understood: she'd spent weeks organising, gathering signatures. But he also understood the police point of view: Spurling was a public relations nightmare, and Wendy was a close friend of the man's main victim. He explained this, adding, 'And they probably know about you and me.'

Some of the tension went out of her. She placed a hand on his leg. Presently she leaned closer, peered evilly into his face, edged her hand up his thigh. 'Hope I'm not distracting you.'

'You are a bit.'

She slid her hand higher. 'Is that better?'

Hirsch coughed; his voice didn't come out right. 'Much.'

He drove on down the valley, trying to ignore the warm pressure. 'What about the no-confidence motion?'

'I asked Bernie Love to present it.'

Love was the publican of the Woolman Hotel. He'd offered to hold the protest meeting in his function room—so he could keep the bar open, according to the local wags, but Hirsch suspected he wanted to stick it to the Redruth police, whom he blamed for keeping patrons away from his door. Either way, he'd been refused in favour of the town hall.

'I guess I shouldn't sit with you,' Hirsch said.

Wendy rubbed his leg. 'Best not.'

'Look, the whole thing could be a fizzer.'

Wendy folded her arms. 'Not if I can help it.'

The Adelaide press put the attendance at 500. Significant, given that the population of Redruth was 1300 and the greater area 3500. Standing room only, and Hirsch found himself propping up a side wall, on his left a primary-school teacher, on his right the elderly neighbour of the woman who'd fallen through her back door on grand final night.

'Hear you got yourself shot,' the old man said.

People up and down the district were making that mistake. 'Almost shot,' Hirsch said. 'How's Crystal?'

'She died.'

Hirsch felt crushed. He should have checked on her.

The old man touched his sleeve. 'Not because of the fall. She was out of hospital in no time. Just old age.'

Hirsch surveyed the rows of cheap metal chairs, the heads neat and ragged, the summery shirts and worn, comfortable bodies. A few young people, but most were aged between thirty and sixty. A media presence at the back: TV cameras, and a range of metropolitan and national newspaper reporters. The hall itself was a carbon copy of Tiverton's: wooden floors, pressed-tin ceiling, some fancy plaster work, a stage at the far end. In front of the stage and facing the audience were four unoccupied chairs set at a couple of trestle tables.

'Do you need a seat?' asked Hirsch.

'Got my walking stick,' the old man said.

Presently Kropp and his wife came threading through to the row of reserved chairs at the front of the room, the sergeant grinning and shaking hands left and right. No one greeted his wife, and Hirsch wondered how she felt. Invisible, maybe.

There were no grins and handshakes when Nicholson and Andrewartha appeared. 'Who's the woman with Nicholson?'

'His wife.'

Hirsch grunted. Did she know about the girlfriend? 'And with Andrewartha?'

'Wife.'

Two burly men and their burly wives, they pushed through to the front with jutting chests and chins, and sat, solid and aggrieved, the men in uniforms so tight, their upper bodies so beefy, they couldn't fold their arms properly. Hirsch glanced about for Wendy, finally spotting her on the far side, watching him from the end chair of a row a third of the way back. She rolled her eyes: *that took you long enough*, grinned and turned to the front again.

The room was rowdy but fell silent when four men emerged through a side door and sat at the trestle tables.

Two were senior policemen in full uniform: Cremen, the new area commander, and Wright, an assistant commissioner from headquarters in Adelaide. A third man wore a suit but had the hard, guarded look of a policeman. IIB, guessed Hirsch.

The fourth man stood as soon as he'd sat. He was sun-creased, diffident, wearing a sports coat over an open-necked white shirt. His big hands mangled each other as he spoke. 'I'm Des McEwan, CEO of the regional council. I've been asked to chair tonight's meeting.'

And not taking much pleasure in it, thought Hirsch.

McEwan introduced Cremen and Wright but not the stony-faced man wearing the suit, then drew a breath. 'To begin: almost six hundred people signed a petition which said, quote, *The law in Redruth is being administered in a harsh and uncompromising manner*, and so here we are.'

The audience stirred, muttered, squeaked about on the cheap seats.

McEwan added hastily, 'We don't want a witch-hunt or a show trial or an opportunity to get even with anyone. We don't want rumour and innuendo. But six hundred signatures is significant, and tonight is your opportunity to air your concerns in a fair and reasonable manner.'

Told to push the fair and reasonable line, thought Hirsch. He waited, arms folded, for the floodgates to open. But the audience, although restive, kept their hands in their laps. Nervous? Self-conscious? Intimidated by the men at the trestle tables? Afraid that Kropp, Nicholson and Andrewartha had eyes in the backs of their heads?

Finally a hairdresser from the Redruth salon waved her arm.

'Yes, Sylvia.'

She stood, middle-aged, awkward, shoulders hunched. 'I work right on the square and every day I see what it's like for anyone unlucky enough to cross paths with the police. I really feel for our old people, getting shouted at in such a rude, arrogant ... Well, it's demeaning. Sometimes it's downright frightening.'

'Too right,' murmured the old man at Hirsch's elbow.

Bernie Love made his way to the front of the room. The publican was a glossy, grinning man with a hard mercantile core. About sixty, he wore a black silk shirt and new-looking jeans.

'You know me, I run the Woolman. Simply put, patronage is down thirty per cent because of these bozos.' He gestured at Kropp, Nicholson and Andrewartha. 'Intimidation's what it is. Patrol car parked outside the main entrance so no one wants to come in. Or they come into the bar and just stand there, giving everyone the evil eye. It's a bloody disgrace.'

He glared around to make his point, then returned to his chair. Raelene Skinner, owner of the motel, took his place. She was hunched over, squeaky with nerves, reading from a sheet of paper. 'People think of Redruth as a wheat and wool town, but it's also a *tourist* town. Except the tourists aren't coming, or they're not staying, because the police are always breath-testing people or setting speed traps outside the motel. I used to employ eight people; now I'm down to two.'

She scurried back to her chair. The supermarket manager bobbed up, said rapidly that no one shopped in Redruth anymore, and sat again. Then silence, then a couple of other people had their say, one tongue-tied, the other blustering but vague.

Hirsch watched the superintendent, the assistant commissioner. They were less remote now, full of little nods and headshakes, taking pains not to look at Kropp, Nicholson and Andrewartha. You could almost hear them tut-tutting, oh-dearing. It was meant to be reassuring, and Hirsch rated it as a solid professional performance.

Then he thought: they're *relieved*. The townspeople—awkward, decent, well-mannered—were simply reporting a few instances of over-enthusiastic policing. Nothing serious. No criminal acts. A bit of tea and sympathy and we can all go home. And thank God for that, after the Spurling business.

He looked for Wendy. He couldn't see her. Should *he* say something?

Des McEwan cocked his head at the crowd. 'Anyone else? No? Perhaps—'

The assistant commissioner stood. 'Perhaps Sergeant Kropp might be invited to respond?'

'Yes, of course,' babbled McEwan.

Kropp rose massively, turned to face the audience. His gaze raked the room, steady, reasonable, fair.

'The police motto,' he said, 'is leading the way to a safer community, so we make no apology for reducing the road toll through random breath tests and speed detection.'

He was about to go on but a couple of *hear hear*s went

around the room and a man stepped away from a huddle of men on the opposite wall. He stared at the chairman, who said, 'I invite Eric Dawe of the State Emergency Service to say a few words.'

'I'm a hundred per cent behind Sergeant Kropp,' Dawe announced. 'Who gets called out when some tanked-up idiot runs head-on into a tree or worse still, another car? Me and my men. We're sick of it. It's heartbreaking.'

People muttered. A woman stood. 'I know this makes me unpopular, but in the midst of his own troubles, Sergeant Kropp got my son off drugs and into football.' She shut her mouth with a click and sat. Kropp, embarrassed, returned to his seat.

'What troubles?' murmured Hirsch as a hum of comment rose from the audience.

The teacher at his elbow said, 'His kiddie was run over and killed a few years ago. Only three years old.'

Oh fuck, thought Hirsch. Meanwhile arguments ranged about the room, people craning around in their seats, saying, 'Yeah, but . . .' and 'On the other hand . . .' Perhaps sensing that he'd lost the advantage, Bernie Love strode onto the cleared area in front of the trestle tables and bellowed, 'Oy!'

He waved a sheet of paper above his head. The noise abated.

'Before we start passing out sainthoods,' he shouted, 'I'd like to move a motion.'

McEwan checked with the assistant commissioner, who shrugged guardedly. 'Go on, Mr Love,' McEwan said.

Love thumbed a pair of glasses onto his nose and read:

'*I move that the residents of Redruth and its surrounds have lost confidence in the policing abilities of Sergeant Kropp and Constables Nicholson and Andrewartha, and that they be replaced with officers respected, knowledgeable and experienced in community policing.*'

Cremen jumped to his feet. 'May I suggest an amendment?'

'Go ahead,' McEwan said.

'That a police investigation be allowed to run its course before the issue of no confidence is considered, and that this meeting elect a committee to hear community complaints and liaise directly with the investigators.'

The assistant commissioner joined him. 'That way no one need feel intimidated. Have faith in us to do the right thing. The formal complaints investigation process really does work.'

Before Love could object, McEwan said, 'Shall we vote?'

Hirsch watched and waited. He didn't vote. 175 voted for the amended motion, 136 against.

Jesus. That went off like a damp squib, Hirsch thought despondently, watching people shift in their seats, grab their handbags, stand ready to leave. He still couldn't see Wendy. He pushed away from the wall, anticipating her disappointment.

A ripple passed through the room.

Wendy walked onto the stage and stood in a commanding position, looking down on the men at the table, the shuffling audience and clanging chairs. Beside her stood a girl, barely mid-teens, holding a baby. They waited. A gradual calm settled.

McEwan, following the direction of the stares, turned around. 'Mrs Street?'

Wendy ignored him. She gestured to the wings. Bob Muir emerged, crossing the stage in his unhurried way, nodding to the men and women he recognised. He was accompanied by Nathan Donovan, who looked terrified.

'What's this?' shouted Nicholson.

'Mrs Street?' said McEwan. 'We've passed a motion.'

'We've passed a motion to investigate a bit of over-enthusiastic policing,' Wendy said. 'I'd like to move a new motion.'

'You can't,' Nicholson yelled.

Wendy glared at McEwan. 'Mr Chairman, have you formally declared the meeting over?'

'Well, no, we still have to form a committee, but—'

'But not everyone's had their say. I'd like to introduce Cristobel and Nathan. They have experiences they'd like to share.'

The girl was tremblingly brave. She gestured with the baby. 'This is Travis. I'm not sure who his dad is. Him,' she said, pointing, 'or him. They done me one after the other.'

Nicholson, Andrewartha, both men sinking in their seats. Nicholson's wife stood, bulldozed her way out of the hall. Andrewartha's wife seemed unsure what to do.

'She was fourteen at the time,' Wendy said.

'If you don't believe me,' the girl spoke clearly in the hush, 'DNA'll prove it.' She turned to Nathan. 'Your turn.'

Nathan hunched his shoulders, frozen in place. Muir touched his elbow. The boy swallowed visibly and walked to the edge of the stage. He pointed, his voice strained: 'Them two pricks have taken me out east and bashed me up. Left me to walk home. Done it like, every coupla months.'

He stepped back out of the limelight.

Wendy gave him a smile of great warmth, then gazed out over the room again. 'And so you can see, Mr Chairman, why we need to consider a new motion.'

37

Hirsch returned from patrol on the Monday to find Kropp waiting for him. He appeared to be dozing behind the wheel of a Redruth patrol car. Head tilted back, eyes closed, hands in his lap.

But he was quick to sense Hirsch. In a couple of economical motions he was out and onto the footpath as Hirsch's key slid into the lock. 'Sarge,' said Hirsch, one arm out to hold the front door ajar, giving the sergeant plenty of room.

'Constable.'

Hirsch opened the connecting door to his private quarters, again making space for Kropp, as if the pair of them might explode into violence if sleeve brushed sleeve. Kropp shook his head. 'Your office will do.'

He took the plain wooden chair. Hirsch, a little tense now, swung into the swivel chair behind his desk. He didn't feel intimidated or deferential. He felt . . . what, exactly?

More victims had come forward at the protest meeting. No one raised any real accusation against Kropp himself, but they made it apparent that he had lost control, letting his men run his patch as if it was their personal playground and he the ineffectual principal. A dinosaur who'd forgotten who he was supposed to be and what he was supposed to do. Had he been complicit? Blind, certainly; and people had stories about verbal abuse. But he wasn't bad in the way Spurling was bad. He'd sensed something about Logan and Coulter. And plenty of people had stood up for him.

Hirsch would reserve judgment.

Kropp folded his arms. 'You could have called me the day those pricks tried to kill you,' he said. 'I'd have done the right thing.'

'Sarge,' Hirsch said. There was no way he would have called the man. Kropp would have been compromised, or he'd have believed Spurling and the Latimers. And if Nicholson and Andrewartha had come along for the ride, it might have proved fatal.

Kropp saw the story in Hirsch's eyes. He slumped and shook his head, all elasticity vanished. He drew one huge dry palm down over his face, trying to rub something out. 'What a fucking mess.'

Dying to know the score, Hirsch asked, 'What's the new super going to do?'

'The boys are going down, I know that much.'

Boys. As if Nicholson and Andrewartha were unruly kids, not serial rapists. 'Going down how, Sarge?'

Kropp looked fully at Hirsch. 'If the bashings and sexual assaults can be verified, they're looking at jail time.'

'And you, Sarge?'

'Remains to be seen. Asked to resign? Disciplinary hearing and busted to Traffic?'

'When?'

Kropp shrugged bitterly. 'No idea. All I know is I'm on leave, starting tomorrow.'

'With pay?'

'Fuck you.' Kropp shook his head. 'Took my eye off the ball.' As if it was a game, being a cop. 'My officers let me down.'

Hirsch had had enough. 'You allowed them to.'

A flash of the old quick surging power, Kropp snarling, '*You* going to lecture me about *my* conduct?'

Hirsch tensed and said nothing.

'Your girlfriend got what she wanted. Put-the-boot-into-your-local-copper.'

'Oh for fuck's sake. There were plenty of formal and informal complaints long before I arrived in the district. All my "girlfriend" did was get people off their arses.'

Kropp snorted. 'Yeah, right. Didn't get any pointers from the kind of cop who dobs in his colleagues.'

'Go to hell,' Hirsch said. 'They stitched me up. They threatened my parents. They *frightened my mother and father*, worthless fucking cowards that they are.'

'You do *not* drop another police member in the shit,' Kropp said, sticking his bulky jaw out.

'If not me, who, then?' Hirsch demanded. 'We let murdering, raping, racist cops get away with it?' He stared at Kropp, daring him.

Kropp stared back. 'What did I ever do to you?'

'You did it to yourself. You know I was asked to spy on you? I didn't.'

'Bullshit.'

'*You did it to yourself.* They have files full of complaints, going back years. Internal Investigations, even Spurling kept a few.'

'You spied on me.'

'No I didn't, I was asked to. There is a difference.'

'You spied on Quine easy enough.'

Hirsch said, 'Quine was a criminal. He committed criminal acts. He corrupted junior officers and got them to commit criminal acts, and the Internals knew all about it, and now he's in jail.'

'Holier than thou Hirschhausen.'

Yeah, well. Maybe a touch sometimes, when the wind's in the right quarter, Hirsch thought. Didn't make him wrong, though. 'Quine set me up to take the blame. He threatened my life. He frightened my parents. This is news to you? Why are you defending a man like that?'

'He's a colleague,' Kropp said, jaw out.

'So anything's allowed? Because you both wear the uniform and swore the oath, *he's* allowed to commit crimes? *You're* allowed to be a fuck-up?'

'I didn't fuck up.'

'You took your eye off the ball, you said it yourself. You turned a blind eye to Nicholson and Andrewartha's bullying, their sexual assaults. You turned a blind eye to them harassing a female constable you were supposed to train and protect. You ran interference for criminals just because they belonged to your footy club. And meanwhile you were running some catering business in police time using your mail-order bride.'

Kropp came out of his seat, red and frothing. 'You do *not* talk that way about her, you fucking prick. You don't know anything about her. She's been living here since she was a kid.'

Hirsch knew he was wrong—but fuck it, he was on a roll. 'Thought the town'd let you in if you ingratiated yourself enough with people like the Latimers? You're a disgrace.'

That was what Spurling had said.

Kropp sat, dangerously still in the chair, tendons standing out in his neck. 'You're this close to a thrashing.'

'Fine. Bring it on.'

Eventually Kropp made a curt gesture and said, 'If I laid a finger on you I'd probably get a bloody reprimand.'

He's making a joke? Hirsch watched and waited, wondering what was happening inside Kropp.

The man exhaled. Dropped his head and said mildly, 'I want you and me to take a little drive together.'

'What, out east? Some convenient mine shaft?'

'Mate, I'm not a killer.' A crooked grin appeared briefly. 'I'm just a fuck-up and a disgrace. All right?'

North along the Barrier, Kropp driving, into a day of rusty winds and black, staring birds dotted along the swooping wires.

Silence all the way until Kropp said, 'I've seen the forensic report on David Coulter's vehicle.'

Hirsch, lulled by the motions of the car, sat up straight. 'And?'

'The driver's side headlight and quarter panel had been replaced at some point.'

Hirsch heard a 'but' in Kropp's voice. 'Okay . . .'

'I checked with the panelbeaters at Redruth Automotive: it was one of their repairs, and they did it *before* Melia Donovan was run over. The rest of the car's never been damaged.'

'Damn.'

'Yeah. What's more, they told me Judd had a laugh about it one evening after a few beers. Coulter had let the girl drive, and she'd run into a tree.'

'Oh, right,' Hirsch said. 'A couple of people told me Melia had been in an accident. So where does that leave us?'

Kropp stared ahead, tethered grimly to the wheel. 'Why don't you have a bit of a think about it.'

Hirsch looked out at the dust and the fence wires. No inspiration there. 'One of the others did it? Or Coulter used someone else's car?'

'Nup,' said Kropp emphatically. 'They're all clean. Come on, if you eliminate Coulter and the others, who are you left with?'

The road north swam in mirages, stretching to the dry horizon, the pink and grey hills. Hirsch was half fond of the place now.

'Sam Hempel,' he said.

Sam and his stalking. Sam tailing Melia Donovan because he wanted her, not because he thought she needed protection. She belonged to him, and if he couldn't have her . . .

'Give the lad a cigar,' Kropp said sourly.

'He blamed Coulter,' said Hirsch, 'because Coulter was sleeping with the love of his life.'

'Not only that. Coulter put him in jail for six months a couple of years ago. If you'd done your homework, you would have known that.'

He *should* have known that. He thought again. 'But I've seen his car. I've driven it. It's a shit heap, but there was no recent damage or signs of repair.'

No reply. At the sign for Muncowie, Kropp turned off the highway and onto a single vehicle track, two stripes of gravelly dust stretching to the hills. One kilometre, two, and they were out where the battlers lived in corrugated iron shacks set amid dead grass and rusted car bodies, where cats slunk away and the dogs were nothing but ribs and a prick.

Pulling into a weedy yard, Kropp switched off and the air was still and hot when they got out and slammed their doors. And there was Sam Hempel's Commodore, uniformly sun-faded and pock-marked. An exhausted dog watched them and no curtains stirred. A plate, knife and fork sat on a stump, a smear of tomato sauce blackening in the sun. A hand mower sat at the end of a stripe of cropped grass and would have finished the job if there'd been a will to push it. A David Jones bag had been snagged by untamed rose canes; someone had coughed blood into the tissue Hirsch spotted beside a canvas chair grey with sun and water damage. And sure enough, there was the sound of a woman hacking her lungs up inside the house.

'Sam's mother?'

Kropp nodded. 'Father shot through years ago.'

He didn't approach the house but led Hirsch to the rotting sheds at the back, where a rust-fretted Land Rover sat on weak tyres among the nettles.

Slamming his meaty palm on the dented nose of the vehicle, Kropp said, 'If you'd done your job right, you'd have found this fine example of English automobile engineering registered to one Mary Kathleen Hempel.'

He stared intently across at the house.

Hirsch followed his gaze. Sam Hempel stood at the back door, shoulders slumped. No fight in him and nowhere to run. The boy who borrowed the Land Rover whenever his own car wouldn't start.

'Still got your copper's instincts, Sarge.'

Kropp bristled. Seeing no disrespect, he stared out over the touch-and-go paddocks, the blurred horizon, and finally at the miserable house and the man he'd come to arrest.

'Me,' he said, 'I'm going out in a blaze of glory.'

Read on for the first chapter of

PEACE

*The next gripping novel in the Hirsch
series, coming soon from Viper*

1

This close to Christmas, the mid-north sun had some heft to it, house bricks, roofing iron, asphalt and the red-dirt plains giving back all the heat of all the days. And this Thursday morning a grass fire to top it off.

Hirsch toed a thick worm of softened tar at the edge of the Barrier Highway, watching the mop-up. Country Fire Service trucks from Tiverton, Redruth and Mount Bryan in attendance. One of them at the seat of the fire behind an old farmhouse set back from the road, the second chasing spot fires, and the Tiverton unit patrolling the fence line. Not a blazing fire—a slow creep through sparse wheat stubble—and not a big one, only a corner of the farmhouse cypress hedge and the road paddock. No wind today. Cloudless, as still as a painting.

A suspicious fire, though.

'Suspicious in what way?' Hirsch asked.

He'd parked his South Australia Police 4WD nose-up to

the words *Tiverton Electrics* on the tailgate of Bob Muir's ute. If Hirsch had a male friend in the district, it was Muir. A man mild, unhurried, but capable of a hard, exacting competency whenever he used his hands or his brain. He was what passed for the local fire chief.

'Not a firebug, if that's what you're thinking,' Muir said. 'I'll show you once they've given the okay.'

All Hirsch could see right now was a corrugated-iron roof with flakes of farmhouse-red paint still clinging, and a towering palm tree.

The Tiverton unit drew near, Kev Henry the publican at the wheel. Two men on the back, hosing fenceposts: Wayne Flann and some guy Hirsch didn't recognise. A shearer? Windfarm worker? Didn't matter. Flann mattered, at least to some extent. He was mid-twenties, with sleepy eyes, loose limbs, almost good-looking. Always privately amused, as if he was one up on the world. Getting a kick out of this fire. Flicked his wrist when he spotted Hirsch, landing a loop of water on his uniform shoes.

'Knock it off, Wayne,' Muir said.

The truck trundled on and then a radio crackled. Bob Muir listened, said, 'Good oh,' and jerked his head. 'This way, Constable Hirschhausen.'

A long, rutted driveway took them down to a gap in the hedge and the house and sheds on the other side. The house had been unoccupied for years, the stone walls ceding to the dirt, the rocks and the dying grass. Ants teemed where once had been lawns and flower beds. A wheelless pram beside a crooked garden tap; a ladder busted down to three or four rungs leaning against the tank stand. Nothing seemed whole. Cracked windowpanes, grass in the rusted and drooping gutters. Only the palm tree showed any splendour, and its base was littered with dead fronds.

Hirsch parked behind Muir in the side yard and got out. Here the smoke was more acrid—burnt vegetation with an overlay of scorched rubber? The sunlight was queer, too, winking hazily where it came through the ragged fringe of palm fronds, casting blurred shadows on the dirt.

Looking up, Hirsch said, 'These old country places with their palm trees.'

Muir grunted. 'Over this way.'

He took Hirsch along the flank of the house and around the tank stand to the back yard. The cypress hedge sheltered the house and garden on three sides, Hirsch realised. To his eye, the fire had started in one corner, charring the patchy grass before scorching its way through the hedge, leaving a spidery tangle of blackened, leafless twigs in its hunt for better fuel on the other side—the wheat stubble.

'What do you make of that?' Muir said, pointing at the blackened dirt.

Hirsch looked down. Ash on his toecaps now, not only dust. He felt sweaty, greasy, a sensation of grit in his teeth. And still early in the day. 'Kids playing with matches?'

Muir might have been disappointed in him. 'Mate, the wire.'

Coiled in the ash at the base of the hedge was a length of insulated cable. Now Hirsch understood the smoke's acrid taste: molten plastic. But mostly his gaze was caught by a stripe of copper glowing bright.

'Ah.'

'Exactly,' Muir said, spreading his arms. 'I mean, why go to the bother of slicing off insulation with a knife when you can burn it off? Lovely hot summer's day, dead grass all around . . .'

Hirsch grinned. 'Maybe they felt better-hidden in here.'

Muir pointed to the dead ground between the house and the sheds. 'They would've been just as invisible from the road over there in the dirt.'

'Who called it in?'

'Your girlfriend, in fact.'

Hirsch visualised it. Wendy Street heading down to Redruth at 7.30 to arrive at the high school by eight, same as usual. Saw the fire, called Bob, knew Bob would call him.

'Early start for your average copper thief,' Hirsch said. 'Maybe it's the country air.'

Back in his CIB days in the city he could rely on the bad guys sleeping till noon. He glanced dubiously at the old house. 'They didn't strip it out of there, surely?'

'Nope. Not worth their while. What this is, is their base. Big metal skip full of copper in the barn.'

Hirsch gazed across a stretch of dead soil broken only by abandoned harrows, a rusty fuel drum and a silvery gumtree. A barn, an open shed collapsed at one end like a mouth in rictus. 'So they've been at it for a while.'

'Be my guess,' Muir said.

Hirsch recalled a department memo: two thousand

reported thefts of semi-precious metal in South Australia this year, estimated value $2.5 million. Mostly copper, mostly from building sites; also powerlines, rail networks and storage depots. Electrical wiring, antenna cables, transformers, hot-water pipes. Police members advised to keep an eye open for unusual activity or reports that might indicate blah, blah, blah . . .

He ran a mental gaze over the district, the thousands of square kilometres he patrolled. A couple of new houses going up in Redruth, but that was his sergeant's headache, not Hirsch's. Some kitchen remodelling here and there. The long-abandoned railway service. Not much in that. Maybe the stuff was brought here from far and wide to be stripped, stored, shipped elsewhere. He didn't know where to start with it. Sometimes, it seemed to Hirsch— newcomer to the bush—that his job was as much probing the landscape as probing the circumstances of the crimes committed in it.

'Prints,' he muttered, thinking of the paperwork ahead, wondering about the likelihood of getting a forensic team here so close to Christmas.

Hirsch photographed the wire coil in the ashes, the charred grass around it and the skip piled with stolen copper, much of it dulled by oxygenation. Then he looped crime-scene tape across the entrance to the shed and called his sergeant, who was underwhelmed but promised to notify CIB in Port Pirie.

Finally, Hirsch reassessed the day ahead. On Thursdays he took a swing through the back country south and west of Tiverton, on Mondays he patrolled north and east. Hundreds of kilometres a week, checking in. An elderly grazier here, a widow with a schizophrenic son there. A police presence—meaning a cup of tea, a chat, a follow-up. I'm afraid your car was found down in Salisbury, burnt out. Your neighbour claims your dogs have been troubling his sheep. I'm required to ensure that your rifle and shotgun are properly secured. Any further sightings of that mysterious truck you saw last week?

Some of the people he called on were lonely, others vulnerable. Some got into trouble through a lack of foresight; a handful were actively dodgy. It was the diversity of the people and experiences, that's what Hirsch enjoyed about his Thursday and Monday patrols. He liked to start early, about 7 am, but today it was almost 9 and he was still only a few kilometres south of Tiverton. He'd have to take a few shortcuts to make up the lost time. Phone some of the people on his rounds rather than dropping in.

'You off?' Muir said.

'Yep.'

His face a picture of innocence—so that Hirsch was instantly on guard—Muir said, 'All set for tomorrow night?'

In a moment of weakness which he'd been trying to spin as building good community relations, Hirsh had agreed to be Tiverton's Santa this year. He'd be distributing presents to the town and farm kids on the side street near Ed Tennant's shop, then announcing the winner of the town's best Christmas lights, while looking ridiculous in a smelly red suit.

'Fuck off, Bob.'

'That's the spirit,' Muir said, clapping him on the back.

Hirsch set out south along the Barrier Highway. Window down, Emmylou Harris in the CD slot, a hard country lament that suited his mood—the isolation, the bushwhackery he sometimes encountered. Down the shallow valley, low dry hills on either side, greyish brown with the darker speckles of shadows or trees clinging to the stony soil. Stone ruins close to the road, distant farmhouse rooftops, a line of windfarm turbines along a nearby ridge—the settler years, the struggling present and the future, all in one. Halfway up a sloping hillside a motionless dust cloud. A vehicle on a dirt road? A wind eddy? It all seemed unknowable, a world poised for action, but unable to proceed. Hirsch had been the Tiverton cop for one year now and was waiting for a mutual embrace, but the place kept him at arm's length. If life was the search for a true home—a welcoming place, a constant lover or a mind at peace—then he was still looking.

Kind of. There was Wendy in his life. In the eyes of the district they were 'going out,' and that was just fine with Hirsch. And he was close to her canny, amusing daughter Katie, who'd saved his life last year. He had plenty to be thankful for.

Hirsch turned west onto Menin Road, the boundary between the Tiverton and Redruth police patrol areas. Place names mattered up here, where they didn't in the city, it seemed to him. Menin Road, Lone Pine Hill, Mischance Creek, Tar Barrel Corner, Mundjapi—all putting down layers of meaning and significance. Menin took him up into better wheat country. Better rainfall west of the Barrier Highway than east of it. 'Barrier': another signifier. Better crops and fencing, better roads, shorter distances between farms. But, all the same, Hirsch drove for a further twenty minutes and saw not a soul.

And then he saw Kip.

He was past the dog before he realised it and braked hard, sending road grit and choking dust over the poor mutt. He got out, crouched, offered his upturned palm. The kelpie halted, skin and bone, ribs and prick. Panting, deeply fatigued. A low growl in his throat—it seemed to break free before he bit it back as if ashamed.

'Kip,' Hirsch said. 'Kippy. Here, boy.'

The world stopped. Not a breath of wind and the day soundless but for galahs screeching in the gums beside a cracked-mud dam and the tick of the cooling motor. Kip gave a slow tail wag.

'You're thirsty, right?' said Hirsch.

He always carried plenty of water. In the rear compartment of the Toyota, where he sometimes had to transport prisoners, was a locked metal compartment for spare handcuffs, flares, ropes, a torch, evidence-collecting bags and a couple of Tupperware containers. Hirsch tipped a shallow layer of water into one of those and set it down on the crown of the road, halfway between the driver's door and the dog.

Kip dropped to his belly, stretched and twitched his nose. Got to his feet, limped forward, dropped again. Then, by degrees, he was at the water, testing it. Started lapping all at once, drops flying about, before looking to Hirsch for more.

'Not yet, bud. Too much, too soon, bad for you.'

Hirsch drew near, reached a hand to the bony skull, stroked the dog between the eyes. Kip turned, licked his hand, and let himself be coaxed by the collar into the passenger seat, where he circled twice before curling head to tail as if he'd come home to his favourite blanket. Snout on paws, alert to Hirsch's every movement but trustingly alert. Trusting Hirsch to know the way home.

'Poor old boy,' Hirsch said, giving the dog a last pat before turning the key. 'You've been in the wars, haven't you?'

Cuts, blood flecks, a torn ear, the sheen gone from his tawny pelt.

Hirsch glanced at his watch, did the maths again. He'd lose even more time returning Kip to his owners. He checked for mobile reception—zilch.

Half a kilometre along, steering with his right hand, one eye on the road, the other on his phone signal, he suddenly had two bars. Stopped, got out, consulted his notebook and made four calls to his non-urgent clients. Wouldn't matter if he didn't pay these people a visit this week.

First Rex and Eleanor Dunner. She picked up. Sorry, but he had no leads on the graffiti artist who'd tagged their heritage-listed woolshed.

'That's very disappointing, Paul.'

Hirsch took that philosophically. He was always disappointing someone.

Next he told Drew Maguire it wasn't a police matter if

the neighbour's sheep strayed onto the Maguire property through a hole in the fence.

'What if I flatten the bastard?'

'Then it becomes a police matter.'

Next, a call to the owner of a wallet that had been handed in. No cash or cards in it, but he'd drop it off next Thursday. Finally he checked on Jill Kramer, a single mother who'd been robbed and hospitalised by her ice-addict daughter.

'She's in rehab.'

'Doing okay?'

'Well as can be expected.'

That was a kind of mantra in the bush. Hirsch heard it once or twice a week. Acceptance. Not daring to hope for better times. 'Will she come home to you when she gets out?'

'She's got nowhere else to go.'

'Let me know when,' Hirsch said ... And I'll check in more often than once a week.

He drove on, past a homestead with a windsock on a landing strip, down and around and in and out of old, eroded cuttings in the folds of the earth. Along a sunken road between quartz-reef hillslopes, and across the Booborowie valley, a patchwork of wheat stubble, crops awaiting the harvester and dark, green-black lucerne—darker where massive, computer-controlled sprinklers crept over the ground.

Then up. Over Munduney Hill and onto a side road—and now Kip knew his home was drawing near. Climbed to his feet, stuck his snout into the airflow and barked.

'You bet,' Hirsch said.

He slowed for the cattle grid at the front gate—not that the Fullers ran stock anymore. Then onto a track that wound past star thistles and Salvation Jane to a transportable house on stumps. No weeds here. It was as if a switch had been flicked: vigorous couch-grass lawns, rosebushes and native shrubs. No sign of Graham Fuller's old Land Rover in the carport, but—perfect timing—Monica was there, unloading groceries from the open hatch of her Corolla. She turned with an expectant smile, a lonely country woman who didn't get many visitors, the smile growing curious when she saw she had the police on her doorstep.

Then she spotted Hirsch's passenger and simple joy lit her face. She let the shopping bags go, wiped her palms on her thighs and came at a little run to yank open the passenger door. 'You found him!'

Kip whimpered and slobbered, his tail whipping the seat.

'Where have you been, you monster? You poor thing, you're filthy.'

A glance at Hirsch as if uncertain of the proprieties. 'May I?'

Hirsch grinned. 'He's not under arrest, if that's what you mean.'

Monica Fuller laughed, helped the kelpie to the ground. 'Thank you so much. Where on earth did you find him?'

Hirsch explained, Monica cocking her head as if mentally tracing a route on a map. 'So he was more or less on his way home,' she said. 'God knows where he's been. Come and have a cup of tea. I'll text Graham, he'll be that thrilled.'

She chattered on, a simple release of tension. Within minutes she'd settled Kip on the veranda with a bone to chew, stowed tins and packets into pantry and refrigerator, and placed a mug of tea and a slice of Christmas cake at Hirsch's elbow. A tired kitchen, a hint of 1970s orange here and there, Formica and laminated chipboard. A house where there was a kitchen re-fit on the to-do list, but money was tight. Some meagre light came through a window above the sink, more from a screen door to the veranda. Hirsch could see staked tomato plants in the back yard, an old stone dunny and an implement shed. No implements these days, only rusty ploughshares and rotting hay and empty grain sacks.

Monica's phone pinged. She was round-faced, comfortable in herself, her wiry black hair laced with silvery filaments. About forty, a face in the crowd if you saw her on the street, but Hirsch sensed her shrewdness, her quality of watching and waiting. She read the message on her phone and grinned happily at him.

'Graham says he owes you a beer.' She frowned. 'Is that allowed?'

'I've been known to go off-duty.'

She grinned again. 'So I've heard. Mrs Street, Wendy, teaches my youngest.'

I'm the talk of the high school? wondered Hirsch. 'I'll take down the wanted posters when I get back to town.'

She laughed. 'Wanted posters.'

Graham Fuller had come into the police station on his way to work Monday morning with a dozen A4 printouts in his hand: a photo of Kip on his haunches, sizing up the photographer. *Have You Seen Kip? Reward Offered* in big black letters. Hirsch had pinned one to the wall next to the wire rack of police, district council and public health notices, and all week he'd seen Kip's face elsewhere in town: on power poles, fenceposts, the shop window. Privately he'd thought it a lost cause. Kip had been bitten by a snake or shot by a neighbour or stolen. Or, worst case, he'd run away because he'd been beaten once too often.

Now Hirsch was wondering if perhaps the Fullers' dog had been stolen. He sipped his tea. 'I understand Kip has won some ribbons in his time.'

Monica shrugged, modest. 'Best sheepdog at the Redruth show, four years running—back when we had sheep.'

It was a common story. The family farm no longer sustained a family. It was either sell out to a richer neighbour or a Chinese-owned agri-company, or shift career gears and stay in the district. Graham Fuller now serviced windfarm turbines; Monica worked two days a week at the Clare hospital. A lot of driving involved.

Hirsch said, 'All those prizes . . . How did the other dog owners take it? Anyone get their nose out of joint?'

Monica moistened her fingertip, dabbed at the crumbs on her plate, looked at him wryly. 'It was ages ago. And I mean . . . the Redruth Show? It's small-time.'

'People store grievances.'

Monica shook her head. 'Actually I'm wondering if it's related to the time our phone line was cut—though I don't see how.'

One evening last January, Monica and Graham had just gone to bed when they heard noises in the yard and a knock on the door. Kip barked and strained at his chain until it broke—Graham was just in time to see him charge into the darkness—as Monica tried to call the police and realised the phone was dead. Kip returned eventually. Meanwhile Graham found the phone line severed, a neat, clean snip through insulation and wiring, and some garden tools missing.

Copper, again. Not much copper, though, and it had simply been cut, not stolen. 'A long shot,' Hirsch said.

Monica waved a hand as if to deny the direction her mind had taken her. 'I know, I know; hard to imagine they saw the kennel and thought, ah, a dog, we'll come back and steal him at the end of the year.'

'Anyway, he's back, that's the main thing.'

Still, two incidents involving police within twelve months. That was well over par for this area. Hirsch stood, stretched his back, said he'd better be going. He could see, through the little archway that dated the house, a sitting room with a small, overdecorated pine Christmas tree, cards on a string looped beneath the mantel above a fake log gas fire, loops of red, green and silver tinsel. 'Season's greetings,' he said, 'thanks for the cake.'

'You too. And thanks heaps for bringing Kip home,' Monica said.

She took him out onto the veranda, watched him bend to knuckle the kelpie's head. 'Those cuts—someone took a stick to him.'

Hirsch allowed that that was one possibility. 'Or he got into it with another dog.'

'No, that was a stick,' Monica Fuller said flatly.

She walked with Hirsch to his 4WD. 'I hate to add to your workload, Paul, but there was a bit of excitement in town just now, while I was doing the shopping.'

No one had notified Hirsch. Maybe he'd been out of range. 'Do I want to know?'

'Brenda Flann.'

'As I thought, I didn't want to know,' Hirsch said.

ABOUT THE AUTHOR

Garry Disher is the author of more than forty titles in multiple genres, including *The Sunken Road*, shortlisted for the NBC and South Australian Festival awards, *The Divine Wind*, winner of a NSW Premier's Award, and *The Bamboo Flute*, winner of the CBC Book of the Year award. Garry's Wyatt thrillers and his Peninsula mysteries have garnered acclaim worldwide, winning awards in Germany and appearing on best-books-of-the-year lists in the USA. *Chain of Evidence*, the fourth Peninsula mystery, won the 2007 Ned Kelly Award, and *Wyatt* won the award in 2010. He has received the Ned Kelly Lifetime Acheivement Award.

garrydisher.com